SWORD AND SERPENT

TAYLOR R. MARSHALL

SAINT JOHN PRESS
MMXIV

This book is a work of fiction. Any references to historical events, existing locations, or real people, living or dead, are used fictitiously. Other names, characters, places, and events are the creation of the author, and any resemblance to actual events, locations, or persons, living or dead, is coincidental.

Saint John Press
800 West Airport Freeway, Suite 1100
Irving, Texas 75062

Printed in the United States of America
Acid-free paper for permanence and durability

ISBN: 978-0-9884425-5-9

Cover design by W. Antoneta
Book and map design by SisterMuses

Please visit Sword and Serpent on the web at: www.taylormarshall.com

*For my children Gabriel, Mary Claire,
Rose, Jude, Becket, Blaise, and Elizabeth:
Cum gladio et sale interficite dracones.*

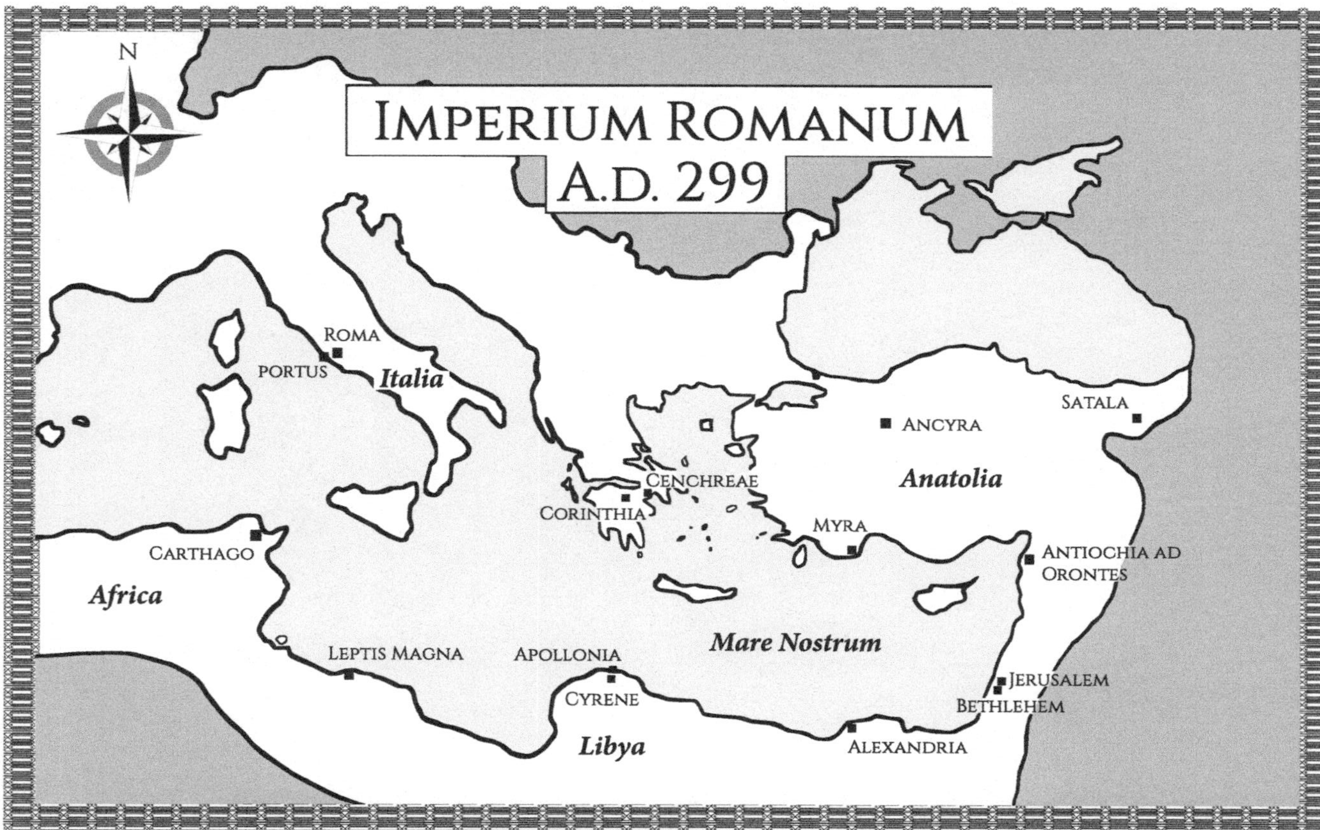
Imperium Romanum
A.D. 299
N
Roma
Portus
Italia
Satala
Ancyra
Anatolia
Cenchreae
Corinthia
Myra
Carthago
Antiochia ad
Orontes
Africa
Mare Nostrum
Leptis Magna
Apollonia
Jerusalem
Bethlehem
Cyrene
Libya
Alexandria

PROLOGUE

ANTIOCHIA AD ORONTES, A.D. 299

"*DOMINE*. THE GODS ARE SILENT."

The words came as a whisper, under the breath, as quiet as the end of times is ever proclaimed.

The *haruspex* bowed as he spoke, cringing between the stony stare of Jupiter Capitolinus, towering in carved marble over the altar behind him, and the deadlier, weightier stare of the divine Diocletian, Emperor of Rome. The priest kept his gaze on his bloodied hands, shaking from three days of ritual fast, and prayed to the silent gods that Diocletian would not command him to take the sacrificial victim's place.

Several minutes slipped away before the *haruspex* finally lifted his eyes. The light of the ritual fires caught the smooth line of Diocletian's clenched jaw and glimmered in the brilliant azure of his eyes. In the deep purple of his toga, he was as imposing and beautiful as a god himself.

And, the haruspex realized, just as silent.

Diocletian beckoned him closer. The priest stumbled toward him, hunched in a bow, fingers half-curled like lifeless talons.

"Faustus," the emperor said, his voice quiet and terrible. "The portents."

"None, *domine*. Apollo sends us none. The gods are silent."

"How is that possible?"

"I don't know! The victim was untainted. No *vitium* corrupted the sacrifice. But I read nothing in the lamb's vital organs." His voice pitched up, threaded with panic. "The gods are silent!"

Diocletian never moved. "Do it again," he said. "I don't care how long it takes. Repeat it!"

Faustus' tongue flicked over his cracked lips. He could taste the birth of fear in the smoke-haze of the temple. The attendant stationed at the brass tripod was trembling with it, barely keeping the incense burning. It was in the pale faces of the few members of the imperial household, clustered near the great doors of the Temple. But it was in the heavy silence that Faustus could taste it, bitter as the tang of blood running over the altar stone.

Faustus staggered back toward the altar. Fear was never without his companion Rumor. If Faustus repeated the sacrifice, there would be no stopping either of them.

Not that it mattered now. It was all coming to an end.

As he neared the altar, one of the servants by the door moved. The *haruspex* watched sidelong as the man raised his hand and made a slow, curious gesture, brushing his right thumb over his forehead, down, then across.

Faustus stiffened. It was a subtle gesture; it might have been nothing. But he knew better. He'd seen that sign before. It wasn't Roman. It certainly wasn't Etruscan. It belonged to the strange new cult that had risen in this gods-forsaken region and now infected even Rome herself, and it had no place in the great Temple of Jupiter, Jupiter the All-Powerful, Jupiter the Victorious.

He moved to rebuke the man, but stopped when Diocletian shifted his weight. The gods might be silent, but the will of the emperor was clear.

He turned back to the bloodied altar, calling for a new victim. His attendant dragged a young sheep forward, and Diocletian stepped forward again with the ritual knife.

Four times they repeated the sacrifice.

Four times Faustus failed to divine the will of the gods.

It was no use. For thirty-nine years he had read the lines of livers and hearts, and counseled generals and emperors with the messages he found there. But not now. The gods were most definitely silent.

Rome was forsaken.

When the fifth victim failed, Faustus fell on his knees before the altar, soaking his toga in the blood that ran like water down the sanctuary steps. The mangled carcasses of the spoiled victims lay strewn around him, unfit to be burned, all wasted.

"Speak, Apollo," he whispered to the smoke and the silence and the deepening shadows. "Declare your will..."

He tore at the veiling fold of his toga with bloody hands, staining the white wool crimson. As his frantic thoughts scattered in panic, his eyes fell on the servant who had made the strange sign. And in that moment, all his fear turned to rage.

"We are lost," he hissed, standing to face the emperor. "The impious defile the sacrifices. Apollo will not speak while we tolerate their blasphemies."

Diocletian's face hardened. "What impious?"

"Rullus, there," Faustus said, pointing at the servant. "He made an impious sign. He has desecrated this sacred place."

The emperor kept his gaze fixed on the haruspex. "Rullus called on his own god, and you found yours silent? I don't wonder at your panic. Perhaps you are sacrificing at the wrong altar."

"*Domine meus!*" Faustus recoiled. "You can't mean that."

Diocletian did not answer. He glanced at his secretary, who came immediately with a profound bow.

"The gods are angry with us, Piso," he said. Faustus watched the blood drain from Piso's face, but Diocletian had his gaze fixed on the stained altar. "Send word to all the Legions calling for public sacrifice. We will unite the empire in blood, it seems."

Piso bowed and withdrew, leaving Faustus alone with the emperor again.

"Jupiter has always guided me," Diocletian said, touching his forehead before gesturing at the massive statue of the god in all his glory. "If our tolerance of some foreign deity has angered him, then Jupiter must be appeased. Let the upstart god be silenced."

1

Satala, Anatolia

Standing at the edge of the dusty village of Satala, Jurian watched as a small crowd gathered outside the walls of the Legion fortress. Even from his distance, he could easily see what made them push forward in hushed expectation—the Emperor's *signum* flashing in the cold autumn sunlight near the fortress gate, signaling the arrival of an imperial messenger. This far out on the Empire's frontier, the *signum* was a rare sight, rare enough that it lured even Jurian's younger sister Mariam toward the village, all curiosity that she was.

Jurian followed her uneasily. When they reached the crowd he snatched her arm, stopping her, as if she'd strayed too close to a chasm.

"What's going on, Jurian?" she asked.

He was tall enough to see past most of the people, but it did him no good. From this vantage he could make out nothing but the *signum* and the plumed helmet of the messenger giving his report to the Legate. They were too far away for Jurian to hear what the man said. He doubted any of the people could hear him either—and the messenger was certainly speaking in Latin, anyway—but that hadn't stopped them from pressing toward the walls to gawk.

"I can't see anything," Jurian said, squinting against the cold sunlight. "And you wouldn't be able to either."

"Let go. I want to get closer."

"You'll get smothered by *Matrona* Priscilla there," he said with a smirk, gesturing toward the wide back of a woman standing on tiptoes a short distance away. "And how would I explain that to Mother?"

Mariam's grey eyes widened, then creased with a sudden smile. "You're horrible," she said. "Come on, Jurian!"

Jurian sighed. He let her take his arm and pull him toward the front of the crowd, though he smiled as she steered well clear of *Matrona* Priscilla. The pit of his stomach crawled, but he held his head high, refusing to let it show. He would rather die than let the Legate see his uncertainty. Even after so many years, Jurian still couldn't look at the man without seeing his father—his father, who had worn that toga with so much more strength and authority than Marcus the Pompous Valerius Flaccus.

His father, who had died when Jurian was fourteen, barely three years ago. Three years that felt like one…or a thousand.

Jurian jerked his gaze from the Legate and buried the pain deep inside.

By the time he and Mariam threaded their way to the front of the crowd, the messenger had already been escorted into the fortress. The Legate remained behind, standing pale and shaken in the shadowed archway. Marcus Valerius should have been ashamed, Jurian thought, letting the crowd and his own Guard see him so unnerved. Jurian's father would never have been so weak. His jaw tightened.

I will never be so weak.

The Legate lifted his hand and the crowd grew deathly silent. Speaking Greek for the lower-born citizens to understand, Marcus Valerius said, "The Divine Emperor Diocletian *Augustus* has ordered all Legions and all the Empire to offer sacrifice to the gods, to plead their mercy and favor. A great darkness has fallen over the world." He paused, his hand restless on the hilt of his sword. "The portents have failed. The Emperor's *haruspex* and now even the augurs cannot divine the will of the gods."

A gasp rippled through the crowd. One matron standing near Mariam wailed and pulled her *palla* over her head like a mourning veil. Mariam caught Jurian's eye, a faint line of confusion between her brows. Jurian shook his head subtly. Now was not the time for her questions.

The Legate's raised hand quieted the people again. "We will begin sacrifices at the Temple of Apollo tonight at sunset. Go now. Honor the gods."

Jurian took Mariam's elbow and propelled her back the way they had come, hoping to slip away before anyone recognized them. But he was too slow. Just as they reached the edge of the crowd, someone sidled up behind him and dropped a flaccid hand on his shoulder.

Jurian's grip on Mari's elbow tightened. Then he released her and turned around, barely stifling a groan when he realized the hand belonged to Casca, the son of *Legatus* Marcus Valerius. Even two years Jurian's senior, Casca was barely Mariam's height, and he had the unfortunate aspect of a newly beached fish—he always looked surprised and a bit breathless, his face a little too pale and eyes a little too wide.

But for all his flabby, goggle-eyed looks, Casca was a snake in the grass, and he'd been singling Jurian and Mari out ever since the Valerii had come to Satala. Jurian did his best to keep Mari clear of him, but there was no avoiding the confrontation now.

Casca squinted up at him, smiling nastily. "What's wrong, *Georgios?* Running away?" He jabbed Jurian in the shoulder. "Only the guilty run away. Is it your fault the gods are silent? You and your half-breed sister?"

Mariam stiffened beside him.

"Don't call me that. And don't *ever* call her that again, *Flaccus,*" Jurian said, his voice low.

"That's not funny!" Casca said, glaring at Mariam as if she'd put Jurian up to saying it. "That name has belonged to my family for hundreds...maybe *thousands* of years!"

"Of course it has," Jurian soothed. "It perfectly suits your family. Or wait, are you ashamed of it?"

Mari's breath escaped in the barest whisper of his name.

"No," Casca said. "I think you're jealous of it. They say green eyes are a sign of jealousy." His lip curled. "Or mixed blood."

Jurian swallowed back his burning anger, forcing an easy smile that he was sure barely concealed his desire to break Casca's nose. Some of the town's citizens had stopped to watch them, and Jurian knew that an audience would only make Casca more vicious. The snake loved to make a scene, and even though they were speaking Latin, the meaning was obvious. He couldn't give Casca the satisfaction of baiting him in front of a crowd.

"Nice seeing you, Casca," Jurian said. "I'm sorry we missed your father."

He tried to turn away, but Casca grabbed him again, this time twisting the neck of his wool tunic in his fist.

"You're trying to call me fat, aren't you?" he demanded, deliberately raising his voice to capture the crowd's attention. "You insult me, and you insult my family! I'm not fat!"

Jurian's hand flashed up and gripped Casca's wrist until he squawked and released Jurian's tunic.

"I know," he said. "And I'm not Greek. I'm *Roman*."

"You'd never know it by that barbarian name you call yourself, *Jurian*," Casca snapped, slinking in a circle around them. "Seems you don't even know what you are. And besides, your father was Greek. Hardly a real Roman, not to mention the biggest disgrace in the history of the *Apollinaris* Legion!"

Jurian's eyes narrowed. "What do you call a real Roman, Casca? Everyone here is some kind of Greek." He nodded toward the small crowd. "Would you like to explain to them how they aren't real Romans? Oh, wait. I forgot. You don't speak Greek. Should I do it for you?"

Jurian toyed with the idea of repeating it all in Greek for the crowd, but thought better of it. A quarrel between families was one thing. A rebellion against the Roman Empire was something else…and great fires could be kindled by a lone spark.

"You wouldn't dare," Casca hissed.

"Anyway," Mari interjected before Jurian could answer. "Father was a friend of the Emperor's. You have no right to insult his memory, Casca!"

Casca snorted, shaking a limp lock of dark hair off his forehead. "So you say. But where's the Emperor now? Friends take care of each other, don't they?" He tapped his forehead. "So remind me where you live now? And why my family was sent to this gods-forsaken vestibule of Pluto's hell in the first place?"

Jurian made no answer, and Casca's teeth flashed in a grin.

"Right," Casca continued. "We wouldn't want to say, would we? Because friends don't let that happen to friends, do they? Seems like our divine *Imperator*, gods long protect his rule, forgot all about his dear friend's barbarian children and the widow who's too frail to—"

Jurian swung his fist. Just before it slammed into Casca's jaw, a hand caught his wrist with painful strength and drove him back.

"Is there a problem here?"

Jurian twisted to see the Legion Tribune, Titus Terentius Varro, standing beside him. Varro dropped Jurian's hand, his grey eyes dark and stern beneath his plumed helmet. Jurian squared his shoulders but dropped his gaze, feeling suddenly, strangely, ashamed.

"This isn't your affair," Casca sniffed, brushing off his toga. "I'm just having a chat with my *friend* here. Nothing the Tribune need be concerned about."

Jurian's jaw tightened as Varro swung around, dismissing the little knot of spectators without a word. As soon as the people had dispersed, Varro frowned down at Casca.

"Your father is looking for you," he said. "I suggest you don't make him wait."

Casca's mouth twitched, but he nodded and turned away, spearing one last spiteful glance at Jurian as he left.

"Mariam," Varro said, smiling at her as he dropped a heavy hand on Jurian's shoulder. "Would you give me a moment to speak to your brother?"

Mariam swallowed and glanced anxiously at Jurian.

"Don't worry," Jurian said. "Go make sure Mother doesn't

need anything."

Mariam caught his gaze and nodded at the warning she read there. She turned to leave, but paused and inclined her dark head to Varro, murmuring, "Thank you, *domine*."

"Whatever for?" Varro asked.

She smiled faintly. "Preserving the peace."

Jurian watched her hurry away, hardly daring to breathe.

But Varro didn't rebuke him, or threaten him with arrest. He only released Jurian's shoulder and said, "Walk with me."

Jurian followed him wordlessly toward the Legion fortress. His breath caught as they passed under the broad stone archway into the *castra*. It had been three years since his father's death and the arrival of the Valerii…three years since he'd walked within these walls.

Three years since his family had been turned out of their home and left forgotten in the streets of Satala.

He tried not to stare at the *praetorium* gleaming golden under the late afternoon sun, with its Roman columns and the fruit trees that he and Mariam used to climb. It was just a building now, not a home. He'd trained himself to forget this place…to forget what it felt like to be respected and honored.

Varro stopped at the *quintana* a few streets from the *praetorium*. The air here was thick with the smell of hot bread and spiced meat, and noisy with the calls of merchants and the too-loud conversations of a handful of Legionaries. He plucked a handful of ripe figs from a basket at one of the market stands and flipped the merchant a few bronze coins.

"Now then, Jurian," Varro said, offering him a fig. "Would you have actually struck Casca?"

Jurian regarded Varro for a moment, a bit surprised at the boldness that blazed through him. Maybe it was the air of this place that gave him courage.

"Yes, *domine*. I would have. And…I wish you had let me."

"I respect your honesty," Varro said, nodding his approval. "What did he say to you?"

Jurian hesitated, but he'd already gone too far for caution.

"He insulted my father. He said he wasn't a true Roman. That he was a disgrace to the Legion."

He kept his eyes fixed on Varro, determined not to show the shame and fear that roiled in his gut. Varro's expression remained perfectly neutral, all but the slight tightening of his jaw.

"Well," he said, his mouth quirking in a smile. "I probably would have punched him too." He glanced across at the Legionaries, then down at the fig in his hand. "Don't make the mistake of thinking we all believe as the Valerii do about your father. Gerontios was a true leader and a noble man. I admired him greatly."

Jurian frowned. For so long he had wanted to talk to someone—anyone—about his father. His mother was too grieved and too weak, and his sister, sympathetic though she was, could never really understand. Now when Varro gave him the chance, the words seemed to catch in his throat, and he didn't even know why. Jurian knew his father had trusted Varro. He wanted to trust the Tribune, too, but trust was a hard commodity to come by.

"I understand, *domine*," he said at last. "But when the Legion returned defeated by King Narseh, they said that my father dishonored himself in battle, that his failure had caused the Legion's defeat." He dropped his voice and added, "And even worse, that my father killed himself to restore his own honor, but left *Caesar* Galerius to be humiliated by Diocletian." He gritted his teeth. "I have to know the truth, *domine*. Is that what happened?"

For several long moments they stood side by side in silence under the shade of the pomegranate tree, then Varro said, carefully, "I wasn't there when your father died, Jurian."

That wasn't what Jurian had hoped to hear. He set his jaw and stared at a group of Legionaries across the *quintana*, who were laughing over a game of dice. From somewhere deeper within the *castra* came the sounds of steel striking steel in soldiers' drills, the steady rhythm of a smith's hammer.

"Do you understand what I'm trying to tell you?" Varro asked, gripping Jurian's arm. "I can offer no witness. And my position forbids me to contradict the official report."

Jurian frowned. "Do you mean—"

"I mean," Varro interrupted, his voice a harsh whisper, "that I couldn't say anything even if I believed your father had died under peculiar circumstances. Or if I thought his death was untimely and a great loss to the Legion, or if I believed superstition smothered common military sense. These things would be forbidden for me to say, even if I believed them. I wish that I could give you some consolation, but as you see, I cannot."

He swung his gaze away and dropped Jurian's arm.

Jurian swallowed hard. Were Varro's suspicions correct? Had his father been killed by his own Legion? And what if the Emperor didn't know the truth? If he could be told...perhaps he would restore the honor of Gerontios' name. Restore his family's honor. They could go back to Rome, or to Antioch, and leave Satala forever. They could live as they were meant to live...as respected Roman citizens, not outcasts.

But what did it really matter? As long as the Valerii believed that Gerontios was a disgrace, and as long as they ruled in Satala, nothing would change for Jurian's family.

The truth didn't matter.

"Are we clear?" Varro asked.

"Clear, *domine*," Jurian said, startled by how unsteady his voice sounded. "And thank you for...for preventing me from getting into trouble with the Legate."

Varro smiled. "As I said, I admired your father. I like to think we were friends, even." He contemplated his handful of figs. "I would do more for you if I could, Jurian. Has anyone taken your father's place in your training?"

"Not exactly. My father's younger brother might have, but he and his Legion are fighting near the Danube."

"I see."

"But my father had been training me. Weapons, fighting, tactics, governance." He lowered his gaze. "If I'd known how things would turn out, I would've studied harder."

"Then you've not trained at all these last three years?"

"Oh," Jurian said with a short laugh. "I've done my best. Leptis runs through drills with me when he isn't on duty. And our servant Erastos still teaches us. Or did, until very recently."

"Leptis is a good soldier," Varro said. "I'm glad to hear he is working with you. And this Erastos, he was your servant? Not a slave? Where has he gone?"

Jurian shifted uneasily. "He was a freedman," he said. How could he explain that Erastos wanted to dedicate himself to the service of God, and that his mother had let him go? He couldn't, no matter how much he trusted Varro. Instead he said, "He left of his own accord a few months ago."

Varro measured him a long moment. "And have you assumed the white toga yet? I see Casca parading around in his as often as he can."

"My father was going to bestow it on me after the campaign."

"Then it's high time, I should think," Varro said. "And your uncle is posted up north. Do you have any other family?"

"My father's older brother is in Rome. I don't know of any other family."

"And your mother never married again?"

"Could anyone take my father's place so easily?"

Varro didn't seem impressed by his outburst. "To provide for her children, perhaps."

"She's too ill." The words came out stark and cold.

Varro dropped his gaze abruptly but couldn't hide the sudden flash of grief in his eyes. "Well, in that case," he said, quiet, "I'll ask the Legate if I may stand in your father's place to recognize your majority. No need to wait for the next festival day." He clapped Jurian on the shoulder. "We take such occasions as we can find them, here on the frontier, don't we? Gods know when a chance might be your last. Speak to your mother. I'll see it done."

Jurian bowed. Varro tightened his grip on Jurian's shoulder briefly, then stepped away and straightened his helmet.

"I have my duties," he said. "But we will see you this evening, I'm sure, for the sacrifice."

Only Jurian's practiced mask of indifference concealed his sudden rush of panic. He bowed again and mumbled, "As the God wills it."

2

Cyrene, Libya

THE FOUR DAYS OF CLEANSING rites had finished. The old god in the hills had been placated, sated with sacrificial blood for another month, and his sole priestess Sabra, tending his Temple under the earth, could barely recall the victim's face. Barely.

That is, until she left the undying fire of the inner sanctuary and faced the total darkness of the Temple's underground passages, where no light could chase away the vision of the child's face and the torment of Sabra's grief. She bit her lip and prayed to forget as she felt her way through the twisting corridors toward the world above. Years of practice steadied her steps along the uncertain path between pillars and over broken stones—years of practice, and more falls and bruises than she would ever admit.

The darkness had terrified her at first, when the last priestess of the Temple had taken her down into the belly of the earth and showed her the rites of the god she was marked to serve. How foolish, she thought now, to be afraid of the dark. It was almost a comfort to her since she had come to know the terror of god.

Her legs shook, weak from her four days of ritual fasting, and a headache throbbed behind her eyes, but she forced herself to keep moving. If she stopped, she would lose her sense of place, her sense of direction. The underground Temple was laid out like a labyrinth, its twists and corridors designed to keep the unconsecrated from the sanctuary, but it had almost snared her—her, the god's voice, the god's hands—more times than she cared to recall.

She passed a gap in the right-hand wall and marked it off on her mental map. Three steps later her left hand brushed a raised stone and she turned, feeling her way into the branching tunnel that followed. As always, a breath of warm, dry air sifted over her, strange after the clammy coolness of the deep sanctuary. It was the only reassurance she ever had that she hadn't gotten lost. Ten more strides and another left turn, and all at once the corridor brightened enough for her to see her hands and, just ahead, the outline of the stone steps where they lurched up toward the street.

She reached the bottom of the steps and drew a deep breath. The sky over Cyrene opened above her, a pattern of pearls set in midnight silk, wide as the endless sea. After the blindness of the Temple, the dark of night felt strangely empty. There was no comfort in the stars.

As she dragged herself up the steps, a shower of golden torchlight spilled down the stairs from the street above. She stifled a cry of surprise, recoiling, and threw a hand over her eyes.

"Mistress Sabra!" a voice called from behind the brightness.

Her breath slipped out in relief as she recognized Hanno, one of her father's Libyan eunuchs. He was only a few years older than she was, though he stood nearly a whole head taller than her and was twice as broad. Hanno's mother had been Sabra's own nurse, and she and Hanno had shared food and toys and secrets until Hanno had been whisked away to learn his duties for the governor and Sabra had been ushered into the service of the god under the earth. He was the closest thing she had to a friend, and she trusted him even more than her own slave Ayzebel.

Sabra fumbled her way up toward him, still wincing from the torchlight. As soon as her feet breached the threshold of the Temple she said, her voice a rasping whisper, "Hanno. Can you put that out? It's too bright."

"I'm sorry, mistress," he said. "I forgot about the darkness."

He extinguished the torch in the urn of sand by the Temple

stairs, returning the night to moonlight.

"Did my father send you?" Sabra asked. She pressed her fingers against her eyes. "I'm in no danger."

"He thought you might not be able to make it back up the hill."

Sabra gave him a dubious look and Hanno grinned.

"All right, he didn't. *I* thought you might not make it." The smile was already gone from his face. "The god can't be pleased to see you so spent in his service, tottering around like an old grandmother when your life should be blossoming."

Sabra forced a weak laugh, throwing it like a veil over her fear. Deep inside she always worried that the god was indifferent to her. She could serve...or not. She could die...or not. Another priestess would do just as well, or perhaps better. Who could tell what the god was thinking, or what might please or anger him? At least the gods of the Greeks and the Romans—and even that strange new god that some in Cyrene had come to serve—at least their will could sometimes be discerned.

All Sabra could hope for was that her prayers and fasts were enough to keep her god deep in the earth. She never wanted to imagine what might happen if the rituals failed, but she knew she would never forgive herself if they did.

Sabra realized she was shaking, and not just from hunger. Dreams of death, of dry stones and fire and blood, had plagued her since she was a child, even before the mantle of the priestess had been laid on her shoulders. And though she tried to dismiss them as only dreams, she couldn't escape the terrible fear that they were a promise...a portent of what would happen if she should fail.

"Mistress?" Hanno asked, touching her arm. "Should I call a litter for you? You're white as sand."

"No," she said. She must not be weak. She must be strong, always strong. "I just need some water."

Hanno disappeared without a word, his absence making the darkness deeper. Sabra rubbed her hands over her arms, chilled in spite of the warm wind that blew in from the south. The abandoned streets around the temple district of Cyrene usually didn't bother her. Despite a lifetime of solitary hours spent in the darkness of the temple, Sabra had never felt alone.

Tonight was different. Tonight she was afraid, and she was alone.

Hanno returned with a dripping gourd of water, and Sabra swallowed it all in a few gulps that left her chest burning.

"Better now?" Hanno asked, watching her carefully.

Sabra handed him the gourd, tasting the drops of water that clung to her trembling lips. "Did you taste the water, Hanno?"

Hanno frowned. "No. Was it sour?"

"I'm…I'm not sure." She licked her lips again, trying to catch the taste that had surprised her, but it had gone. "Does that ever happen to you? Something troubles you, and you can't recall what, and it just festers in the back of your mind like a thorn." She shook her head. "It was there a moment ago. Something about the water. Now it's gone."

Hanno bent his head. "I should have tasted it first," he murmured. "I'm sorry, mistress."

"I'm fine," she said, clasping his arm. "It was just…I'm tired, that's all. And hungry. My mind is playing tricks."

He nodded and looped the gourd onto his belt. Then he guided her arm around his neck and started for the long hill that led up to the governor's palace. Sabra leaned more and more on Hanno as they went, but he never complained.

She drew a ragged breath and murmured, "It was so hard this time. I don't know why."

"They're drawing the name tomorrow, aren't they?" Hanno asked.

She glanced up at him, surprised to find sadness in his eyes. Sadness and fear, and something like hope.

"Yes," she said. "In the evening."

"Are you worried?"

She stopped and faced him, pulling her arm free from his shoulder. "I serve the god without fear, Hanno," she said, hoping the tremble in her voice didn't betray her as a liar. Then she dropped her voice to a whisper. "But these are the days I hate above all others."

"It never gets easier?"

Sabra hesitated. Against her will, her eyes dropped shut, and she remembered the last sacrifice as clearly as if she stood before the god's cave again. High on a hill outside the city, gaping like a maw among the houses of the dead, the cave waited to swallow the victims she provided. Deep in the corners of her memory she could still hear the faint haunting melody of a distant flute, the drums echoing the chaos of her own pulse, the weeping of a child.

The dry wind stung her eyes and she lowered her gaze. It was only when her lashes brushed her cheeks that she realized they were wet with tears.

She swiped at her cheeks. "I don't regret," she whispered. "I don't fear. I don't fear."

Hanno muttered something under his breath and started again for the palace. She stumbled beside him, biting her lip to keep from crying, staring fixedly at the plain tips of her shoes faltering over the paving stones. Somehow Hanno managed to get her all the way up the hill, though she felt so heavy she wondered how he could move with her at all.

She mumbled a greeting to the sleepy slave who met them at the door and let Hanno guide her into the open peristyle. Her servant Ayzebel knelt beside a low coal brazier under the portico, coaxing the embers back to life. She rose when she saw Sabra, but even then she kept her head bowed and eyes averted.

Sabra sighed, too weary to be saddened by the girl's withdrawn attitude. Ayzebel had served her for nearly seven years now—almost half their lives—but the girl never seemed comfortable in Sabra's presence. At first Sabra thought she was just timid, but lately she'd begun to believe Ayzebel simply hated her. And nothing she did seemed to change that.

Sabra collapsed onto a pile of embroidered cushions close to the fire, enclosed in its warm circle of light. A cool autumn breeze trickled through the columns of the open peristyle, trembling the leaves on the slender branches of the fruit trees. She leaned toward the brazier to escape the chill, letting the fire's warmth soothe away the numbness and the aches she'd collected in her vigil at the Temple.

She stared at her hands, watching the low firelight burnish her too-pale skin. Her father's complexion showed his Numidian lineage, and, though she couldn't remember her Roman mother, Sabra imagined that she must have had beautiful olive skin. But Sabra resembled neither of them, with her pallor and her strangely golden eyes. She looked nothing like the sun, and everything like the grave. Marked by the god himself for his service, the old Priestess had said. Serving him was her fate.

A kitchen slave approached with a dish of dried fruits and nuts and a flask of water. Hanno took them and dismissed the boy, then settled cross-legged beside her.

"Mistress, eat something," he said, and nudged the dish toward her.

She reached for a raisin, mumbling, "Too tired."

"Eat first, then sleep," he said.

He was scowling at her with a look black as thunder, and Sabra couldn't help a smile.

"Oh, have it your way," she said. "Hand it here."

He gave her the plate and she picked through the offerings, leaving the walnuts and eating the almonds and hazelnuts instead, washing them down with tepid water. She caught Hanno eyeing the leftover walnuts.

"Eat them if you like," she whispered.

Hanno peered around the open courtyard, but Ayzebel had disappeared to prepare Sabra's bed and no one else was around. Only his fingers moved then, sneaking up to the plate and scooping a few walnuts into his palm. Sabra tried to smother a laugh but failed.

Hanno grinned. "I haven't heard you laugh in months."

"I laugh!" she protested, her smile faltering, but the words didn't convince her. Then, "Months?"

"Months," Hanno pronounced, setting his jaw. "It just gets worse and worse. I hate to see you like this."

Sabra stared at him, then shrugged. She was too tired to argue. "I'm not unhappy, Hanno. I wish you'd believe me."

He gave her such a skeptical look that she found herself smiling again.

"And don't blaspheme the god, either," she said, when he opened his mouth to speak. "I know what you're going to say. I don't want you to say it."

He shook his head and shoved the rest of the walnuts into his mouth so he couldn't say anything. Sabra followed his example, stuffing a handful of raisins into her mouth and savoring their sticky sweetness. Ayzebel returned as she finished, waiting with an oil lamp to take her to her chamber. Sabra avoided her gaze and handed the plate to Hanno.

"See to that. I'm going to bed."

"Sleep well, mistress," he said, standing and helping her up. "I pray that the nightmares leave you in peace tonight."

Sabra shuddered. "Those nightmares spoke of future days," she whispered. A cold dread seeped through her veins and she looked up into Hanno's dark eyes. The words were out before she could stop them: "I don't need them anymore."

3

Satala

Jurian made his way home as the sun slipped toward the horizon, turning the fields around the village a burnished gold. Besides the low hum of insects and the scratching of the wind through the scrub, everything was perfectly silent. At times like these, Jurian could imagine he was the only person alive, and the sensation both exhilarated and terrified him.

Halfway back to the house, he spotted the slow churn of movement in the undergrowth, higher on the hill and a little south from where he walked. It was a boar, judging from the way the grass stirred—violently, slowly, methodically. The wild hogs had strayed too close to the village lately, until the Legion had put a price on the destructive nuisances. Jurian had made a fair bit of coin bringing in their carcasses before, but tonight he had a different end in mind for the beast.

Jurian put a hand instinctively to his shoulder and swore softly when he grabbed nothing but air. He'd left his bow at home that morning, since he'd meant to do his day's food foraging in the market, not the fields. But then the messenger had come, and he'd forgotten. Now, with the market stalls closing early on account of the public sacrifice, that boar would be his only option for his family's meal.

He fingered the hilt of the long hunting knife that hung from his belt, pulling it free with a quiet rasp of steel on leather. The blade had belonged to his father, picked up from a barbarian enemy on some campaign in the deep forests around the Danube. His father had called it a *seax*, and he'd told Jurian that it was a fitting weapon for a Roman boy with a Germanic name.

It was a cruel-looking weapon, with strange runic letters etched above the blade and a twisting knot carved in its grip. Its blade was shorn off at the end as if the tip had been broken, but his father had said it was forged that way on purpose. It felt solid in his grip, solid and dependable. And he knew that its razor edge was more than capable of piercing a boar's hide.

His mouth twitched in a smile as he flipped the grip on the knife and edged through the grasses, low and lithe like a hunting cat. As he got closer, he got his first good glimpse of the boar. It was young and small—that would make an easier fight and a lighter burden to drag home.

The boar stopped rooting in the dirt, the whites of its eyes showing as it glared warily in his direction. Holding his breath, Jurian eased his way forward until he was a dozen feet from the animal. Then he stopped to watch and wait. The boar would either charge or flee; if it charged, Jurian would have one good chance for a killing blow. If it ran, the hunt was off. He would never be able to catch it on foot.

When the boar relaxed, Jurian crept forward again. His heart pounded, blood and fear and the fire of excitement rushing through him. Just a few more steps. But suddenly the boar lifted its head, eyes rolling and ears flicking madly. Jurian froze as he heard what had startled the hog.

Hoofbeats.

Seconds later he saw them. A handful of Legion riders crested the hill, cantering straight toward him and the boar.

The boar screamed and bolted in Jurian's direction. It didn't slow and didn't swerve. Jurian shifted to the balls of his feet. Just before the boar trampled him, he dove sideways, driving the vicious blade into the boar's neck, down past the vital cord toward the heart. With another terrible squeal the boar lurched and collapsed, paralyzed, the dark blood pooling on the pale dirt. Jurian picked himself up, gasping for breath, and delivered one last blow up under the boar's jaw to end its suffering.

He sat back on his heels as the world returned in a rush. The horsemen broke through the brush and wheeled to a halt. Nine officers from the Legion's cavalry unit loomed over him, some armed with bows, others with long spears, all of them scowling. One edged forward and Jurian squinted up at the rider. The Legion Decurion, one of the cavalry commanders.

"You spoiled our hunt," he said in Greek.

Jurian flicked a glance over the other riders, but none of them so much as smiled. He stood, holding the bloody knife at his side in a way he was sure they would call disrespectful.

"Should I have let him gore me, *domine?*" Jurian asked in Latin.

The Decurion exchanged a surprised glance with the horseman closest to him, who said, "That's *Legatus* Lucius Aurelius Gerontios' son."

"Are you?" the Decurion asked Jurian.

Jurian studied him in silence, weighing his options. "I am," he said finally.

The Decurion leaned his forearm on the saddle horns. "And you took down this boar, knowing we were hunting it?"

"No," Jurian said. "I took down the boar when he charged me, but I thought he was my quarry. I meant to take him to my mother. She's ill. The doctor said she needs meat for strength."

The Decurion frowned. "The doctor? Which doctor?"

"He never said his name. I think he was the *sapsarius*."

"Well, and you killed the boar with what, just that knife?"

"Yes, *domine*."

The Decurion's brows arched, impressed, and he cast an appraising glance over the boar and the two wounds that had killed it. Jurian's blood warmed with a flicker of satisfaction. He imagined his father would have been proud. And his father would have let him keep it. But if the Decurion asked him for the carcass to feed the troops at the fortress, Jurian would have to yield it, and his family would go hungry.

He couldn't let that happen. He would have to be bold; he would have to take a gamble.

"*Domine*," he said, "Take this boar as a gift and an apology."

A strange smile fractured the Decurion's stony look. "That alone convinces me that you are Gerontios' son." He glanced again at the horseman on his right. "Well. How much meat would you say you would need to feed your family tonight?"

Jurian contemplated the boar. Neither his mother nor Mariam ate much meat, and he could make do with very little if it meant making a good impression on the Legion officers.

"A shoulder should be enough."

"Then you'll have it."

"There's nowhere to field dress it here," Jurian said, gesturing at the treeless sweep of land, "but our house is just a little farther up the hill, if you would let me slaughter it there."

The Decurion waved a hand and one of the horsemen dismounted with a length of rope. Jurian smiled. He'd been troubling over the best way to get the carcass home ever since he'd spotted the boar, but with the man's help they easily dragged the boar the remaining distance to the house. Jurian tied the hog up by its hocks and slipped inside to get his carving knife.

The old farmhouse had little of the Roman design besides the simple stone *lararium*, the Roman altar for the household gods near the door, which now stood empty and covered in dust. Jurian cast an anxious glance at it as he passed into the kitchen, praying that the Decurion wouldn't decide this was a good time for a social call. The last thing they needed was Legion officers traipsing through their house and mocking their poverty—and seeing their empty shrine.

He grabbed his carving knife from its hook near the blazing *fornax* and returned to the horsemen just as Mariam appeared, climbing the long hill toward the house. When one young eques spotted her and dismounted, Jurian gritted his teeth and stuck the carving knife through his belt, and stalked out to meet her.

"Mari," he whispered. "Where've you been? You should have

been back an hour ago."

She flicked a curious glance at the horsemen, smiling cheerfully at the one who had dismounted.

"Julia and Claudia caught me as I was coming out of the village," she said. A blush crept over her cheeks, and Jurian knew it had nothing to do with the two girls and everything to do with the horseman behind him.

"Do you know him?" he asked. "That *eques?*"

Her eyes widened. "No, but he keeps staring at me! What am I supposed to do?"

Jurian tried to stifle a grin but failed. He clasped her arm and leaned closer to her, teasing, "Well, don't *smile* at him! You'll just encourage him."

She tucked a loose strand of dark hair behind her ear and nodded, trying her best to look serious. "Why are they here? Have they come because—"

"They're here for the boar. I can't explain right now. Go and check on mother. And for goodness' sake, stop fluttering your lashes at that *eques*, or we'll never be rid of them!"

Mari edged past him and favored the young horseman with a final bright glance as she left. Jurian sighed. He had once tried to put her off the Legionaries by telling her that they couldn't marry, but they both knew that no one followed that law any more, especially not out in the borderlands. But Mari should have understood that something deeper divided them. Something far more dangerous than some antiquated law.

Jurian went back to the hog, butchering it with little fuss as he listened to the men's conversation.

"His name was Marcellus," one of the men was saying. "Renounced his oath and everything."

"He was executed?" asked another. "Treason?"

The first nodded. "As I heard it, it all started with the Legion sacrifices. He wouldn't participate."

Jurian swallowed, the knife hilt suddenly slick in his hand. He wiped it and his palms on a bit of leather and carried on his work with intense focus.

"Why not?" one asked. "What makes his cult so special? We set up a *castra*, we build altars. The more altars, the better! Why would this Marcellus be so un-Roman? Doesn't his god play with others?"

Un-Roman. That word rang in Jurian's ears. Casca had accused him of the same fault. He clenched his jaw.

"Boy," one of the men called to him suddenly. "Lucius Aurelius. What do they call you?"

Jurian swallowed. "Jurian."

"Jurian! By the gods, did Gerontios really give you a barbarian name?"

Jurian lowered the knife and turned to face the horseman. He expected mockery, but the man's smile was curious, not cruel, so Jurian bit back his sharp retort and instead told the man the truth.

"It's actually Georgius. Lucius Aurelius Georgius. But my father always called me Jurian. A Germanic man saved his life, up along the Danube. He was a farmer. Called himself Jurian. So, that's what my father always called me." He shrugged. "He meant to honor the man, I suppose."

The man nodded. "And you don't go by Georgius?"

"We don't have much use for formality out here, *domine*."

"And was that your sister we saw just now?"

One of the men muttered something to the *eques* who had dismounted before, and the man grinned broadly.

"Yes," Jurian said, sharp.

"Isn't she part of some Cult of the Lady? All these new cults popping up, hard to keep them straight. My Julia goes there sometimes. What's a father to do, eh?"

Jurian hesitated. The man probably meant the Cult of Aphrodite, which had recently become popular among the younger women of Satala. Jurian had never had the slightest interest in it the way some of the village boys did.

Like Casca, he thought before he could stop himself.

All Jurian knew was that Aphrodite was nothing like the Lady his sister and mother honored. He also knew that if his father was still alive, he would never have allowed Mari to be involved in such a cult.

"I wouldn't know, *domine,*" he said awkwardly.

"Ah, well," the old horseman said. "And what about you? Since we're talking of gods, which is your favorite?"

Jurian hesitated for an awful moment. What could he say, when he knew so little of his family's faith? And now that it was under suspicion, to admit anything would be a death sentence.

He smiled suddenly, recalling something his father had told him about the soldiers in his Legion—a blessed ambiguity that just might get him out of this conversation.

"Oh," he said, with a hidden smile, "you know, I favor the virgin-born God."

Several of the men exchanged knowing looks and grins, and the one closest to Jurian bent and clapped his shoulder, saying, "Ah, excellent, *frater!* I thought you had something of the soldiers' god about you."

Jurian kept the smile frozen on his face. From his father's stories, he knew that the followers of Mithras considered themselves as a sort of secret brotherhood. He'd counted on them thinking he meant the soldiers' god and not the Christ, but a cold wash of fear suddenly swept over him.

What if they invite me to join their rites?

For one heart-stopping instant, he waited for the blow to come. Blessedly, it never did.

"Indeed," one of others said, nodding at the butchered boar. "That was work worthy of the god, to be sure!"

Jurian nodded his thanks and turned to pack the butchered meat in a reed basket, all but the shoulder for his family's stew. He carried the basket to the young *eques* who had been watching Mari and shoved it up to him unceremoniously.

"Your flesh," he said, with just the hint of a malicious grin.

The older horseman cackled with laughter. "Watch out, Dacien. I don't think he likes you looking at his sister."

Dacien took the basket, and as he turned to lash it behind his saddle, he said with something like respect, "That girl is lucky, you know. Having you for her brother."

Jurian managed a half-smile and inclined his head. The men headed off at an easy canter toward Satala, the sounds of their laughter fading long after the sound of hoofbeats. Jurian waited until they had disappeared, then headed back into the house with the hog's shoulder.

Mari had already set a pot of water to boil and stood at the board slicing beets. She said nothing as he came in, and her face seemed drawn. Jurian sighed as he spitted the hog meat and rubbed it with salt and spices, then set it to roast in the *fornax*.

"Mari, I'm sorry," he said. "About the *eques*."

"Oh," she said, her hands going still. "That's not—"

In the ragged remnant of daylight slanting in through the window, Jurian caught the shine of tears in her eyes. He kissed her forehead gently.

"What is it then?" he asked. "What happened?"

"It's Mother," she said. She shook her head and started carefully slicing a small mound of carrots and turnips for the stew. "I…I don't know how to help her."

Jurian sighed and went to wash his hands of the boar's blood, then he slipped into the small peristyle where he found his mother asleep on a low couch near the coal brazier. Even so close to the fire and huddled under a thick wool blanket, she shivered as she slept. With his heart in his throat, Jurian knelt down beside the couch and gently touched her shoulder. She was so thin, so weak, her cheeks gaunt and grey. Some days she hardly seemed to wake up at all, and no amount of medicine seemed to make any difference.

"Jurian," she whispered suddenly, her eyelashes fluttering against her cheeks. "Is that you?"

Jurian swallowed hard. "Yes, Mother," he said. "Do you need anything? Water?"

"I need…"

Her voice trailed off and she turned her head on the cushion, her once lustrous hair falling in a brittle cascade over her cheek. Jurian glanced over his shoulder and saw Mari standing pale in the doorway, her hands full of vegetables, tears in her eyes. He held her gaze briefly, then turned back to his mother.

"Tell me," he said, trying to sound strong.

The ghost of a smile touched her lips and her hands stirred on a scrap of bloody rag, her fingers reaching for his. He took her hand in both his own, choking back an unsteady breath.

When she spoke, he barely heard her. "I need the priest."

"The priest? What priest?"

Mari came and knelt beside him. "Do you mean Eugenius?"

She nodded. "By the bones of the rock," she said in Greek, "I'll wait for you to bring him."

Her eyes drifted shut and her breathing steadied, and Jurian got up and backed away from the couch. Mari followed him into the *culina*. He braced his hands against the board, head bowed, jaw tight. The blood simmered in his veins like anger, but he didn't even know why.

"The bones of the rock?" he echoed. "What does that even mean? And who is this Eugenius?"

Mari put a hand on his shoulder. "He's the priest that sometimes comes," she said, quietly. "I don't think you ever met him. You never come to offer thanksgiving with us."

"Of course I haven't met him," Jurian snapped. "I've only just been trying to keep this family from falling apart since Father had to die in disgrace and leave us in ruins." He slammed his fist on the board so violently that Mari jumped. "Why isn't he here?" he cried, almost shouting it. "Why did he leave us—leave *her*—like this? If he were here, she wouldn't be dying!"

Mari stared at him, then threw her arms around his neck. He bristled, furious that she thought he needed comforting, but after a moment he realized, stupidly, that she was the one who needed it. Letting out his breath, he held her close. For all he'd prayed, he could never bring his father back. For better or worse, he and Mari only had each other.

"Where does this Eugenius live?" he asked softly.

"South and a little west, maybe a five or six hours' walk," she said, the words stumbling through her tears. "He lives in a hut up in the hills."

"How am I supposed to find him?"

She laughed and released him, wiping her cheeks. "You'll smell it. His woodsmoke always smells of herbs."

Jurian nodded and went to grab his bow and quiver and his father's military cloak. When he came back into the *culina,* Mari stood at the spit of boar meat, turning it over the flames.

"I'll miss the stew," he said ruefully.

Mari smiled. "I'll save you some, don't worry. But take some bread and pomegranates. At least it's something."

She packed a few things into a cloth parcel, tying it with string before handing it to him. He hesitated.

"Mari, can you find the doctor? He may be able to give her some comfort while I'm gone."

"Of course," she said. "Don't worry. With everyone distracted by the rituals, I won't be in any danger."

"Just stay clear of the Legion," he said, winking at her over his shoulder.

4

CYRENE

MORNING CAME TOO SOON AFTER Sabra's long vigil at the Temple. She had barely drifted into a troubled sleep when the jubilant crowing of a rooster broke through her dreams. She groaned, pressing her hands into her eyes. The splintering headache she'd hoped sleep would cure was still there.

Another rooster close to her window took up the morning call, and Sabra forced herself out of bed. In the half-light of dawn, Sabra dressed quickly in her plain robe. She was still fastening the laces of her sandals when Ayzebel came to tend to her hair.

Sabra frowned at her somber reflection in the polished bronze mirror as Ayzebel brushed out her dark hair. The priestesses of the Roman cults glittered in embroidered robes, their hair braided and bound with beaded fillets, as bright and shining as the gods they served. They didn't realize that their rites meant nothing. Empty words spoken to empty ears.

And yet, all Sabra could think was how she looked nothing like them.

Her plain dark robe and loose hair were a sign to everyone around her that she was untouchable, that she served an older god, a darker god, than the gods of the Romans. No wonder Ayzebel could barely look at her.

"How long before the children come?" she asked quietly.

Ayzebel's hands faltered. "An hour, mistress. Will you eat?"

"Maybe a little," Sabra said. She studied the girl's somber reflection, then, before she could stop herself, the words were out of her mouth. "Ayzebel, are you afraid of me?"

Ayzebel froze, meeting Sabra's gaze in the mirror.

"I don't understand," she said, but for once she didn't immediately glance away. Then she added with something like defiance, "I'm not unhappy."

Sabra swallowed. Had Ayzebel been in the peristyle when she had said the same thing to Hanno? Why else would she speak so boldly, with that bright gleam in her eyes?

"You may go," she said, pulling her hair free of Ayzebel's hands. "I'll eat later."

"You've been fasting for days, mistress," Ayzebel said. "You should take a real meal."

Sabra hesitated. The fact that Ayzebel was talking to her was curious enough to keep her from brushing off the girl's concern.

"I suppose you're right," she said.

She sighed and turned, and found herself face to face with Ayzebel. The girl stood with her hands in loose fists at her sides, her cheeks pale and her amber eyes troubled.

"Mistress," she said. "How do you do it?"

"Do what?" Sabra asked.

"This morning you will teach the children about the god. And tonight one of them will be chosen for the sacrifice. How do you do it? How do you teach them how to die?"

Sabra swallowed, tasting dread like bile at the back of her throat. "I don't," she murmured. "They teach me."

AFTER FORCING DOWN a brief but hearty meal of grains and fruit, Sabra set out alone for the school in the Greek *agora*. Many of the city's children received their normal lessons there, but not today. Today was the day of the winnowing—the day, second only to the day of sacrifice, that Sabra dreaded most.

As she made her way down the hill, head high, eyes down, she remembered what the old priestess had taught her about this day. Even now she could remember the smell of amber from the woman's necklace, the dry rustle of her dark robes over a floor strewn with reeds.

"There was a prophecy," the woman had said, standing at a tall window and staring out at the crumbling streets. *"The god thirsts for blood, innocent blood...or do they say, flawless blood? Who knows what the sayings of seeresses mean? But he desires blood, and if we do not offer it willingly, he will stop the fountain and wait for us to fall wasted in the streets."*

After that, Sabra's nightmares had begun. The dry spring, blood in the streets. Sabra shook her head, forcing the terrible images from her mind. She had enough to worry about without tormenting herself with specters.

When she arrived in the *agora,* a few of the ramshackle shops had just opened—dreary little stalls filled with broken bits of unwanted trinkets, forlorn merchants watching Sabra pass with only idle interest. Sabra kept her eyes down, her heart aching. Cyrene was dying. This city, its people...all dying.

Sabra stumbled and forced herself the rest of the way down the market street to the school, which was little more than a room nestled behind the decadent aromas of the baker's shop. Sometimes the baker would bring the children scraps of dough fried up and laced with honey, but he had stopped bringing them for Sabra years ago. She'd always hated that she had to refuse them, but the god's service was not for the weak. Even when she was free of her ritual fasting, she was forbidden to taste wine, meat, honey or sweets. She couldn't even lawfully touch the steel of a knife, not even to save her own life.

Sabra edged inside the school, standing for a moment in the half-light filtering through the tree just outside. The long wooden benches squatted in a semi-circle, waiting for the children whose names had been enrolled in the lottery for the first time. These were the ones who needed to learn what they were facing, what honor would await them if their name was chosen. Eventually, if her father could sway the elders to the god's purpose, she would teach all the children in Cyrene. But not everyone served the ancient deity, though his worship kept them all safe—the vapid gods of the Romans held sway still. And then there was that new god, the virgin-born. His cult was growing.

Perhaps that is why the god is angry.

Sabra realized that she was holding herself tightly. She didn't understand why her father permitted these heresies to flourish. Time and again she had tried to tell him, to warn him. But he was too far under the sway of Roman politics to listen to her premonitions.

She heard voices behind her and moved quickly into the chamber. The children slipped into their places on the benches, their smiles extinguished like candles in her presence. Most were girls, some as young as seven years old. As she studied their fresh faces and wide, frightened eyes, she felt suddenly weary, soul-tired as she had never felt before.

It was best just to get it over with.

She began quietly, lifting her eyes to look at each of the children in turn as she spoke. "You are here because you may be asked to give the greatest measure of service to our god. When he first reached these shores, a terrible earthquake heralded his arrival. The ground broke open and brought forth the Kyre, the spring that gives water to our city. The Greeks called it Apollo's, but in truth it is the old god's alone. It flows, or not, by his will alone. Almost forty years ago there was a new earthquake, and great waves lashed the shores of Apollonia, our sister city. Temples fell, the great library was destroyed. Death and disease followed in its wake. One by one the priestesses of the god fell ill and died, until only one remained."

Sabra paused, just long enough to see the fear-white faces of the children staring back at her. One small girl on the front bench hunched over, her dark hair spilling over her face. Sabra knew from her trembling shoulders that she was weeping, and wished she could spare the girl from the terror that was coming.

"The priestess had long felt the anger of the old god," she continued. "Strange things were happening near the god's cavern in the Green Mountain. Smoke and fire, the earth shaking as if stirred by the steps of an enormous beast. Some people claimed they saw the manifestation of the god himself, prowling the hills wrapped in flame and shadow, questing for something to quell his appetite. The god, you see, was hungry."

One of the boys actually gasped, and several other children started whispering nervously. Sabra held up her hand and they fell silent, all at once. So, they had come to *that* moment, the moment she always dreaded. She had told them of the god, of his manifestation and his hunger, and now they had pieced it together with what they knew about *her*. This dark god—this was who she served. She was the voice of the god, no, the face of the god. So now, she was the one they feared.

She sighed and went on, "The priestess continued to offer prayer and ritual fasts to show the god that he hadn't been forgotten. Some believe he revealed himself to her. She never told me if it was true. But she knew the god had to be appeased."

"Have you seen the god?" one of the children asked.

Sabra drew a slow breath and pressed her hands together, trying to hold back the dread bubbling up inside her.

"I…I'm not certain," she admitted. "But it doesn't matter. The last priestess was given a vision foretelling the great destruction of all Cyrenaica unless the god could be satisfied, but she didn't know how. My father sent a messenger to the Delphic oracles, requesting guidance. How could we stave off the destruction he was planning against us?"

The little girl in the front shuddered and said, "Sacrifice."

"Sacrifice," Sabra repeated, quietly. "The oracle said that each month we were to offer to the god an innocent life. At first, we tried to offer what we offer to all the other gods. Spotless beasts—goat kids, sacred chickens, unblemished lambs. We even offered first-born calves and the finest stud colt in my father's stables. But the god only got angrier and angrier. People went missing. Traders left the city at night and never reached Apollonia. The ground began to tremble and break, swallowing herds, destroying homes. Foul vapors seeped from fissures in the broken earth. And the priestess, now an old woman, finally divined the meaning of the god's desire. The oracle asked for *innocent* life. Animals can be spotless, but they cannot be *innocent*. The sacrifice would have to be a human child."

The boy began to weep openly. "You mean," he gulped, "when you talk about us serving the god, you mean we get served *to* him?"

"What do *you* think happened to Juba when he was led up the mountain?" one of the older girls asked him, stoic.

"He got *eaten?*" he gasped. His voice broke on the word, and he stared at Sabra through terrified eyes.

"He was accepted by the god and the city survived another month," Sabra said. "There is such honor in that! Each month, one of us has the chance to keep our people safe. If the god is satisfied with us, he will leave the rest of the city in peace."

"Us?" asked the girl in the front.

Sabra lifted her chin, because this was her best chance of making them brave. "Yes, *us*," she said. "My name is there with yours in the lottery."

As she expected, they stared at her with a new regard.

One of the girls asked, "Are you afraid?"

Sabra smiled faintly. "Who wouldn't be? But that doesn't mean I am unwilling. I will do whatever the god asks of me, if it means keeping our city safe."

"What if no one got sacrificed?" the little boy asked.

Sabra shook her head. The voice had come muffled to her ears, as if from far away. She stared at the cracked stones beneath her feet, dry and barren, dazzling in the blazing sunlight. A desiccating wind buffeted her, thick with the smell of burning grass, burning flesh. Turning away from the fierce afternoon sun, she gazed at the city spread in panorama before her.

Empty streets. Empty markets. All empty.

Nothing remained of her beautiful city, nothing but smoke and shattered stone. She turned and found herself facing the Fountain of Apollo, the narrow cavern from which the Kyre flowed…or used to flow. The rocks were dry. The moss on the stones had turned to patches of brittle grey. The conduit that once carried the water to the city...empty.

"Empty," she whispered, and the cavern echoed back to her a word that she had not spoken: "*Dead.*"

She leaned into the low mouth of the cavern, and saw Death itself staring back at her.

"Mistress Sabra!"

She reeled back, torn from the vision by the child's frantic cry. The room cut into focus around her, stark and dim, quiet but for a chatter of noise seeping in from the market. And in front of her, thirteen children stared at her open-mouthed.

"Mistress Sabra, are you all right?" the dark-haired girl asked.

Sabra blinked and slowly unlocked her fingers from the edge of the podium. Her palms were damp with sweat, but her whole body shook from a sudden chill. Gradually her heartbeat slowed its hectic chattering.

"I'm all right," she murmured.

"You just went completely white," the girl said. "And your eyes...you kept staring at the ceiling, like you saw something there. Something terrible."

"And you were muttering," the boy said. "But I couldn't understand any of it."

"Was it a vision?" the older girl asked, voice hushed and almost reverent.

Sabra shuddered. "I'm not sure."

If only the old priestess were still alive, she could explain all of this. Was that what she had seen, that terrible vision of a forsaken city? And what did it mean? Sabra didn't even know who to ask. She alone served the god and knew the secrets of his worship. There was no one who could help her.

She drew a deep breath and managed a faint smile. "You asked what would happen if we failed in the sacrifices. We would lose everything. That is why you should consider yourselves fortunate, even blessed. If you are chosen to offer your blood, you will redeem the whole city."

"I don't want to die," the older girl said suddenly, with unabashed honesty. "I don't want to be a sacrifice."

Sabra stepped away from the podium, tucking her hands in the dark folds of her robe. "I know it sounds terrible. Your older sister is Jezbel, am I right?"

The girl nodded, curious.

"I taught her, too, at one time. Think about it this way. What if someone told you that either you or Jezbel had to die, and you had to choose which of you it would be. What would you do?"

The girl paled and sat up straight, then she whispered fiercely, "I'd never let anyone hurt Jezbel. Never."

Sabra didn't answer; she didn't need to. The girl's words hung heavy in the air, as the other children grasped the meaning of what she'd said. They were always smart that way. Gods help them, but they were smart.

"What does the god look like?" another girl asked. "You said the old priestess saw a manifestation of him?"

"My grandfather told me he saw the god up in the hills," the older girl said. "He said he had the horns of a bull."

"Ten horns!" another interjected.

"And wings like a bat," the little boy said. "And smoke comes off him like he's on fire."

"I heard he has fangs like a snake!" another girl cried, almost shouting to be heard over the other children's chatter.

"Teeth like a crocodile," the older girl corrected.

"That's enough," Sabra said, feeling queasy. "It is blasphemous to speak so freely of the god."

Most of the children bowed their heads, chastised, but the older girl held Sabra's gaze.

"Please tell me one thing, Mistress," she said. "Do we see the god, there at the end?"

Sabra swallowed hard. "I don't know."

Was she supposed to tell them they would be blessed to receive a vision of the god? Or that they might die of fear? Part of her hoped that it wasn't true, that the victims died suddenly, without time to feel terror. But she didn't know. She had never stayed at the god's cave longer than she was permitted.

When the girl didn't keep questioning her, she murmured,

"You are all free to go. Fortune favor you tonight."

They got up one by one and slipped past the curtain, letting in fickle shafts of dazzling daylight and the smell of roasting meat and nuts. Only two girls remained—the little one in the front row and the stoic older girl. Sabra went and sat on the front bench, facing them.

"Is everything all right?"

The younger one sighed shakily and nodded; the other shrugged and kept her gaze averted.

"What are your names?" Sabra asked.

"Elissa," the little one said. "My father works for your father in the Prytaneum."

"I'm Dido," the older girl said, then added, "Yes, named after the famed queen of Carthage."

Sabra smiled. "Did you need to ask me something?"

"How do you keep from feeling afraid?" Dido asked. "I'm so scared of the lottery. I don't even want to go." Tears started to her eyes, and she blinked them away in embarrassment. "I just turned fourteen," she whispered. And then, all in a rush she said, "And…there's a boy, and he smiled at me yesterday as if I was the prettiest thing he'd ever seen. What if he really cares about me? Is it so wrong of me to want to live? I don't want to die. I'm not ready."

Elissa ducked her head, smiling in spite of herself. But Sabra couldn't smile, not even at Dido's honesty about the boy. Her heart felt strangely sick, something like doubt or dread gnawing a hole deep inside it. She knew what she should say: Dido ought to be honored at the idea of giving her life to the god. Fear was weakness; fear didn't belong to true piety. But somehow, she couldn't say any of those things.

All she could say was, "None of us knows when we will die. And we shouldn't live in fear because of that. I just know that, when my time comes, I want to be able to face that dark gateway and say honestly, *I did all I could.*"

Dido nodded unenthusiastically. Sabra didn't really blame her. No matter how carefully she cultivated her sense of duty, her piety to the god, deep inside there was always a remnant of dread. Better not to dwell on it, though, lest the god mistake it for apostasy.

"And you, Elissa?" she asked, forcing the thought away.

"I'm not afraid to die," Elissa said, more boldly than Sabra expected. Then, voice hushed, "I'm just afraid of the god."

"That is not unwise," Sabra murmured.

"But you serve him!"

"Listen, Elissa. Have you ever been to the contests where they bring out a lion and make it fight against a man?"

Elissa nodded, crinkling her nose.

"Well, someone has to bring it food and water, right? To keep it alive?"

"So the god is like a lion?" Elissa asked, eyes wide. "I see. The lion-keeper serves the lion, but he isn't friends with it, because he would be stupid to try. The lion is too dangerous."

"Yes," Sabra said.

"So you're the lion-keeper."

That would be so much safer, Sabra thought, but she only nodded.

"And we might be the man in the ring, only we would have no weapons." Elissa hesitated, turning rather grey. "Actually, we might be the next dinner."

"Oh, Elissa!" Dido cried, and clapped a hand over her mouth.

"But I saw a man kill the lion once," Elissa went on, undeterred. "Does that mean…is it possible someone could kill the god too?"

Sabra flinched instinctively, throwing one hand before her in a sign against evil. Elissa just watched her through wide, innocent eyes while Sabra held her breath, expecting the god to strike one or both of them dead at any instant. When nothing happened, when the breeze carried on and the people kept chattering in the market, she sighed and bowed her head.

"We don't talk of the god that way," she whispered. "It is impossible even to imagine. Forget the lion. It was just an example, and a poor one at that. Now, go on, you two."

Dido got up first, bowing her head. "Thank you, mistress. I'll try to be braver."

Sabra smiled at her in farewell, and jumped in surprise when Elissa suddenly threw her arms around her neck.

"I think you're too pretty to be the god's priestess," she said.

"Silly!" Sabra laughed, patting the girl's back awkwardly.

Her eyes burned and she found herself trying—and failing—to recall the last time anyone had embraced her. Even Hanno never did that any more.

5

Cyrene

Sabra pushed her way through the crowded *agora*. Her throbbing head, coupled with the press of heat and noise, made her vision swim and her thoughts wander. She was halfway through the marketplace before she realized that the crowd was no milling throng of idle midmorning shoppers, who spent as much time gossiping by the fountains as they did browsing the wares. They were all heading one direction, pushing through the Greek market to the Roman forum.

She trailed after them and realized they were gathering around the *rostrum*. There, to her surprise, she saw her father standing with an imperial Roman messenger.

Her father raised his hands, and the crowd quieted to listen.

"People of Cyrene," he said. "We have just received word from Diocletian *Augustus*. The auguries and haruspicy of the priests of Apollo have failed. Public sacrifice is called for throughout the Empire." He paused, looking down at his hands. "Since tonight is the night of the winnowing, we will hold the public sacrifice tomorrow at sunset."

He stepped down from the *rostrum* and the people drifted away, murmuring among themselves.

"No," Sabra whispered, standing still in the midst of the swirling crowd. It was all so clear. "Don't you see?" she asked of no one in particular, but no one paid her any mind.

Darkness was threatening to pull her under. She was caught in the eddy of it. She had to get out, to get away. Sabra pushed her way through the straggling crowd and fled back up the hill to the governor's palace, where she cowered in the far corner of the peristyle, knees drawn up to her chin.

She didn't know how long she'd been there when Hanno finally found her. He didn't say anything, but he knelt on the mosaic floor beside her, one hand gripping her shoulder.

"They don't understand," she said, her voice wild.

"Understand what?"

Sabra suddenly became aware of his hand on her arm and drew back instinctively. A brief warmth stole over Hanno's face and he dropped his hand and his gaze. Somewhere inside, Sabra was furious with herself for flinching, and furious with him for respecting her reaction so quickly. He was concerned about her, even if no one else was, and she had pushed him away.

"Did you hear the news?" she asked. "The Roman priests can't read the auguries or the haruspices. They say the gods are silent, that Apollo is hiding his message. But don't you see?" Her voice trailed off, then she whispered, "Why can't they see?"

"I don't understand, mistress," Hanno said.

"It isn't Apollo. It's the god. *Our* god. The auguries run dry, but not because the priests have failed. Apollo has failed. Molech is angry at the whole world, and he is silencing all others. And the spring they call Apollo's will run dry, but not because of Apollo. The port city they call Apollo's will crumble in the shaking of the earth, but not because of the thunder of Apollo's feet. The Emperor is calling for public sacrifice to Apollo, but it is not Apollo who must be appeased." She snatched Hanno's arm. "Hanno! We are all going to die."

"Mistress, no," Hanno said, but she couldn't focus on his words. "Sabra!" he said, sharp. That finally brought her attention to him. He gripped both her shoulders, his dark gaze holding hers. "Intercede for us. You can save us!"

She pulled away with a shattered gasp. Terror spiked through her, and she couldn't understand why. Everything around her was cast in stark relief—blackest shadows twisting against blinding light, and everything in chaos. She flung her hands up over her eyes and scrambled to her feet. In the last calm corner of her mind she saw Hanno staring at her in dismay, fear, grief.

As if he knew the meaning of those words. But none of them knew. Not really.

Not yet.

She thrust a hand back toward him away and fled to her chamber. In the middle of the room she knelt down on the stone floor, throwing her hands wide and bowing her head.

"Let me save them," she whispered frantically. "Whatever you need, I will do. Just let me save them."

She strained to hear the god's answer, but only the silence grew, pressing around her like the darkness of a crypt.

AS NIGHT FELL, everyone gathered in the massive theater west of the Sanctuary of Apollo. Sabra could see its faint glimmer of lights from the portico of the governor's house, where she waited with her father and the chief members of the household.

She stood in her full priestess regalia—dark robe and dark *palla*, a whisper-thin veil drawn across the lower half of her face. A gold amulet weighed heavily from her neck, and on her ankle she wore a tiny bell that jingled faintly when she walked, meant to lull the god back to his sleep if he happened to wake before his time. Before the ceremony, she had marked her forehead with a stain, tracing a thin line from her hairline to the bridge of her nose in a red ink so dark, it looked like blood.

Her father held a large reed basket containing the names of the children eligible for the lottery scribbled on scraps of papyrus. On the broad steps below the palace, some of the people had gathered to watch Sabra's choice, even though the name would not be announced until they stood on the stage of the theater. Sabra tried to ignore them. She could barely concentrate anyway, with her stomach roiling and the ache in her head turned to a sharp, constant pounding. In a way Sabra was glad she had eaten so little during the day, or the queasiness of dread might have made her ill.

In the folds of her robe, her hands were cold and shaking.

"The time of the winnowing has come," her father said, raising his voice so the gathered people could hear. "Let the god choose his sacrifice." He turned to Sabra. "Choose, Priestess."

The governor spoke softly, but the words were a laceration. She cast a furtive glance up at him. Time had been kind enough to Lucius Titianus, leaving his hair still dark and ungreyed, but the burden of governing through Diocletian's meddling had left its mark in the grim set of his mouth and the hardness of his eyes. But those eyes were gentle now, even compassionate. Sabra wondered if he understood how difficult this moment was for her, how it got more difficult each month when it should have gotten easier, the way the tailor's fingers got worn and calloused from so many needle pricks.

She drew a deep breath and reached into the basket, whispering her usual prayer to the god to guide her choice.

The god chooses, she told herself, sifting through scraps of thin papyrus. *I am nothing but his conduit. I'm not the one condemning anyone to death.*

Am I?

Choose, Sabra.

Her fingers rested on a scrap and she drew it slowly from the basket. Without looking at it she held it out to her father, who handed the basket to a slave and accepted the papyrus. He held her gaze, then, trying a frail smile, he bent his head to read the name. Sabra saw the precise moment he finished, because his shoulders drooped and a thin sigh escaped his lips. When he glanced up, his face had turned rather grey, drawn with grief.

"Who is it?" she asked.

"The daughter of my friend and colleague, Aqhat," he said. "Elissa."

Sabra stared at him. Her stomach churned, and she swallowed back bile.

"No," she whispered.

With so many eyes on her, she couldn't react, couldn't cry out, couldn't weep. She was the priestess of the god. Who was she to protest his choice?

She blasphemed the god, a voice whispered in the back of her mind. *Is it any surprise that she was chosen?*

Sabra squeezed her eyes shut and bit down on her lower lip. Her hands knotted behind her back as if she could seize the pain like a white-hot poker until she didn't feel it any more. It was the only weakness she could allow herself.

Her father rested a hand briefly on her shoulder. She stumbled into step beside him, wishing she could plead a headache and escape to her chamber, knowing she had no right to flee. Not when it was her duty to lead a sweet child to her death.

Elissa. Oh, child, I'm so sorry.

What is she to you, compared to the god? the little voice said.

She shook her head and fixed desperate attention on the smooth white stones of the street, the way the cypress trees shook in the wind, the quiet tinkling of the bell on her ankle. They wove their way down the long steps through the bitter smoke of charcoal fires and torches, through the thundering, expectant silence of the crowd. The walk lasted a thousand years, tracing down past the Prytaneum, through the Roman forum and the Greek *agora,* past the Sanctuary of Apollo where the spring still gushed its water.

Sabra paused there a moment, staring into one of the narrow conduits that channeled the water to the city until she'd convinced herself that the spring was in fact still flowing. At least that had not changed.

As they approached the theater she caught the noise of flutes and drums, the musicians playing the wild cacophony of sound that they would play again on the night of the sacrifice…on the night she would lead Elissa up into the hills and leave her to die.

Somehow she and her father arrived on the raised stage. She didn't know how. The last few moments had passed in a blur. As the music died down, the crowd stopped murmuring and a silence heavy as night fell over the city. Sabra's gaze drifted over the people, shadowy in their mourning colors, and a chill crept over her.

This was a side of her people she never liked to see. On these nights, they didn't wear their somber robes in grief or piety for the honored dead, but with a sort of macabre exultation. They *craved* these nights. Craved them, just as much as they hated them. They stared as greedily at Sabra and her small entourage on the stage as the spectators had once stared at the man who got devoured by the lion, repulsed and bewitched all at once. She and her father had a strange sort of power, she realized, standing there on that stage, and it terrified her.

Her father stopped in the center of the stage. He stood straight and still beside her, but Sabra could feel his grief as strongly as her own. Just for an instant, she reached out her hand and clasped his. He glanced down at her in surprise, but all he could offer her was a strained smile.

"The god has spoken," he called out, his voice carrying easily through the theater. "The name has been drawn. She who is called to serve the god for our protection is…" He faltered. Sabra had never seen him so unnerved, gazing out at the people as if choked by fear. She knew better; it wasn't fear that silenced him, and she loved him for his compassion. He swallowed and finished, "Is the daughter of Aqhat, Elissa. Let her come forward."

A raucous drum beat followed the announcement, but it couldn't drown out the crowd's dismayed cries. Sabra stared straight ahead. She didn't know how her father had managed to speak at all; her own throat had closed with grief long ago. And when she saw the little girl's weeping mother guiding her through the crowd, it took every ounce of her will not to break down. Elissa climbed the steps to the stage stoically enough, and a slave handed Sabra a crown of yellow flowers, a foreshadowing of the wreath the girl would wear on the night of her sacrifice.

Sabra took the crown numbly and stared up at the star-scattered sky to avoid seeing the mother tearfully embracing her daughter. After a moment she glanced down just enough to watch Elissa gently push her mother back with one fierce kiss on her cheek. Then she turned and approached Sabra, her face pale but calm in the torchlight.

"You chose me?" she whispered.

There was no fear in her eyes, no resentment, just a confusion that tore at Sabra's heart more than all the anger in the world might have done. She placed the crown on the girl's dark head.

"The god chose you, Elissa," she murmured.

And I wish he had not, she wanted to add, but that would be impious.

"Mistress Sabra, I lied," Elissa said. "I *am* afraid to die."

6

Satala

Jurian headed steadily southwest, picking his way over the broken earth under the last fading daylight. He counted steps, counted stones, tried to focus on everything except his mother and the fear that he would come back too late. He listened to the grass and brush rustling under his feet, and ignored the echo of her words in his mind.

He had walked a few hours when he realized that he could hear other steps echoing his own. Cautiously he slowed down, canting his head back to catch the noises coming from behind him. Someone, or something, was close on his trail, crashing through the scrub like a panicked beast. He turned and crouched close to the ground with one hand on the hilt of his *seax*. In the deepening twilight he could see nothing at all.

After a moment, the noise of pursuit stopped, then a thin voice threaded through the dark.

"Jurian?"

He jolted upright. "Mari?" he called, fear turning his mouth dry. "What's wrong?"

Mother must be dead. Oh, God…

What else would send her chasing after him in such a panic? Sick with dread, he waited as she raced up to him and skidded to a halt, bending over her knees to catch her breath.

"Saints, Mari, what happened?" Jurian asked. "Are you all right? Is Mother…is she all right?"

Mari peered up at him sidelong, still doubled over and gulping air, her face grey with exhaustion. Her dark hair drifted around her face in a wild chaos but she didn't seem to notice. Her eyes were wide, he realized—wide, but dry.

Fear, then. Not grief.

"I went to the village…to get the doctor, like you asked," she gasped, swiping her hands over her forehead.

"And?"

"Oh, Jurian," she whispered. "I heard them…they were saying such awful things. I was so afraid, I didn't go to the doctor. I just came to find you."

That didn't make any kind of sense. Mari was usually sensible, but this…this was foolish, and dangerous. He frowned and handed her his leather waterskin, watching her drink greedily.

"How'd you know where to find me? You could have passed a few feet from me and never even seen me!"

She shrugged. "I knew I'd find you. Listen, I heard the Legion soldiers talking."

"How did you even get close enough to hear them?" Jurian interrupted.

She glowered at him. "All right, I wandered a little too close to some of them. But I'm glad I did, because…otherwise I wouldn't have overheard them." Her eyes widened. "They were talking about *us*."

"What, our family?"

"The Christians in Satala," she said, peeved that he'd misunderstood her. "They're saying it's our fault. The gods and the sacrifices and everything that's wrong in the world. They said they would hunt us all down and offer *us* as sacrifices to the gods. One of them said that anyone who doesn't honor the gods is a traitor to Rome and deserves to be executed. And…"

There's more? Jurian bit back the question, gripping the hilt of his *seax*.

"And it's Casca."

"What is? What's Casca got to do with any of that?"

Mari handed him the waterskin. "The soldier said that Casca was going to lead the hunt." She paused, searching his face in the half-light. "Jurian," she said, "he *hates* us."

"I know that."

"Jurian—"

"I *know!*" The words came out more harshly than he meant, and he collected himself. "I'm sorry. I know. It's just…tonight, of all nights, we're going to fetch a priest."

"You're not saying to give up, are you? Mother said…she *needs* this."

Why? he wondered with a flicker of annoyance. *She needed the doctor more than anything. And now neither of us can get her one, because there's no way I can send Mari back into that pit of snakes.*

"Of course we have to keep going," he said, pacing a few steps. "If it's what she wants. We just have to be careful, and we have to make sure no one sees us coming back with him."

Mari let out her breath and managed a smile. She took a few more seconds to catch her wind, then she pointed a little west.

"You're not quite on the right track," she said.

Jurian hugged her gently around the shoulders. "Then I'm glad you came. I can't get lost with you here." He paused, then added, "And you were right to come and tell me what you heard."

Mari smiled up at him and set off confidently in the direction she'd indicated. Jurian followed, keeping a watchful eye on the wide sweep of the countryside around them. Anyone could have followed Mari from the village; anyone could be stalking them now, waiting to see where they were headed so late at night, so far from home. When no one appeared, he relaxed a little and moved up to walk beside her, but neither of them spoke.

Jurian tried to keep them going at a steady pace, but he worried about Mari's stamina. She didn't falter, though, even as the miles stretched to leagues and the full moon crawled across the sky. They both kept their attention on the uncertain ground, which buckled and pitched under a treacherous net of weeds and scrub. Farther down the slopes, the silhouettes of trees fractured the grass like a mosaic, but here on the hilltops there was nothing to see but sky and stars.

The silence had grown so thick that when Mari finally spoke Jurian winced as if she'd shouted.

"There it is, see the smoke?" she said, pointing.

Jurian scanned the sky until he saw a thin curl of smoke, just slightly paler than the night darkness, drifting up from the valley below them. He sniffed experimentally and grinned.

"See it and smell it, just like you said."

They hurried the remaining distance to the priest's house, slipping down slopes of shifting dirt, clambering over hillocks thick with weeds. Jurian studied the house curiously, but Mari seemed as familiar with it as with their own home. It was a respectable place, though small, surrounded on every side with waving cypress and fruit trees. Bushes of fennel, bay and sage lined the path to the door, their exotic aromas lacing the night air with every breath of wind. All the windows were dark, but Mari went straight to the door and pounded on it like a thunderbolt.

"Oh, I hope he's not asleep," she whispered to Jurian, and hammered on the door again.

A few moments passed, then they saw the flicker of an oil lamp coming to life in the atrium. The door inched open.

"Eugenius? It's Mariam."

The door opened fully, revealing a small man in simple garb, his bald head shining copper in the warm light of his oil lamp. The priest's eyes shone with a kind of light that made him look far younger than the web of wrinkles on his face suggested. The lines around his eyes deepened as he gave Mari a warm smile.

"I hope we didn't wake you up," Mari said.

Eugenius waved a hand and stepped outside to join them. "No matter. Any time is a good time to see a friend," he said. A shadow darkened his eyes and he murmured, "And I was expecting you."

"Expecting us?" Jurian asked, sharp, frowning at the priest. "How could you possibly?"

Eugenius cast an appraising eye over him and, ignoring his

question entirely, said, "So, this is Lucius Aurelius Georgius."

"Jurian," he said stiffly.

The priest seemed unperturbed. "Yes, I'd heard about this curious name of yours. And more as well."

Jurian shot Mari a dangerous look but she just smiled sweetly and said, "Nothing but good things, Jurian."

His mouth twisted and he glanced away. "*Domine*, we can't stay long. We only came to ask if you would come back with us."

"Has something happened?" Eugenius asked.

"Mother asked us to bring you," Mari said. "She's very ill, *domine*." Her lip trembled and she bit down on it, hard. "She's..."

Jurian added, quietly, "I'm afraid we don't have much time."

Eugenius frowned. "You must be exhausted. That's no small walk from Satala. Can I offer you food, something to drink? Whatever I have, it's yours if you need it."

Jurian glanced at Mari, but she only lifted her chin and said firmly, "There'll be time to sleep and eat tomorrow."

"Well enough. Let me just fetch my things." The priest turned to Jurian and added in a conspiratorial whisper, "I know better than to argue when either she or your mother get that look."

Once Eugenius had disappeared into the house, Jurian turned to study Mari. She still seemed pale, the skin under her eyes bruised with fatigue.

"Are you sure you're not too tired to walk all the way back?"

"You're probably more tired than I am," she shot back.

Jurian grinned and held up his hands in surrender. "You found me out."

Eugenius returned a moment later with a walking stick and a small leather satchel. Jurian eyed it curiously, but Eugenius offered no explanation of what it was. It looked rather like the bag the doctor carried, but Jurian didn't think Eugenius was any sort of healer. But if his mother believed that he could do something to help her, he wasn't about to argue.

He set out in the lead, walking as fast as he thought Eugenius could manage. Mari followed silently, but presently Eugenius quickened his pace to walk beside him. They continued without speaking for some time, but Jurian got the strange sense that Eugenius was waiting for him to say something. Finally he sighed and turned to the priest.

"Can you heal our mother?"

"*Heal* her?" Eugenius asked, surprised, and gave him a strange sort of smile. "I suppose that depends on your perspective."

Jurian blew out a breath of frustration. "Did you hear the news from Diocletian's messenger?"

"No, I've not been to the village all day. What is it, more Persians? Another battle? By the holy rock, please don't tell me they've changed the currency again."

Jurian chuckled in spite of himself. "No, not that I know of." He explained what the messenger had said, and then, though he couldn't say why, he found himself telling Eugenius about the dealings of the rest of the day—the fight with Casca, his conversation with Varro, the meeting with the mounted troop, Mari's discovery of the conspiracy in the village. Eugenius listened attentively, lips pursed and brow drawn in a frown.

"You seem worried," Jurian said when he finished. "I thought you didn't believe in the auguries of the old gods."

"Old gods," Eugenius echoed with a laugh. "They are not so old as you imagine. Not old enough. And no, that's not what has me worried."

Jurian gestured for him to continue. Eugenius carried on in silence for several more minutes, instead focusing on keeping his footing over the rugged earth.

"You said they were conducting a sacrifice tonight," he said, finally meeting Jurian's gaze. "The whole town."

"That's right."

Eugenius winced. "And you say Mari overheard them planning some kind of punishment for our people?"

Jurian shrugged. "A few soldiers said it. I'm not sure it means anything…but if Casca is involved, I'm worried. He's—"

"He's a bully," Eugenius said bluntly. "A miniature dictator abusing his power over anyone weak enough not to put up a fight." He cocked an eye at Jurian. "Which wouldn't seem to be you, Georgius."

"Jurian." He shook his head. "No. Like I told you, I would have given him cause to hide his face for a while if Varro hadn't stopped me. But I'm afraid that makes him hate our family even more than he already does. And if he has a pack of Legion dogs nipping his heels, he'll be bold." Jurian glanced over his shoulder at Mari and dropped his voice to a whisper. "I fear for her, *domine*."

"You may have good cause," Eugenius said. "I've seen the Legion hunt our people down before. And now…" He stopped on the hillside, waiting until Mari joined them. "You are both in terrible danger."

"No one saw us leave," Jurian said. "We can get to the house from the west, and no one will even know you've been there."

"It doesn't matter that no one saw you leave. It matters that no one will have seen you at the sacrifice."

He pressed on, hunching his shoulders. Jurian exchanged a glance with Mari and jogged a few steps to catch up with him.

"Do you mean to scare my sister?" he asked, sharp. "Satala's a big village. Do you really think we'd be missed?"

"Of course you'll be missed," Eugenius said. He turned to Jurian, tapping him roughly on the shoulder. "*You* are the children of the former Legate, a Legate who is a bit more famous than most. You may imagine that you've been shuffled off to a corner of the town and forgotten, but you ought to know better. Do you really think Casca won't be watching for you? Waiting for you? Now you are following your father's footsteps, and you think no one will notice? Holy saints, boy, you have no idea the knife's edge you're walking."

Jurian stopped, laying a hand on the priest's arm.

"Wait," he said. "My father's footsteps?" His voice was a bare whisper. "What do you mean?"

Eugenius gave a heavy sigh. In the silver moonlight, they all looked ghostly, Jurian thought—the shadows of people.

"Titus Terentius Varro told you something of your father's death," Eugenius said. "Superstition getting the best of military sense? What do you suppose is going on in the village tonight? What is that if not superstition besting common sense? They are looking for someone to blame. It's just what your father's comrades did when the renowned *Legio Apollinaris* failed to achieve what should have been a sure victory over the Persians. Who is easier to blame for the ill-will of the gods than the one who refuses to sacrifice to them?"

Anger flared hot in Jurian's blood. "You really think my father was killed because he didn't burn a lamb to Apollo or Sol Invictus?"

It all seemed so pointless. Was it worth so much? Was it worth the loss of his father's life? Their shame? Mari would say yes, but she'd always been so much surer of these things than he. For all he tried, he could never see anything but the emptiness in his house and the loss of everything he'd ever known. And there were times he hated his father for it. Hated that he could so easily leave them all for something Jurian barely even comprehended.

And if what Eugenius said was true, who would believe it? How could he explain it to anyone without risking the same fate for his mother and sister? It was impossible.

Just like that, his dream of restoring his family's honor and righting all the wrongs in his life shattered around him. And here was this priest, with his steady certainty and his infuriating insinuations. Jurian gripped the handle of his *seax* as if it were the only solid thing left in his reality.

"Then do you believe the story Marcus Valerius has spread like poison through Satala?" Eugenius asked, measuring him quietly. "Do you believe that your father died by his own hand, in the cowardly attempt to restore his own honor while leaving another to take the fall?"

"That's not fair," Jurian snapped. "It doesn't have to be one or the other."

"Jurian," Mari said, touching his shoulder. "Can't we argue about this later? Let's just get home. Please."

Jurian took a slow breath and buried the anger deep inside where Mari couldn't see it. "Let's go," he said, but he didn't take his gaze from the priest's. "It's not as if it matters."

He spun away from them. He could hear Eugenius and Mari quietly shuffling after him, the low murmur of their voices floating to him on the whisper of a breeze.

He didn't want to admit that the priest's words had alarmed him, but his anxiety grew with every step. It was true—Casca would have waited for them at the sacrifice. And when they didn't show…what if he led his soldiers to their house and found its empty altar and the foreign symbols over the doors? He didn't think his mother's illness would stop someone like Casca.

The full moon was sinking toward the horizon when Jurian finally spotted their house, betrayed by the smoke from the peristyle's coal braziers. Eugenius must have noticed it too, because his hands flashed out and caught Jurian and Mari.

"Listen to me, both of you," he said, turning them so they could all see each other. "I'm going to tell you something now, because I'm not sure I will get another chance. You need to leave Satala. Tonight."

"I'm sorry?" Jurian said, recoiling. "This is our home! And our mother is too sick to travel. Where would we even go?"

"Oh, Jurian," Eugenius said, a sad, gentle smile in his eyes. "She will not be going with you. But this was her wish."

Jurian jerked his arm out of the priest's grip, his hands knotted in fists. "Look, the house is right there! Let's go so you can get to work healing her. You can tell us whatever you need to later."

Eugenius drew a thin breath and bowed his head. "As you wish, *domine*."

7

Satala

Jurian strode past the priest, his thoughts pulling a hundred different directions at once. None of this mad night made any sense. His feet slipped in the scree on the slope behind the house, but he didn't slow down until he reached the door. Inside he lit an oil lamp and, without waiting for Eugenius or Mari, slipped into the peristyle to find his mother.

To his surprise, he found her sitting up on the narrow couch, her thin hands clasped between her knees and her head bowed, the red glow of the fires warming the pale translucence of her skin. She lifted her head when Jurian approached, and with too much effort she held out her hands to him. Jurian knelt in front of her, taking her hands gently in both his own.

"Did you find Eugenius?" she asked, her voice fragile as spider silk.

"He's coming," Jurian said. "Can he help you, Mother?"

She smiled, untangling her hand from his and brushing it through his thick hair. "My fire-haired boy," she whispered. "Look at you now. You carry so much pain in your heart. Don't grieve for me! Eugenius will set me right in the way that matters most." She cupped his chin, and her eyes brightened with a sudden fierce light. "You and Mari must leave Satala. I told Eugenius to tell you."

Jurian gritted his teeth. "Yes," he said. "He did. But we won't leave you. How can I leave you?"

"Oh, child. I'm not the one you must worry about now." She coughed shallowly, pressing the edge of her mantle against her mouth. "You must take care of Mariam. She needs you...now more than ever."

Those words sounded too much like a farewell, and it was almost more than Jurian could bear. His throat tightened and he bowed his head, fighting to find the words he wanted, fighting the grief that threatened to drown him.

But instead he heard himself asking, "Where can we go?"

He wondered if she even comprehended his question. Her eyes were dull, and she stared quietly at the embers in the brazier. "There's fire in the darkness, a beast of fire and rage," she murmured, slipping back into Greek. Jurian winced and held her hand silently. "Rome will run red with blood, blood poured out on the bones of the rock, and so much fire... Like a phoenix, eternal Rome rises from a storm of fire and blood." She swayed and put a hand to her forehead. "What am I saying? Jurian, Jurian, remember this. Steel can kill but the wood will set you free. The rock holds the steel and will hold it again, but first it must pass through fire and over a sea like glass."

"Mother," Jurian said, fear closing his throat. "You're delirious. You need to rest."

"I'm not delirious now," she said, and smiled. "And here are Eugenius and my daughter."

They were standing motionless in the archway of the peristyle, and Jurian wondered briefly how long they had been there. He kissed his mother's hands and backed away to give Eugenius room. His mother tried to rise as the priest approached, but Eugenius hurried forward and gently laid a hand on her shoulder to stop her.

"Now, Polychronia, what have I told you?" he asked. "Save your strength now."

"It was good of you to come," she murmured, and relaxed back against the couch.

Eugenius found a low bronze stool along the wall and carried it over to the couch. "Please, Jurian, Mari," he said. "I am going to ask your mother her accusations. But if you could, go back onto the slopes behind the house. I believe we passed some hyssop shrubs near the top of the hill. Could you bring me some? It will soothe her cough."

"It will come, Jurian," his mother said, fixing him with a brilliant stare. "Steel and fire…and blood. And these are not things to mourn. But you must be ready."

Mari backed away, pulling Jurian along with her. As soon as they were out of the peristyle, she turned and fled from the house. Jurian rushed to catch up to her.

"Mari," he said, stopping her outside the door.

"I'm fine," she said, but she kept her dark eyes downcast, avoiding his concern. "Really. I just…want to be of some help." She glanced up and whispered, "Did you see her face? Just now, before we left?"

Jurian sighed. After all that his mother had said to him, and the way it felt like she'd been saying goodbye, he expected to see sorrow, fatigue, illness, maybe even resignation or despair in her face. But he hadn't.

"She looked…happy," he murmured.

She nodded and they climbed back up the long hill, weaving back and forth as they searched for the shrub. With the moon low behind the slope it was darker than ever, and Jurian wondered aloud how they were ever going to find the plant. Mari said nothing, which meant she was terrified. Jurian wished he knew how to comfort her.

"What did Eugenius mean?" he asked after a while, bending low to peer at a plant through the shadows. "All that about hearing mother's accusations? Who is she accusing? Does she know something about father's death?"

Mari stopped a little lower on the slope. Jurian couldn't see her face, but he could tell by her silhouette that she had her fists on her hips. "It's not about him, Jurian. She's accusing herself, making an account of her sins before God to seek forgiveness.

Don't you know anything? Haven't you paid attention to anything she's tried to teach you?"

Jurian grumbled and straightened up, kicking viciously at the plant that wasn't hyssop. He opened his mouth to retort but closed it suddenly, hard. Why could he see Mari's silhouette? The moon was behind the hill, not behind her. There hadn't been any light there before…

"Mari," he said. He swallowed hard. The last thing he wanted was to frighten her more, so he took a few steps higher up the hill. "Come here. Is this hyssop?"

She marched up the hill to crouch beside him. "Saints, Jurian, that doesn't look anything like hyssop. Don't you know—"

Jurian paid no attention. He stared past her down the hill. Half a dozen torches gleamed off polished Roman armor, fracturing the darkness. A slow chill spread through him, and he gripped Mari's arm and pulled her lower into the scrub, gesturing toward the house before she could speak. A muffled sob escaped past the hands she clapped over her mouth.

Four Legionaries clustered near the front of their house, each carrying a torch. Jurian's stomach twisted with sick fear and dread.

No, it's not possible. What are they doing? What do they want?

Time churned to a sluggish crawl. Jurian couldn't move, not even to release Mari. He couldn't breathe. He just stared and kept staring at the silent men, willing them away, wishing he could unmake everything that was happening.

It was their silence that paralyzed him, even when his hand itched to draw his *seax* and rush down the hill. There was no passion in their movements. No frenzy of hatred, no mania of zeal. They were cold. Calculating. Deliberate. And they were waiting for something.

He heard the horses' hoofbeats before he saw the riders, and he didn't even need to look to know who rode at their head.

"Jurian, it's…" Mari's horrified whisper choked past the fingers she held curled at her lips.

"I know."

Jurian held Mari tight against him, blood boiling as he stared down at Casca. He'd dressed himself in all his finery for this, Jurian noticed. And he could just imagine how Casca must be relishing this moment.

Two soldiers emerged from the house. In the torchlight, their swords gleamed darkish, like ink stains. They approached Casca's horse and bowed, striking their fists to their breasts. Jurian couldn't hear what they said, but he could see Casca's face twist in the flickering light.

"Burn it."

Those words echoed clearly across the hills. Mari gave a strangled sob as one by one, the soldiers tossed their torches—some at the thatch roof, some through the open windows. The flames gnawed at the fuel, slowly snaking through the thatch.

No. Jurian bit his lip so hard that it drew blood. *No. No.*

This isn't happening.

Mari's sobs sounded like muffled screams now, and he couldn't look at her. Her grief would tear him apart.

As the flames stretched greedily to heaven, Jurian thought he heard singing.

They're alive. They're still alive. Oh God, I have to save them.

"Mari!" he whispered, fierce. "Stay here! Do you understand? Stay here and don't move!"

He crept forward a few paces and drew his *seax*, but just before he broke cover, he hesitated. Another Legionary was striding up the slope from Satala with a torch of his own, its light bleeding over the red plumes of his helmet.

"Jurian," Mari pleaded. "What are you waiting for?"

The Legionary had almost reached the house when the flames caught in the roof and the wood furnishings inside, and smoke poured from every opening like blood. The man broke into a run, shoving past the other soldiers, disappearing into the thickening smoke.

"Too late," Jurian gasped, but he didn't know if he was telling himself or Mari, or the Legionary. He tried to breathe but his lungs felt empty, broken. "It's too late."

The Legionary stumbled back out of the house, coughing into his cloak as the smoke coiled around him. Jurian swallowed as the man's torchlight shone on his face.

Varro.

He strode up to one of the soldiers who held a blood-stained *spatha*. Jurian couldn't hear more than a murmur of their voices over the snap and roar of flames, but then, without any warning, Varro drew his knife and slashed it across the man's throat. Dark blood washed over the soldier's gleaming armor. An unclean death, a coward's death. Even when Jurian closed his eyes he could see the man's eyes wide with surprise, his mouth clenched in a grim line, his skin flecked with blood.

But in his mind it wasn't Casca's soldier he saw. It was his father…his father falling under a comrade's knife…

He flinched, shattering the vision, and watched in horror as Casca edged his horse toward the Tribune.

And then the unthinkable happened.

Mari was up and past him before he could stop her.

"No!" she cried, but her voice came thin and feeble, swallowed by the night.

She had taken barely a step before Jurian caught her again. They both crashed against the ground, and this time she stayed still, shoulders shaking as she fought back tears. Jurian glanced toward the house, praying every prayer he knew that the soldiers hadn't seen or heard them. His heart sank; Varro was staring straight at the spot where they lay, pressed close against the earth in the shadows.

A sick ache tugged the pit of Jurian's stomach. In the fickle torchlight, Varro's face was drawn, creased with pain and loss. The other Legionaries still stood staring in shock at the Tribune and their fallen comrade and hadn't seemed to notice anything.

"You shouldn't be here, Tribune." Casca's voice reached them faintly. "You have no business here."

"You had no right." Varro's voice was taut but firm. "On whose authority did you burn these people alive?"

"On mine, Varro. Mine."

For one awful moment, the two faced each other. The Legionaries stood like statues, waiting. Only Casca's horse beat the ground with a hoof, snorting in the smoke and ash.

"I will not forget this," Varro said. With one last glance around at the hills, he bowed to Casca. "I will never forget."

He strode away from the blaze, viciously kicking a stone in his path as he went.

Casca edged his horse forward, directly toward them. Jurian held his breath but Casca stopped there, his eyes sweeping beyond the place where they lay concealed in the bracken.

"So to all traitors to Rome!" Casca shouted. "Do you hear me, *Georgios?* Do you?" He waited for a moment, listening.

As if I'd be stupid enough to charge out at him, Jurian thought.

Casca's face twisted in frustration. "I will find you! I swear to the gods above and below that I will hunt you down, you and your sister both! And then I will break you!"

He wheeled his horse and cantered back to the soldiers. One of the men gestured toward the fallen Legionary's body, and Casca jerked a hand toward the burning house. Then he rallied his mounted troop and they galloped back toward Satala. The remaining soldiers dragged the Legionary's body to the house and committed it to the flames.

"Burning that heathen's body with Mother's," Mari choked. "Oh, God, have mercy!"

Jurian nudged her into silence and they watched the Legionaries march away, leaving their life smoldering in ashes.

8

SATALA

JURIAN PRESSED HIS HEAD AGAINST the dirt, while Mari huddled beside him and tried to stifle the sobs that racked her body. Behind them the smoke roiled against the night sky, staining the air with the stink of burning thatch and wood.

"They…killed them," Mari wept, the words shattered. The flames were so bright now that they cast a faint red glow on the hillside, turning her tears crimson. "She was so…so sick." She slammed her fist on the ground, then bent over it, shoulders shaking. "Jurian…I didn't even…I didn't get to say goodbye."

Jurian shuffled to her and wrapped his arms around her. Closing his eyes, he forced the grief and rage and despair deep down into the inmost corners of his heart. Then, exhaling slowly, he clasped both of Mari's shoulders.

"Eugenius told us we would need to leave," he said. "I don't know why, but I have the strangest feeling that he knew this would happen. And Mother too."

Steel and fire, she'd said. *Is this what she'd meant?*

These are not things to mourn.

The sorrow threatened to break him again, and he gritted his teeth to drive it back.

"Come on, Mari. Let's go. There's nothing for us here. And Casca will come back in the morning to sweep the area. We need to be long gone."

"But..." She pointed at the burning house. "Can't we..."

He leaned his forehead against hers. "No. There's nothing left. I'm sorry, but we've got to run now."

"Where?"

He got up, pulling her to her feet. For a few long moments they stood side by side, staring down the hill, their faces echoing the firelight. Jurian clasped Mari's hand.

"I don't know," he murmured. "Maybe we should go to Rome."

"Rome," Mari said, expressionless. "Why?"

"Father's older brother is in Rome. And Mother said something about it before...before you and Eugenius arrived. She kept talking about the bones of the rock, remember? From how she talked about them, I thought she meant that they were in Rome, whatever they are." He turned to face her. "And honestly, Mari, I don't know anywhere else to go."

"The bones of the rock," Mari echoed. "I always wondered what it meant. Maybe we can find someone who can explain it. So." She straightened up, taking a deep breath and wiping her cheeks dry. "So. Rome?"

"Rome. Which means, we should stay close to the Roman road heading west, but I don't think we should actually use it. Casca will be following us. You know he won't stop."

Mari nodded mutely.

"But...we're going to need provisions. I don't know if miracles work on pomegranates."

She smiled. "I know where we might get some. I mean...I hate even thinking of it, but...don't you remember what Eugenius told us? He said that anything he had is ours if we need it."

"True," Jurian said softly. It was just one more thing the priest had said that made Jurian believe he'd known what was coming. "Come on. We've no time to lose."

Mari shifted her gaze from the burning house to the village spread in the valley, identifiable only by the distant lights of sentries' torches on the *castra* walls.

"You know, somehow I always hoped that everything would un-happen," she said. "Father's death, moving out of the *praetorium*, Mother's illness. Do you remember those days, Jurian, before it all fell apart? I don't remember much of Palestine. Satala has always been home."

Jurian nodded. He had only a faint scattering of memories from Palestine, where he'd been born and where they'd lived before his father had been assigned as Legion Legate to the *Apollinaris*. Everything he'd ever known, everything he'd ever loved, everything he'd ever hated…had always been Satala.

Satala, he thought, *has betrayed us.*

All but Varro.

Jurian wished he could have thanked the man…though he wasn't even sure what for. For killing a man? For caring when no one else did? For his silence? But they would probably never meet again. Once he and Mari left, they would never be able to return.

He clenched his hands and burned the village to ruin in his heart until there was nothing left.

"Jurian!" Mari gasped suddenly. "What about the others?"

"The other who?"

"The other Christians! They're all in danger now, too."

"How many?"

"A hundred?" She bit her lip. "Maybe two?"

Jurian groaned and ran a hand through his hair. "Mari, we don't have time to warn two hundred people before dawn."

But can we just leave them? Can I let them burn, like Eugenius? Like Mother?

"We don't have to tell two hundred people," she said. "We just have to tell one. He'll make sure the rest are warned."

"All right, I'll do it. Who is this person?"

"No, *I* will do it," Mari said. "Olennius doesn't know you. And besides, it would be impossible to explain where he lives."

"I'm not letting you go into that village when half the Legion is out looking for us!"

Mari drew the hood of her cloak over her head and gripped

his arm. "Jurian. You have to let me do this."

"Will you at least let me come with you?"

"No," she said. "Too noticeable."

"What's noticeable is a young girl wandering the streets in the fourth watch."

"Don't you trust me?"

Jurian held her gaze. "It's nothing to do with trust. It's just that you're all I have left."

That tempered the fire in her eyes, and she bowed her head. "Fine. But put up your hood at least. I swear your hair is like a torch all on its own."

He obeyed and followed her down the hill. Once they reached Satala, he realized why Mari hadn't wanted to give him directions—she wove through side streets and down alleys, back and forth until Jurian was dizzy. Finally she stopped at a small house and knocked violently at the door until it creaked open.

She exchanged a few quiet words with the person on the other side, then told Jurian, "I'm going in to speak to Olennius. Keep watch out here."

She slipped into the house and Jurian edged into the shadows. The street seemed quiet enough, filled with the ordinary night noises of mewling cats and infants crying through open windows. As time crawled by, Jurian fought a surge of impatience. Any minute the streets would come to life—the fullers and bakers rising early for their tasks, the Legionaries taking up their drills in the *castra*.

He grimaced and turned to survey the street westward, and found himself face to face with Varro. His fingers flashed to his knife hilt, but Varro held up a hand to stop him.

"Don't be alarmed, Jurian," he murmured.

"How'd you find me here?" He peered past the Tribune, searching the shadows. "Where are the others?"

"I saw you coming into the village. I was waiting to see if you would come down from the hill." He paused, then murmured, "I'm sorry."

"Then why didn't you stop it?" Jurian hissed.

"I would have if I could," he said. "But I didn't know."

"Why don't you arrest us?"

"For what crime?" Varro asked. "Listen, Jurian. I know what your father was. I know your mother shared his piety, and I assume that you and your sister do too. What is that to me? We're Romans. Aren't we supposed to be the great civilization that unites the world? We made a grave error under Nero, but I like to imagine that we've grown wiser, not weaker, in two hundred years. Even Emperor Decius knew better."

"I wish more of the army shared your view," Jurian muttered.

"We aren't all like Casca. Maybe we could be better, if there were more young men like you in our ranks." He surveyed Jurian briefly. "Well, where will you go now?"

"To Rome, I think. For…many reasons."

"Everyone ends up at Rome," Varro said, smiling, "if they follow a road long enough. But remember me, Jurian, if you ever need a friend in Satala. And if ever my path crosses Casca's in such a way that gives me cause…" He left the rest unsaid, but Jurian bowed his head in gratitude. He glanced at the house and added, "I'm not going to ask what brought you to this house in the middle of the night."

Jurian grinned faintly. "No, *domine*. Even if I believed there were others like us in this village who might need protection against Casca and his followers, I couldn't tell you."

Varro laughed quietly and clapped a hand on Jurian's arm. "Fair enough."

A murmur of voices drifted through one of the house's open windows, drawing steadily closer. Varro took a step back.

"I'll go now before they see me. But don't worry about them. I won't let anyone else be taken by this madness if I can do anything to prevent it. Fortune favor you, Jurian, and may the God you worship watch over your journeys."

He turned and disappeared so suddenly that when Jurian finally remembered to whisper, "Goodbye," the street was already empty.

9

Cyrene

THE THEATER HAD FINALLY CLEARED, leaving only Sabra and Elissa in her crown of yellow flowers standing on the stage with the night darkness pressing around them.

"What happens now?" Elissa asked. She straightened her shoulders and drew a breath, but Sabra could see the fear in her eyes.

"Now you belong to the god," Sabra said. The words tasted like ash in her throat. "For the next few weeks you will live under my care at the palace."

"But why can't I stay with my mother until…until the night comes?"

Sabra smiled gently and crouched down to the girl's level. "I know it's hard. But think how much harder that would be for your mother."

It would be so much more painful, but is that always a bad thing? she wondered, and shook the thought from her head.

"I think I understand," Elissa said, though her eyes welled with tears.

"Come on, then," Sabra said, standing and holding out her hand. "It's not all bad. We don't talk about the god and the sacrifice every minute of the day. There's space for living, too."

She tried to sound cheerful, but the words felt hollow. Elissa said nothing, but took Sabra's hand and walked quietly beside her, back past the Sanctuary of Apollo and the Greek and Roman markets, and up the hill toward the governor's palace where she would live the rest of the month...the rest of her life...with Sabra.

The priestesses of the old god had once lived in a house together near the Temple, but after the old priestess had died and left Sabra alone, she had returned to her father's house. One day, when she was ready to choose a successor, she might move back to the priestess's house, but for now, she had her suite in a secluded wing of the palace. Her own chamber was the largest, and there were two smaller rooms attached—one for her slave Ayzebel, the other for the sacrificial victim during the time of preparation.

Sabra showed Elissa the small bedchamber that would be hers, which was as plainly furnished and comfortable as her own. Elissa hesitated in the doorway, staring at the narrow bed and the clothes chest, her face pale with fear or revulsion.

Sabra knew what she must be thinking: *this is the room where so many other children have stayed, and now they are all dead.* Sabra could still see each of their faces, so clearly.

Too clearly.

Finally, Elissa glanced up at Sabra and ducked into the room with a whispered goodnight. Sabra let the curtain fall across the door with a sigh and went to her own bed, where Ayzebel waited to take her robe.

"Is that her, then?" Ayzebel asked. "The next one to die?"

The words had a bite to them, and they lodged in Sabra's heart. She straightened up from taking off her bell-adorned sandals, throat knotted, and couldn't think of an answer.

"Go to bed, Ayzebel," she said finally. "I'm not going to sleep tonight. I need to pray."

Ayzebel bowed. "Then I will pray too," she murmured, and disappeared into her own room.

Sabra paused outside Elissa's chamber. She could hear the girl's broken breath, her stifled sobs, and she listened until her heart was breaking with the sound.

"Never comfort them the first night," the old priestess had com-

manded her. *"They must learn what it is to be alone. Never trust another human, Sabra. They will only forsake you. Much better to learn to stand on your own, and face the god and the end of things with courage."*

With her head hurting worse than ever, Sabra turned and fled, seeking solitude in the trees and the night wind in the slopes behind the palace.

In all of Cyrene, there was only one place that she felt at peace—an old grove of juniper and pines that time seemed to have forgotten. There, in a little clearing open to the night sky, she sat down in the grass and drew her knees to her chest. She'd meant to pray for forgiveness, for strength, but now the prayer died on her lips. What if the god hadn't noticed her weakness? Did she really want to draw his attention?

No. Better to avoid his notice, as much and for as long as possible.

She leaned back on her elbows and stared up at the star-crusted sky. Three years. Three years she had been the sole priestess of Molech. Three years she had been instructing the victims, some not much younger than herself, and leading them up into the hills to die. Three years—and they felt like three thousand.

I'm a coward, she thought, and pressed her hand against her mouth as if the god might hear even her inmost thoughts. *I hate this so much. Why did the old priestess choose me? Why not someone else…anyone else? She closed her eyes and breathed the spice of pine deep into her lungs. Even if I could… I can't leave, or everyone will die. I'd do anything if it meant the god would leave us alone once and for all.*

If the histories were true, this manifestation of the god was something new. Centuries ago he had been worshipped in one place, in the form of a massive, terrible idol that devoured children in a belly of fire. But then his followers had dispersed through the Empire, and the god…the god had followed them, demanding new rites, new sacrifices, new worship. Who was she to argue? She couldn't imagine the gods would like to be forgotten, or supplanted by new pieties. It was no surprise that hers had grown so angry and vengeful.

Sabra lifted her hands up. The backs shone pale in the starlight, but when she turned them to see her palms, they were swallowed in darkness. Maybe they were just so stained with blood that they matched the shadows.

So much blood. So much death.

She lay there a while longer, until she'd gathered enough scraps of calm to see her through the next day. When she almost fell asleep on the grass she got up and made her way back to the palace, letting herself in as quietly as possible. It was almost morning. A few slaves might be up already, starting the day's baking, but most of the household would still be asleep.

At the thought of food, Sabra's stomach rumbled fitfully. After her ritual fasting, Sabra felt eternally hungry, and no amount of bread and nuts ever seemed to fill her up.

She slipped down the long corridor toward the kitchen, her bare feet padding silently over the cool mosaic floors. Ahead she could see the walls of the *culina* warm with firelight, casting back the shadows of the kitchen slaves. She could hear the low murmur of their voices, speaking Punic, and she would have ignored it until she caught one word.

"...the prophecy?"

She knew that voice—it was Abdosir, one of Hanno's close friends.

"As if we wouldn't know what it really meant," said another, a woman she didn't recognize. "*Innocent* blood indeed."

A blush of anger curled up Sabra's neck. How dare this woman try to interpret the Oracle's prophecy, the message of the gods? What could she possibly know that no one else would?

At the same time, Sabra had a sudden, horrible thought.

What if they had misunderstood the Oracle? What if they were still offering the wrong sacrifice?

And what if her father knew it?

She clenched her hands in fists and retreated down the corridor. Food could wait until she'd had time to think.

A FEW HOURS later, Sabra was starting to regret her impulsive piety of the previous night. With her eyes heavy and gritty and her stomach woefully famished, she went to fetch Elissa for their morning meal.

The girl was already awake and dressed when Sabra knocked on the doorframe. She looked terrible, with her hair all a mess and her eyes red-rimmed and puffy from weeping. But she smiled when she saw Sabra, and that cut Sabra's heart more than the thought of her weeping.

"Ayzebel," Sabra called. "Can you help Elissa get ready for the day?"

Ayzebel flicked a glance over the child and swallowed, hard. "Of course. Come here, child," she said, beckoning Elissa. "Look at all that lovely hair you have!"

Elissa smiled at her and went to stand where Ayzebel instructed her. Sabra watched, bemused at Ayzebel's gentleness as she combed out the girl's thick dark hair and brought her a cloth soaked in cool water.

"Here," Ayzebel said, with a mock warning look. "We can't have you look like you've been crying all night!"

Elissa scrubbed the cloth over her face and took a deep breath, then suddenly held it out to Sabra. "You can't look like you've been crying, either," she said.

Sabra caught herself laughing in surprise. Ayzebel looked a bit chastised, but Sabra only took the cloth and patted it against her eyes.

"There. Much better," she declared, and handed the cloth to Ayzebel with a flourish.

Ayzebel gave her a puzzled smile and a little bow, and disappeared from the room.

"Now then, Elissa, are you hungry?" Sabra asked. "Come with me."

ALL THROUGH THE morning meal and Elissa's lessons, the question about the Oracle's prophecy needled Sabra's mind, but it wasn't until afternoon that she could retreat to the cool, shaded porticoes of the peristyle to think. She had walked the entire circuit around the inner garden twice when Hanno appeared suddenly, pacing beside her with his hands behind his back and head bowed as if he'd been there forever.

"You're very quiet," he said presently.

She smiled at him. "I'm always quiet."

They walked a little while in silence, then Hanno said, "I saw the girl, Mistress. The chosen one. She's very young, isn't she?"

"Barely seven," Sabra murmured. She turned suddenly to face him, darting a glance over the peristyle to make sure they were alone. "Hanno…am I a coward?"

His mouth opened in surprise, then folded down into a frown. "Why would you even think that?"

"Because…I *hate* it," she hissed. She winced and clapped a hand over her mouth, but no bolt of lightning struck her down. "I hate it but I never stop. I take them…I leave them… I just don't know any more." She pressed her hands against her head, staring hopefully at Hanno as if he could make sense of the world. "Where is this terrible fear coming from? Why am I suddenly afraid of…"

"Of what?" Hanno asked.

She swallowed and dropped her gaze. "Of…myself. Of what I am capable of doing. And how can I stop? If I abandon my duty… everyone will suffer. Doesn't the good of the city outweigh the good of some few individuals—these children, even my own? Why do I suddenly doubt that? What is one life to thousands? But how can I be the one to destroy a life like Elissa's? Even for the god? I don't know what to do. I don't know what's wrong with me." She peered up at him, wrapping her arms around herself. "Would you be able to do it? If you knew that one life could save the city, could you be the one to take that life?"

Hanno rubbed a hand over his bald head.

"I'm not sure," he said slowly. "I like to think I could. But to do what you do?" He shook his head mournfully.

Sabra frowned. She wasn't sure if she should take that as praise or condemnation. Was it courage and strength that helped her carry out her duty, or had she just passed totally into the darkness? The priestess had always said that those in the service of the gods were not like the rest of men. Maybe this was what she'd meant.

"What other god threatens his followers with destruction? It's strange, don't you think?" She flicked a glance up at Hanno. "Am I blaspheming?"

"No. I don't think you are."

"I think you're wishing I had stayed quiet," Sabra said with the faintest whisper of a smile.

Hanno grinned and gave her a mock bow, which made her laugh.

But after a moment her smile faded and she bent her head. "All this doubt…it must be because I'm being weak. I'm too attached to that girl. But I just keep thinking that, if we just gave the god the right sacrifice, all this madness would stop." She thought about the slaves' conversation in the smoky kitchen. "He would be appeased once and for all and leave the city in peace. Ten years now we've been offering him the blood of innocents." She looked up at Hanno. "Since I was Elissa's age. You'd think he'd be satisfied by now if the sacrifices were right."

The muscle in Hanno's jaw tightened.

"Do you know something you ought to tell me, Hanno?" Sabra asked. "I heard someone talking about the Oracle. About how we interpret her message."

Hanno faced her, crossing his arms. "Mistress, I'd only be spreading rumor if I spoke. What I heard, I heard from another slave, who heard from another, who had it from the slave who was present when the Oracle's message was received."

Sabra frowned. "A slave? But the message would have been delivered in Greek. How would he be able to understand it?"

"He speaks Greek, too, not just Punic. Most of us didn't even know that he did, until then."

"Well, what did he hear?"

Hanno lifted his hands. "I don't know, Mistress. I don't speak Greek."

Sabra glared at the fountain sparkling under the afternoon sun, chewing the inside of her cheek with frustration. "Do you know his name?"

"I shouldn't have spoken," Hanno said, and took a few steps away from her. "Forget what I said, Mistress. It's rumor. It's not important. It will only distract you from your duties."

"Hanno!" she called, watching him stride away without a backwards glance.

He was lucky he was her friend, she thought bitterly, or she would have had him punished for disrespect.

She sighed and pressed her hands to her forehead. Would she really? She didn't even know that any more.

10

ANATOLIA

JURIAN AND MARI HEADED WEST and a little south after leaving Eugenius' house, walking until the sun rose in a haze of late autumn glory. If they kept on in that direction, Jurian knew they would eventually cross the Roman road that led to Ancyra. He had some memories of poring over his father's Legion maps of Anatolia, and though he'd never gotten a good sense of how to measure distance, he knew this much: they were in for a long walk.

They had been walking for a few hours when Mari stumbled beside him.

"Are we far enough from Satala yet?" she mumbled. "We've walked for *forever*."

Jurian stopped and turned. There was nothing but rolling hills around them now, dusted in browns and drab greens to the southwest, brilliant emerald to the north where the land buckled in massive hills. Satala and the walls of the Legion *castra* had long since disappeared from view, but Jurian feared that at any moment, Casca and his horsemen would appear over the ridge just behind them.

"I think so," he said, and Mari promptly collapsed on the ground where she stood.

Jurian smiled and dropped down beside her, stretching out

full length with his hands behind his head.

"You know, you should have picked a spot that wasn't facing straight at the sun before you sat down," he remarked, plucking a long strand of sweet grass to chew. "And we can't stay long. Just a bit of a rest, all right?"

"Whatever you say," Mari said, her voice muffled in her arms.

She was asleep a moment later, sprawled on her stomach in the grass, her hands wrapped over her head to block out the light. Jurian threw an arm over his eyes and tried to follow her example. But even though his legs ached and exhaustion soaked every muscle in his body, his restless mind kept him from sleep.

Over and over again he saw his mother's face, heard the echo of her last words. The Legionaries with their blood-stained swords, Varro's grief and fury. The burning house. The singing. Casca's vow to hunt them down and break them.

His throat tightened and a clawing ache gripped his heart. But he drove the grief back, swallowing the numbness and all the pain. There would be time to mourn later, when they were safely away from Anatolia. Casca would make good on his threat if he could, especially if he caught them in the wild. He would have to be vigilant.

It was almost midday before he drifted into restless, dreamless sleep.

He woke with a start a few hours later, heart pounding, his throat thick with dust and thirst. Mari was sitting up beside him, nibbling a handful of walnuts they had found in Eugenius' house. She looked better for having slept, but her hair had fallen out of its knot into a dark tangle and she had a streak of dirt smudging one cheek.

"Feeling better?" Jurian asked her.

She gave him a smile that tried too hard to be enthusiastic. "I wish that nice *eques* had given me his horse, though," she said.

"Right," he said. "Can you imagine? Us with a horse?"

Her eyes got a dreamy faraway look and she said, "Oh, I can imagine it."

Jurian rolled his eyes and sat up, brushing grass and dust

from his tunic. "Well, keep imagining it, because that's as close as you'll get. Where are the nuts?"

She tossed him a small linen bag and he scooped out some almonds still in their shells. Mari watched him use the hilt of his *seax* and a smooth rock to crack the shells, then held out her hand expectantly when he finished.

"Smash your own," he said, pitching the bag back at her.

She jutted her lower lip and didn't move her hands, but couldn't hide the mischievous gleam in her eyes. Finally Jurian heaved a long-suffering sigh and deposited three almonds into her waiting palm. She grinned triumphantly and ate them all in one mouthful.

"We should reach the road by late afternoon," she said when she had swallowed.

"How do you even know that?"

She shrugged, combing her fingers through her tangled hair and tying it back at the nape of her neck. "I used to look at father's maps, too."

"You did?"

"I was bored. They were interesting. So?"

He smiled and gestured to the walnuts in her hand. "Finish those. We need to keep going."

Mari nodded and shoved them into her mouth. As he waited for her, Jurian checked his quiver—only ten arrows left. He would need to make more once they got out of the hills and into the woods, and he'd need to start watching for game. Mari coughed suddenly, startling him out of his thoughts, but for his concern she just pointed at the nuts in her other hand. He tossed her their waterskin and got to his feet, Mari joining him a moment later.

It was late afternoon when they finally spotted the Roman road. The slanting light glanced off the road's paving stones, so bright that Jurian had to shield his eyes.

He stopped some thirty feet away to contemplate it. "Well, there it is."

"Yes," Mari said, folding her arms with mock seriousness. "Should we cross it?"

"Well..." His voice trailed off, and he turned a slow circle. "The land is gentler on the north side, at least for now. But there are more trees for cover to the south." He shaded his eyes and looked along the road in both directions. "We'll stay off the road itself. It's too exposed."

"So which side will it be, then?" Mari asked, a wicked twinkle in her eye. When he hesitated she said gravely, "It's quite obvious. Once we pick a side...we can never go back."

Jurian had to laugh. "I'm not *that* bad," he said, and she smirked. "Let's go. I think I'll have better luck hunting on the other side."

He led Mari across the road and they continued west, walking until the sun set in a blaze of rose and amber. As the shadows deepened, Jurian tracked south into the trees where the ground would be softer. But it was already getting dark under the canopy of leaves, so he found a spot that seemed fairly level and dry and spread his cloak on the ground.

"I'm going to hunt," he said, unslinging his bow and leaning his weight against the lower limb to string it.

Mari paused in the middle of sitting down. "I'll get some wood."

Jurian waved over his shoulder. "And look for a spring if you can. We're going to need more water."

He roved into the woods, trying to quiet his steps over the dry leaves and needles. The stand of trees wasn't particularly large, but he could hear movement in the undergrowth. Small movements, so, probably a rabbit or a fox. His mouth watered—they had eaten nothing but dried figs and nuts since they'd left Eugenius' house. He picked his spot and didn't move again, even when the sounds seemed to retreat further into the trees. Better to be patient than risk scaring his prey with a misplaced step.

It didn't take long for the rustling to return. Jurian's eyes, now adjusted to the shadows and moonlight, caught the occasional red gleam of the animal's eyes as it foraged. He'd already nocked an arrow on his bowstring, and as soon as the creature turned its head, he drew and released. Silence. He let out a breath. Silence meant he had killed it with one blow.

When he returned to the camp, he was already holding up the skinned rabbit for Mari's admiration, but his sister was sound asleep next to a small pile of wood. Jurian studied her anxiously, but he wasn't really surprised at her exhaustion. He dragged the wood away from her and got a fire going. Once he had coaxed it into a low flame, he spitted the rabbit and set it to roast.

The warm aroma of cooking meat woke Mari, and she blinked at him across the fire, bleary-eyed and disoriented.

"Did you happen to find any water?" Jurian asked gently.

She nodded and pointed to the low tree branch where she'd hung the water skin. "I didn't quite fill it up. I thought we could fill it again in the morning."

Jurian frowned but said nothing. Mari wasn't a hunter, and she wasn't a fighter. She was barely fifteen, and though she'd had strength enough for both of them in Satala, out here in the wilderness she seemed so young. So lost.

He returned his attention to the roasting rabbit. The silence was unnerving. He had never minded the quiet before, but usually he couldn't even bribe Mari to stop talking. Studying her across the firelight, he didn't know if it was sorrow or exhaustion that stole her voice. He wished he knew what to say.

In the end, he just said, "The rabbit's done."

Mari gave him a smile that pretended enthusiasm. "You should eat it," she said. "You need the meat most of all."

"We both need it," Jurian protested. "With all this walking, you'll need it too to keep up your energy."

"Really," she said, and wrinkled her nose. "Rabbit's not…my favorite."

"You don't have to pretend for my sake. There's more than enough for both of us."

"I'm not hungry, Jurian," she said finally. "All right? I don't want food. I just want to sleep."

With that she curled up in her cloak, facing away from him. Jurian stared at her, the skewer of rabbit meat dribbling hot grease on the leaves at his feet.

Oh God, why am I such a failure? he thought. *I should never have dragged her out into the wilderness. I'm sure this isn't what Mother or Eugenius had in mind when they told us to leave.*

The thought of Eugenius quieted his inner voice. How could a man knowingly walk into the place of his execution? Eugenius had *known*. Jurian didn't understand how, but he was convinced the man had seen his own death approaching. And yet he had gone anyway. Why hadn't he turned them away at his door? He would still be alive and safe if he had.

Or, maybe…

Jurian's mind shifted against his will toward the thought he'd been desperately trying to avoid since they'd left Satala.

Maybe Eugenius and Mother would still be alive if I hadn't been such a coward.

"What if I could have saved them?" he whispered out loud, challenging the night to answer him.

Part of him hoped that Mari would still be awake, that she would hear him and comfort him, telling him there was nothing he could have done. She didn't.

And even if she had, Jurian wasn't sure he would have believed her.

THE CHILL SUNRISE brought brighter spirits to their little camp. Mari finally accepted a few pieces of rabbit meat left from the night before, and once they had both eaten, they headed on.

Mari had trouble maintaining a brisk pace for more than a few hours at a time, so Jurian tried to keep a steadier, slower pace that she could manage. Still, he knew that the nights would quickly turn a brutal cold, and the last thing he wanted was to be stranded on the plateau when the snows came.

And then there was Casca. Always, Jurian thought he could hear hoofbeats pursuing them. He kept turning to look over his shoulder, scanning the empty landscape rolling away behind them while the crawling dread in his gut only grew stronger.

Mari hummed as they walked to keep herself occupied. After a while she started singing in earnest and goaded Jurian to join her, insisting it made the walking more bearable. He had never felt comfortable singing, though; he had a decent enough voice, low and a bit husky, but he never knew if he was singing exactly the right pitches. For a while he listened to her, but it wasn't a song he recognized. To amuse her he tried to join in anyway, but he kept guessing the wrong word to sing and finally she dissolved into laughter. The laughter turned to coughing and it took her a few minutes to get her breath back.

"Saints, it's no use," she said.

That night when they camped, Jurian watched Mari across the dancing flames of their tiny campfire. She seemed thinner than he remembered.

It's just the walking, he told himself. *The walking and little food to make up for it.*

It made perfect sense, but when he closed his eyes to sleep, all he could see was his mother's wasting, and how fast it had all happened at the end.

In the middle of the night, a sudden sound startled him awake. As he lay there, heart pounding, trying to figure out what he'd heard, the sound came again.

Mari was coughing.

THEY WALKED FOR five more days before they saw sign of anyone else. The first thing they noticed was the smell of a cooking fire, then a massive plume of smoke appeared around a bend in their path. Jurian stopped short when he saw it, hurrying Mari farther from the road and into a stand of trees.

"That's a lot of smoke for one or two people," he whispered.

In the occasional gusts of wind from the northwest, he caught the sharp noises of clashing metal and—more than that—he could smell the thick odor of animals. A lot of animals.

"Legion camp," he said. *Could Casca have missed us somewhere?*

Mari's eyes widened. "Out here?"

"Maybe it's a different cohort," Jurian said. "Maybe there's another battle with the Persians coming." He waved a hand at Mari. "Wait here. I'm going to sneak ahead and see if I can make out their *signum*."

He slipped away from the trees, drawing the hood of his cloak up to cover his unusual—and all too visible—red hair. He edged across the road, then crept up the low hill that had blocked their view of the smoke.

Once he'd gotten high enough for a good view, he eased forward until he could see down into the valley below. To his left, the road bridged a broad river, and, as he expected, a Legion camp spread on its opposite bank, north of the road. A few Legionaries stood posted at either end of the bridge. The camp was too far away for him to identify the emblem embroidered on their red *vexillum*, but this wasn't a large troop, and no military expedition either. The men milled about, with no semblance of the strict order he expected from a well-drilled Legion.

Just as he was about to turn away and head back to Mari, movement at the marquee tent in the center of camp caught his attention. The tent flap was slapped back, and out stepped Casca.

Even at this distance, Jurian knew it was him. There could be no mistake. He stood a head shorter than the officer who attended him, and only Casca gestured that way as he spoke—hand dancing like a hooked fish on a line. A moment later, another soldier brought around two horses, holding them steady for Casca and his attendant to mount.

Jurian pushed himself into motion, half-sliding, half-running down the hill. He had to get Mari out of here…but how?

Casca's troop barred the only bridge over the river that they'd likely find for miles, and if he found them, he'd kill them. Jurian hesitated in the shallow gully next to the road, staring towards the bridge, waiting for the inevitable sound of hoofbeats.

None came. Casca must have gone the other way.

Jurian darted across the road and back to the copse where he'd left Mari concealed in the shadowy underbrush.

His heart stopped.

Mari lay curled up under a tree, still and pale as snow, and over her stood the largest man he had ever seen.

11

ANATOLIA

JURIAN'S HAND FLASHED TO HIS bow, and before he could think, he had an arrow nocked and drawn, sighted on the giant.

"You!" he gritted. "Get away from her!"

The man spun around, holding out his hands. Jurian swallowed hard and fought back a flicker of fear. The man was even larger than he'd thought, over a foot taller than Jurian himself, and Jurian could stand shoulder to shoulder with most soldiers in the *Apollinaris*. Jurian couldn't see if he carried a weapon, but his hands were massive. Jurian knew that he'd never stand a chance against a blow from one of those fists. But he edged forward anyway, circling toward Mari.

"Back away and tell me what you've done to her! If you laid a hand on her..." His eyes flickered to Mari, fear lodged in his throat. "Mari, wake up!"

"Peace, peace," the man said, his voice the lowest rumble Jurian had ever heard. And then, to Jurian's surprise, he knelt down there in the dirt and fallen leaves with his hands over his head. "I mean no harm. Not to you, not to her. I only found her like this a moment ago, and I was afraid she might be dead. If she was, I only meant to give her a proper burial."

Sudden panic drowned his rage, and Jurian let the bowstring go slack as he rushed to Mari's side.

"No, no," he whispered, kneeling beside her, hands shaking as he touched her shoulder.

She stirred suddenly and twisted halfway onto her back.

"You're back already?" she mumbled, and opened her eyes.

Jurian held up his hand just as her face blanched with terror. She bit her lip, hard, eyes wide and staring at the man behind him. She didn't cry out, but she shuffled away from him.

"Let me deal with him, all right?" Jurian said softly. "I don't think he's dangerous, but I need to find out."

She nodded and sat up, clutching her thin arms close around her. The giant, Jurian noticed, was murmuring something under his breath, his whole face etched with relief. Jurian's mouth twitched and he scooped up his discarded bow and arrow, holding them by his side as a warning as he approached the man. The giant met Jurian's gaze quietly.

He couldn't have been much older than Varro, Jurian realized, though it was hard to tell past the thick length of black beard that he wore far too long to be fashionable. And his eyes—Jurian had never known someone who could look so terrible and yet so kind at the same time.

This is the sort of man, Jurian thought, *who would face a lion without flinching, and bow to a child without shame.*

He wore an ordinary tunic, though it was too worn and stained to be called white. The cloak slung over his shoulders was much like Jurian's, and it didn't quite conceal the band of leather he wore around his upper left arm. On the ground beside him he had a long staff for carrying a bundle of provisions, much like a Legionary's *sarcina*.

"Are you Roman?" Jurian asked at last.

The giant sat back on his heels and squinted at him with a faint smile. "Aren't we all Romans?"

"That's not what I meant," Jurian said. "You said something about a burial, earlier."

The man held his gaze and reached a thumb to his forehead, brushing it down and across in the shape of a *tau*. Jurian stared at him, but Mari gasped behind him and mimicked the gesture.

When Jurian just stood motionless, Mari leaned forward and slapped his leg.

"Jurian! Make the *signum!*"

Jurian shot her a puzzled glance and did his best to imitate the motion, feeling foolish.

"Ah," the giant said, smiling. "I thought so."

"What do you mean, you thought so?" Jurian said. "Why won't you answer my question?"

The man gave him a patient look. "Look, boy, are you going to put that bow down and be civil, or do you think that twig will actually work on me?"

Jurian bristled. "I'm not a boy. I'm the only man of my house."

Not that I have a house to be man of, he thought.

The giant laughed, long and rumbling, then he sobered and cast an appraising eye over Jurian. "Remains to be seen."

Jurian crouched in front of the giant, setting down his bow and quiver and drawing his *seax*.

"I'm going to ask you just once more," he said. "Tell me who you are and what business you have in these parts."

The man just chuckled. "Ah, yes. That's much more impressive." He glanced at Mari. "Can you ask him to stand down?"

"Jurian, please," Mari pleaded. "Just—"

"You're taking *his* side?" Jurian cried, gesturing at the giant with the point of his knife. "Really?"

Mari shrugged and smiled. "Jurian, he's a fellow traveler!" She smiled, eyeing the giant from under her sweeping lashes. "And I like him."

After a moment, Jurian shook his head and stood, sheathing the knife. He helped Mari to her feet, then turned back to the giant.

"Thank you for your concern," Jurian said. "But we have to be on our way."

"East or west?" the giant asked.

"What does it matter?"

The man stood and picked up his provisions. "If you're going west, you might want to know there's a Legion camp just ahead. I presume that's the way you're going, since you're here, and you're not wet."

"We are going west," Mari said promptly.

Jurian slapped his forehead in frustration. "Mari!" he cried, then frowned at the man. "What did that mean, we're here and not wet?"

"You're here, so you didn't cross the bridge, and you're not wet, so you didn't cross the river. Means you must have come from the east. But you're not traveling on the road, so I imagine you'd rather not meet the Legion up ahead—God knows, I don't care to. Am I right so far?"

"Perfectly!" Mari said, smiling. Jurian glowered at her and said nothing.

"Well, then I'm also right in saying you're about to get very wet, because there's no way to go any further west without crossing the river."

"Thank you for clarifying the obvious for us," he said. "We'll be on our way to the river now."

The giant regarded him skeptically but said nothing, only pointed toward the west with something like a mock bow.

Once they'd gotten out of earshot, Mari sighed and said, "We should have asked him to come with us."

"Why are you so quick to trust him?" Jurian asked.

"He gave the *signum*, didn't you see?"

"And that makes him trustworthy, just like that? What if he was trying to trap us? Maybe he was scratching a gnat bite and you think it makes him a believer. Maybe he's looking for runaway slaves and thinks that's what we are."

"And maybe you just think too much!" she said, too loud—the violence of her voice brought on another fit of coughing.

She leaned on a tree trunk to wait for the spasm to pass, and Jurian watched her anxiously.

"Mari," he murmured. "You're not well. Why do you keep trying to hide it?"

She stared at him, the backs of her fingers still pressed against her mouth. Finally she drew a shaking sigh and said, "Because I was afraid if I said anything, it would make it true."

"Make what true?"

"That I…that I have the wasting illness. Just like Mother."

Jurian recoiled.

"No," he said, his blood turning to ice. "No, that's not possible. It's just the weather. Sleeping in the chilly air. All this dust. You'll get well again as soon as we get off the road!"

"Jurian," she said, letting go of the tree to take his arm. "It's been happening for much longer than all that. You want me to stop hiding it? Then that's the truth."

He spun away, feeling like his lungs had failed. It couldn't be true. He wouldn't let it be true. When he felt her hand on his shoulder he stopped his frantic pacing and drew a long, steadying breath.

"I'll keep walking as long as I can," she murmured, giving him what she meant to be an encouraging smile. "But—"

"Don't. Just don't even say it." Jurian hugged her fiercely for a moment, then took her hand and led her forward.

The trees gave way all at once to the broad sweep of the river. Jurian had led them a little southwest, hoping to get far enough from the bridge that Casca's Legionaries wouldn't see them crossing. He'd succeeded in that much—the hills blocked their view of the bridge from here—but still, Jurian stopped in dismay on the bank.

The river was so wide. The water snaked past in swirls and eddies, white foam slapping against a scattering of jagged rocks. Jurian dipped his fingers in the water, gasping at its chill.

It was useless.

"How're we going to get across this, Jurian?" Mari whispered, wrapping her arms around herself.

"I could build a raft," Jurian said. But one more look at the river and he had to shake his head. "But the rocks are too rough, and the current's too fast…we would get swept right under the bridge. And then Casca would know we're here."

"Casca?"

"And I don't have any rope anyway."

"Jurian."

"But I could make something out of thin branches, maybe. I could weave them like a mat."

"Jurian."

"What?"

He turned and found her pointing behind them. Jurian spun and saw the giant standing at the edge of the trees, watching them quietly.

"Why are you following us?" Jurian asked, frustration bubbling up inside him.

"I came to offer my services." The man gestured at the river. "Planning to swim?"

"I..." Jurian gritted his teeth and looked away. "I can't swim. I thought we could walk across."

"Will you give me the courtesy of listening to my experience?" the giant asked, a bit sternly. Jurian sighed and nodded. "I've crossed this river more times than I can count. At its deepest, it reaches my chin."

He didn't need to elaborate; the top of Jurian's head wouldn't have reached the man's chin, even standing on his toes.

"So, no walking across," Jurian said. "Well. You've crossed it. Do you have a boat or a raft?"

The man grinned, his white teeth flashing behind the dark bristle of his beard. "No. But I'll show you what I do have."

He approached them, and for the first time Jurian noticed he was barefoot. The man planted his massive, dirt-crusted foot between them. His little toe was the size of Jurian's largest toe, but the largest was almost the size of a small spring onion. But stranger than that, between the two he had four more toes. Jurian stared, not sure whether to be fascinated or disgusted, and he exchanged a quick glance with Mari.

"So...you have six toes?" he asked, uncertain. "I'm sorry, I'm not following. What does this have to do with the river?"

"Five toes are good for gripping, but six are even better," the giant said, with a flash of something like pride. "When I was your sister's age I found them terribly embarrassing. Wouldn't you?

Always barefoot, so that people could stare. After all, who makes shoes for a six-toed boy? And how could I have money to pay a cobbler for shoes made just for me? Anyway, I found them useful in the end. A blessing, even. They've helped me carry many a burden across many a river, including…" He turned away, staring down the river with the strangest light in his dark eyes. "Including the most precious burden of all."

Mari watched him, obviously hoping he would explain, but he just shook his head and smiled.

"So you're saying you can carry us across the river?" Jurian asked.

"I'm suggesting that you have very little alternative than to trust me."

Jurian gritted his teeth. The man was right. Unless they wanted to risk Casca and the Legion, there was no other way.

"All right, but take her first," Jurian said, nodding at Mariam. He unslung his bow, staring the giant coldly in the eye. "And I'll be watching you the entire way."

"Oh, for pity's sake," the giant said, and asked Mari, "Is he always like this?"

"He didn't used to be," she said wistfully.

Jurian's jaw spasmed, but he didn't put the bow away. "I'm sure you understand," he said to the giant. "She's all I've got left."

The giant put a heavy hand on his shoulder, just briefly, then stooped to a low crouch. "Climb onto my back, girl. I'll take you safely."

Jurian helped her scramble onto the man's broad back. She glanced down at Jurian, anxiety flickering in her eyes.

"Can you hold on the whole way?" Jurian asked. "You tell him if you start to slip, do you hear me?"

"I'll be all right," she said. "Stop worrying."

Jurian circled around to face the giant. "Listen," he said. "I'm trusting you. She's not very strong. Please keep a tight hold on her, will you?"

The man offered no flippant answer this time. He only nodded and turned to the river, plunging one foot in, then the other, pausing at each step to get a purchase on the slick riverbed rocks. Jurian watched anxiously as he used the long pole of his *sarcina* to test out his footing, the water twisting and rushing around his massive legs, then his torso. Mari clung to his neck, her face buried in the folds of his cloak. They reached a sudden rush of water and Jurian's heart launched into his throat as Mari's arm slipped and she scrambled to grab hold again.

The giant froze, reaching back to steady her, then slowly moved on, angling his body upstream to take the worst of the current's force on his chest. They sank lower and lower, until all Jurian could see were their heads and the tall pole.

Jurian held his breath until they started to rise again, and finally let it all out when he saw them come safely ashore. Once he had set Mari down away from the river's edge, the giant made his slow, careful journey back across the water. He came out dripping and shook himself like a dog, scattering icy water all over Jurian. Jurian took off his cloak and wrapped it around his bow and quiver, sealing the arrows in.

"All right, your turn," the giant said. "Up you get."

"Thank you," Jurian muttered. "For taking such care of her."

The man gave him a broad, warm smile and turned his back to Jurian, crouching down so that Jurian could climb onto his back. After a few awkward attempts Jurian managed to get up.

"Are you sure I won't be too heavy?" he asked.

He felt more than heard the man's rumble of laughter. "I've carried the heaviest burden, boy. You're nothing compared to that."

"There must be a story in there," Jurian said, trying not to gasp as the first wave of icy water rushed over his feet. He held onto the giant's neck with one arm, the other hand balancing his bundle on top of his head. "The most precious burden and the heaviest burden? What were they?"

"The same," the man said. "Another time, I'll tell it to you. Now let me concentrate. Keep distracting me and we'll both get washed away."

Jurian complied, though this was perhaps the first time in

his life that he would have preferred conversation to silence. He didn't need to worry though; the giant carried him across with just as much carefulness as Mariam, and none too soon he was slogging up onto the river bank. Jurian leapt down and rushed over to Mari. She smiled at him, but her teeth were chattering violently and her whole body shook with cold.

"Are you all right?" he asked.

"Fine," she said. "Just frozen."

"Let's take that cloak off. It's soaked through and won't do you any good."

She nodded, her fingers faltering over the cloak clasp, but finally she managed to get rid of it. Jurian freed his own cloak from his bundle and threw it over her shoulders. He was about to ask the giant to start a fire, but found that he was already busy mounding tinder in a hollowed pit.

As soon as they had a good blaze going, Jurian helped Mari over to the warmth, showing her how to sit with the cloak spread out behind her to trap the heat against her body. They all hunkered close to the fire, shivering as the sun seeped toward the horizon.

"We should camp here," Jurian said. "We're far enough from the road for a fire. I'll see about getting us something to eat."

"We're next to a river," the giant said, giving Jurian a reproachful look. "Why not fish?"

"I'm not much of a fisherman," Jurian admitted.

"Ah, come on. I'll teach you."

The giant laid down his provisions, carefully extracting what at first looked like just a jumble of thin ropes. But as the man spread it on the ground, Jurian realized it was a woven net, easily large enough for both him and Mari to climb inside. Along one edge, it was fixed with stones, but along the other edge the giant wove a straight branch he'd found on the river bank. He carried it into the water and held it out to his side, angled up toward the rushing current. Jurian saw how it worked easily enough—the branch kept it spread wide, and the stones weighted the bottom to keep it open.

"That's all there is to it?" Jurian called.

The man shot him a look of exasperation and amusement. "All there is to it, hah!" he retorted. "I'd like to see you standing out in this water, boy."

"My name's Jurian."

"Strange name," the giant said. "Barbarian?"

"Germanic."

"Like I said." The giant twitched the net, then edged a little farther into the river. "Well. Perhaps you are a bridge."

Jurian scooped a smooth, flat rock into his palm, weighing it before tossing it into the water.

"If I were a bridge, I wouldn't have needed you to carry me," he called.

The giant gave a great bellowing laugh. "Very true. Well, since you've finally decided to be civil, I'll tell you my name." He bowed his head to Jurian. "Menas. At your service."

12

Cyrene

SABRA STOOD AGAINST THE WALL in her chamber, watching as one of the slaves measured the lengths of Elissa's arms with a piece of knotted rope. The girl stood precariously still, like she might fall over any moment, her eyes following the woman's every move with open curiosity.

"What's this for?" she asked Sabra, her arms dipping with fatigue.

The slave clucked and nudged her arms back up.

Sabra hesitated. "They're measuring you for a new robe," she said. "You're in the service of the god, now. You need a robe fitting for your new role."

"Will I look like you?" Elissa asked, twisting to see herself in the bronze mirror, oblivious to the slave's frustration.

"Yes, rather. Near enough."

She swallowed the rest of the answer she should have given—Elissa was also being measured for her sacrificial garment. Sabra's throat tightened and she turned to stare out the low window. They dressed the girls up like brides before leaving them to die. Long white tunics, beaded and embroidered at hem and throat, with a white veil instead of the bride's typical orange, to remind the god of the perfect innocence of the offering.

As if the god could fail to notice.

At one time, the symbolism of it all had seemed so rich and beautiful to Sabra. Now it only made her sad. There was something wretched about a god who called innocence to a bridal dance in death.

Shouldn't the gods be about life and love instead?

At the thought Sabra recoiled from the window, her hand clutching at her throat. Her weakness terrified her. And Elissa was only making it worse. No matter how often she told herself to harden her heart, to see the girl as nothing more than a lamb or goat kid for the god, she couldn't do it.

"What happens after I get my robe?" Elissa asked.

"Once you're ready, we will go down into the Temple, and I will teach you the rites so you can participate in them with me."

The beautiful warmth of Elissa's cheeks paled and she dropped her gaze. "I'm going to help worship the god?"

Sabra nodded slowly, noticing with some curiosity that when Elissa glanced up, she looked not at Sabra, but at Ayzebel lingering in the shadows. It didn't surprise her that Elissa had grown attached to the slave; Ayzebel had made a great effort to take care of the girl, more than she dedicated to the previous sacrifices. A corner of her heart wished that Ayzebel would show her the same kindness—or even just friendship. But that was pettiness unworthy of the priestess of the old god, so she pushed the regret away.

"Once Asherah is done with you, you are free for the afternoon," Sabra said.

"Can we walk down to the markets?"

Sabra hesitated, then murmured, "I'm sorry. Once you have your robe, perhaps then we can go. But it wouldn't be fitting for you to go down as you are. Do you understand?"

The girl heaved a long sigh and bent her head.

"Very well, Mistress Sabra."

Sabra nodded and left the chamber, realizing after a few steps that Ayzebel had followed her.

"Is it right to deny the child any sight of the outside world?" Ayzebel asked, joining her with a deferential bow. "Mistress. Not to question your judgment, of course."

Sabra bit her lip on telling Ayzebel that she had wanted to say yes. It wouldn't be proper to admit weakness to a slave.

Proper.

"Could I say yes, now that I've said no?" she asked instead.

Ayzebel's eyes widened, their curious amber irises luminous against the warmth of her skin. "Why not? To show mercy after judgment? What can be the harm in that?"

"Ayzebel, it would be *weak.*"

"Is that so important?" She paused, then blurted, "Why not show her that you're *human?*"

"If only it were that simple," Sabra said.

She headed down the corridor, but Ayzebel followed her all the way out into the peristyle.

"What harm can it do, mistress?"

"What harm?" Sabra asked, turning back to her. "Can you imagine if her mother saw her? Would you be that cruel to that poor woman?"

"You think that would be cruel?" Ayzebel asked, eyes widening. "To let the woman see her child again before she loses her forever?"

At almost the same moment Sabra said, "To tear open a wound that has begun to heal?"

"Who are you to say it has begun to heal?" Ayzebel cried, taking a step closer to her.

Sabra stared at the girl. There was a fire in her that Sabra had never seen, and it steeled her into cold resolve.

"Back away, Ayzebel," Sabra said, going very still. "And do not speak so freely to me again. I've made my decision."

Ayzebel hesitated, then backed away, head bowed. "Forgive me, mistress. I meant no disrespect."

"My answer is still no."

Sabra turned and headed into the cool, dark atrium. The silence of the house felt suffocating. All she wanted was to be outside, to be free and alone. There was no prohibition against *her* walking the city streets, but when she thought about doing so after denying Elissa the same pleasure, it felt strangely like a betrayal. Still, if she didn't get out now, she would go mad within these walls. The days were dragging by with such painful torpor.

Finally she called to a passing slave and sent him to find Hanno. Except for the days of the winnowing when she went down to teach her students, she never went into the city alone. Her father insisted on it. It wasn't fitting, he said, for the governor's daughter and the priestess of the old god to wander the streets alone. So she took Hanno when the household could spare him, since he was the only person she ever felt truly comfortable around.

Hanno appeared a few moments later, and without a word they left the palace. Sabra wondered if Hanno was still angry with her over the conversation about the Oracle, but he seemed relaxed enough. Just quiet, which was exactly what she had wanted.

When they reached the forum, he finally glanced at her and asked, "Are we going anywhere in particular, mistress?"

"No," she said. "I just needed to breathe."

She crossed to the large stone fountain near the *rostrum*, sitting on the rim while Hanno stood, arms folded, at her side. A deep quiet lingered over the forum, and not only because of the late afternoon hour. She could *feel* the city's suffering. Her job was underground, with the fire and the dead—perhaps that was why she could feel the decay settling like rot in the bones of the city she loved so dearly.

Maybe the god had already cursed them. If he was still angry with them, perhaps he had caused the dwindling of the silphium crops that, for better or worse, had always been the principle trade for the city. As the trade failed, the city crumbled.

If only I could heal it. If only I could find the way to bring peace and life back to this place.

Her gaze drifted across the dismal buildings, the cracked stones of the street, the fullers' receptacles in the alleys that stunk of urine. She shuddered.

"I need to go to the Kyre," she said. "I keep dreaming that it is running dry."

"Look behind you, mistress," Hanno said gently.

She didn't want to; he was being sensible, but she didn't want to hear sense. Still, to gratify him she glanced at the fountain behind her, its water gurgling cheerfully into its broad basin. If the Kyre had dried, of course the fountain would have, too. But she didn't care. She wanted to see the spring...she wanted to look into the cave, and make sure she wouldn't see Death staring back at her.

Hanno followed her, patient and uncomplaining as ever, as they made their way to the shaded silence of the Sanctuary of Apollo. The whole way up the narrow path to the cave, Sabra stared at the water swishing past in the conduits, but none of it satisfied her need to see the spring itself. Finally they reached the mouth of the cave, which was little more than a hole in the hillside. From within its cool, humid space, Sabra could hear the quiet splash of water, but she planted her hands on the rough stone and stuck her head inside. As her eyes adjusted to the dim light, she saw the clear water gushing down the slick stones. Smelled the damp rock and the tangy, almost decaying scent of moss. Felt the spray of the water on her cheeks.

"Satisfied now?" Hanno asked.

She glanced over her shoulder. He stood with arms folded, but it was worry, not annoyance, she read in his eyes.

"Does the spring seem weaker than before?" she asked. "Please. I want to know."

He sighed but gave a respectful gesture to the god of the spring, and bent to look in. After a moment he withdrew, slowly. For a long time he didn't speak.

"Well?" Sabra asked.

"Yes," he said, almost whispering it. "I think you're right."

A wave of panic surged up from her stomach. "You're not just saying that to tease me, are you?"

He shook his head. "No, mistress. I wouldn't tease about that."

"Hanno, if this spring dies, we all die. The Kyre is the only reason this city stands here." She bit her lip, then grabbed his arms. "As the god's voice, I command you to tell me what the Oracle said. I need to know."

"By all the gods, mistress, please don't ask me!" Hanno cried, eyes wide. "Ask Abdosir."

"I don't want to ask Abdosir. I want *you* to tell me, now."

Hanno's eyes shone and the muscle in his jaw tightened, but finally he turned and sat on the low edge of the cave's mouth.

"The slave who heard the messenger was Hiram," he said. "After you and I talked the other afternoon, I asked him to explain it to me."

Sabra sat beside him and waited for him to continue. The air from the cave breathed over her, clammy like the underground temple of the god, like the fingers of the tomb.

"The message from the Oracle was this: *Blood flows not water dries. The hungry one will rage until he receives the blood of the innocent. Your city's salvation awaits the wood.*"

"Yes, yes," Sabra said, frowning. "That's the Punic translation. I've heard it before. So, what was the confusion? Most people debate about the first sentence, or the meaning of the wood, but the slave I overheard seemed to fix on the word for *innocent*."

Silence.

Then Hanno said, "*Amymon*."

"That was the Greek word?" Sabra asked, and tapped her lip. "*Amymon* means innocent. But…it also means excellent."

Hanno hid his face behind his hand and murmured, "Gods pity me. Oh, mistress, it also means *noble*."

Sabra froze. The air from the cave slipped around her neck like dead fingers, and she gasped. "Noble *and* innocent? Hanno! In this whole city, who could that possibly mean?"

Hanno wouldn't answer.

Finally she said, "*Me*. I'm the one the god wants. Marked for his service from my birth, indeed! I've *always* been the one he wanted. And all this time…oh, gods…all those children…"

She stared out at the city, hands shaking, but she couldn't make sense of the turmoil of emotions churning inside her. The burn of anger, the cold trembling of fear, dull resentment, and… somehow…the giddiness of joy.

Joy?

She jumped up, trembling. Finally she knew what worship the god really wanted. She knew how to save the city, how to restore the Kyre and keep her nightmares from coming true.

She knew how to save Elissa.

Because if it was her blood the god craved, why shouldn't he have it? She could die and sate the god's hunger once and for all. The Oracle had spoken. It had to be true.

"Don't you see what this means?" she cried, and laughed.

Hanno stared at her as if she'd gone mad.

"I can save them. Hanno! We can end this."

"Mistress," Hanno choked.

Sabra stopped pacing and spun to face him. "My father *knew*." Just like that, her joy faded, swallowed in shaking anger. "He heard the Oracle. He knew what she meant. And he let all those children die in my stead."

Rage shook the pit of her soul. She wanted to strike something, break something, scream as loud as she could. But there was nothing to strike, nothing to break, and she couldn't scream in this holy place. Finally she threw herself at the rocky cliff face and slammed her fist against it until the skin tore and bled. Hanno grabbed her shoulders and pulled her away, not letting go even when she turned to strike his chest instead.

"Ten years, Hanno!" she cried. "*Ten!* How many lives? How many poor children have we fed to the god and he knew all along! He knew the truth and he didn't even care that I'd have to live with myself, with the guilt that *I* left them to die. I died with that first child I left on the cliffside! I've been nothing but a broken shell ever since, hollowing into madness and despair."

The last few words were lost in a wrenching sob. Hanno stood perfectly still, holding her by the arms as she wept against his shoulder. She knew he couldn't embrace her, because he had no right to touch her, but she wondered if he loathed her too, because of her blood-stained soul.

After a few moments she collected herself, splashing a handful of cold water over her face with a whispered *thank you* to the god.

"What will you do?" Hanno asked as she dried her face on the sleeve of her robe.

"First I'll talk to my father," she said. "Come on."

They arrived back at the palace at the same time as a Legion Legate and his Tribune. Sabra frowned. There were no Legions stationed in Libya, but occasionally they saw the *Augusta* or the *Traiani* collecting auxiliary archers for some campaign or other. Sabra didn't much care who they were or what business they had there. She only cared that they would be occupying her father's attention when she so desperately needed it.

She exchanged a glance with Hanno and followed the men up to the house. The Tribune glanced back as they crossed the threshold, his eyes fixing briefly on hers. Sabra watched the predictable change of his features: surprise, interest, uncertainty, reserve.

"Forgive me," he said. "Were you here to see the governor?"

She didn't answer, but folded her hands in her robe and bowed her head. It wasn't fitting for her to look too steadily at a man, or for one to look at her…even though some days that was the hardest part of her priesthood.

"The priestess is the governor's daughter," Hanno said.

The Tribune might have looked surprised. Sabra wouldn't know. She only heard him draw a slight breath and saw his sandals shuffle back to give her room. As she slipped past him, she heard Hanno say to the officers,

"I will tell the governor that you are here."

Once in the solitude of the peristyle, Sabra hesitated. She longed to tell Elissa what she had learned, but she couldn't imagine the horror of telling the girl that she could live, and then finding out that she was powerless to stop the sacrifice. For now, she would wait until she could talk to her father. Surely he would make things right, when he saw her willingness to embrace the destiny the Oracle had named for her.

All would be well.

13

Cyrene

Ayzebel found Sabra pacing in the peristyle what felt like hours later.

"Mistress," she said. "Your father wants to speak with you."

"Now?" Sabra asked. "But doesn't he have guests?"

"They had business to attend to in the city before dinner."

Sabra nodded and headed to her father's small office, situated between the atrium and the peristyle. He was inside, poring over some parchments on a tall desk, his forehead creased with worry or concentration. The look vanished when she came in, and he smiled warmly at her.

"Ah, Sabra."

"You wanted to speak to me?"

"Hanno hinted that you might have something you wanted to discuss with me. Is something troubling you?"

Sabra twisted her fingers together. She'd been contemplating what she would say to him while she'd waited in the peristyle, but now it had all vanished. When she didn't speak, her father seated himself on the stone bench by the wall and patted the spot beside him. Holding her breath, Sabra sat down stiffly and folded her hands in her robe.

"What did the Legion officials want?" she asked.

Her father waved his hand. "Oh, you know. The Legion is

returning to Numidia, so we have the pleasure of entertaining its officers tonight." He gave her a serious look. "But that is no matter. What's troubling you?"

"Father," she said, her voice a bare whisper. "The Oracle..."

He straightened up, bracing one hand on his leg, but when he didn't speak she swallowed hard and pressed on.

"I fear we might be wrong about the sacrifices. I fear that... perhaps the god doesn't want children's blood at all. Maybe the old priestess chose me—"

"Enough!" he barked, holding up a hand. "Have you been listening to slaves' chatter? The Oracle's message was clear. We were sacrificing goats and chickens. In that context, the meaning is evident. The god wanted human blood, not animal." He pressed the bridge of his nose. "Honestly, Sabra, I'm more concerned that we might be feeding a monster and not the god at all. When our ancestors worshipped the god, he had no physical form. They made an idol of bronze and fire, and they offered him sacrifice by casting their offerings into the flames. But this? This is something new. We believe the god wants blood, but you've seen the altar up in the cliffs after the sacrifices."

"Have you?" Sabra asked, stunned. She didn't think he'd ever gone up there. She'd thought it was forbidden.

"Yes. There are no blood stains. No remains but bones, as if the flesh had been completely burned away. This creature that lives in the cave...it consumes them. But it consumes them in fire. What if this is not the work of the god at all? What if the beast is something else?" He hesitated for one awful moment, then added. "What if it is something we can destroy?"

"Father!" Sabra cried, casting the sign against evil. "You don't mean that! I'm the priestess of the old god. Wouldn't I know—"

Wouldn't I know if the sacrifices were failing?

But they are failing. Isn't that what this is all about?

Sabra shook her head and pressed her hands against her eyes. "Then did we ever offer sacrifice to the old god? Why did we start chaining children to the rocks in the cliffs, if not to appease Molech?"

This was a nightmare. Her world was dissolving around her.

Did her father not believe? Had she been fed lies all her life, and pressed into the service of some monster? And for what?

Had it all been for nothing?

Her father was speaking again, though Sabra could barely make sense of his words.

"This creature, that…dragon… By all accounts, it crawled out of the sea some fifteen years ago and terrorized the coastland. Then it came to settle in these cliffs. We've been trying to appease it with sacrifices ever since. We always believed it was a manifestation of the god, but part of me wonders now if we were wrong."

"But what about the Oracle?" Sabra whispered, breathless.

"'The Oracle spoke of 'the hungry one.' She never named him as the god, or the 'divine hungry one.' He is the ravager. The destroyer. But she did not name him Molech."

Sabra clutched her hands inside her robe as if by sheer force she could hold the pieces of her world together.

"No," she managed, "Molech *is* the hungry one, the fire that consumes. Why would he not manifest himself like some sort of dragon, if that was his wish?" She stood unsteadily. "I think you're afraid of the Oracle, so you're trying to explain away the sacrifices. You've never wanted to believe the truth. You know that my blood is required, so instead you blaspheme the god!"

Her father opened his mouth to answer, but she swept on, "And what of Elissa? Are you going to send her to feed a monster that you don't even believe deserves the honor of due sacrifice? What should I think of that, Father?"

He tipped his head back to meet her gaze, his face etched with weariness. "I don't know what to believe any longer. Everything is crumbling and all the things we used to believe are shaking in their foundations. What are we to do?" He sighed and bent his head. "Never mind my prattling. I'm only tired, and every child we offer to that beast breaks my heart."

Sabra winced, hearing the pain in his voice that so perfectly echoed her own.

"Do you truly believe that we are placating the god when we

offer these sacrifices?" he asked, his voice low.

Sabra hesitated. But the answer was quick in her mind: *No.*

Finally she said, "I believe…I believe it is the god we are trying to placate. But I don't think he is happy with our efforts."

"And now the auguries of Apollo are failing," her father said. "Perhaps none of the gods are happy with us." He sighed. "Don't fret about the Oracle, *cara*. Your name is in the lottery too, Sabra. If the god really desired your blood, your name would be chosen."

But you instituted the lottery, she thought. *You started the lottery when you knew it was me he wanted all along!*

"So Elissa must be offered?"

"The god chose her, didn't he?" her father asked, but she stood, silent and still, waiting. "The god chose her this time, Sabra. Not you."

She closed her eyes, everything she wanted to say catching in her throat.

"Now," her father said, "would you like to take dinner with us this evening? I know you're accustomed to eating alone, but you are always welcome."

Sabra stared at him. *Have I always been welcome? Was this just another scourge I punished myself with for no cause?*

The thought of eating with the officers made her strangely nervous, but she caught herself murmuring, "Yes, thank you."

"Then we will see you for dinner." As she turned to leave, he said softly, "Take comfort, Sabra. It's always darkest before the dawn."

WHEN EVENING CAME, Sabra made her way to the large *triclinium*. She was dressed formally in her Priestess regalia, all but the veil over her face that would have made eating impossible. Her father and the officers had arrived just before her, so she did her best to lift her chin and make a bold entrance. But no sooner had the Tribune caught her gaze than her self-confidence shattered. She ducked her head and cursed herself for accepting her father's invitation, and longed for the concealing security of her veil.

A number of other government officials joined the party with their wives, and though some of the women were only a little older than Sabra, none of them so much as glanced at her. In fact, they all seemed intent on *not* looking at her. Sabra sat rigid and silent, nervous even when she spotted Hanno along the far wall. She watched the others feasting on lamb and pork, washing it back with bitter wine mixed with water and honey, and somehow she didn't feel the slightest bit hungry.

"What's the news from the rest of the Empire?" her father asked the officers.

"Nothing unusual," the Legate said. "They're finally concluding the Peace of Nisibis in Anatolia, so that will end the Persian campaigns once and for all. Then there's all this business about Christians deserting the army, betraying Rome to serve their own king, or so they say. I don't know why they're so bothered about it. We've lost a few in our Legion in recent years—it's not all that new. One a few years ago refused to serve at all. Maximilian, I think. How's that for *pietas?*"

"What happened to him?" one of the wives asked.

"Executed, of course," the Legate said smoothly, as if he couldn't believe the question. "He was a traitor."

Sabra forced herself to keep chewing her mouthful of almonds, but they stuck in her throat when she tried to swallow.

Did we always talk so freely about death? she wondered. *But why should it bother me? Death is my domain.*

"Surely you don't think all those people are traitors?" another woman asked.

Sabra glanced at her curiously. Cyrene had its share of Christians, she knew. She'd even heard rumor once that someone important to that faith had come from the city, centuries ago. She didn't know the full story, and she'd never bothered to study faiths that were not her own.

Is this woman one of that cult? It's a dangerous question to ask so freely.

"Who can say?" one of the men said.

Another disagreed—Caius Dignianus, her father's second-in-command. "I can. They refuse to honor the emperor. They prefer some other king to Diocletian *Augustus?* Then they aren't truly Roman, and, what's more, they support a foreign power."

"It's not a foreign power," another man countered. "They serve a god. His kingdom—if he's got one—isn't of this world anyway. So what's Rome so nervous about?"

"Now that the auguries are failing, I'd say we've got cause to be nervous," the first man retorted. "And it means that this new cult is something more dangerous than we thought."

"Rome must have unity if she is to survive and expand," the Legate said, waving a hand to quiet the argument. "Once Alexander ruled the whole world, then Caesar surpassed him by going beyond the limits of the known world. We can only follow in his great footsteps if Rome is united. Gods, we're inviting so many foreign cults and foreign cultures into Rome, it's remarkable we have any sense of who we are any more. But at least most of them are willing to assimilate." He shook his head, addressing Sabra's father. "These Christians are dangerous because they stand apart. They seem to believe they're somehow special, that their beliefs are the only ones that are true. You know, they remind me of the Jews. That's where they got started, over there in Palestine."

The men murmured in agreement, all of them hanging on the Legate's words like they were dripping honey.

"And I will give you all a little prophecy of my own—the fate of Rome herself is tied to what happens to these people. I think as one grows, the other must diminish, and if we have to encourage that with a little force, then so be it."

"But they aren't dangerous, are they?" the first woman asked. "I've heard they mostly just keep to themselves."

"Does it matter?" Dignianus asked with a snort. "Only the good of Rome matters."

Sabra swallowed. She wondered what they would say if they knew about her sacrifices, her service to the old god. Would they say she should be serving Venus or Vesta instead of Molech? Was he too foreign a god for their tastes, with his dark and unquenchable thirst for blood?

As if he'd read her thoughts, the Legate suddenly said, "I've heard rumors that you have strange goings-on around here. What is this talk of some kind of creature up in the hills?"

Silence.

After a moment, Sabra realized that everyone was staring at her. She froze, her tongue stuck to the roof of her mouth.

What do I tell them? If I tell the truth, will we be traitors too? Or do I lie and offend the god…and look like a fool?

She tried to swallow again and managed to meet the Legate's gaze evenly. "A dragon, you mean?"

The Legate laughed. The Tribune studied her curiously, but he at least wasn't mocking her.

"A…dragon?" the Legate echoed. He glanced at the Tribune as if to say, *Gods, haven't we civilized these people yet?* "I'm sure you know that dragons are a myth, girl."

And what is your faith but myth? she thought, her eyes boring into the Legate's until he looked away.

"I am the sole priestess of the old god and the voice of his manifestation," she said, the words burning through her. "I am not a child. You may mock me if you choose, but I know what I have seen."

She didn't dare look at the Tribune, but the Legate sat back, both brows arched in surprise.

"Many of us have seen the dragon," one of the women murmured.

"A dragon?" the Tribune asked, softly, his gaze fixed on Sabra so steadily that she blushed. He was asking *her*. He dared to speak to *her*, and he wanted her to answer.

"I am the voice of his manifestation," she repeated, "and I know what I have seen."

When the meal finally ended, the guests withdrew to the peristyle where the coal braziers burned bright and a musician played a lyre quietly from the shadows. Several slaves stood scattered under the portico, holding trays of wine or sweets. The stone walls echoed the guests' laughter and conversation, almost drowning out the music and the soft splash of the fountain. Sabra intended to walk straight through to her own chamber, but she'd only gotten halfway through the courtyard when someone stepped out in front of her. She groaned inwardly. It had to be the Tribune, with his kind eyes and striking looks.

She dipped her head and tried to move around him, but he held out a hand to stop her.

"Please, Priestess," he said. "I'm sorry if I offended you earlier. I wasn't trying to doubt you. Can you forgive me that, at least?"

She met his gaze briefly before turning away again, biting her lip. Tears burned in the back of her throat. Of course, the first time in her life that a man had seen her as anything more than a robe and an executioner, and she wasn't even allowed to explain why she couldn't speak in her own voice. And by her silence she would only offend him, and if he hated her for it? So much the better.

"The Priestess is not permitted to speak to men," someone said in Punic, stepping up behind her.

Sabra let out all her breath, mentally whispering a *thank you* to Hanno.

"Not at all?" the Tribune asked, the Punic words heavily accented. Sabra wondered if she was imagining the disappointment in his voice. "But I saw you two speaking earlier, coming up the road."

Hanno bowed his head and said simply, "I am a eunuch."

The Tribune's face registered brief surprise, but he only nodded and said, "I see. I envy you, though…at least in one way."

He gave Sabra a slow bow, his gaze holding hers briefly, and strode away to join the Legate. Sabra pressed her knuckles against her lips.

"I'm sorry," she whispered to Hanno, though she didn't even know what she was apologizing for.

Hanno frowned. "No need to apologize, mistress. Are you all right? This was your first public dinner in years, wasn't it?"

"Yes," she said. "And I shouldn't have come." She slid a hand under her hair, feeling her neck damp with sweat. "I'm going to suffocate in here, Hanno. It'll be a fitting end after offending everyone, I suppose.""

"You didn't offend the Tribune," he said gently. "Disappointed him, I would guess, but that's to be expected."

She closed her eyes. "I'm going out. Can you come with me? Please, Hanno."

"You don't ask me. I'm here at your command."

But you're my friend, can't you see that? I want to ask you. I want you to come because you're my friend…not because I command you.

It had been so long since she'd had any friends, though, she wondered how she knew what the word meant any more.

With Hanno following at a respectful distance, she turned and fled the house. They wound back down through the streets, and Sabra realized with a jolt that her feet were carrying her straight toward the Temple of the god. She hadn't meant to go that way. Was the god calling her in to punish her, for disgracing him in public?

She hesitated in the middle of the street, and at that same moment, a terrible scream shattered the night silence.

She met Hanno's startled gaze, and they both took off running in the direction of the noise.

A small crowd had already gathered on the street when they arrived, clustering around the door of a senior official's house. The door stood gaping open, filled with enough light from torches and oil lamps that everyone on the street could see inside the atrium. There, in the depression in the floor meant to catch the rain, the body of the official lay in a pool of his own blood.

Hanno turned away, muttering under his breath, but Sabra stood and stared, refusing to be repulsed. She should be used to death, after all, even though she never saw it like this.

She couldn't see any other officials in the crowd, so that made her the highest ranking person present—and a religious figure besides. Taking on that office, she chose a random bystander and asked, "What happened?"

The man paled when he saw her, and bowed his head. "Who can say, Priestess? One of his slaves just discovered him."

He pointed at a Numidian slave standing close by, wringing

his hands. Sabra picked her way over to him.

"Did you find your master's body?"

"Yes, oh—Priestess. Yes," he said, lifting his hands and casting his head back to the night sky in supplication. "I heard someone running. Didn't see who, but it sounded like bare feet."

"So, another slave?"

He said nothing, just turned his head and stared at the body. Sabra sighed and went to Hanno.

"Summon the Guard, will you? I suppose I should go and tell my father."

14

Anatolia

Menas tugged the net from the water, frowning when he saw a scant handful of fish trapped in its fine strands.

"Won't that be enough?" Jurian asked from his perch on a riverside boulder.

"Hah!" Menas shook his head and cast the net again. "Maybe for you and your sister. Not for me."

Jurian smiled in spite of himself and turned back to the straight length of stick he was smoothing for an arrow.

"Where are you from, Menas?" he asked, hoping to get an answer now that they were on friendlier terms. "Are you traveling somewhere?"

"Not traveling, if you assume there's a destination." He paused, reflecting. "Well, I have a destination, but God only knows when I'll reach it. And I won't reach it with these legs, anyway."

"Are you always this cryptic?"

"Possibly."

Jurian laughed. "And my first question?"

"I've come from…so far away. And I have so far to go. I'm from darkness and guilt."

Jurian glanced up. Menas was staring fixedly at the water with the strangest expression in his dark eyes..

"That's really not what I was asking," he called.

Menas turned and grinned at him. "I thought my height would make it obvious."

"Are you a Philistine?" Mari asked, wandering over to them with Jurian's cloak still clutched tight around her.

"A what?" Jurian asked, racking his memory of his father's maps. "I've never heard of such a people."

"Nor will you," Menas said. "My people were conquered and reconquered so many times that not even our name remains to us. We're just a part of Rome, now. Isn't that the way of it? Once we were the most feared warriors in the world, giants in size as well as ambition, killing dragons of the sea and toppling empires, only to be brought low by our own pride."

Jurian frowned down at Mari. "What do you know about his people?"

"Oh, saints, Jurian, didn't you listen to any of the stories..." Her voice faltered and she turned to stare out at the river.

"I wish now that I had," Jurian murmured, his throat tight. "What story did Mother tell about Philistines?"

"How David killed Goliath," she said.

"What, was David some sort of Philistine warrior?"

Mari exchanged a glance with Menas that made Jurian feel incredibly ignorant, but Menas just grinned and tugged his net from the river.

"Should I tell the story or do you want to?" he asked Mari, sloshing his way to the river bank.

"You, please," Mari said.

Once they had the fish speared on green wood and staked over the fire, Menas settled on the ground and folded his hands.

"David was not the Philistine," he began. "David was an Israelite."

"A Jew."

"Yes."

"So he was the warrior?"

"Jurian," Mari hissed. "Let him tell the story!"

"David wasn't a warrior. Goliath was the warrior king of the

Philistines. He was so tall, even I would be nothing next to him."

"So if David wasn't a warrior, what was he?"

Menas smiled and smoothed the damp strands of his beard. "David was a boy. Younger than you. Probably Mari's size."

Jurian settled against a tree trunk and laced his fingers behind his head. "Well, this all sounds ridiculous. How could a boy kill someone so strong and powerful? Did he trick him? Poison him?"

"No, no. Single combat," Menas said impressively. "Goliath had his sword, which probably weighed more than you do, and a spear that would make a Legionary's *spiculum* look like a twig. David wasn't supposed to fight, but he took his sling and five smooth stones out into the field."

"Why smooth stones?" Mari asked.

"They're easier to cast and aim, and they fly more evenly," Jurian said.

Menas nodded. "So David went out to face Goliath and all his army, and challenged Goliath to single combat."

"That can't have ended well," Jurian said.

"David cast a stone, and it struck Goliath here," said Menas, thumping his finger against his forehead. "Killed him with one blow. Then David cut off Goliath's head with his own sword, and took his sword and spear as his trophies."

"But you said the sword weighed more than me," Jurian said.

Menas speared him a sharp glance. "Wasn't the killing miraculous enough? You allow that he killed a giant with one stone and then complain about him picking up a sword?"

Jurian's mouth tugged into a grin. "So it's a fable? Just another myth?"

"No, it's true," Mari said. "It really happened. Eugenius told me once that things can be true and a foreshadowing at the same time. Not like the pagan Oracle's prophecies which are all smoke and shadow. Sometimes things happen that are mysterious and strange, and they also point ahead to other things that *will* happen, someday."

Jurian eyed her skeptically, but after saying so much Mari had gone a little grey, and he didn't have the heart to question her.

"Stranger things have happened," Menas said with a curious smile. "And there are stranger things in this world than giants." He scratched his beard and cocked a bright eye at Jurian. "I've got this feeling you might see a few of them yourself."

The fish were crackling over the fire, steaming with a fresh, sweet aroma. Menas pulled them from the heat and passed the skewers around once they had cooled.

They ate in silence for a while, then Jurian asked, "So David defeated the entire Philistine kingdom, just like that? Were they assimilated like the barbarian enemies of Rome?"

"Far from it," Menas said. "They never submitted. Better if they had—maybe they would have survived. But as I said, they were conquered and reconquered until they were just a legend, lost to time, with only a handful left who can claim that lineage. So it seems it was up to me to make up for my ancestors' failings."

"How so?" Mari asked, picking at her fish.

"My ancestors never bent a knee to David, even when he became king. So now I bend mine to his heir."

Jurian's mouth twitched. "So, do you live somewhere, Menas? You can't have always wandered this wilderness."

Menas gave a rumbling laugh. "I'm not in the wilderness any more. And no, I don't live anywhere in particular. Here in the forest, along the rivers, wherever I find myself. We're all wanderers. I just choose to live that a bit more literally than most."

Jurian sighed and finished his fish. He wasn't sure why Menas was so reluctant to talk about his past, but he wouldn't press the matter. After all, wouldn't he be evasive if Menas asked him about his own past?

Strange he hasn't even asked, he thought, licking his fingers.

Mari slipped away from the fire for a few minutes, and when she returned she simply wrapped herself in Jurian's cloak and laid down under the tree. When she had fallen asleep, Menas turned to Jurian with a grave look.

"She's very ill, isn't she?"

"We lost our mother only about a week ago. She was dying from some wasting illness, but…" Jurian sighed and stabbed a stick into the embers. "That wasn't what killed her."

Menas glanced pointedly upriver toward the bridge, and Jurian nodded once, fierce.

"I'm sorry," Menas said and bowed his head, murmuring something under his breath. "I wondered how you two came to be out in the wilderness."

"Some Legionaries found out that we're Christian," Jurian said. "The Legate's son. He hates me anyway. And since the auguries failed...well, it was a handy excuse, I suppose."

"The auguries are failing?" Menas asked, eyes glinting. "How interesting."

"Yes, well, I guess they wanted someone to blame. Apparently a priest and a dying woman were good enough."

Menas reached over and clasped his shoulder. "This darkness has been a long time coming. The failure of the auguries might just be the tipping point."

"Anyway," Jurian said, brushing the uncomfortable thought aside, "I think Mari caught whatever our mother had. I saw what happened to her. Will I have to watch Mari wither like she did?"

"Perhaps some medicine would help her?"

Jurian gave a desolate laugh. "No. There's no cure. Even the doctor in Satala couldn't do anything except make our mother more comfortable."

"So you're fleeing the Legate's son and his cohort," Menas said, "and going where, exactly?"

"We're trying to get to Rome."

"Rome?" Menas rubbed his beard, then his hand drifted down unconsciously to brush the leather band around his arm. "What do you hope to find there?"

"Answers. Family, maybe. A purpose? I don't know."

"Perhaps all of them," Menas said. After a moment's silence, he roused himself. "Well, you won't get far if you don't sleep." He tugged off his thick cloak and handed it to Jurian. "Go on, take it. I'll watch here by the fire for a bit. That'll keep me plenty warm."

"Thank you," Jurian murmured.

15

ANATOLIA

MORNING COULDN'T COME TOO SOON. By the time the sun crawled over the eastern hills, Jurian was stiff, cold, and exhausted from a near-sleepless night. As he tried to stretch the aches from his arms and legs, he noticed that Menas seemed bright-eyed enough. Even Mari had more color in her cheeks than the night before, which kindled a little hope in his heart.

They ate a cold meal around the ashes of last night's fire, and as they finished, Jurian said, "I can't thank you enough, Menas, for helping us across the river. And for the fish."

"Nonsense. It was my pleasure."

Jurian turned to Mari. "Are you ready? We should get started. I don't know if Casca's moved his men out yet, but every moment we stay, we risk discovery."

"Of course." She clasped Menas' hands. "Thank you."

"If I might," Menas said, and cleared his throat gently. "Perhaps I could travel with you awhile. There may be more rivers on the way. I can take you across all of them…and I wouldn't mind a change from walking alone."

Mari's face lit up, looking so happy that Jurian couldn't imagine disappointing her.

"I'm sure I couldn't stop you," he said with a laugh. "I tried that once already, and see how that worked out."

"Ah, true," Menas said, smiling ruefully. "But it's nicer to be wanted than to tag along like a homeless dog."

"Of course we'd love you to come," Mari said. Then, glaring at Jurian, "Wouldn't we?"

Jurian smiled at her. "You probably know these lands," he said to Menas. "We'd appreciate a guide…and the company."

Menas buried the ashes of the fire and they struck off into the woods, veering southwest away from the road. By midmorning, Jurian realized just how grateful he was for Menas' presence, when Mari suddenly stumbled and Menas, without missing a step, shoved his *sarcina* into Jurian's hands and swept Mari into his arms.

As Menas settled Mari's head against his shoulder, he glanced at Jurian, unmistakable alarm in his eyes. Against Menas' solid bulk, Mari looked so frail. She reminded Jurian of his mother's alabaster comb—a piece so thin and delicate that the sunlight shone right through it.

At midday they stopped for a small meal, but Mari refused to eat. She huddled against a tree, coughing uselessly into her cloak, spots of fever red on her cheeks. Jurian's heart plummeted when he noticed flecks of blood on her chin. He poured some water onto a scrap of cloth and knelt beside her, but she wouldn't look at him as he dabbed the cloth against her skin.

"It's no use," she whispered. "I'm just slowing you down."

"Why, am I in a hurry?" he teased gently.

"You know we are. If Casca catches us, he'll murder us both." She laid a hand against his cheek, and he flinched at the lifeless chill of her touch. "I can't keep going. I just want to sleep. Oh, saints, is this how Mother felt at the end?"

Jurian glanced at Menas for help, but the giant just met his gaze quietly, his eyes dark with grief. Jurian's blood simmered with anger. He would never give up on her. He would never let her die. She was still alive, and grief was for the dead.

"We have to be close to a village by now," he said. "I know it's not completely uncivilized between Satala and Ancyra."

"I've wandered this region a long time," Menas said, voice

low. "I don't think there are any towns for another day or so. And not many towns have skilled healers."

"All right," Jurian said, getting to his feet. "How long can you carry her?"

Menas smiled at Mari. "She's no burden at all."

"Then let's get going."

He picked up Menas' *sarcina* and settled the shaft of the pole against his shoulder. Menas lifted Mari, cradling her in his arms like a child, and they set off.

Jurian paced ahead, gripping the pole until his fingers ached. Menas had to be wrong; there had to be a town close by. He sharpened his senses, alert to the slightest change in noise or smell. Dusk had just fallen when he suddenly stopped.

"There! Do you smell that?"

Menas turned his nose to the breeze, sniffing around and then shrugging. "I'm not sure I'm smelling what you are."

"A fire. Peat. Something cooking? Vegetables, probably. I don't smell meat."

"What are you, a hound?"

"A hunter."

"Well? Where is it coming from?" Menas asked.

Jurian turned a slow circle, finally pausing as he faced south. "That way."

He wove through the trees, grateful for the sparse undergrowth. As they went, the smells grew stronger until even Menas commented on them. Jurian picked up his pace.

"Maybe it's a village," he said, glancing over his shoulder. "Maybe—"

He plowed into something, and stumbled back in surprise as the something grunted in pain. Gradually he distinguished the shape of a man standing in front of him, bent over and rubbing his foot. He was all in dark cloth, even his hood, which made him almost invisible in the dusk.

"What's wrong?" Menas asked.

The man snapped up with a startled cry. "What are you?"

Jurian recovered. "That's not very nice."

"How many are you?" the man whispered. "I'm...I've got nothing to tempt you. I have no money. Leave me in peace!"

"Is there a town nearby?" Jurian asked.

"A...a town?" The man bent to massage his foot again. "No, no towns anywhere, not for another day's walk or so. Was that your foot that maimed me or did you smash it with a club?"

"I'm sorry," Jurian said. "I didn't see you at all."

He glanced at Menas, hoping for a little help, but Menas just chuckled and said nothing.

"Listen, I need a doctor. My sister is very sick and I'm afraid she doesn't have much longer to live if she doesn't get help."

"Where is she? I'll come with you."

"You?"

The man gave an exasperated sigh. "You did ask for a doctor, didn't you? Maybe I can help."

"She's right here."

The man shuffled forward until he almost bumped into Menas. "I think this is a giant, not your sister. Unless your sister is a giant? That would be awkward."

"The girl's in my arms," Menas said, his voice a low rumble. "Haven't you got a torch or something?"

"Never needed one before. But here, I've got some candles... somewhere..."

They listened to him rummaging in his belongings, then he thrust two tawny candles into Jurian's hands.

"Hold these," he said.

"I am."

The man snorted. A moment later they heard the sound of steel striking stone, and a spark danced out over the candles. The first wick caught, then the second, and the man peered at Mari in the fickle light. He was no taller than Jurian, with a thick dark beard and a bald head that glistened in the candlelight under the arch of his hood. His eyes were a startling light grey, surrounded by creases that deepened as he studied Mari.

"Well," he said. "I suppose you'd better come with me."

"Where?" Jurian asked.

"My home, of course. You didn't think I lived out in the woods like a beast, did you?"

"*He* lives in the woods," Jurian said, jerking a thumb in Menas' direction.

The man surveyed Menas head to foot. "He is a beast," he said, so mildly that it was impossible to take offense. "Come on. No time to waste."

He shuffled off into the trees with a slight limp that Jurian hoped he hadn't caused. Jurian and Menas followed him, and the smell of peat smoke grew steadily more powerful. At last Jurian spotted the smoke curling out from a wide cave, the fire inside lighting it up like a glowing scar in the mountainside. The man ushered them in, watching skeptically as Menas had to stoop low to get inside.

Jurian stared around in surprise. The cave was much larger than he had expected, its roof soaring away into the shadows, its farthest wall well beyond the ring of firelight. Besides a crude wooden table there was no furniture, only a few pots for cooking and a scattering of furs over the dusty floor to serve as rugs and a bed. Leaning against the wall was a crude wooden cross almost half as tall as Jurian.

Jurian caught Menas' gaze and nodded toward it, watching a broad smile fracture the wary look on Menas' face.

The man noticed them staring and froze in the middle of dragging a fur closer to the fire, alarm stark on his face. Jurian glanced at Menas but the giant was still holding Mari, so, to appease the man, he held his gaze and brushed his thumb over his forehead, down and across.

The man dropped his head and laughed, then finished hauling the fur to the fire.

"And God sends me wanderers in the wilderness," he said, half to himself. "Fellow travelers." He beckoned to Menas. "Lay her down on this."

Menas obeyed, kneeling and gently depositing Mari on the fur. She stirred but didn't wake. The man lifted her wrist, feeling the prominent bones before searching for her pulse. Either he couldn't find Mari's, or what he found he didn't like, because he frowned and peered at her face. She had coughed up more blood the last few hours, speckling her skin.

The man observed all of it, then sat back on his heels and met Jurian's gaze quietly.

"I'm sorry. There is no medicine that can heal what she has."

Jurian winced, though he'd been expecting those words.

"How do you know?" Menas asked. "Are you a doctor?"

The man frowned up at him. "Why, I'm Blasios, of course. You…you knew that, didn't you? Isn't that why you're here?"

"Not exactly," Jurian said. "We were looking for a town."

"And something brought you to me instead, of course." Blasios nodded, as if that made all the sense in the world. "Well, if it's any comfort, I have been a physician for many years. Recently retired from the world, though I still see my share of patients who come looking for me."

Jurian sighed and sat by her head, grief and despair threatening to overwhelm him. He was so tired, and he'd put so much hope in finding a doctor who could help…and instead they had met some crazy recluse in the woods who could do nothing but confirm what Jurian had feared all along. Mari was dying, and he couldn't do anything to save her.

"So you can't heal her," he murmured.

Blasios lowered his gaze, his hands quiet on his legs. "I didn't say that exactly."

Mari coughed again, blood flecking her hand, but still she didn't wake. Jurian winced and used the edge of her cloak to wipe the blood gently from her chin.

"Hand me that candle, young man," Blasios said.

Jurian handed it to him in silence, wondering what he meant to do with it. Burn some herbs and make Mari breathe the smoke? But Blasios just paired the candle with his own and blew them both out. Then, gripping them at right angles to each other, he held them over Mari's chest, then laid them against her throat, murmuring something under his breath all the while. Jurian tried to listen, but couldn't make out the words. They didn't sound like

Greek or Latin. He clenched his jaw. It was as he feared—the man was insane.

The air around them brightened, and Jurian glanced at the fire where Menas sat, head bowed, hands folded. It wasn't until Jurian turned back to Mari and Blasios that he realized that nothing had changed except Blasios' face, which held a radiance as if the candles were still shining full on him. Suddenly Mari stirred, drawing back with a grimace. Her lips parted and she tipped her head back, and one thin breath hissed through her teeth. And then she was still.

Jurian lurched forward, lifting her up and cradling her against his chest.

"What did you do?" he shouted. "You killed her!" Frantically he smoothed her hair from her face, pressed his lips to her forehead. "Please," he whispered. "Please, God…let her stay…"

He laid his cheek on her forehead, holding his hand to his face so they wouldn't see the tears he could no longer suppress.

Menas' heavy step thundered toward them, and Jurian glanced up to see rage like lightning in his eyes, and Blasios holding up his hands in a desperate gesture for peace.

"Look," he said. "She isn't dead!"

Jurian's heart froze. Mari opened her eyes, blinking drowsily before staring straight up into his worried eyes.

"Jurian?" she said. "Why are you looking at me like that? You're squeezing me half to death. And…where are we?"

16

Anatolia

Jurian stared at her. "Mari..." he began, but his voice faltered. "Are you all right?"

She pushed away from him, studying Blasios with some curiosity. "Hello," she murmured. "I feel like I've met you before."

Blasios smiled enigmatically. "You have, in a way."

"What is going on here?" Jurian asked. He glanced at Menas, whose anger had vanished behind a visible respect. "Am I the only one here who doesn't understand what's happening?"

Mari turned to him. He expected her to tease him, or rebuke him for overreacting, but instead she leaned over and embraced him. She didn't say a word.

"Do you...feel any different?" he asked her, feeling foolish for asking it.

Her forehead puckered and she stared at him, frowning in confusion. "I...oh, saints." She twisted around and faced Blasios, eyes wide. Then suddenly she laughed and said, "Yes, different. I'm starving."

Jurian began to laugh, and he held Mari tightly until she pushed him away.

"But the illness?" Menas asked. "You still feel that?"

"No. I feel...fine?" She clapped a hand over her mouth, then dropped it to reveal the biggest smile Jurian had seen in ages.

"Jurian! I'm all right."

Jurian stared at her, then at Blasios and Menas, a wave of confusion washing over him. Everything was spinning out of control around him, and he couldn't even figure out where he was.

He pushed himself to his feet and strode out of the cave.

Out in the silence and the chill of the night, he leaned against the cliff face to stare at the stars and pray for something to make sense. Deep in his thoughts, he felt the simmer of anger and resentment, and that made less sense than any of it.

Some time later—minutes or hours, he wasn't sure—a shadow moved in the cave, and then Menas stood beside him.

"Now that I think of it," Menas said presently, leaning against the rock beside him, "I *have* heard of this hermit Blasios. I may have even escorted a few people over a river who were searching for him."

"What just happened in there?" Jurian asked. "She was...it was just like with my mother. She was dying."

Menas lifted his shoulders. "Blasios is powerful with God."

"What does that even mean? Surely you don't think that God bends on a whim to do whatever some hermit asks?"

"Why not? He is God, after all. Don't you remember the Roman centurion?"

"I remember altogether too many Roman centurions," Jurian muttered. "Which one did you have in mind?" When Menas didn't answer, he said, "Is this another story? Like the boy and the rock that brought down an empire?"

"This is better," Menas said, unmoved by Jurian's tone. "A centurion went to the Christ and asked Him to heal his slave who was sick. The Lord said He would go with him and heal the man, but the centurion protested, saying that the Lord could simply say a word, and it would be done. The Lord marveled at his great faith and did as he asked. The servant was cured from that hour."

"Well...if we believe the Christ is God, of course He could do such a thing," Jurian said. "What could He *not* do?"

"So, what do you suppose just happened with Mari? We don't have a centurion, just a little old hermit. But his faith is as great as that soldier's...and God honored his request."

"But the soldier and Christ...that was centuries ago, during His life. Things like that don't happen anymore, do they?"

"I know what I have seen," Menas said simply. "And I believe my own eyes. Don't you? Or do you doubt even more than Thomas?"

Jurian waved a hand. "I'm going to assume that's another reference to a story I don't know."

Menas' face creased in a puzzled smile. "How does your sister know all these stories, and you don't?"

"She and my mother would go listen to the priest Eugenius, and he would tell these stories. I was busy training with Leptis, trying to keep us alive." He took a breath and studied the stars. "My father was the Legate, you know. I've always meant to join the Legion too. That's part of the reason we're going to Rome."

"Hmm," Menas said. For a few moments he said nothing else, but joined Jurian in contemplating the stars. "Most people who don't share our faith will not understand what we believe, or why. The world is a turbulent place right now. We've been left in peace for a time, but things are happening that people don't understand and can't explain. When that happens, people look for someone to mock and ridicule, for someone to blame. Even people in positions of great power find it convenient to have someone they can accuse for their own failings."

Jurian flinched. He'd never told Menas about his father and *Caesar* Galerius, but that seemed to be exactly what the giant was talking about. Galerius had lost the battle, and his father... his father had been a Christian. He had probably refused to participate in the sacrifices before the battle, to invoke the aid of Jupiter the Victorious, to burn incense to the emperor Diocletian. And then the battle turned against them.

It was just like Eugenius had said. His father had been killed by his own Legion and his reputation had been destroyed after his death when no one would dare to defend him.

"Galerius?" he whispered.

"He's one of the worst. And he has more power over Diocletian than I think the *Augustus* would willingly admit. Not political power, but force of character." He tugged a bit of rock loose from the cliff face and crumbled it between his fingers. "What happened with Nero will happen again. The great storm of persecution is already starting. They think we Christians are an easy target, because we don't fight back."

"We don't?" Jurian asked.

Menas smiled. It looked almost wolfish in the moonlight. "They don't understand *real* power." He jerked his thumb toward the cave. "*That* kind of power."

Jurian frowned. And before he understood why, he said, "Is it wrong that I'm angry?"

"About what?"

Jurian gestured behind them. "All this. What just happened."

Menas' brows shot up in surprise. "But why would that make you angry?"

Jurian stared out at the deep of the forest, as if he could find the answer there to the darkness he felt in his own heart.

Finally he said, "I keep wondering why he couldn't have been there for my mother, too. If he could save Mari, he could have saved her. But…it's more than that." He hesitated, then added, "I think I'm angry at myself most of all, because *I* should have saved her from those soldiers. But I didn't. I didn't do anything. She needed me, and I just stayed on that hill and I watched it happen. If I'd done something, maybe we all could have come to Blasios and he could have cured them both." He knotted his hands, closing his eyes as he struggled to control his breathing. "It's my fault she's dead, Menas. Their blood is on my hands… hers and Eugenius' both."

It sounded so much worse than he'd imagined, admitting his guilt out loud to Menas, but Menas didn't turn away from him. He just stood quietly beside Jurian, his huge frame blocking the light from the cave, his arms folded over his chest.

"We've all done things we're ashamed of, Jurian. Things that could paralyze us with horror if we let ourselves think too much about them. We can't stare too long into that darkness. It makes us forget what the light looks like."

Jurian glanced at him, curious. "You?" he asked. "But you seem so sure of yourself. So...*good*." He grimaced. It sounded childish, but it was the best word he could think of.

Menas laughed, low and long. "The fiercest battles are fought within. And they are fought daily, sometimes. I told you that I was making up for my ancestors' failing by bending my knee to David's heir. But I followed their path for a long time before I followed His."

He fell silent, and Jurian waited, breathless, for him to continue. After a moment, Menas said, "I was mocked as a child, you know? Because of my size, my twelve toes. Even though I was twice as big as all the other children, they thought I wouldn't retaliate. They would group together...little packs of hatred. They believed I was slow-witted. Too stupid to know or care what they were saying." He lowered his gaze, studying his hands. "I wanted to prove them wrong. I wanted to be strong and powerful. I vowed I would make them all quail in fear. I wanted to be a defiant king like Goliath, and watch my enemies run from my sight."

Jurian swallowed hard. "What did you do?"

There was a long, terrible silence.

"I discovered I *was* strong," Menas finally said with a sigh. "And I used it. Oh, God forgive me, I used it. Even when I wasn't much older than you, my life would have horrified the most hardened criminals in the Empire. If I'd met you and your sister in the woods then, I might have robbed you and killed you for the fun of it, and enjoyed every minute of it. And I was so, so proud. I thought I was the mightiest man on earth and needed to bow to no one. I fought my way out of arrest countless times, and finally I swore that I would never serve anyone, until I could find someone stronger and more powerful than me. I could rule the world, I thought, and no one would be able to stand up to me."

He sank down to sit against the rock wall, and after a moment Jurian slid down to join him, sifting his fingers through brittle pine needles as Menas continued his story.

"My life had carried me into the deepest pits of darkness. I didn't think there was anything wicked that I hadn't dared to do. After all, what were laws to me? Who could enforce them? So I went on living as I pleased, and I began to gather followers, wicked men who were attracted to my impudence."

Menas grew suddenly quiet, shuffling stones between his fingers. Jurian thought he caught the whisper of a prayer on Menas' lips, and then the giant continued, his voice low.

"One day, as I was traveling in the hills, I met a certain…creature. At first I thought it was a man, because he stood tall as an ordinary man, and dressed rather like a Roman cavalry officer. Only he wore a black embossed breastplate and black-plumed helmet, and the faceplate was the most hideous thing I'd ever seen. If the face of the creature matched that mask, I never wanted to see it. But I could see his eyes, and they were black from lid to lid, swallowing the light like slate."

Menas paused, pressing his fingers against the bridge of his nose. Inside the cave, Jurian could hear Mari's laughter mixed with a quiet stream of chatter as the smell of cooking grew steadily more fragrant.

"I asked him who he was," Menas said at last. "He wouldn't answer. Instead, he picked up a rock and, staring me straight in the eyes, he crushed it in his hand, turning it to gravel. I took it as a challenge, so I picked up a rock of my own and crumbled it to dust. He turned and leapt from the peak of the hill we were standing on, landing on his feet some twenty feet below without the slightest bruise. Impressive, I thought, but not *that* impressive, so I showed that I could do as much. Then he beckoned me and I followed him to the top of another hill.

"Below stood two armies arrayed against each other, preparing for battle. I realized my companion had left me, so I went down to get a closer look. No one paid me any regard. When I got to the front line, I saw the black-helmed man standing between the two forces. I approached him to ask what it all meant, but he didn't need to speak to explain. He raised his arms and the armies crashed together, and the screams of the dying and the silence of the dead swallowed me. And as I watched the carnage, something rumbled over the lines. A sound…like dark laughter. He was laughing, my companion. Laughing."

Jurian shuddered and stared at the stars, and said nothing.

"When he clenched his fists, we stood alone in the valley, and I bent my knee to offer my service. This at last was something I couldn't do. I couldn't reach into the hearts of men and turn them against each other, to raise up wars for no purpose but to laugh at the slaughter. I heard his voice in my head, promising me strength and power beyond my wildest imaginings, and then he dissolved in smoke and shadow, and was lost in the wind. From that moment on, I had his voice always in my head. Driving me to worse and more savage crimes."

"What happened? " Jurian asked.

Menas smiled, enigmatic. "The cross. One day I came to a small wooden cross by the roadside. The voice in my head screamed and screamed. I've never felt such terrible pain, like my skull would split open. I was sure I was going to die. My knees gave way, and as soon as they hit the ground before that cross, the voice left me. I could swear it manifested in the dirt like a miserable little snake, writhing as if poisoned by its own venom. That was enough for me. Obviously my former master hadn't been the most powerful being, if a simple piece of wood could make it squirm in the dirt like a worm with a crushed head. So I vowed to find the meaning of the cross, and serve the power behind it. But He found me first. And even though I'd carried that demon within me for so long, still, He found me and He let me carry Him…"

His voice broke on the last words, and Jurian darted a glance at him. His fingers pinched the bridge of his nose, his hand hiding his eyes, but Jurian could see his shoulders shaking. Feeling suddenly like an intruder, he got to his feet, clasped the giant's shoulder briefly, and slipped back into the cave.

Mari smiled at Jurian as he came into the firelight, her cheeks rosy with the bright glow of life. A rush of relief washed over him that almost brought him to his knees. He crossed over to Blasios and bowed his head.

"Thank you, *domine*, for saving my sister," he murmured.

Blasios laughed. "I'm no lord, *frater*, but you are very welcome. Now, where did that big friend of yours go? There's soup cooking. Should be nearly done, if you're willing to share a poor man's supper."

"We'd be grateful," Jurian said. He eyed the pot. "If you like, I could hunt for some game."

Blasios waved a hand. "Eh," he said, "if you need meat, please help yourself to the forest. I don't eat it anymore, but I won't stop you from cooking it on my fire."

Jurian smiled and exchanged a skeptical look with Mari. Without another word he strung his bow and set off into the night.

17

Anatolia

When Jurian woke the next morning, Blasios was already gone. Jurian couldn't help wondering if he'd been driven away by the reverberating echo of Menas' snores, which had nearly chased him from the fire and out into the cold in the middle of the night. Blasios had left them a pot of porridge, though, and as they sat close to the fire eating their breakfast, Jurian drew a crude map of Anatolia in the dirt with the charred end of a stick.

"I'd say we're somewhere about here," he said, pointing to a spot near the center of the peninsula. "Halfway between Satala and Ancyra. If we go north by Byzantium, we could go by land at least part of the way and avoid the rough seas this time of year. But if we go south and catch a merchant ship out of Myra, we could get to Rome much quicker."

Jurian contemplated the sketch, rubbing a hand through his hair.

Mari touched his knee and asked, "Which way will Casca go, Jurian?"

Jurian shook his head.

Before he could answer, a voice behind him said, "Planning on sailing across *Mare Nostrum?*"

Jurian glanced over to see Blasios in the mouth of the cave, his hands full of herbs and mushrooms.

"It can be a treacherous sea," Blasios continued. "Steer clear of the southern waters if you can. I've heard of strange things going on around Apollonia and Cyrene."

"The merchant routes between Rome and Myra stay to the north, I think," Jurian said, but then he frowned and asked, "What strange things?"

"The way they talk, you'd think the dragons of the old myths had come back," Blasios said, and shuddered. "God help them, they keep trying to placate the beast with sacrifices." He shook his head. "I don't think it's having the desired effect."

"Dragons aren't necessarily a myth," Menas said, his voice lower than usual. "I've seen things in my day..." He flicked a glance at Jurian. "There are things in this world we still don't understand. As wise and learned as we are, we still can't get everything right." He laughed suddenly. "Saints, these Romans still think the way a chicken scratches the dirt can predict the outcome of a battle. We aren't as wise and mighty as we think."

"You don't think this dragon is just another chicken, do you?" Mari asked.

Jurian laughed out loud, and even Menas chuckled.

Mari looked a bit flustered and said, "I mean, calling it a dragon because they can't explain it otherwise, like using chickens to predict something they can't otherwise be sure about." She scowled and brushed her hair off her forehead. "It made more sense in my head."

"Well," Blasios said, smiling. "Even if the dragon is a chicken, I don't think *I'd* want to be sailing too close to that region."

Jurian fixed his gaze on the map. He hadn't drawn in any of Africa but he knew where Apollonia was, and, roughly, Cyrene, the capitol of the Roman province of Libya Pentapolis.

"What is the dragon—or whatever it is—doing in Cyrene?" he asked.

"God knows, I don't," Blasios said. He deposited his herbs and mushrooms on the table and dusted his hands off on his robe. "But the last patient I saw, oh, a week ago now. He had recently come from Egypt, near Alexandria, where he'd heard all manner of rumors about their western neighbors. He said the beast in the hills would snatch random travelers, people who strayed outside the city at night, even cattle and sheep. The earth tremors more than ever in that region, and people claim it's from the beast walking about in his cave. That bit sounds rather superstitious if you ask me. Anyway, the people have been offering sacrifices to the beast for over a decade now, hoping they will keep it from destroying the city."

"What sort of sacrifices?" Mari asked.

Blasios studied her in silence, then exchanged a glance with Menas. "Not the civilized kind. I can't begin to describe them."

Mari shuddered visibly and set down her bowl. "Those poor people. Imagine how terrified they must be. We see how awful it is, but to them, they're just trying to stay alive."

"Fear makes men do terrible things," Menas said, quiet.

Mari shook her head and added, "I don't mean to excuse them. I only feel sorry for them. Why doesn't anyone try to kill the beast?"

"They believe it's a god," Blasios said. "They think it's a manifestation of Molech, that if they anger it, he will dry up the spring that supplies the city with water and kill them all."

"Dangerous ignorance!" Menas growled, his dark eyes flashing. "They don't know what they're dealing with."

"But Menas, you only know it's ignorant because you know the truth," Mari said, laying her hand on his arm. "To them…they think it's the truth. They don't know any different. Not yet, at least." She frowned and grew quiet, staring into the fire.

Jurian swallowed. Mari couldn't know what the giant actually meant. His words had come from experience, not the safe sort of knowledge born from hearing the right kinds of stories. He felt Menas' gaze fixed on him, but he kept his eyes on the map. Though he felt inclined to trust Menas, a doubt lingered in his mind. By his own admission, Menas had once been utterly wicked. Had anything survived of that man who had so gloried in his crimes? Could anyone ever change completely?

Mari would say yes; he wasn't sure if he could agree.

He rubbed his jaw and idly sketched the northern African coast, letting the tip of the stick rest on the location of Cyrene. The dragon bothered him. Until he'd met Menas, he would have laughed off anyone who claimed they'd seen something so mythical as a dragon, but…he'd seen the fear in Menas' eyes. Real fear. And something that could make Menas afraid couldn't possibly be a mere fancy. So what could have the people of Cyrene so terrified that they would offer unspeakable sacrifices to save themselves?

"Enough talk of dragons," Menas said, startling him out of his thoughts. "What's our path? If anyone wanted my opinion, I recommend Myra. I know a good man there, and the port is always busy with merchant ships. Besides, that land journey past Byzantium would just take too long."

"Always better to let a boat do the traveling than your own legs, I'd say," Blasios interjected.

"All right, so, Myra," Jurian said, tapping the south coast of Anatolia. "Should we go by Ancyra, or cut southwest from here?"

Menas eyed the map thoughtfully. "Ancyra would be the easier journey, but longer, and I've heard that it's dangerous for our people these days. And then there's your friend Casca. I wager he'll head to Ancyra in the hope of catching you there."

"And we can't avoid the cold and the snow no matter which way we go," Jurian said.

"I vote the shortcut," Mari said, then added softly, "I've had enough of Legions."

"Can you lead us to Myra?" Jurian asked Menas.

The giant nodded. "I've traveled this region long enough. I know the easy paths and places where we can shelter if the snow gets too thick."

"And you're up for it, Mari?"

"I feel like I could walk forever," she said, her smile like the summer sun.

"Well, no time to waste. Blasios, thank you for your care and hospitality," Menas said. He stood and crushed the hermit in a tight embrace.

Blasios wheezed and thumped Menas on the back until he let go. "God save you," he gasped. He gripped Menas' arm, staring him long and hard in the eye. "Take care of these two," he said. He frowned and added, "And yourself. I don't think we will meet again."

Menas looked ready to protest, but Blasios turned away and picked up the two candles they had used the night before. Drawing Jurian aside, he pushed the candles into his hands.

"You're going to Rome. It's a pilgrimage we all must take, but some of us can only go in our hearts. Take these and remember me when you're there. Light them at the tomb of the rock. Light one for yourself, for guidance on the dark paths you will walk. And light one for him." He nodded at Menas. "He will need it in the days to come. I see a great sadness in him." He glanced upwards briefly, then drew Jurian's head down and kissed his forehead. *"Let the high praises of God be in their throats, and two-edged swords in their hands,"* he murmured. "These words are for you. Keep them close."

18

CYRENE

SABRA RETURNED TO THE SCENE of the murder early the next morning with her father and Hanno. The city guards had placed a perimeter around the house, keeping out everyone except the household slaves. They let her father through without question, but Sabra noticed the way their eyes slid to follow her. After the events of last night, the look on their faces hurt more than usual—that curious blend of suspicion and awe, fear and respect. She bit her lip. Why did it suddenly bother her, to be known as simply The Priestess? She wasn't even The Governor's Daughter, but she would have preferred that to The Priestess.

She was never just Sabra.

With a sigh she shook her head and dismissed the thought. Now wasn't the time to agonize over her loneliness. A man lay dead in his own house, the *impluvium* filled with his blood instead of rainwater.

She stumbled and pressed her hand against her head, but the image wouldn't fade: the rocks inside the Kyre's cave seeping blood, blood pouring down the conduits to the city, the forum's fountain gushing red with it, the pools of the bathhouse like steaming seas of crimson. A wave of nausea washed over her and she covered her mouth.

A moment later she realized that someone was holding her

upright. Hanno.

"Mistress?" he asked, almost a whisper.

She glanced around. The guards had taken a few steps away from her, leaving her like an island in the middle of the street. Her father hadn't noticed anything; he was busy inside the official's house, questioning the slaves and examining the body before the burial cult came to claim it.

"I'm all right," Sabra said. She swallowed hard, willing the sick pang to go away. "Is it possible to dream when you're awake? Can nightmares come during the day?"

Hanno said nothing but bent his gaze away from hers. Sabra gnawed her cheek in frustration. The only reason he wouldn't answer was that he was a slave and she was the governor's daughter, and they were surrounded by staring people. The fact that the Tribune had seen them talking yesterday was bad enough; neither of them could afford the whole city to see it.

She pulled her elbow free of his grip and strode over to the house.

"It was Adad," a slave was saying as she entered the atrium. He knelt in the corner, his hands over the back of his head as if he expected someone to strike him. "I know it was. He whispered against our master. He thought we would sympathize with him, but we never did!"

Sabra's father frowned. "You're accusing a man of murder simply because he murmured against his master? Murmuring isn't prohibited. He could even have safely complained about Aulus Arrius to me, by the law of Rome."

"He refused to pray for him," the slave whispered. "We offered sacrifices for his health and safety, and Adad refused to come."

The governor let his breath out in a hiss. "Does anyone else wish to accuse Adad, or defend him? Where is this slave now?"

"Hiding, *kyrie*."

"Why?"

"Because he's guilty. Because he was afraid of us."

"Of you?"

The slave nodded. "Adad is a Nazarene. He murdered Aulus Arrius for a blood sacrifice. He fears we will tell everyone about his dark rituals! But we know all about them. The Legionaries have seen enough. You should hear their stories!"

"Enough!" the governor snapped. "I have no care for hearsay."

Sabra heard murmuring behind her, and glanced over her shoulder to see one guard speaking quietly to another…but not quietly enough. The bystanders outside the villa had obviously overheard them, because suddenly they began whispering to each other, arguing back and forth, straining for a better look into the atrium.

That is how it always starts, Sabra thought, shivering. *A whisper, under the breath, caught on a breeze.*

They had barely finished questioning Aulus Arrius' household when a member of the Guard came to report that Adad had been found, stoned to death in an alley behind the Greek *agora.*

"This is honestly getting ridiculous," Sabra's father said, kneading his forehead as he paced in his *tablinum.*

A few days had passed since Adad's murder, and the city hadn't quieted down yet. Sabra sat on the low stone bench, a few reports from the guards held neglected in her hands. More reports lay scattered on her father's desk, some read, others ignored. From the sheer number of them, Sabra was surprised her father had read any of them.

"What are these all for?" she asked.

He swept one off the table, glanced it over, and then slapped it back down. "This murder…these murders, I should say. The whole city's gone mad. Do you know how many of my own officials I've had come to accuse their political rivals of being Christians, just to get them out of power?"

He laughed and waved a finger at her. "You know, yesterday at noon Caius Minnucius came to tell me that Manius Tetius was a Christian. Not three hours later, Manius Tetius popped up requesting that I arrest Caius Minnucius as a Christian and a traitor.

What am I supposed to make of all this nonsense? The city is pushed to the breaking point as it is, with the crops harvested almost to extinction and the economy failing and this…this dragon in the hills making everyone afraid of their own shadows. You know, I even had someone tell me that the Christians are making the dragon angry, and that we should feed all the Christian children to it as a ritual cleansing of the city."

Some part of her wanted to agree with them. These people with their strange piety and their new god refused to enroll their children in the lottery and spurned the public sacrifices. They wouldn't even burn incense to Diocletian. It wouldn't have surprised her if the whole pantheon of gods was angry with them. Maybe the Legate and all these people were right to blame them—if they could get rid of the Christian problem, maybe the god would be placated, and Elissa could be spared.

"I think they're right," she said, startling herself with the violence of the words. "The god *is* angry. Let them appease him. They shouldn't be afraid to, should they? If they don't believe he is a god, they must not believe he has any power. Let them go and see what power he has!"

"Sabra," her father said reproaching her gently. "I know you're anxious about these portents and the sacrifices. But isn't it the Roman way to show patience and consideration for foreign cultures and beliefs?"

"Maybe that's our problem," she said, standing and dropping the sheaf of reports on his desk. "Maybe that's why the Empire is in so much trouble."

She slipped out of the office, heading back to her own chamber. Elissa was there with Ayzebel and Asherah, who were busy making last-minute adjustments to her dark robe. When Sabra saw the girl, somber and melancholy with the red ink staining her forehead, she covered her mouth and prayed that when she spoke, her voice wouldn't break.

"Elissa," she said. "How does it fit?"

Elissa twisted around so she could look in the bronze mirror.

"Perfectly," she said, quiet with fear. "I look like a priestess."

"Tomorrow night it will be time for you to come with me to the Temple."

"Why?" Elissa whispered.

"It is the halfway point between the night your name was chosen and the night of the sacrifice."

Had the time gone so fast? Sometimes it felt like years had passed, sometimes minutes. She wasn't sure which was worse.

Elissa cast an anxious glance at Ayzebel, then straightened her shoulders and said, barely louder than before, "I don't think I want to go into the Temple."

Sabra gave her the most patient, encouraging smile she could muster and crouched to meet her gaze. "It's not so bad, Elissa. It's actually all very simple." She paused, her eyes drifting toward Asherah and Ayzebel. "But I'm not permitted to talk about these things freely. I'll explain our duties when we go into the Temple."

She left the room, waiting in the peristyle until she saw Asherah carrying away her basket of supplies. A few more minutes passed, but Elissa and Ayzebel didn't come out to join her like they usually did in the afternoons. Curious, she wandered back to her chamber and stopped outside the doorway when she heard the low murmur of their voices. Respect told her to leave, that she had no right to listen to their conversation, but it wasn't true. One was a slave and the other an offering to the god under her rule—or at least, that was what she imagined her father would tell her. They could say nothing that she didn't have a right to hear.

She eased forward a few more steps until she could understand their words.

"You can still pray, you know," Ayzebel was saying.

"But is it wrong? It seems like pretending, and…and what if there are other things I have to do? I'm afraid I'll do something wrong."

Sabra heard Ayzebel sigh. "I don't know. I wish I could tell you what to do. Let me talk to Theodorus, and see if he can give you any advice. All right?"

"All right. But please hurry."

That sounded like the end of the conversation, so Sabra

slipped silently back to her usual place in the peristyle. Confusion tangled her thoughts. *You can still pray?* Of course Elissa could pray—that was the whole point of their rituals. But who was this Theodorus? She'd never heard his name mentioned before. It wasn't a Punic name, which meant he likely wasn't one of the slaves, so how did her own slave have dealings with him?

Maybe if she just ignored the problems with Ayzebel, they would simply go away. That was what she always hoped, but it never worked out as neatly in practice. She pressed her fingers to her forehead, glad that her priesthood meant she didn't have to manage a household. Technically she wasn't even subject to her father. She wasn't subject to anyone but the deity she served, like the Vestals of Rome, though without nearly as much glamor and respect.

Elissa came into the peristyle a few minutes later, a leather ball in her hands.

"What's that?" Sabra asked, tilting her head. "I recognize that ball. Toss it here."

Elissa smiled and passed her the ball—a weak throw, but Sabra caught it easily. "Ayzebel said it was yours when you were little."

"She's right. I thought I lost it years ago." She weighed the ball in her hand, then pointed across the peristyle. "Go on, over there. Can you catch?"

Elissa bounded across the trimmed grass to the other side of the fountain, where she stood dwarfed by the statues edging the portico. Sabra threw the ball gently and Elissa missed catching it, but she laughed as she chased the ball across the mosaic floor. As soon as she grabbed it she spun and flung it wildly back at Sabra, sending it bouncing harmlessly off the stern face of a statue of Mars. She clapped a hand over her mouth, giggling while Sabra tried to give an apologetic salute to the god as she scrambled after ball.

They tossed it back and forth until even Sabra was breathless with laughter. When they finished a slave brought them cups of cold water, and as they sat side by side on the fountain's edge,

Sabra thought with a twist of sadness that this was the happiest she'd ever seen Elissa.

And it was the happiest she'd been in ages.

"Where is Ayzebel?" she asked, trying to sound casual.

Elissa shrugged, kicking her sandals against the stone basin.

"Elissa, is there anything you want to talk about?"

The girl's eyes flashed to her face, wide and surprised. "I don't know...why?"

"You seemed sad earlier," Sabra said. She tipped her head back, staring at the cloudless sky above. "If you have any questions about what's going to happen, you know you can ask me."

"But you're so sure of yourself," Elissa said.

It was a strange thing to say, Sabra thought. Did her certainty make Elissa want to hide her doubts? A voice in the back of her mind whispered that Elissa was far from the truth. For two weeks she'd been fighting uncertainty, fighting doubts, fighting questions. 'Sure of herself' was exactly what she *wouldn't* call herself these days. Could Elissa see that? Maybe even Ayzebel saw it. Maybe everyone could.

"Do you ever wish you could leave Cyrene?" Elissa asked.

"I've never even thought about it. Where would I go? My duties are here."

"But what if you didn't have any duties?"

"I—" Sabra hesitated. She'd never even imagined what her life would be like without the god dictating every day of it. "I don't know."

"I wish I could go to Britannia," Elissa said, her face lighting up with excitement.

"Britannia! What do you know about Britannia?"

"It's the very edge of the world." Her joy faded into shadow and she added, "It's as far away from here as I could get."

"I'm sorry," Sabra whispered. Even that felt like a betrayal of the god, but she couldn't stop herself. "I don't know how you can even bear to look at me."

"Because we're both sacrifices," Elissa said quietly.

19

Cyrene

THE NEXT DAY DAWNED COOL and damp, with a faint drizzle that lasted until midmorning. Elissa was pensive, but Sabra had barely slept all night—not because of her upcoming duties in the Temple, but because Ayzebel still hadn't come back from wherever she'd gone. Sabra tried to ask Elissa again if she knew where the slave had gone, but Elissa either had no idea or had proved herself to be a stubborn and convincing liar.

Sabra was halfway through her morning recitation of prayers when a commotion on the street shattered her mental sanctuary. She stumbled over the words of the prayer, losing her place. Fear snatched at her heart—she had never made a mistake before. The old priestess had been right to live secluded from the world, she thought. She would never have let herself get distracted by anything.

Sabra closed her eyes, determined to start over and repeat the prayer flawlessly.

"Mistress Sabra!" Elissa shrieked, bolting into her chamber.

Sabra opened one eye and saw the girl planted in the middle of her floor, both arms stretched out and terror all over her face. Elissa didn't even seem to recognize that she'd interrupted anything. Sabra closed her eye to continue her prayer, but her mind wouldn't focus. Not with the quiet broken by the sound of Elissa weeping.

"What is it?" she asked, whispering a silent apology to the god and praying that he wouldn't slay her for her disrespect.

"They've got Ayzebel," Elissa said, as if that explained everything.

Sabra swallowed hard and got to her feet. Ayzebel had always been difficult to deal with, but she had never gotten herself in any real trouble.

"Where?" Sabra asked.

"Hanno said…down in the *agora*," Elissa sobbed.

"All right. I'll take care of it," she said, hoping she at least sounded more confident.

She wasn't sure she could bring herself to dismiss Ayzebel if she'd been caught doing something forbidden, but she didn't think she could punish her either. But if Ayzebel was guilty, Sabra would have to do one or the other. She alone was responsible for her slave.

Sabra sighed and left the palace alone, since Hanno was nowhere to be found. A small crowd had gathered in the *agora*, laced among the statuary near one of the state buildings. Ayzebel stood in the center of the market surrounded by a handful of city guards and a few slaves Sabra recognized.

The girl looked perfectly normal to Sabra, dressed in her plain tunic with her hair neatly bound back, but her eyes were red from crying and Sabra saw vivid streaks on her arms as if she'd been struck. Sabra drew a thin breath to bridle her anger.

"What's all this about?" she demanded.

"Priestess, we found this slave plotting against you here in the agora late last night," one of the guards said. He tightened his grip on Ayzebel's arm, but Ayzebel didn't even wince. "We've been trying to question her but she won't talk."

"Let go of her arm," Sabra said, her voice low and cold.

"Priestess, I—"

She fixed the guard with a deadly stare and he turned several shades paler, dropping Ayzebel's arm as if it burned him. Ayzebel crumpled, dropping to hands and knees on the smooth stones.

Sabra's heart launched into her throat but she forced herself to stay calm.

"You questioned her," she said blandly.

"She was being stubborn," the guard said, but he wouldn't meet her gaze.

"You maimed my slave without my permission."

"She was plotting—"

"So you said, but you've offered nothing to prove it. You should have brought her to me. Or do you think I am incapable of dealing with my own slave?"

"She's a traitor to the city, to the Empire."

Sabra's hands knotted. "You said she was plotting against *me*. Don't try to deceive me."

"What's going on here?"

Sabra glanced over her shoulder as her father swept out of the crowd, his eyes rimmed with fatigue. Hanno came a few steps behind him. As a unit the guards straightened up, but the governor was frowning at Ayzebel, still crouched on her hands and knees.

"Perhaps they'll give you a straight answer," Sabra said. "Ayzebel, can you stand?"

Ayzebel shuddered and shook her head. Cold and sick with dread, Sabra bent and lifted the hem of the girl's tunic to reveal the bloody and torn skin of her calves. Sabra let out all her breath in a sharp hiss, her hands shaking in fists.

"You tortured her," she said, fixing the guard with a frigid stare. "Did you even give her a chance to plead her case? Or did you just assume she was guilty?"

"I heard her myself!" the guard snapped, red-faced, then he bowed and mumbled, "Priestess."

"Heard her saying what?" Lucius Titianus asked.

Sabra crouched beside Ayzebel, clasping her shoulders, but the girl refused to meet her gaze.

Why? she wondered. *Even now, when I want to help her, why does she hate me?*

"She was speaking to another woman," a guard said. "We

couldn't see who, but I heard them say that the abominations had to stop. That the Priestess had to be stopped."

Sabra released Ayzebel's shoulders, lowering her hands slowly to her sides.

"We had a tip from someone who knows her, so when we saw her sneaking around the city we knew we had to find out what she was about. That's when we overheard her conspiring against the Priestess."

"What sort of tip?" Sabra asked, hoarse, unsteady.

"That girl is a traitor. She's a...*Christian*." The guard almost spat that word, and one of the slaves made a sign against evil. "She was plotting to obstruct our sacrifices, to take the girl meant for the old god and use her for her own dark rituals. I heard it all."

"Ayzebel," Sabra whispered. "Is it true?"

Ayzebel said nothing.

"Gods, now it's infecting my own house!" Lucius Titianus shouted. "Will we never be rid of this annoyance?"

"I wish to speak to her alone," Sabra said.

The guards shifted, uncertain, but the governor jerked his head at them and they withdrew, driving the onlookers back with them. Sabra knew what people would say, seeing her kneeling on the ground beside a slave, but she didn't care.

"Is this why you've always hated me?" she murmured.

Ayzebel lifted her face. Crying had left her eyes more brilliant than ever, and her lip trembled. "I've never hated you, mistress," she said. "I've only wept for you."

Those words cut deep, and Sabra bowed her head. "Is it true, what they're saying? Did you mean to steal Elissa for some other ritual?"

"God help me, no," Ayzebel gasped. "I know you care about her. I do too. I thought perhaps...perhaps I could rescue her."

"Ayzebel," Sabra said, clasping her arm. "You know that would have meant a death sentence for you, if you'd succeeded."

To her surprise, Ayzebel only smiled.

"Why?" Sabra whispered.

"I've never wished you ill, mistress. I've seen the sorrow in your heart and I've prayed for a way to save you from it. I did my best, but it wasn't enough."

Sabra swallowed and stood. The guards took that as a signal to come forward, forming a loose ring around her and Ayzebel.

"I find no fault in the girl," Sabra said, staring the oldest guard straight in the eye. "She is not to be harmed."

"The girl professes to be a traitor. Don't you?" He nudged Ayzebel sharply with his foot. "Answer! Are you a Christian?"

Ayzebel held Sabra's gaze. "I am."

Sabra took a shallow breath.

"From her own lips, see?" the guard scoffed.

"What harm has she done?" Sabra cried. "Whom has she hurt except me? And I say I find no fault in her."

"We know who she was planning to hurt, Priestess. We know she cares nothing about the laws of the city, or the good of Rome."

"She says one word, and you can condemn her for all of that?" Sabra said. "Where is justice?"

"Priestess, stand aside. This is our domain, not yours. She has admitted her guilt before a dozen witnesses."

"She's *my* slave!"

The guard stepped closer to her, eyes sharp with defiance. "You serve the old god. You have no possessions by right. Isn't it enough that you take our children?"

Sabra recoiled, stunned breathless. Only years of training kept her face neutral. Somewhere beyond the hammer of blood in her ears and that chaos of words in her mind, she realized the people were clamoring, some shouting in agreement with the guard, others—followers of the old god—calling up prayers for the man's apostasy. Someone threw a handful of wilted lettuce at Ayzebel. The governor held up his hands to quiet the mob, but the tension simmered under the surface even when the clamor died down.

One of the other city officials pushed free from the crowd to join them. Caius Dignianus, she realized sourly, who had dined with them the other night. He always seemed to know exactly when to make an appearance. For a while he rubbed his jaw and contemplated the scene, as if anyone had asked him to pass judgment.

"This is quite easily resolved," he said. "Governor, all the slave needs to do to is come with us to the statue of Diocletian over there and offer incense for the health and success of the emperor. That is Rome's way, and it is sure testimony to guilt or innocence in the matter of treason against the Empire."

Sabra swallowed. She knew—and Dignianus knew—that no Christian would pass such a test. The snake. What did he mean to gain by this? What business did he have meddling in her affairs? And why did her father say nothing to stop the madness?

"Did the gods give you the power to judge this case?" she asked, her voice strong and clear.

"I'm the only one here impartial enough and powerful enough to do so, don't you think?"

"Mistress," Ayzebel whispered. "He can't hurt me."

Dignianus must have heard her, because his lip lifted in a sneer and he flourished a hand at her. "Stand up, girl. Let's get this over with so we can all go back to what we were doing before you interrupted us."

"Father," Sabra murmured. "You can't allow this. I don't believe she has injured me."

"She isn't being punished," the governor said, but he sounded weary. "She is just going to silence her naysayers."

Sabra shook her head. In the folds of her robe, her hands knotted and unknotted, shaking with anger and fear. She felt so powerless. Usually her word was enough. Ever since she was thirteen, she'd had the power to forgive criminals if she had a mind to, to save them from the executioner if they begged her mercy. And now she was powerless to save a slave who had done no wrong—and her own slave, for that matter. When had everything turned sideways?

But now the guards and Dignianus had created a public spectacle out of Ayzebel's trial. Her father wouldn't risk the mob's wrath, not with instability already rife in the city. Rome's iron fist was closing around them. Her father ruled at Rome's pleasure, and showing sympathy for the girl now could unbalance his own rule.

A guard moved toward Ayzebel, meaning to haul her to her feet, but Sabra stepped quietly between them.

"Priestess," the guard said. He at least was deferential, unlike the other guard, and his face betrayed his uneasiness. "Please."

"Do you mean to anger the god by interrupting the justice this girl must face?" Dignianus asked her, eyes wide in astonishment.

She studied him carefully, but his horror seemed real. Either that, or he was a master of theater. But even if he only meant to mock her, his words curdled her blood with fear. Because he was right—could she serve the god faithfully if she interceded for those that hated him? And if these Christians were offending him, what new punishments would she call down by her interference?

Her gaze shifted to Ayzebel kneeling behind her, braced on shaking arms. Could she turn her back on her now?

"Father," she murmured. "I can't intercede for her…not directly. Caius Dignianus is right, the god would be offended. But please…do something."

He met her gaze with a quiet sadness. It was just as she'd feared; he wouldn't help her. Not today. There was a quiet shuffling behind her and she turned to find the guards with Ayzebel sagging upright between them, blood staining through the bottom of her tunic from her lacerated legs.

"No!" she cried. "No, you can't—"

"Priestess, stand back," the snide guard interrupted, flashing a hand toward her.

Rough hands clamped on her arms and she gasped, doubling over. Who had dared to touch her? Didn't they know that threatening the Priestess of Molech meant death? She twisted around and found two guards gripping her firmly, the pair of them white-faced with fear.

Good, she thought, anger roiling through her. *At least they understand what they've done.*

20

Cyrene

SABRA TRIED TO TWIST FREE but the men were soldiers, nearly twice her size, and she had never trained in wrestling at the gymnasium with the other girls and boys. She'd never had a need to. A moment later she noticed two other guards keeping her father from rushing to her.

Fury stained his cheeks like blood, but he said nothing.

The guards half-dragged, half-marched Ayzebel to the Caesareum, where a massive statue of the *genius* of Diocletian loomed over a small marble altar. Gleaming coals filled the bowl on the altar, waiting for a pinch of incense to honor the divine *Augustus*. The guards escorted Sabra and her father into the temple, still holding Sabra's arms and maintaining a respectful distance from her father. At the head of their little procession, Dignianus carried himself with all the air of an emperor himself. He'd always coveted her father's office, Sabra knew, but this was beyond ridiculous.

"Here, then," Dignianus said, scooping a bead of incense from the waiting dish and tossing it on the coals.

A pungent smoke rose up, coiling around the marble legs of the emperor. Dignianus beckoned the guards to bring Ayzebel forward. Sabra bit her lip.

Just do what he says, she thought, wishing she could say it out loud. *Please, Ayzebel. What does it matter? Why are you fighting?*

Dignianus took Ayzebel's hands, smoothing her fingers open in a gesture that would have seemed tender, if not for the spite in his eyes. He placed two beads of incense in her palms. Ayzebel stared at the golden tears, but Sabra's eyes were riveted on her.

It was so small a thing. So small.

Surely Ayzebel's God wouldn't mind if she tossed them on the coals for their emperor? Not if it saved her life?

Ayzebel tipped her head back to regard the stony countenance of Diocletian *Augustus*. She smiled and, staring Dignianus in the eye, let the incense fall to the marble floor.

"I will not," she said.

"You are a slave! If your mistress commands you, you must do it!" Dignianus said. He fixed Sabra with a cold look. "Surely your mistress wills that you honor the emperor."

Sabra swallowed but couldn't drive away the lump in her throat. "Please, Ayzebel. It doesn't mean anything."

"It means more than you know," Ayzebel whispered.

"See how she flaunts her disobedience!" Dignianus cried. "If this is how one slave treats her mistress, imagine how the whole cult of these infidels will treat Rome! Traitors, the lot of them!"

He seized the bronze tongs from the altar and pulled out a glowing piece of coal. Then, without a word of warning, he grabbed Ayzebel's hand and dropped it into her palm. Another followed the first before anyone could move.

"Stop!" Sabra screamed, wrenching against the guards' grip, unable to break away. "You're hurting her!"

Ayzebel stood frozen as Dignianus picked up the fallen tears of incense. With a little flourish he placed one on each smoldering lump of coal.

"There now. Just let them go," he murmured. "Drop them right there in that bowl. That's all we're asking you to do. Look at your hands, girl. They're burning."

Ayzebel's face turned a ghastly white, but she lifted her chin, lips pressed in a thin line, and refused to move. Her hands shook as the coal scorched her skin.

"Ayzebel!" Sabra wept. "Please!"

She wanted to look away, but couldn't. She wanted to break free and bowl the girl over, to force her to drop the coals, but she couldn't. She stared at Dignianus' face, with its sick blend of fascination and disgust, and wanted to feed him to the god. But she couldn't. She could do nothing. Except...

In despair she thrust out her hands and cried, "Cursed be this place and everyone in it if you don't stop this madness now!"

Dignianus hissed in anger and slapped the coals from Ayzebel's hands. They scattered across the marble floor, leaving a trail of embers in their wake, and a frail curl of incense smoke with no statue to embrace. For a long moment no one moved. Ayzebel kept her head up, pain in every line of her face, but Sabra couldn't tear her gaze from the girl's charred hands. Sobs racked her body.

But Dignianus hadn't finished. He speared a glare of veiled hate and fear at Sabra, then snapped his fingers at Ayzebel's guards and strode out of the Caesareum. The guards followed, dragging Ayzebel between them.

"Stand aside," the governor said to the guards around him, his voice low and cold. They still hadn't touched him, but they hemmed him in, preventing him from leaving. "This is insanity, and I won't have it in my city."

"Caius Dignianus is right. Traitors must be punished," one of the guards said.

"She's not—" Sabra started, but her voice failed her.

"You saw what she did, Priestess. Defiant treachery."

"Follow them," she said. "I have the power to pardon any criminal if it's my will." A strangled cry drifted into the cool silence of the temple, and the blood plummeted to her feet. "Follow them, now!"

"It's too late, Priestess."

She pushed back, hard. The sudden motion made up for her lack of skill, and the guards staggered back. One of them lost his grip, and she spun toward the other and slammed her fist down on his extended elbow as hard as she could. He cried out in pain and let go, and Sabra took off for the door of the temple, ignoring her father's cries. She stumbled out into the chill daylight and flung her hand over her eyes, her gaze following knots of running people until she found the object of their curiosity. A choked scream lodged in her throat and she flew down the temple steps. People moved aside instinctively as she rushed by. If they were scandalized to see her running, so be it. She didn't care.

She didn't stop until she reached the stone pillar where criminals were publicly flogged. Her heart stopped; her lungs forgot to breathe. Ayzebel hung from the binds on her wrists, her hands deformed and blackened from burns, her back open under a brutal web of lashes that wept a sea of blood. She wasn't moving.

Vaguely Sabra felt her feet stumbling into an unsteady run. She dropped to her knees beside the girl's limp figure, reeling with nausea at the barbarity of it all. Her fingers grazed Ayzebel's shoulder, but the girl didn't even flinch. Just rested there with her head leaning against the pillar, her eyes like chips of amber staring at nothing, a smile on her face.

Ayzebel was dead.

Tears burned like fire in Sabra's throat, her whole body shook with rage. She lifted a trembling hand to smooth back Ayzebel's braided hair, then planted a kiss on her blood-speckled temple.

"I pray your God smiles on you for honoring him with your life," she whispered.

She stood, slowly, and turned. From the corner of her eye she noticed her father standing nearby in horrified silence, but she ignored him, fixing her gaze instead on the guards and Dignianus. The guards who held the bloody scourges bowed their heads under her stare, and even Dignianus licked his lips nervously.

"May the gods forget you for all eternity," she hissed. "May your names and the names of all your kin be stricken from their tablets, and may the old god feed on your corpses."

THAT NIGHT, SHE took Elissa down to the *adyton* of the god's Temple, the secret inner sanctuary where only she and the sacrificial victims were allowed to walk. The girl knelt in the middle of the floor and sobbed as if her heart had broken. Sabra didn't stop her.

Elissa wept for them both.

21

Anatolia

The journey to Myra seemed to last forever. The first few days out from Blasios' cave, the weather was cool but mild, and Mari's high spirits and Menas' tales kept everyone moving. Then, without warning, winter came. It hit like a tempest, plummeting the temperatures to a frigid cold and bringing a rage of snow in its wake.

Jurian had heard horror stories about the winters in central Anatolia from the Legionaries who had the misfortune to make that march, but he'd always assumed they were exaggerating to impress their friends.

They hadn't been.

For a while they walked in the shelter of the low mountains, but eventually the snow and the wind seemed to forget about things like windbreaks and swirled all through the valleys, driving white drifts into every crevice and hollow. When Jurian spotted a narrow cave in one of the rocky mountainsides, they holed up for warmth for a day until the blizzard passed, eating dried meat and raisins and lamenting the lack of a fire.

"This isn't the worst I've seen," Menas said mildly.

He sat closest to the cave's mouth, his cloak over his head and his bulky frame blocking out most of the wind. He crouched awkwardly, trying to wrap his purple, swollen feet in the hem of his cloak for warmth. Only a few scraps of daylight slipped in past his shoulders, leaving the tiny shelter a confusion of shadows.

"What was the worst?" Mari asked.

She sat huddled against Jurian's side, her wool cloak pulled up over her nose. Jurian wrapped his own cloak around both of them, still afraid that she would fall ill again at any minute.

"Well, that would be, hm, five years ago, I suppose? I was walking up from Myra, and had just come into the mountains when the snow came. It got so cold I had to look to make sure the sun still existed, but of course, the sky was so full of snow that I couldn't see the sun at all. Needless to say, that didn't improve my mood. But the snow kept coming until I couldn't even see the hand in front of my face, and my eyes burned so badly from the cold that I thought they'd crack and fall out if I stared too long anyway. Then, without warning, I hit the edge of a ridge and fell a clear fifty feet before I hit the ground."

"Fifty!" Mari interrupted, laughing. "Not likely."

"Well, maybe it was closer to forty."

Jurian cocked a brow at him.

"Well, maybe thirty. Anyway, it was a long drop. And I landed right in a drift of snow. Surprisingly, though, it felt a bit warm in there, so I just wrapped up in my cloak and went to sleep. Slept for three months, just like a bear, and came out when the snow started melting."

"Three months!"

He winked at her. "Three blessedly warm, quiet months."

"Days?" Jurian asked.

Menas coughed.

"Hours?" Mari asked, a note of despair in her voice.

"All right, three hours. But it felt like months. And I suppose I climbed out again before it melted. It was like climbing a mountain! The snow had piled up ten times my own height."

By then Mari couldn't stop laughing long enough to protest, but Jurian was almost more entertained by the satisfied smirk on Menas' face. The giant had obviously been a bit lonely in his travels. Jurian wondered how he could have survived so long without an audience for his stories.

Thinking about that, he asked, "Do you escort many people through this region?"

Menas grew thoughtful. "Oh, quite a lot. Once I carried ten people across the same river, all in the same week." His eyebrows shot up and he jutted a lip, adding, "And once I carried ten people across a river…all at the same time."

"No you didn't!" Mari laughed.

"Well, it felt like I did," he huffed.

"You were going to tell us that story, Menas," Jurian said. "About the heaviest burden you ever carried."

Menas hunched his shoulders, letting a thin whimper of wind into the cave. "Do you know what it was?"

They shook their heads, Mari enraptured, Jurian curious.

"A child."

Mari looked like she wanted to laugh again, but then seemed to realize that Menas wasn't embellishing this time. "A child?" she murmured.

"It was not long after…after the devil had left me. I was on the river, fishing for my dinner, when I looked up and saw this beautiful little child, only about three or four years old, standing on the riverbank across from me like he'd been there forever. I was afraid he would wander into the water, so I rushed across the river toward him."

"Where were his parents?" Mari asked, horrified.

"That's what I asked him. He just fixed his gaze on me with the faintest smile on his lips, and didn't say a word. That child's eyes…" His voice drifted away and he stared a while into the shadows. "Like the night sky. You know how it seems so close but so far away, so clear but so fathomless? His eyes were like that. He just stared up at me, like he could see right through me, see all I had ever done, and yet he looked at me without fear, without hatred. Like I meant something to him." He bowed his head, threading his fingers through the length of his beard. "I asked him if he wanted to cross the river. He said yes, so I knelt and lifted him onto my shoulder. He was the first person I ever carried across a river. I wasn't worried. The boy was tiny and light, and he didn't move at all. I was afraid he would start wiggling as we got into the water, and make us both fall."

"What happened?" Jurian asked.

"Well…that was the most dangerous crossing I've ever made. I thought I was going to drown. I thought I would die."

Mari straightened up, frowning. "But if he was so small and light…was the river too deep?"

"No," Menas said, a strange smile flickering in his eyes. "No, the river was quite shallow. It barely reached my chest. But as I came to the middle of the river, the weight on my shoulder grew heavier and heavier. It pressed me down, bowing me over, crushing my legs. I was sure I would collapse and get swept away, and that would be the end of me and the child. A last frail remnant of the old me whispered that I could save myself if I left the child, but I refused. I would carry that child safely even if I died at the end of it. Finally, when my legs had nearly failed me, I cried out to the child. I think I said, 'You are too great a burden.' That same moment, the weight became bearable again. I made it the rest of the way as carefully, but as fast, as I could, and set the child down on the riverbank."

A shriek of wind tore past Menas, blowing his hood over his face and scattering snow over Jurian and Mari. Mari drew back into her cloak, batting the wet flakes off her face.

"Did you find out why he was so heavy?" Jurian asked.

Menas smiled, slowly. "I did. I said to the boy, 'I've never carried a burden as heavy as you.' The child said, 'You have seen this burden before. It stood at the side of a road, and even then, it brought you to your knees.' It seems foolish now, but at first all I could think was how strange it was that the child could talk to me like a grown adult. Then I realized that the child wasn't a child, but a man, his forehead bruised and pierced, wounds in his hands and in his feet, and eternity in his eyes."

Mari gasped and clapped a hand over her mouth, and, more slowly, Jurian caught the implication. He stared at Menas, bewildered, uncertain, but nothing in Menas' face seemed to suggest he was teasing them. Instead, his eyes glittered with the strangest light—wistful sadness mixed with deepest joy. Jurian shifted his gaze away after a moment. He didn't understand that look. Part of him wondered if he ever would.

Menas added, "He told me that the weight I had carried across the river was the weight He had carried up the mountain, the weight of all the sins of the world. I know I didn't feel the full burden of it. He spared me that, on account of my weakness. So that was how I found my answer. I had been searching and searching for this Lord of the Cross, and in the end, He found me when I was least expecting Him."

AFTER A WEEK of hard traveling, the snows gave way to a milder climate, the air growing warmer the farther south they walked. Finally, mid-afternoon on the eighth day, they reached the top of a low ridge and saw the great sea sprawled beneath them in a chaos of grey and azure. Mari turned to stare at the march of snow-crested mountains behind them, as if they belonged to some other world. Hunger, cold, and exhaustion gave Jurian little patience to enjoy the beauty, and Menas seemed to agree; his gaze was fixed on the city at the water's edge—and the curls of smoke that suggested a thousand cooking fires.

They had all felt the pangs of the rough travel. Their clothes were meant for warmer climates, and miles of trekking across rocky ground had shredded the leather soles of their shoes long before they hit the numbing wetness of the snow. Food was even worse. Blasios had provisioned them with some dried fruit and nuts, and Jurian had done his best to hunt along the way, but with the deep snow he'd found little game. In the end, all he'd accounted for were an unfortunate rabbit and one lone mountain goat, neither of which stretched very far with Menas in their group. Still, though they all looked a bit worse for wear, they'd survived, and now had the prospect of warmth and comfort spreading below them.

"Come on," Menas said, grinning broadly at Jurian and Mari. "I need to pay a visit to a dear friend."

"Saints, I hope there'll be food at the end of it," Mari sighed, one hand clamped around her waist.

"Nikolaos isn't a wealthy man, but somehow he always has enough to share," Menas said.

By early evening they had reached the outskirts of the city. They skirted a massive necropolis of brightly painted tombs cut in the cliffside and passed under the shadow of the Temple of Artemis Eleutheria. Mari stared; Jurian wasn't surprised. From what Menas had told him, everything in Myra was Greek but the laws, even more than in the Legion town of Satala.

Menas led them into a humbler quarter of the city, nearer the Andriake port with all its traffic, noise, and filth. The sea wind carried the sharp smell of brine and fish. Mari had a strange look on her face, and Jurian chuckled as he realized she was trying—unsuccessfully—to breathe without smelling the stench. She glanced skeptically at him as they followed Menas through the mazy streets, but Jurian just shrugged. If Menas' friend lived in one of these hovels, who was he to scoff?

The sun had set when they reached a sparsely inhabited district of the city. They had left the last shops some time ago. Here there were a few small houses, but the road was no more than a dirt track. Menas pointed out their destination—a simple house of Greek design at the end of the road, with a carving of a fish at the doorway instead of the customary statue of Hermes.

"Fish?" Jurian murmured to Mari.

She shrugged. "Maybe he likes fish."

Menas rapped at the door, the sound echoing through the inner courtyard. A moment passed, then the latch lifted and a pool of lamplight spilled over the threshold. Jurian blinked in the sudden brightness. The person who opened the door was even shorter than Mari, and at first Jurian thought they were being greeted by a child. Then the lamp shifted aside and Jurian saw a young man, completely bald though he looked no older than thirty, with a curly black beard and deep complexion. His dark eyes shone almost golden in the lamplight, and for some reason he was grinning as if he'd just won a bet.

"Well, it's about time," he said with a bright laugh. "Did you get sidetracked? I was afraid the meat might get overdone."

They stared at him. Then Menas gave a deep, rumbling laugh and crushed the man in an embrace, all the more comical because of the enormous difference in their heights.

"All right, yes, I'm here," the man said, eyeing him sidelong. "You giants are all the same. Sentimental and overly dramatic."

Jurian's brows shot up, but the man glanced at him and gave him a faint wink.

"How'd you know to expect us?" Jurian asked, folding his arms, even though something about the man made trusting him feel instinctive. "We didn't even know we were coming before we decided in the wilderness."

"Details," the man said, and waved them into the inner courtyard. He squared his slim shoulders, tipping his head to study them. "Eh, you're all tall! That's to be expected, I suppose. I'm Nikolaos, if you didn't know that already."

Jurian nodded, accepting the man's hand. "Jurian. This is my younger sister, Mariam."

Nikolaos clasped her hand briefly and beamed a warm smile at them. "Any friend of Menas is welcome here," he said. "Well, come on. You look half-starved, the lot of you. I've got a little feast prepared. Nothing as fine as tomorrow's will be, but I thought you would appreciate it."

Menas and Mari followed him eagerly, but Jurian hesitated near the door, bewildered.

"How—" he started but no one was there to hear him, so he flung his hands in the air and strode after them.

Mari had already ducked into the tiny kitchen to offer her help to Nikolaos. The warm aromas of roasting pork and honey drifted out through the narrow doorway with a stream of golden light, and Jurian's stomach complained in answer. He leaned against the doorframe across from Menas, arms crossed.

"Can you explain this?" he asked, nodding at the small man inside the kitchen.

Menas grinned and drew a deep, noisy breath, taking in the

cooking smells. "I've missed this place. Nikolaos always knows how to entertain a guest, though half the time I've no idea where his food comes from."

"Who is he, though?"

Nikolaos laughed. "This kitchen is not that large, son."

Son, Jurian scoffed. *He's younger than Menas!*

Nikolaos glanced at Menas and they exchanged some wordless communication, ending with Menas nodding solemnly.

Nikolaos' smile flashed again and he said, "I'm a presbyter."

"You're a priest!" Mari gasped. "Did you know Eugenius?"

Nikolaos hesitated. "There aren't many of us yet, but I haven't met all my brother priests. I never met your Eugenius, but I know him."

Jurian pressed his fingers against the bridge of his nose. *And I thought Menas was bad.*

"No need to weep, daughter," Nikolaos said to Mari, seeing the grief in her eyes. "All is well with him. He does not need our tears now."

He served them slabs of pork coated with honey and roasted nuts, with olives and crumbling goat cheese, and they sat down to eat on bronze benches near a coal fire in the courtyard. There was bitter wine mixed with water and spices in the Greek fashion, but only Menas seemed to actually enjoy it. Jurian and Mari chose to drink water instead.

"This feast was amazing," Mari said, cleaning honey off her fingers. "What did you mean about tomorrow being better?"

"You...don't know what day it is," Nikolaos said, flatly.

"We've been walking a long time. The days all sort of...run together," Menas said.

Nikolaos leaned back, folding his arms on his narrow chest with a look that Jurian would have called smug, except that there was nothing arrogant about Nikolaos. "Well," he said. "Tomorrow is the eighth day from the *kalends* of Ianuarius."

"Jurian!" Mari exclaimed. "That's the day you were born. Mother always said so."

Nikolaos regarded Jurian curiously.

Jurian shrugged. "She told me that once too. I never saw why it mattered, though." He frowned at Nikolaos, rubbing a hand through his hair. "You didn't have to…that is, we never celebrated it before."

To his surprise, Nikolaos laughed. "Don't be embarrassed, Jurian. Our feast tomorrow is meant to honor the other nativity we observe on that day."

"Whose?"

Menas chuckled.

"Oh," Jurian said, because it was the only thing that would make sense. "You mean Bethlehem? The nativity of the Christ? That was…"

"The same day as yours, apparently." Nikolaos sighed, staring into the fire. "The pagans just had their mad Saturnalia, but tomorrow is the day the world once bowed in silent adoration before a poor Child in a cave." For a moment no one spoke, then he slapped his hands on his thighs and leaned forward. "Will you stay and join the feast?"

Jurian finished his barley bread and settled back on the bench. "I think so. But we can't stay any longer than that. We'll need to get down to the port tomorrow and see about a ship."

"Heading to Rome?" Nikolaos asked, staring at his dish.

"How—?"

Nikolaos just gave him a look, and Jurian's mouth quirked in a smile.

"There's a merchant ship pilot," the priest said. "Macarius. He should be able to give you passage. Tell him I sent you."

Jurian gave Menas a skeptical glance but neither of them said anything. Under the night sky, the air turned dank and chilly, but even the bite of the sea wind felt mild compared to the bitter cold of the mountains. Nikolaos stoked up the fire.

"A family gave me this house to use," he said. "There are plenty of bed chambers, one there where I usually sleep"—he gestured behind them—"and a few upstairs, all furnished. There should be spare blankets in the chest in the hall if you get too cold. There's a well near the kitchen and the washroom just beyond it."

"I'll just make myself comfortable out here," Menas rumbled, stretching his toes toward the fire. "I sleep under the stars every night, and I doubt you have a bed large enough to fit me."

"True," Nikolaos laughed. "And I'm no Procrustes." He stood, drawing up his dark hood. "I hope you all sleep well."

Mari yawned and pushed herself off the bench, murmuring a good night before slipping upstairs. Menas found a large, heavy wool blanket in the storeroom and rolled himself up in it near the fire. Jurian took that as his cue to leave, but, even after so many days of rough journeying, his mind was wide awake. He paced in the courtyard while Menas fell into a deep, sonorous sleep. When the fire started to die he built it up again and sat a while near its warmth, but that didn't help either.

Finally he slipped out and headed down to the beach, where the surf washed the sand like a slow breath. Low clouds hid the stars, but the night was bright enough to see clearly. Jurian sat on a low sea wall and buried his head in his hands.

When he lifted his eyes, he stood face to face with a massive lion. Panic surged through him with a force like fire, but the lion waited, perfectly still, staring at him through lucid blue eyes. Every instinct told him to run, to get to safety, but his legs wouldn't move. The lion sidled up and rubbed its head against him like a cat, the muscles in its shoulders rippling as it curled around him.

Blood pounded in Jurian's ears, so loud he was sure the lion could hear it. Slowly he lowered his gaze. The lion stopped in front of him, close enough that Jurian could feel the heat of its breath on his chest. Its eyes locked with his and its mouth gaped open, wider and wider, its lips peeling back as its cutting teeth stretched into fangs. The tawny fur shriveled to black scales, the tufts of its mane sharpened to spikes, and Jurian found himself staring not at a lion but a leering dragon, its body coiled tight around Jurian's. He tried to shout but the dragon lunged first, mouth impossibly wide, an inferno blazing in its throat...

"Jurian!"

He stifled a cry of surprise and jerked around, only to find Nikolaos crouched beside him, staring at him in concern.

"Everything all right?"

Jurian scanned the beach frantically but the lion, or dragon, had disappeared.

"It's nothing," he said. His voice rasped, hoarse. "Just…a dream, I guess."

"I know something of those," Nikolaos said, sitting down on the wall beside him. "Anything you wanted to talk about?"

"It was just a dream," Jurian repeated, eyeing him skeptically. "It's not important."

"Sometimes they are."

Jurian shook his head and faced the sea. "When my father left with the Legion to fight against Narseh, I dreamed about an eagle devouring a fish. I never thought about it again until the priest Eugenius told me my father had been killed because of his faith. But still, it didn't completely make sense to me until I saw the sign outside your door."

Nikolaos leaned onto his knees, his dark eyes bright even in the uncertain light. "The eagle should be careful. A day may come when it stoops to catch a fish and finds it has met its match."

22

CYRENE

IN THE DEEP DARKNESS OF the Temple, with only the feeble light of the altar fire to banish the shadows, Elissa looked less like a bride and more like a specter. She stood perfectly still, her hands loose at her sides, as Sabra fastened her robe down her arms with jeweled pins. The soft silk of the white robe caught the firelight, gleaming like it was flame itself. Sabra swallowed and tried not to notice, because she could barely summon the will to continue without having visions of Elissa's death torment her.

"Mistress," Elissa whispered. "Why do I have to look like a bride?"

Sabra's hands faltered. "Because a marriage is a contract of fidelity," she said. "It binds two families, makes them share each other's successes, prevent each other's failures. We offer a bride to the god for the same reason, to bind our city to the divine. We hope that, if he accepts her, he will prevent our demise, and we will share in his favors."

Elissa nodded. "What about Juba?" she asked quietly. "He was a boy."

"I don't know why sometimes a boy is chosen. But I think it is to encourage us not to rebel. It's like when a man takes his enemy's son captive, that captive becomes a pledge of the enemy's obedience. Only in this case it's a reminder that we are all the god's captives, in a sense."

Elissa said nothing. She stepped obediently into the embroidered white shoes that Sabra set before her, and lifted her chin as Sabra draped the whisper-thin veil over her head, fixing it with a wreath of white flowers. Sabra shuddered. The brides in the city covered their heads with a *flammea,* a veil of brilliant orange that symbolized the blaze of fire. Her sacrificial victims needed no symbolism. The fire would be real.

I can't do this. Oh, gods forgive me, I can't.

Fear curdled in her veins as a dark certainty edged into the corners of her thoughts.

I serve the god without fear. Who is she to me, compared to the will of the god?

They will all die if I fail.

"You're shaking, mistress," Elissa said, and threaded her fingers through Sabra's. Sabra covered her mouth. "I'm not afraid anymore."

"And the god?" Sabra asked. Her voice was unnaturally high. "Do you still fear him?"

Elissa smiled. "No. Ayzebel taught me not to fear him." She met Sabra's alarmed gaze with terrible certainty. "I know you think Christian children should be fed to the god. I just want to be as brave as Ayzebel."

Sabra let out a strangled breath that sounded like a sob. "Elissa…you know I didn't mean that. You know…I was only afraid."

"Don't be afraid."

The girl bowed her head and turned to the doorway of the *adyton.* They were supposed to burn incense to the god before leaving his presence, but Sabra had been ignoring Elissa's refusal to obey all along. She bit her lip and tossed the beads of incense into the brazier, whispering a prayer for the god to be pleased with their worship. Then she hurried after Elissa, who still hadn't learned the twists and turns of the labyrinth.

They emerged at last into the cold night air, where half the city lined the road with torches in their hands. Somewhere in the background ritual musicians played a cacophony on their flutes and drums, the sound of it setting Sabra's teeth on edge.

No one spoke.

The musicians emerged from the crowds and followed Elissa and Sabra up the road toward the hill where the god lay in wait, playing so loudly that Sabra almost didn't hear the sound of a woman weeping in the crowd. Almost. At the base of the hill the musicians stopped, and Sabra and Elissa went up alone.

I'm just like that guard, Sabra thought, steadying her shaking hands so they wouldn't rattle the links of the chain she carried. *I'm just like Dignianus, shoving coals into Ayzebel's hands.*

This is different, the warring voice in her head countered. *Dignianus was trying to make a political point. This is real worship. This is what the god demands. You can't flout the divine will to satisfy your own sentimentality. It's got nothing to do with you and what you want. You are the god's voice, his hands, his instrument. Act like it.*

It should be me. It should be me. I should let Elissa go and take her place.

The god didn't want you.

This is all wrong.

Elissa drew a sharp breath, startling Sabra out of her inner debate. They had nearly reached the crown of the hill. The moonlight reflected off the whitened skulls of a hundred offerings, all lining the dirt track with wreaths of dried flowers still on their crowns. Somehow the flowers always survived. Sabra had never wanted to wonder how. But it was a macabre sight, and Elissa trembled beside her. She couldn't blame her; she was trembling too. Being this close to the god always threatened to drown her in fear.

A sick stench crept over the outcrop of rock above them, seeping out from the fissure in the cliff face. Elissa's breath came fast and loud, every exhale wanting to scream.

"Does your God give you strength?" Sabra murmured.

Elissa only nodded.

I wish He would give me some of it.

The girl walked up onto the outcrop and stopped when she saw the stone pillar gleaming bone-white near the fissure. Even the ground beneath it had a silver sheen, mercifully free of bloodstains. At least that; if the place looked like a butcher's shop, Sabra would never have the strength to come alone, let alone bring anyone with her.

She turned to the fissure and called on the god, reciting the prayers and invocations she'd known by heart since she was a child. Her blood thudded, cold and sluggish, freezing her where she stood. Elissa watched her, wide-eyed, backing away step by step without realizing it until she reached the pillar.

"Sabra," she gasped. "Sabra, I'm scared. Don't leave me here. Don't leave me to die!"

Sabra lowered her hands. She couldn't look the girl in the eye, so she fixed her gaze on the pillar above her head. Her stomach heaved, threatening to send up the ritual meal they'd just shared.

"You are the salvation of Cyrene," she said, her voice sounding dull and flat as the stone beneath her feet. "You save us all in the shedding of your blood. As your blood flows out, so the waters of the Kyre will not fail. As you stand steady, so the earth will not quake and devour us. You honor us, and will walk boldly into the embrace of your ancestors."

Elissa whispered, "Though I walk through the valley of the shadow of death…"

Sabra clasped the chains around her wrists, binding her to the pillar.

"I fear no evil."

Sabra backed away, stricken. "But I do."

SABRA CROUCHED AGAINST the stone wall deep in the Temple's labyrinth and sobbed into her hands. Her body shook uncontrollably, weak from retching in the shadows until there was nothing left. She knew she had to return to the *adyton* and offer prayers and incense to the god to begin her ritual fast, but she couldn't force herself to move. Her thoughts churned chaotically, her heart failed and failed again, shattering into a million broken pieces.

She hated it all. Hated what she had done. Hated the priestess who had chosen her. Hated the city that clung to her cult with horrific devotion. Hated her father who never saved her. Hated the god who had such a monstrous lust for blood.

But more than anything, she hated herself.

I'm a coward. I'm weak and a coward. I should have taken Elissa's place, and I was too much of a coward. I could have saved her. Oh, gods, why didn't I save her? Why didn't I save any of them? Juba and Flavia, Agrippina and Melita, Julia and Tanith, Lydia…Agathe…

23

CYRENE

AFTER FOUR DAYS SABRA EMERGED from the Temple, at midnight when the world was dead. Hanno waited for her again at the top of the steps, no torch in his hands but grief in his eyes. When she stumbled he caught her arm, but she pushed him away.

"Don't touch me, Hanno," she said. "I don't deserve your concern."

Hanno hesitated, then he shook his head and drew her arm around his neck. "You know, sometimes you say these things and—at risk of sounding defiant—I honestly just don't care."

Any other day those words would have made her laugh. That night, even the attempt at a smile brought the tears stinging to her eyes.

"Every single child," she whispered. "Every single one of them was a far better person than I will ever be. Gods pity me."

He said nothing, but walked slowly with her up the road to the palace.

It was always the same, she thought as she sat in the peristyle eating a handful of nuts. Every month passing exactly the same way. Was this the rest of her life? A cycle of death and half-life, and never an ounce of meaning?

The next day passed in a dull fog. She went down to the school and taught the children. Returned to the palace to pray and prepare for the winnowing. Ate a simple meal of grain and fruit and, at nightfall, went with her father to stand on the porch to start the cycle all over again.

Her vision blurred as she dropped her hand into the basket, sifting through the parchment scraps, praying for the god to guide her hand. She chose one and drew it out, numb as stone, and handed it to her father. He took it, and she watched him from the corner of her eye with little interest. His face seemed pale, she thought idly. His eyes so much older. When had that happened?

He swallowed, holding the paper tight, and finally lifted his gaze to hers. "Jezbel," he said. "The name is Jezbel."

What will her little sister say to that? Sabra wondered.

Her father said, "I can't do this to my people anymore."

Sabra closed her eyes. "I could end it all if you'd let me."

They went down to the theater and called the girl forward. She was older, almost Sabra's age, and a commotion followed her naming, but she came onto the stage without hesitation and accepted the wreath of flowers in calm silence. Sabra thought she heard a younger girl shouting in the crowd, but it didn't matter. Even if Jezbel's sister wanted to save her, she couldn't. They couldn't save anybody.

They waited for the crowds to clear the stands and then returned in silence to the palace. Sabra showed the girl her room and slipped back out before her new slave, an older woman named Acenith, could stop her. Coming to a sudden decision, she headed directly for her father's *tablinum*. But just outside the door she stopped, because she could hear, all too clearly, Hanno's voice coming from within.

"You have to tell her."

"I can't," her father said. "You know what she will say."

"Lord, you know it would kill her if she learned the truth."

"Enough. I've made up my mind. See it done. And remember, no one can know."

Sabra retreated back into the peristyle before Hanno could find her there. She sat a while on the pile of embroidered cushions, counting the passage of time. After a few minutes she would go and confront her father…not just about the sacrifices, as she'd planned, but this new conversation. What had Hanno meant, *tell her?* Tell who?

She groaned and buried her face in her hands. The palace was too small for secrets, and much too small for lies.

"I thought I would find you here," someone said behind her—Hanno.

He knelt beside her and sat back on his heels, holding a dish and a cup of water.

"What's this for?" she asked.

"You."

She glared at him. The night's proceedings had robbed her of her appetite, but she could feel her hands shaking and knew she couldn't afford to wallow in her grief. She took the dish from him, but for a moment she just pushed the nuts and dates around on the plate.

"How did you know I would be here?" she asked. She wanted to ask him about her father, but was too ashamed to admit to eavesdropping. "I'm only here because I couldn't sleep."

"I knew you wouldn't be able to," Hanno said, shrugging.

Sabra studied him sidelong. He seemed uneasy, troubled, and that troubled her because he had always been so steady. So certain. A voice of reason when her own was far away. Maybe she could wheedle the information out of him without him realizing it…get him to volunteer it. She ate a few of the nuts, trying to come up with a strategy for tricking him, and reached for the cup of water.

"This is all wrong," she whispered. She took a few long gulps of water to clear her thoughts and wash down the bits of almond that clung to her throat. "It should have been me. I can't let this one die too, not after…"

Elissa. She closed her eyes but couldn't drive away the vision of that girl's eyes staring after her, calm and radiant…and sad. It was the sadness she remembered most. Not fear, not grief for her own death, but…for *her*. For Sabra. Elissa had watched Sabra backing away, and her eyes had shone with pity. It cut her to her core now just as it had then, and she clutched her stomach.

"Hanno," she said, licking her lips. "It's the water again. I can still taste it…what is that? Is it the god, cursing us at last?"

"I'm sorry," Hanno murmured.

She blinked and tried to focus on him, but his figure swayed woozily in the firelight.

"For wh—" Her tongue wouldn't move, wouldn't speak.

"For this."

As darkness crashed over her, she could have sworn she heard him whisper, "It was you."

SHE WAS ROCKING.

For a moment she thought she had slipped back into her childhood, to the nights when Hanno's mother used to rock her to sleep. Funny, that was the last time she could remember feeling safe. But she felt safe now, and warm, bundled in on all sides with the ground swaying gently beneath her. Blood flowed like sludge through her veins, and the fog in her thoughts reduced all the sounds around her to a muffled jumble.

Voices.

Quiet…incomprehensible…a low current of conversation and distant laughter…

"…Far enough by now…" a voice said with sudden loud clarity, pulling all the other sounds into focus with it and snapping her out of her haze.

She shifted, but she was so comfortable…and the ground kept moving and the voices kept murmuring… She couldn't feel her arms or legs, only the heaviness of her body dragging her down… down into sleep…

"…Not these days…"

That sharp, clear voice cut through her grogginess again and this time she made a real effort to wake up. Gradually she became aware of herself. She was stretched out on her back, crammed into a narrow space between a few clay *amphorae* packed with straw and a pile of coarse rope. A thick wool blanket that stank of brine lay over her, blocking out most of the cold wind that she felt suddenly on her face. Cold…and wet. She winced as another gust sprayed a fine, stinging mist onto her cheeks.

Nearby she heard the heavy clomp of shoes on wood, and then Hanno's face filled her vision as he crouched over her.

"Are you awake?"

"What does it look like?" she muttered. The ground rocked again, violently, and her stomach pitched. "Hanno! Where am I? What've you done?"

His face fell with genuine grief, and he clasped his hands at his forehead in supplication. "I'm so sorry, mistress. I only did as I was asked."

"Where are we?" she repeated, attacking each word.

"See for yourself."

He stood and pulled her to her feet. She nearly retched when she stood upright, dizzy and disoriented. There was nothing around her. Nothing but stars and…nothing but the sea.

24

MYRA, ANATOLIA

JURIAN AND MARI WENT WITH Menas down to the port the next morning, hoping to find the merchant vessel Nikolaos had told them about. The fog had rolled in over the night and blanketed the city, so thick that they'd had to wait for it to burn off before they could even see Nikolaos' door across the courtyard. Now the city looked sepulchral in the writhing mist, bleak and grey under a flat grey sky. The low tide slapped lazily far down the shore, leaving half a dozen merchant vessels keeled on the beach. Everywhere they stepped they crushed fragments of shells and wet, bubbly seaweed.

Mari held her cloak over her nose as they went. "Maybe Byzantium would've been a better idea," she muttered. "Does it smell this bad when you're at sea?"

"I don't think so," Menas said. "But my nose has never been that keen."

"And there are things that stink worse than fish," Jurian muttered. "Like Legate's sons who flounce around putting on airs."

Mari and Menas exchanged pointed looks.

"Flaccus," Mari said, her laughter bubbling over.

Jurian's mouth quirked in a half-smile. "It doesn't just smell like fish," he said. He scanned the coastline until he spotted a tall, narrow structure that looked like a granary, with a mound of bleached white shells outside it. "I think it's coming from that building over there, do you see it?"

Mari squinted into the fog. "Are those—"

"Shells," Menas said. "I suspect that's where they make the *purpura* dye for the crimson borders of your *toga praetexta*."

"Saints, it stinks!" she gasped. "Can something so pretty smell so bad?"

Menas laughed and swept a curious glance over Jurian, who, knowing what the giant was wondering, fidgeted with the edge of his filthy tunic.

"Have you taken on the white toga yet, Jurian? I haven't seen you carrying one, but if you're going to Rome, you'll probably want to wear it there."

"Our house burned down," Jurian said shortly.

"That's true."

Jurian hesitated, then admitted, "But I hadn't gotten it yet. Not formally."

"Well," Menas said, dismissive. "In the frontier, things aren't as formal as in the cities. You probably could have taken on the toga after your father's death, and no one would have complained."

"The people of Satala?" Jurian spat, his hand curling reflexively. "They would have taken any oddity as a chance to publicly humiliate us."

They walked a while in silence, their feet slipping in a spread of wet silty sand. The sea wind blew off more of the fog, revealing patches of bright azure sky and enough sunlight to cast a stunning rainbow behind the city.

"That life is behind you now," Menas murmured.

"Let's hope," Jurian said. He pushed the nagging thought of Casca's pursuit aside and turned his attention to the beached ships. "They all look abandoned. I don't see any crew."

"They've likely pulled in for the winter," Menas said. "The seas can be treacherous this time of year."

Mari slowed, shielding her eyes as she stared out at the sea. Jurian stopped beside her. From where they stood, the sea looked calm and eternal, a sweep of blue-grey as far as they could see.

"How dangerous?" Mari asked. "It looks so peaceful here."

"Said many a child watching a sleeping lion," Menas chuckled. Jurian flinched, violently, but Menas didn't notice. "Let's just say our sea sends many a seasoned sailor scrambling for land in the winter."

"Should we even be here?" Jurian asked, waving at the beach. "I mean here, looking for a ship. Will any be sailing? What if we have to stay here until spring?"

"I doubt that," Menas said. "Nikolaos would be happy to host us, but I'd rather not impose on his charity. Some ships still sail. Many goods can be stored for the winter, but some can't. We just need to find a ship on her way to Rome from Antioch or Tyrus."

"What would they be carrying?" Mari asked.

"Wheat, let's hope." Menas chuckled. "Or fish. Wouldn't *that* make a pleasant voyage."

Mari wrinkled her nose. "What about this Macarius person?"

"Well, I don't like to doubt Nikolaos, but he hasn't seen Macarius in months." Menas shrugged. "Though maybe he always comes into port this time of year."

They reached the stone docks where, to their relief, they found a few trading vessels and a handful of Roman triremes bobbing in the low water. The warehouses and offices were quiet this early in the morning, but the rest of the docks were a jumble of activity as sailors pulled haul off their ships' decks. Even in the *castra* at Satala, Jurian had never seen quite so much controlled chaos. He and Mari both kept close to Menas to avoid being trampled by the rush of slaves moving back and forth to secure the goods. Gulls cried and circled overhead, eyeing the decks of a few small fishing coracles in search of unprotected catches of fish.

"How are we supposed to find anyone here?" Mari asked, raising her voice to be heard over the din.

"Ask, I suppose," Jurian said, and glanced at Menas. "Any ideas?"

Menas grinned broadly. "Just one." He pushed them behind him, then cupped his hands around his mouth and bellowed,

"Macarius!"

Mari clapped her hands over her ears but Jurian just stifled a laugh. For a moment an absolute stillness fell over the dock. Everyone stopped to stare at the giant, then a man in a dark work tunic stepped away from a broad-hulled merchant vessel just to the left of where they stood. He glanced up and down the dock, looking faintly amused.

"Yes?"

Menas cleared his throat. "Ah."

Macarius wiped his hands off on a bit of wool and came to meet them. He surveyed Menas from head to toe, then cast a cursory glance over Mari and Jurian. Sea and sun had weathered his skin to the color of rich mahogany, but his eyes were bright blue and his hair was fair, almost golden—a strange contrast.

"Did you need me?" he asked. "I'm a busy man. Lots to do before tomorrow."

"Nikolaos sent us," Jurian said.

The pilot's brows jumped and he grinned broadly, seizing Menas' hand, then Jurian's, and bobbing his head to Mari.

"Nikolaos! But how'd he know—"

"Details," Jurian said, his mouth quirking in a smile.

"Of course," he said with a bark of laughter. "Nikolaos. For a priest he's got more news than most town gossips. Half the time I don't know where he gets his information. Well? So, he sent you. What can I do for you? In the market for some wheat?"

"Not exactly. Are you on your way to Rome?"

Macarius scrubbed his fingers through his tangled hair. "We set sail tomorrow morning, soon as we get our wind, and pray that the weather holds good. We should have sailed this morning but the wind didn't cooperate. Squalls off shore, I'd wager."

"Can we buy passage with you?"

"No," Macarius said flatly. Jurian opened his mouth to protest, but Macarius bellowed a laugh and clapped him on the shoulder. "I wouldn't take money from you even if you could pay me. I owe Nikolaos a debt. You're welcome aboard. Can't guarantee it'll be a pleasant journey, but we'll see you as far as Corinth safely. Tomorrow morning before dawn. Before the tide turns."

He jerked his head in a quick nod and swung away, shouting at one of the sailors unloading sacks of grain from his ship. Jurian and the others stared after him, bemused.

"Well, it seems that takes care of that," Menas said. "Let's just hope he doesn't go back on his word."

They returned to Nikolaos' house and were greeted by a rich warmth of aromas—exotic spices, baking bread, and a bright tangy scent unlike anything Jurian had ever smelled. They found Nikolaos busy in the kitchen, stirring a pot of porridge. On the board were several small red-gold fruits, one cut through its thin rind to reveal a juicy flesh inside. They were unmistakably the source of the tangy smell.

"What are these?" Jurian asked.

"They smell so good," Mari said, inhaling deeply.

"It's called a *narang* in Persian," Nikolaos said. "Take one if you like. Don't eat the rind. Smells wonderful, tastes awful. The inside is fairly sweet though."

Jurian picked up one of the fruits and peeled back the skin. He tried to bite straight into it like a fig and ended up with an explosion of tart juice running down his chin and spattering in his eyes. Mari laughed as he blinked and swiped at his face. She daintily divided hers into sections, giving Jurian a smug look when she ate the whole thing without a mess.

"I've never had anything like it," Jurian said. "Are they common around here?"

Nikolaos laughed. "Not at all. They will be one day, I'm sure, as soon as the Romans discover how good they are." He turned back to the *fornax* and swung the pot of porridge off the low flames. "Here, help yourselves. It's nothing fancy, but a merchant I know recently brought me some spices. They make even the worst barley bearable."

He spooned out dishes of porridge for each of them, with coarse bread to dip in sweet olive oil and bitter wine.

"I have something for you, Jurian," he said, as they sat around the courtyard fire.

"For me?" Jurian exchanged a curious glance with Mari. "What is it?"

"Actually, I'll have something for all of you, but yours is on the special side. It's a day of nativities, and though we don't carry on the way the pagans do with their mad Saturnalia, we can have something to commemorate the day, I think."

He scraped the last bits of porridge from his dish with his bread and washed it down with water, then disappeared into the storeroom. A moment later he returned, his arms laden with cloth. He set the whole burden on the bench, and picked up a length of fine white wool.

"I thought it would be fitting that the day you were born should mark the day you become a man. Well." He paused, studying Jurian thoughtfully. "You took on that role years ago, but it's time everyone recognized it."

Jurian received the soft length of cloth, speechless. Finally he managed, "A toga? A white…toga?"

"You're going to Rome. You're beginning the next stage of your life. It's time to put away the things of a child, Jurian. We don't offer sacrifices to the gods on this occasion, but I offer up my prayers for you today. You will face many trials in the years to come. I pray for your strength. Don't falter. Don't lose your purpose."

Jurian bowed his head. *I don't even know my purpose yet,* he thought, but he only murmured, "I can't thank you enough."

He started to unfold it, but Nikolaos stopped him abruptly. "Wait, hold on! Don't put it on yet!"

He fixed Jurian with a mock glare and shook his head, then handed him the next article from the pile—a new tunic to replace the tattered one that nearly a month of trekking through wilderness had ruined.

"I have a new tunic for you too," he told Mari, handing her a long robe dyed in a deep blue hue. "And I would have gotten one for you, Menas, but the weaver didn't have a loom set wide enough. He said it would be finished before you leave tomorrow."

"How did you know—" Jurian started, then just waved his

hand and gave up. "Never mind."

As Mari took the blue cloth gently in her hands, Nikolaos set something on top of the bundle.

"And this is also for you," he said, his voice suddenly soft. "I pray it will give you strength and courage for what is to come."

Jurian leaned over Mari's shoulder as she brushed her fingers over the object. It was a smooth, dark stone, tumbled by the waves of the sea until it had a subtle sheen. On its face was an etching—a fish—that gleamed in the firelight as if threaded with silver. Mari's finger traced the shape, her eyes on Nikolaos.

"It's beautiful," she said. "Did you make this for me?"

A merry gleam returned to Nikolaos' eyes. "I'm not so subtle a craftsman," he said. "But I know where to find what I need."

Mari clasped the stone in her hand and murmured, "Thank you."

"For everything," Jurian added. "For the gifts...and for your counsel."

"Ah, it's the least I could do. Now, if you'll excuse me, I have some other matters to take care of."

He paused, his eyes lighting up with some secret joy, and he disappeared into his chamber. Jurian took the new tunic and an urn of well water to the washroom, where he peeled the half-rotted tunic off his shoulders and splashed water all over himself. When he'd gotten as clean as he could from cold water and a bit of olive soap, he pulled on the new tunic and fixed it with his thick leather belt. It was by far the finest thing he'd ever worn. He couldn't imagine how Nikolaos had managed to afford it; the priest lived in complete poverty, but somehow, like Menas had said, he always seemed to have what he needed.

He left the washroom and refilled the water urn for Mari. A little later she came back into the courtyard, walking carefully as though she might ruin the fine wool of her new tunic just by walking too fast.

Jurian smiled when he saw her. "I hope we don't run into any Legionaries between now and tomorrow morning," he teased.

She didn't laugh the way he expected. Her face paled and she bit her lip, but she didn't say a word. She just sat on the bronze bench beside Menas and twisted her hands in the skirt of the tunic. Jurian frowned. Usually any mention of Legionaries got at least a smile or a blush out of her.

But he couldn't think of any way to ask her why it upset her, so he sat on the other bench and stretched his feet toward the fire. "Where's Nikolaos?"

"He left while you were cleaning up," Menas said. "Looked very sneaky and suspicious, too."

"And he doesn't mind us staying here while he's away?"

"Not a bit. Nikolaos, really? I don't think he would mind if we emptied his storeroom while he was gone. Not that I'm *actually* suggesting such an activity, of course..."

He patted his stomach ruefully, and Jurian laughed. Porridge could hardly have satisfied Menas, who easily ate more than Mari and Jurian combined at every meal.

With nothing else to do, they headed into the city, which was still decked out from the celebration of the Saturnalia, and wandered through the market streets for a few hours to pass the time. They got back to Nikolaos' house minutes before he did, and as he slipped in through the courtyard door they all stopped and stared at him. His dark tunic was streaked with something grey like soot and he even had smears of it on his face, stark against the high color of his cheeks. He was, inexplicably, grinning like a madman.

"I know better than to question that look," Menas muttered to Jurian, folding his arms over his broad chest.

Nikolaos dropped onto one of the benches, laughing to himself until Jurian was smiling without even knowing why.

"Well, that went better than I expected," Nikolaos said, rubbing his hands. "They'll never guess."

"What did you do?" Mari asked, breathless with excitement.

Jurian exchanged a skeptical glance with Menas.

"Just a bit of...problem solving," Nikolaos said. When that didn't satisfy Mari he grinned wider than ever and said, "Some of my little flock here in Myra are very well off. Merchants, traders, government officials, all with more money than they can spend. They bring it to my little *domus Dei* on the Lord's Day and leave it to me to distribute to those who need it more."

"So why do you look like you crawled through an ash pit?" Jurian asked, hiding his curiosity behind a faint scowl.

"Well," Nikolaos said, his voice trailing off on the word. "Some people don't like to ask for help, or be seen accepting it. So I use a little creativity." He tapped his head. "Somehow it's even more satisfying when they don't know where a gift is coming from, than when they do. I just love to see their faces." He let out a satisfied sigh. "One of the men of my flock has three daughters, and not a spare coin for a dowry. What was I supposed to do? I love weddings!"

He straightened up suddenly, his joy fading into a strange intensity. His eyes turned to Mari and Jurian but he seemed to be looking beyond them, or through them. Then his gaze focused, resting on them each in turn.

"She will need you," he said to Jurian. "When you find her, she will be ready for a wedding, but not the wedding she was meant for." He turned to Mari. "And you, daughter. Your wedding day is almost upon you."

25

Myra

Nikolaos was true to his word. He prepared a feast that night that far surpassed anything Jurian and Mari had ever seen. There was roast pork with pomegranate sauce, a slab of lamb meat rubbed with spice, fresh tangy cheese, soft wheat bread, and bowls of the Persian fruits and fresh vegetables. The heady wine far surpassed the vintage they'd had the night before, so even Jurian accepted a dish of it mixed with water, honey and spice.

Nikolaos had filled the courtyard with countless candles, letting their honey-sweet fragrance mix with the aromas of food. Warm golden light flooded the open space, shining on the white walls and columns until Jurian felt like they were standing inside a piece of amber.

"To honor the coming of the Light of the World," Nikolaos said, seeing Jurian's curious gaze.

They ate in comfortable silence for a while, enjoying the food too much for conversation.

"Where did all of this food come from?" Mari asked finally, filling in the corners with a few sweet dates.

Menas disappeared into the kitchen for another thick piece of pork. Nikolaos smiled and patted his lean belly.

"Like I said, some of my flock are very generous," he said. "I don't often eat this well, but it was a special occasion. They make sure I never lack for anything I don't choose to lack."

Jurian frowned but said nothing, focusing instead on sopping up the meat juices and sauce with his bread. Finally even Menas declared himself full, and they all helped to clean up the remains of the feast. Mari went to bed shortly after, and Jurian headed up to his chamber. But again sleep eluded him, and after a while he pushed back the wool blanket and crept down the stairs.

The candles had all been extinguished but Menas and Nikolaos were both still awake, sitting around the coal brazier. Despite his earlier declarations, Menas had a dish of leftover cheese and nuts in his hand that he picked at idly while they talked.

"Will you continue on with them?" Nikolaos was asking, his voice soft, barely audible to Jurian where he'd sat on the stone steps.

"I hadn't decided," Menas said. "I belong here in Anatolia, walking the rivers."

"There's a shadow around those two. I'm not sure what it is, but it troubles me when I look on them."

"I know. I don't know if I could bear their burdens."

Nikolaos fixed Menas with a piercing stare. "You are the *Christophoros*. What burden could you be asked to bear that would be greater than that?"

"I'm not worthy of that title," Menas rumbled.

"I'm not the one who gave it to you."

Menas bowed his head, and for a few minutes neither of them spoke.

"Jurian is destined for great deeds, I think," Menas said.

Jurian's ears burned, and he wished guiltily that he hadn't been listening in.

Still, he couldn't stop, especially when Nikolaos interjected, voice sharp, "And greater sorrows. So don't take away the joys he does have. You should go with him. The rivers will be waiting when you get back, but that boy will need you in the days to come."

Menas gave him a reproachful look. "What boy? He left the boy behind in Satala."

"He didn't leave behind everything of that life. Some of it follows him still." Nikolaos smiled faintly. "But my point remains the same."

"They're going to Rome. You know I'd sooner go to Cyrene than that lion's den."

"You will," Nikolaos said, with a penetrating look. "But not yet. Each journey in its proper time."

"Sometimes I wonder how you know so much," Menas said. "No, that's wrong. I always wonder it. You knew we were coming and where and when we would be going? How?"

Nikolaos gave him an enigmatic smile. "I have reliable sources."

"Eh," Menas said, and waved his hand. "I don't pretend to understand you."

"There we can agree." Nikolaos stirred the coal embers until a curl of flame emerged. "Menas, bring me your staff."

Menas eyed him cautiously, but bent and retrieved the wood pole of his *sarcina*. "You know what it is," he said.

Nikolaos nodded as he took the staff. "I have something for Jurian. But he is not ready to receive it yet."

Jurian shifted uncomfortably, but he couldn't get a good view of what Nikolaos was doing. The priest lifted something up from around his neck, but then he bent over the pole and Jurian couldn't see anything except Menas bowing over his knees, covering his face with his hands.

"Keep it safe for him, won't you?" Nikolaos asked. "You'll know when he needs it."

"I can't carry that," Menas said, his voice so deep Jurian almost couldn't hear him.

"You've carried it before," the priest said calmly. He handed him the staff. "There. The weapon of the conqueror."

Menas received the wood gently, like an infant, cradling it to his chest. "How am I supposed to explain what it is?"

"You'll know. Words will be given to you, dear friend."

Menas sighed and went to reclaim his woolen blanket, lying down on the cold ground with his hands wrapped protectively around the staff. He was snoring almost as soon as he laid down, but Nikolaos remained by the fire, drawing a rolled scroll from inside his robe that he opened near the glow of the embers. The light flickered on his face, his lips moving silently as he read.

Jurian sat motionless, torn between trying to sleep and talking to Nikolaos. He wasn't even sure what he wanted to ask him, but the man had some kind of wisdom that Jurian wished he shared. Finally he crept down the stairs and across the courtyard.

Nikolaos didn't move, and gave no sign that he'd even seen Jurian, but just as Jurian made up his mind to go back to bed, the priest said, "What did you want to ask me?"

Jurian swallowed his surprise. Carefully stepping around Menas' sleeping figure, he sat down on the other bronze bench and held his chilled fingers toward the warmth.

"I want to know about Rome."

Nikolaos laughed quietly. "That would take more time than we have. I can't say it'll be safe for you. Even in Rome our kind are…not highly esteemed. We barely have any houses of worship, even now. Many people still meet in their homes or the catacombs for the thanksgiving. Even our own *pappas* watches his steps in the streets, and word has it that he may have to go into hiding." He rubbed his bearded chin, regarding Jurian thoughtfully. "You should be careful. There's blood in the water."

Jurian frowned, wondering if Nikolaos was referring to the violent, massive sea beasts he'd heard stories about, who went into a frenzy at the taste of blood. Some sort of figure, he thought, and it made sense. He only had to remember their last night in Satala to know what Nikolaos meant.

"I'm not even sure what to do when I get there," he admitted. He leaned on his legs and stared at the glowing embers. "I mean to join the Legion, but I'm not quite old enough. I suppose we'll find my father's brother when we arrive."

"You mean to join the Legion?" the priest asked. "Even after what happened to your parents?"

Jurian's eyes flashed. "*Especially* because of what happened to them. I mean to restore my family's good name, and make them regret ever doing…whatever they did to my father. And I'll make sure those animals who killed my mother never see a promotion."

"Jurian, don't give way to anger."

"Oh," Jurian said with a bitter smile. "I'm in full control of it."

"And now you sound like Menas," Nikolaos sighed.

As if in answer, Menas snored loudly and rolled over on his side. Jurian and Nikolaos both glanced at him, amused, then Jurian let out his breath and dropped his head in his hands.

"Your journey won't end in Rome," Nikolaos said presently. "But it will start there. Go on. Get some sleep now. The ship will sail before dawn."

Jurian got to his feet without complaint, and he only nodded his thanks to Nikolaos before slipping back across the courtyard. At the stone steps he paused and glanced back. Nikolaos had left the bench and knelt on the grass, bracing his forehead in one hand.

"Give them strength," Jurian heard him murmur. "And give me strength to bear it, if You won't let me share their lot."

In the dark hour before dawn, Jurian woke Mari and crept downstairs, hoping to avoid disturbing Nikolaos. But the priest was already awake and busy in the kitchen, pulling a hot, crisp loaf of spelt bread from the oven. Menas was leaning against the doorframe as usual, still half-asleep and so, for once, quiet. He smiled when he saw them.

"Ready?" he asked.

"Eh," Jurian said. "I've never traveled by boat before. Not sure what I should be expecting."

"Just don't think about the motion," Nikolaos said, smiling over his shoulder at them. "And you'd probably do better not to eat before you set sail."

"Why not?" Mari asked. "I'm starving."

Menas chuckled. "Let's just say, breakfast is a meal you should only enjoy once."

Nikolaos grinned and wrapped the bread in a piece of linen. "It's hot," he said, handing it to Menas.

"Your hospitality deserves its fame," Menas said.

Nikolaos waved him off. He slipped out of the kitchen and disappeared into his own chamber, returning a moment later with three small leather sacks.

"What's this?" Menas asked as Nikolaos handed one to each of them.

Jurian weighed the bag, hearing the faint clink of metal.

"My donation to your cause," Nikolaos said. "It's not all for you." He nodded at Menas' bag. "Some is for your journey, to get you where you need to go." He turned to Mari, clasping her hands around the leather bag. "Some is for the poor. I can't always be in more than one place at a time, so please, if you see a beggar, think of me and help him how you can." He shifted his gaze to Jurian. "Some is for our *pappas* in Rome, Marcellinus. I told you before how dire the straits are in the city there, and he has the care of all the churches' true treasures on his shoulders. Give this to him and let him spend it as he sees fit." He gave Jurian a keen, piercing look. "You will give him gold and he will give you steel. They will give you fire and you will give them blood."

Jurian swallowed hard. He wished that just once, someone would give him some straightforward advice. Prophetic statements never seemed to make sense until it was too late.

"Macarius will take you to Corinth," Nikolaos said, as if he'd read Jurian's mind. Jurian wondered uncomfortably if he had. "He will dock at the port of Cenchreae, and you can get passage across the isthmus to Lechaeum, where you will need to pick up a new ship. There's a ship's pilot named Orosius. Aulus Lollius Orosius. Tell him you're looking for a fisherman. He'll take you to Portus. In Portus you should be able to find a rather curious merchant from Celtic Gaul, Dionysius by name." He smiled faintly. "Honestly, it would be hard to miss him. He runs a barge up the Tiber and will take you the rest of the way into the city." He paused, then said quietly, "I'm afraid once you're there, you're on your own."

"Thank you," Jurian murmured.

Nikolaos turned to Mari. "Have courage, Mariam. Your betrothed waits outside the gates."

"Are you arranging marriages for my sister now, Nikolaos?" Jurian asked with a half-smile. "I already have a lot to deal with."

"No," Nikolaos said. "Just offering a bit of fatherly advice. Now listen. Be careful in the city. The lion is coming back to his den, and the cubs will be eager to impress him. Don't cross them."

Jurian stared at him, his face bloodless and cold. He hadn't told Nikolaos anything about his dream. Finally he shook his head, pushing the thought away. The priest was always talking in figures. One more shouldn't surprise him.

"I'm glad to have met you," he murmured.

"We'll see each other again soon, I think," Nikolaos said. "Your way will not always be clear, but I will help you how I can."

Mari took one of the priest's hands and kissed it. "I will pray for you," she said.

Nikolaos studied her with grave affection. "Pray for them," he said, and nodded at Jurian and Menas. "You will lead the way." He patted her hand and turned to Menas. "I don't think we will meet again, River Walker. Go with honor. Go with strength."

Menas startled visibly, looking more discomposed than Jurian had ever seen him. He glanced at Mari. She was biting her lip, her hands twisted in her dark cloak. From the cold pulse in his veins he knew that he must have looked as anxious as they did. This leave-taking was by far the strangest he'd ever seen.

He nodded at Mari and inclined his head to Nikolaos, and they set out into the quiet, fog-laden dark. At the port they found Macarius loading the last few amphorae of exotic spices into his ship's hold. He welcomed them on board, directing them toward the prow of the ship where they could keep out of way until the ship had set sail. Mari sat down on a coil of rope and Jurian leaned over the ship's rail, staring down into the murky sea that lapped quietly against the hull.

"I don't know what you and Nikolaos were talking about," Mari said to Menas. "I can hardly feel a thing."

Menas chuckled and sat on the deck beside her. "Just wait."

It turned out they didn't have long to wait—they had barely

settled when Macarius called for the crew to disembark, throwing off the mooring lines that had held the ship at dock. The crew broke out oars to guide the ship away from the harbor, and the dock drifted away behind them. Mari grabbed the rail behind her as the ship hit its first small swell.

"Oh," she gasped. "*That's* what you meant."

"Yes," Menas said gravely. "We'll have breakfast...after."

"After what?" Jurian asked, glancing at them over his shoulder. "I'm starving. What I wouldn't give for some of the roast pork and cheese Nikolaos had."

Menas stared at him aghast, then his face lost its color and he heaved over the rail. Mari clapped a hand over her mouth but scrambled to her feet.

"Menas!" she cried, wrapping both of her arms around one of his. "Are you all right?"

"Fine," he muttered. "Just trying to...lighten the ship's load."

"I should have brought those last ten *amphorae* of oil, then," Macarius said, coming up behind them. He perched on the narrow rail, balancing precariously. "I left them in Myra on account of our...extra weight. Nikolaos assured me the merchants in Corinth wouldn't complain."

"When did you see Nikolaos?" Jurian asked, since Menas was still contemplating the water over the ship's edge and Mari was distracted with trying to comfort him.

Macarius shrugged. "Last evening. He came by to thank me for agreeing to take you."

Mari straightened up at that, glancing curiously at Jurian.

When? Jurian wondered. *We were with him the whole evening. He must have meant later.*

He shook his head and watched the crew loosing the ship's square sail. As the wind filled the cloth the ship darted forward, and Macarius hopped off the rail.

"That's my cue," he said. "I'd better go direct the long-oarsmen or they'll have us out at sea in no time."

It wasn't until a few days later, when Macarius had brought them into the Aegean Sea and was busy navigating around a scattering of Greek islands, that Mari and Menas finally got used to the rocking and pitching of the ship. Menas stayed in the narrow cabin below the deck as much as he could, but Mari eventually made her way up to join Jurian in the open air.

"I could get used to this," Jurian said, leaning over the rail to catch the sea spray on his face.

The wind that gusted them along stung bitterly cold and the waves chopped with vicious fervor at the hull, making the vessel cant a bit to the side. Apart from the rocky islands jutting up to their right, the wine-dark sea swept away endlessly to the sky, relentless and merciless.

"Look, Mari. See how the ship balances on the waves?" Jurian asked, grinning so broadly that Mari gave him a strange look. "The waves are going one way, but the ship just keeps going where the wind drives it."

"It's beautiful," Mari said. "And terrifying. I could get used to it, but I don't know if I *like* it. It's too big." She braced her hands on the rail, the wind whipping a few loose strands of hair from across her face. "In Satala, everything felt so much larger than us. I was just one person in that whole big town. And then we got to Myra, and I realized that Satala was tiny in comparison. Now we're here on the sea, and Myra would be just a speck in all this space. And do we mean anything at all? We all think our lives are so important, as if anything we do really matters."

"It *does* matter," Jurian said quickly. "I can't help thinking that every person you meet is important for you at that precise moment, and you are important for them." He shook his head and turned back to the water. "I don't know how to explain it. But we might never know how much of a difference we make. One word, one action, spoken to a specific person or done at a precise time, and we could change the whole course of history. We might just be a couple of exiles from a tiny village in a remote part of a frontier region of the Empire, but who knows? Maybe we'll change the world."

26

THE MEDITERRANEAN SEA

SABRA STARED OUT AT THE vast sea, her thoughts spinning wildly out of control. In the night darkness she couldn't see anything but a great blur of nothingness under the glittering sweep of stars overhead. The damp, cold wind bit through the thin linen of her robe, tangling her loose hair around her neck like a hangman's noose.

"What've you done, Hanno?" she whispered.

"Only what I was told, mistress."

He had the decency to look abashed under her glare. "Told by whom?"

A brief silence passed, then he bowed his head and murmured, "Your father."

"Why?" If she had been less furious, she might have wept, but she only gripped the rail of the merchant ship with white knuckles. "Just tell me why."

Hanno shifted and turned his back to the sea. "He…was afraid you were second-guessing the will of the god. He thought you might not go through with the sacrifice this month, and…"

Sabra narrowed her eyes. "You've always been a terrible liar, Hanno. Without me, who has the power to intercede with the god? Who can even offer the sacrifice? He's damned the city. You have to take me back. Tell the pilot to turn around."

"I can't."

"I refuse to leave!" Sabra shouted.

A few sailors at watch glanced over curiously at her outburst, eyes dark with suspicion. Sabra ignored them all. She was shaking with anger, even more than with the unexpected cold, and for a fleeting moment she saw the wide expanse of the sea and imagined the feel of diving into it.

"Sabra!" Hanno cried, reaching out and gripping her arms. "Listen to me. Your father sent you away…because it wasn't Jezbel's name that was chosen."

She froze, her lips barely moving as she whispered, "What?"

He cursed under his breath. "It…it was you."

Time ground to a halt. Sabra stared at him, but he refused to meet her gaze. All her anger, all her confusion slipped away, leaving a numb nothingness in her mind as vast as the sea.

"It was me," she echoed, breathless. "Me? I chose my own name?" Fear launched into her throat and she pulled away from Hanno. "I drew my own name, and he *sent me away?*"

"He saved your life," Hanno murmured.

She didn't think. Her hand flew on its own, slapping him hard across the face. "It wasn't his to save! It isn't even mine to save!"

Hanno kept his head turned aside, but his fingers brushed his cheek where she had struck him. He didn't say anything. Sabra wasn't sure if she wanted him to argue, or if she wanted his silence.

"The god chose me," she whispered. "And now he will only see that I've abandoned my duty. Do you think there is any limit to the vengeance he will wreak on the city? They're all in danger. You have got to take me home."

"Do you love your father?"

She took a step back. "Of course I do. What sort of question is that?"

"What do you think the people would do if they found out he sent you away because your name had been drawn? Some people already believe he knew you were supposed to die at the beginning and made up the lottery to save you. That he was happy to let other parents' children die, but wasn't willing to lose his own. If you go back now, they will rise up against him. You might save your city…but you will almost certainly lose your father."

Sabra turned away, leaning on the rail and bowing her head. A spray of sea foam dusted her cheeks and the wood timbers creaked as the ship crested a small wave.

He chose you because you were doubting, the voice in the back of her mind whispered. *You were weak. The god has no use for weak servants. Are you surprised he finished with you? And now you are running away like a coward, and you don't even try to return to your duty.*

What can I do?

She straightened up and faced Hanno. "Take me to the ship's pilot. Now."

"Mistress, it's the third watch of the night. He must be asleep."

"I don't care. Don't defy me, Hanno."

His jaw tightened but he only bowed his head and led her down to the cabin below the decking. The other members of the sparse crew who weren't on watch slept in blankets among the merchandise, but the pilot had a small room in the cabin near a tiny cabinet that served as a kitchen. No one stood guard outside the pilot's berth, but Sabra wasn't surprised. He was a merchant ship's master, not a pilot of the Roman navy. Merchant ships ran on a ghost crew, no room to spare for idle bodies. Like hers.

Hanno stopped in front of the heavy curtain, and, heaving a sigh, he hammered on the wood doorframe.

"*Kyrie,*" he called. It was one of the only Greek words he knew. "*Kyrie,* my mistress to see you."

Sabra heard a faint rustling, then the curtain drew back and she found herself face to face with a tall, thin man, balding and grey, with severe, hawkish features—the sort of man who looked like he disliked disturbances of every kind, and especially disturbances in the middle of the night. He stared at Sabra in the faint light of an oil lamp, his lips tightened in a thin line framed with deep wrinkles.

"There had better be a good reason for this, slave," he said, spearing a glare at Hanno. Then to Sabra, "What do you want?"

Sabra swallowed. "As sole priestess of the old god, I demand you turn this vessel around and return me to my city."

The pilot snorted. "It was enough trouble to get you on board this ship. There's no way I'm wasting two days' journeying to take you back again. Is that all? Good night."

"Wait," Sabra said, her hand flashing out. "Listen. Believe me when I tell you, you do not want to thwart the will of the god."

"If it's the will of the god for you to get home, he'll get you there. He won't need my help. I've had favorable omens for this journey. *My* god at least is with me."

Sabra stared at him. No one had ever dismissed her god, or her role as his voice, so casually. What sort of heathen were they sailing with?

"Look, girl," the pilot sneered. "I don't know who you are. I know you made me stay longer in a cursed port than I intended, and for that I'm not inclined to help you any more than I already have. But we're putting in at Carthage in a few days. When we do, do what you like. Swim home for all I care. Good night."

He jerked the heavy flax curtain back over the doorway, leaving Sabra and Hanno standing outside in stunned silence.

"I'm sorry," Hanno said.

Sabra forced a laugh. "What for? He proved you right."

"I know you're upset. Do you think I wanted to do this?"

Sabra followed him back up to the deck in the silence, wrapping herself in the fish-smelling blanket and settling down in the shelter of the ship's bulwark. After a moment Hanno sat down beside her, his knees drawn up and wool cloak wrapped around them.

"I don't understand," he said after a while. "Even after I told you what happened, you still want to go back. Why? You know you will die if you return, but...that doesn't stop you."

"I'm not afraid of my own death," Sabra said, but in the deepest reaches of her mind she wondered if it was true. She gave a bitter laugh and added, "After all, it's not as if I've got any life to speak of. My life has always been lived at the whim of the god. Life and death are in his hands. I gave up any right to complain about the one or the other when he chose me." She pulled part of the blanket over her head, trying to block out the reek of fish. "You asked why I wanted to go back."

Hanno nodded.

"I had the chance to end it all," she said, quietly. "And he took it from me."

"Maybe it's not all bad," Hanno said. "This ship is going to Rome. Maybe you can request help from the Tetrarchy."

"What can *they* do?" Sabra scoffed. "They can hardly figure out who's in charge of what. They're more likely to start fighting each other than any outlying barbarians, just watch."

Hanno shrugged. "I never did care much about their problems."

"Me either." Sabra stifled a yawn. "You're lucky I didn't wake up when we were closer to shore. I would have jumped."

"You would have drowned," Hanno said, his voice a low growl. "You don't swim."

She gritted her teeth and closed her eyes.

I'm coming back, she promised the god. *I'll see it done. Don't forsake me now.*

SHE WOKE WITH the first creeping light of dawn, and immediately wondered how she'd managed to sleep at all. On either side of the ship's stern, men plied massive oars to help steer the vessel, and they were shouting across the ship at each other every few minutes with obvious indifference to their two sleeping guests. Almost directly in front of her stood the ship's captain, watching the distant coastline and keeping an eye on the wind in the ship's square sail. The sky hung heavy with a threatening storm and as far as she could see, the choppy waves churned with foam.

She pulled herself to her feet and folded the oily blanket, though the first blast of wind made her reconsider setting it aside. Tucking her hands inside the long, loose sleeves of her robe, she leaned on the rail and stared down into the foaming water left in the ship's wake. Every now and then she spotted a flash of silver, then three lithe dolphins leapt from the water in graceful arcs. She caught her breath and thought about waking Hanno, but he was so soundly asleep she didn't have the heart.

"They're a sign of the gods' favor," a voice said behind her.

She froze, darting a glance over her shoulder to see the ship's pilot close behind her, watching the water like her. Even if she had been able to answer, she wouldn't have known what to say, so she only nodded in silence. She could believe it—she had never seen anything quite as beautiful as those gleaming silver bodies.

The pilot wandered back to his observations, and Sabra wondered if she had offended him by her silence. Deep down she wished for the freedom to speak openly. All her life she had known nothing but the walls of Cyrene—and, more particularly, the walls of her temple. In that city nestled in a valley between two rough hills, she had never imagined that the world was so large. Even here, hardly two days' journey from Apollonia, the god's name seemed unknown, or forgotten. Was Cyrene the only place he was worshipped?

Was it the only place he ruled?

She groaned and leaned her head in her hands. A headache pressed behind her eyes, throbbing relentlessly, reminding her how long it had been since she'd had anything to eat or drink. She was supposed to be in the temple right now, carrying out her ritual fasts with all the long chanted prayers for the god's mercy. No one would be chanting in the darkness of the *adyton* now. Who would lull the god to sleep with bells on her ankles? Who would keep the spring from running dry?

It was no use. She would only drive herself mad with thoughts like those. Perhaps the god *had* willed that she be torn from her duty. Maybe without her there, the city would start to slip into greater ruin, and the people would realize how important his worship really was. Maybe then they would do him the honor he required, and wouldn't spurn his worship to follow other gods…

Like Ayzebel, she thought, choking on a stifled sob. *Like Elissa.*

27

Cenchreae, Corinthia

Five days after the ship had sailed from Myra, Macarius pointed out the port of Cenchreae at what Jurian could only describe as an elbow of land in the middle of the Aegean Sea. The Greek mainland swept up in low ridges to their right, while to the left he could see the jagged coast of the Peloponnese drifting away south. Right at the juncture of the two lay the port, gleaming in white stone and azure blue sea. After days of rough seas and rain, Jurian couldn't imagine a more pleasant sight.

"How far out are we?" Jurian asked, shielding his eyes.

"An hour," Macarius said. "Less if this wind holds up."

Mari climbed up onto the deck to stand beside them, winning a broad smile from Macarius.

"I'll miss having you all on board my ship," he said. "That giant does wonders as ballast."

Mari laughed. "I wish you were going to Rome."

"Eh," Macarius said, shaking his head. "I've been to Rome. Too crowded for my taste. Once you get the open sea in your blood, nothing else will do."

"Is it dirty?"

"Fairly clean, as cities go," he told her. "Just be careful. The Romans' so-called tolerance doesn't extend to everyone any more. You might think the way you act is normal, but it's not."

"I'm not going to change how I act," she said.

"No one's asking you to," Jurian said, straightening up from the rail to look at her. "But changing how you're acting and not acting at all are two different things."

"That doesn't make sense."

Jurian met Macarius's gaze and shook his head. Mari could be astonishingly stubborn at times, but it was a naive stubbornness. She didn't understand how the world worked. Part of him wished he could let her stay in that innocence.

Macarius clapped Jurian on the shoulder and left them to direct his crew, who were pulling out the slender oars to guide the ship into the harbor. Soon they eased the vessel up along the quay and cast the mooring lines, securing them in place. Jurian and Mari stayed where they were, out of the way in the ship's stern, watching the controlled chaos of the crew and dock workers swarming the ship's hold. Menas emerged from the cabin and joined them on the deck.

"Well, you both look ridiculously healthy," he grumbled, casting an appraising eye over them.

Menas seemed a bit worse for wear, Jurian thought. Even after he'd gotten used to the ship's motion, he hadn't eaten much. His skin had a rather dull pallor and he looked a bit unsteady as he reached for the ship's rail.

"When can we get off this scrap?" he asked.

"Soon as those men get the cargo down the ramp," Jurian said. "I'd rather not get in their way."

Menas nodded. "I left our things below."

"I'll get them," Jurian said. "You never did get your sea legs, did you?"

He retrieved their belongings from the cabin and, on his way back, found Macarius sitting on a wooden barrel in the ship's hold, staring at the cargo in utter disbelief.

"Everything all right, Macarius?" he asked.

Macarius just shook his head, mouth agape. "I don't believe it. That rascal!" Jurian gave him an encouraging gesture to explain. "Nikolaos said the merchants wouldn't object to our bringing in ten fewer *amphorae* of oil. Well, the official *mensor* just finished measuring the weight of the oil we brought."

"And?"

"Ten fewer *amphorae*. Full weight of oil. How does that even happen?"

"Maybe you miscounted?"

"I don't miscount!" Macarius cried, but he laughed and scrubbed a hand through his hair. "Nikolaos is truly a marvel. I don't know how he does it." He shook his head again and got to his feet, directing Jurian toward the ramp. "See there on the far side of the docks? There are some wagons that carry cargo from Cenchreae to Lechaeum along the track of the old *diolkos*. It's not more than an hour's ride across the isthmus. You could barter a ride with one of the drivers, or I suppose you could walk."

"I'll see what Mari wants to do. We walked halfway across Anatolia, anyway. Another few miles won't bother us."

Macarius regarded him curiously. "What sent you walking that far in the middle of winter?"

"We had enemies in Satala," Jurian said after a moment. "And one of them swore to make it his life's mission to hunt us down. We cut across the mountains to Myra to avoid his pursuit, after we saw them on the road to Ancyra. I just hope they lost our scent there."

"Sounds like a nightmare."

"Sometimes I wonder how we survived," Jurian said. "By rights those mountains should have buried us."

"And this person who's chasing you? What's he on about?"

Jurian shrugged. "He hates my family. More than anything he hates me. And I think he sees me as his stepping stone to a brilliant career in the Legion…and his father's favor."

"Do you think he'll follow you to Rome?"

"I hope not. Like I said, I hope we lost him in Anatolia. But he's got big ambitions. And he doesn't let go."

Macarius put a hand on his shoulder, more serious than Jurian had ever seen him. "This man…he was with the Legion?"

"His father was."

"Jurian, listen. Rumor flies fast in the Legion. I don't know how, but I swear those birds they use for their auguries carry news from one Legion to another. Your little group is painfully noticeable, and if this man has been talking about his quarry, you're marked targets already. A giant, a strikingly beautiful young woman, and a young man with hair like fire? Just keep your eyes open, and steer clear of the Legion for now."

Jurian's hand tightened. "My whole purpose is to join the Legion," he said. "What else do I have?"

"I'm not saying you shouldn't try. Just be aware what you're up against. All right?"

"Thanks," Jurian said, and he meant it, even if he knew he sounded brusque.

"Now get your crew out of here. Looks like my men are mostly done. Godspeed, Jurian."

Jurian nodded his thanks and turned away, joining Mari and Menas down on the strangely stable dock. As they made their way through the crowd, Jurian told them what Macarius had said about crossing the isthmus.

"We should walk," Mari said. "We've been cooped up on the ship for five days. Besides, it will save us a bit of money."

Apparently without noticing, she opened the bag Nikolaos had given her and dropped a few coins in the palm of a beggar sitting by the roadside. Menas and Jurian exchanged a glance and Jurian couldn't resist a smile.

Leave it to Mari to try to save money while spending it.

They stopped at the dockside market to get some food—anything besides fish, they all agreed. As they waited for their food, Jurian watched a few sailors of the Roman navy standing nearby, drinking the cheap *posca* that sailors and soldiers alike consumed in vast quantities—a nasty, bitter concoction that Jurian was by now heartily sick of.

"I heard it was a dragon," one of the men said. "Can you believe that? A *dragon*. A real one."

"I was there a few weeks ago," another said. "We'd just taken some Legionaries to Apollonia. The Cyreneans were about to send some poor child to her death, thinking it would keep the beast quiet."

"Not a beast," said a tall, narrow sailor with silver in his hair. "Their god. Only human blood will do for him, it's said."

One of the sailors turned his head, brushing his thumb discreetly over his forehead. But not discreetly enough.

"Gods, Tertius, be careful with that. You looked just like one of those Nazarenes when you did that."

Jurian stiffened and stepped closer to Mari. She met his gaze anxiously, pale with alarm. Tertius said nothing but kept his head turned aside, while the other sailors stared at him aghast.

"You're kidding us, aren't you?" asked the first sailor.

"Tertius didn't sacrifice to Mercury before we sailed."

"You're not one of those traitors are you? You put our whole voyage at risk!"

"I did nothing of the kind," Tertius said, quietly.

"We barely survived that squall. Were you trying to kill us?"

"Is that what your God commanded? Kill the nonbelievers?"

"Look at him, he's got guilt written all over his face."

"Where's your God now, Tertius?" one of them taunted. "What does He tell you to do about this?"

He swung his fist and struck the sailor on the jaw, sending him spinning to the earth. The man didn't have a chance to recover before one of the other sailors kicked him, violently, in the back and another drove his foot up under his ribs. The older sailor dragged him halfway off the ground to punch him again. Tertius groaned and twisted, blood pouring from his mouth.

"Fight back," Jurian hissed under his breath, his hands clenching in fists. "What's wrong with you? Fight them!"

He doesn't even have a chance. Not with nine of them all attacking him at the same time.

No one in the market moved. Some watched the scuffle through lidded eyes, through sidelong and hidden stares, but no one stepped forward to intervene. Finally Jurian ground his teeth and started for the knot of sailors, but a hand on his tunic brought him up short.

"Don't be a fool," Menas hissed in his ear. "They'll do to you what they're doing to him."

"Two against nine has got to be better than one." Jurian's hand found the hilt of his *seax*. "And I'm not helpless."

Menas planted a hand on his chest and held up a warning finger, then strode over to the attackers himself and lifted two of them clear off the ground by the backs of their cloaks.

"Back away," he growled at the others.

The sailors he held snatched at the collars of their tunics, faces red. The others froze and stared up at him, mouths open in disbelief, but Tertius lay still in the dirt.

The older sailor measured Menas, eyes narrowed with suspicion or calculation. Finally he jerked his head in a nod, ushering the others back with him. After they'd retreated a few steps they turned and stalked away, and Menas sent the last two sailors sprawling in the dirt. They scrambled to their feet, choking and coughing, and stumbled after the rest of their group.

Mari moved before Jurian could stop her, darting to Tertius' side and kneeling down beside him. She clasped his shoulder with one hand, laying the other on his blood-spattered cheek. After a moment she pulled away, white-faced and shaking.

"He's dead," she whispered, and signed her forehead.

"Mari!" Jurian hissed, glancing around anxiously, but to his relief no one seemed to be watching. "Come away now. Leave him. The port guards will see to him."

"They killed him! They killed him for making the *signum*. Why would they do that?"

"They mock those poor Cyreneans for their barbarous rites and then they do this," Menas said. "They're not so different."

Jurian hurried back to the market stall and scooped up the food the merchant had prepared for them, paying more than they owed in the hope that the man would forget their interference.

"Menas," he said as he came back, and nodded at Mari. "We need to go. Now."

Menas nodded and helped Mari to her feet, guiding her gently but relentlessly toward the track of the old *diolkos*. To Jurian's relief, no one stopped them to question them, and no one followed them, but he didn't slow his determined pace until they'd left the port far behind.

THEY REACHED LECHAEUM by early afternoon, though a blanket of storm clouds had rolled in to darken the sky to a twilight brightness. A chill wind had been chasing them down the paved track the whole way from Cenchreae, as if the low mountains on either side of them had funneled all the wind into the valley, and by the time they stepped out onto the walled Lechaion road near Corinth, Jurian's hands and toes were completely numb and his eyes stung from windburn. Menas grumbled about the dangerous seas between Lechaeum and Portus, but Jurian ignored him. The giant had been in a dark mood ever since they'd docked at Cenchreae.

They bypassed the city of Corinth and walked another hour down the marble road, marveling at the arcades with their shops and the brand new, massive complex of Roman baths. People pressed all around them and stray dogs wove expertly between the legs of the pedestrians, hunting for scraps of food near the market stands. The air hung thick with smells. Some were pleasant—spices and incense, roasting food, the smoke of coal fires. Others were less so, with so many unwashed travelers crowding the road stinking of sweat and brine.

"Saints, there are so many people," Mari muttered, dodging neatly around a man who was either drunk or too long a sailor for dry land.

Menas laughed mirthlessly. "You think *this* is crowded? Wait until you see Rome."

Jurian caught Mari's anxious look and smiled. When she turned back around, he fixed a glare on Menas. "You could try to help me keep her spirits up. Scaring the wits out of her isn't going to make anything better."

Menas grumbled and folded his arms, but he didn't say anything else. With an exasperated sigh, Jurian gave up and led the way, keeping Mari close beside him. Eventually the marble road opened to meet the great port of Lechaeum. Jurian's stomach knotted as he caught his first glimpse of the span of Roman triremes at dock, more than they had seen in either Myra or Cenchreae. But he spotted only one or two navy sailors in the sea of dock workers and merchant crews.

"Orosius," Jurian said. "That's who Nikolaos told us to find. Aulus…something…Orosius."

"Lollius," Mari said promptly. "Aulus Lollius Orosius."

"Thanks," Jurian muttered.

"Did you say Orosius?" someone asked just behind them.

Jurian turned and found a dock worker standing there, his arms laden with cargo.

"That's right. Do you know him?"

"That's him over there," the man said, nodding at a weathered ship a little further down the dock. "Blue tunic. Curly hair. Do you see?"

"I see him," Jurian said. "Thanks."

The man nodded and hurried away, and Jurian led the others toward the pilot. He was a little broader than his height warranted, and he watched them approaching with a closed expression in his dark eyes that verged on suspicion.

"You're Orosius?" Jurian asked.

"That's me," he said. "How do you know my name?"

Jurian hesitated, trying to recall Nikolaos' instructions.

Before he could remember, Mari smiled cheerfully and said, "We're looking for a fisherman."

One of the man's thick eyebrows crept upwards. "Oh?"

"We were told you could help us," Jurian said.

"Nikolaos, eh?" Orosius said with a faint grin. "So I might be able to help you. Depends on what you need."

"Passage to Portus. Soon, if possible."

"How does that rascal know?" Orosius muttered. "Every single time, he knows just where I'm going to be and where I'm headed. Very well. I'm loading up the cargo as we speak. Should be set to sail in a few more hours."

"We can pay for our passage," Jurian said. He jerked his head at Menas. "I know he's a bit heavy."

"The River Walker, aren't you? Heard about you."

Menas colored at that, but he only scowled and nodded.

"I'll have to leave some cargo. Pay me for its value, and we've got a deal."

Menas went with him to calculate the cost of the merchandise Orosius would lose, leaving Jurian and Mari on the dock, watching the workers drag stores of spice and olives into the ship's massive hold. Jurian muttered a prayer of thanksgiving for the lack of fish, and Mari laughed under her breath.

"One more voyage, and then we'll be in Rome," Jurian said. "I'm not sure what to think about that."

Mari hesitated, shifting the strap of the bag she had slung over her back. "What's going to happen to me there, Jurian? Are you going to leave me when you go to join the Legion?"

"That's a long way off," Jurian said. "We'll find our relatives and see what they can do for us." He put his arm around her shoulders, trying to give her comfort when he only felt uncertainty. "Don't worry. Just take it a step at a time. And listen, Mari. You are always most important to me, all right? More than the Legion, more than anything. I'll take care of you. Always."

She gave him her best smile and nodded. "Will you help me find the bones of the rock?"

Jurian let out his breath, because he hadn't even considered asking Nikolaos about those enigmatic words.

"We'll find them, whatever they are," he said. "Someone in Rome must be able to help."

Menas returned to usher them on board the ship, and no sooner had they settled their gear in the cabin's narrow berths than Jurian heard Orosius shouting to his men. The boat rocked beneath them. Menas groused and rolled himself up in his cloak, waving Jurian away when he poked his head into the giant's berth to check on him.

"Wake me up when we get to Portus," he muttered. "If I'm still alive."

"Menas, I need to talk to you," Jurian said, ignoring his request and slipping into the berth. "I'm worried about Mari."

That got Menas' attention. The giant rolled over, but he couldn't sit up without banging his head, so he just tucked a massive arm behind his neck and frowned up at Jurian.

"What's wrong with her? She seems healthy and fine."

"She's fine, of course," Jurian said, exasperated. "It's not that. But what happened in Cenchreae…"

"Tending to a wounded man?"

Jurian rubbed his forehead. "You know that's not what I mean. A man got killed for making the *signum,* and what did she do? The exact same thing, right in the middle of the market where everyone could see. You've got to talk to her. She won't listen to me, I know, but she might listen to you."

"What do you want me to tell her?" Menas asked, his voice dropping impossibly low.

"She just doesn't think. She doesn't seem to realize the danger she's putting herself—all of us—in."

Menas eyed him steadily. "Should she hide her faith out of fear? Is that what we've come to?"

Jurian groaned and leaned his head against the wall. "Just promise me that when we get to Rome you'll keep an eye on her. Make sure she doesn't attract too much attention."

Menas shifted onto his back and closed his eyes. "Right," he rumbled. "When we get to Rome."

28

THE MEDITERRANEAN SEA

SABRA HAD THOUGHT SHE WAS comfortable with being set apart, being the object of awe and even suspicion. But after five hours on the merchant vessel, she was beginning to wish she would never have to see another person in her life. The sailors watched her openly, some curious, some blatantly hostile, others with an interest that turned her stomach cold. She wanted to stay close to Hanno, but apparently part of his bargain with the pilot was that he had to help with the sailing. He stood at one of the oars now with another sailor, a young Egyptian with enough muscles to make Hanno look like a weakling.

Overhead, lightning ripped the clouds, and at every moment the gusting wind threatened to drive them away from sight of land. When the rain started sheeting down, though, it didn't matter how close they were to the coast; Sabra could barely see to the other side of the ship.

"What're you doing, girl?" someone shouted, staggering on the deck in front of her.

She pushed her blanket away from her eyes and found the pilot staring at her as if she were mad.

"Get below deck! I can't be worrying about you flying overboard. Come on!"

He stretched his hand out to her. She took it hesitantly, and he jerked her roughly to her feet, spinning her around and marching her—or, stumbling along with her—toward the steps that led down to the ship's cabin. He shoved her toward one of the narrow berths and she almost fell through the oiled flax curtain it had in place of a door.

"Stay in there until the storm passes!" he said, and disappeared into the rain.

The berth had two narrow slots built into the wall for sleeping on, and Sabra climbed up onto the highest ledge to escape the water sloshing at her feet. Shaking out her sopping blanket as best she could, she wrapped herself up in it and tried to lay still, tried to quiet her shivering by breathing slowly and deeply. The boat rocked and pitched, the timbers groaning under the strain. She listened to the crash of waves against the hull and bit her lip to keep the terror at bay.

The curtain batted back and Sabra lifted her head, praying that Hanno had come to weather the storm with her. He hadn't. In the doorway stood one of the other sailors, his dark hair plastered to his forehead and a malicious sneer plastered to his face.

"Trying to get us to take you home, witch?"

Sabra stared at him. In the confines of the bunk, she could hear nothing as clearly as the pounding of her heart.

"Bad luck, sailing with a woman. Worse luck, sailing with a priestess with a taste for blood. Is that true?" He staggered into the berth, bracing his arm on the wall for support as the ship rolled again. "I should've thought you'd be old and ugly. Don't seem half right, you looking like fair Diana herself."

Sabra's gaze darted frantically around the berth. The space was so narrow, there had barely been enough room for her to stand, and this man was just as large as Hanno. His hand played over the hilt of a short dagger.

"Call off the storm," he said. "Or if you won't, I'll bleed you myself to placate the gods."

Sabra thought fast. If he wanted her blood, and nothing else, then maybe she could use his fear.

"I am the priestess of the old god," she whispered. "If you

harm me, this ship will sink."

The man's hand lashed out, twisting in her hair and dragging her forward until she fell, screaming in pain, onto the floor. The knife flashed in his hand, the tip so close to her neck that one strong wave could send the blade home.

"Pray, priestess," the sailor growled, bending so close to her that she felt his hot breath on her ear. "Pray to save your life. Or do you think your eunuch will come and rescue you?"

"You're a fool if you think the will of the god means less to me than my life," she hissed. "Kill me if you want, and a curse on your blood if you do. I don't need saving."

The man didn't back down. Apparently he wasn't gullible enough to believe he would actually be cursed for killing her.

You said the god's will means more than your life, the voice in her mind whispered. *Are you really unwilling to die for him?*

If I die now, I won't be dying for the god. I'll be dying for this man's superstition.

She eyed the blade of the knife, calculating. Touching steel was forbidden to her, but that didn't mean she couldn't touch the hand that wielded it. Before she could give herself time to think, her hand shot up and batted the man's hand away, and she drove her shoulder into his chest as she lunged for the door. The man stumbled and struck his head on the bunk, and dropped like a stone.

Sabra glanced over her shoulder but she couldn't see the knife any more, only a thin twist of red in the sloshing water. She ran a few steps away, then, muttering under her breath, she returned to the berth and rolled the man onto his back. His forehead bled freely from where he'd hit the wooden slab of the bunk, but the knife had only gashed his arm lightly before spinning off under the lower bed.

Relief washed through her, and she stumbled into the tiny kitchen to wait for the storm to pass. The waves had barely settled to a tenuous calm when she heard footsteps in the cabin, and then Hanno burst into the kitchen.

"Mistress!" he cried, dropping to his knees in front of her.

"Are you all right? There's...there's a man—"

"I know," she said, the words a whisper to keep from breaking, and she told him everything that had happened.

His face darkened, his jaw clenching with stony anger, but when she finished he gave her a strained smile. "I always knew you could take care of yourself," he murmured. "I'll tell the pilot that one of his sailors abandoned his post during a tempest."

Sabra didn't watch the man get flogged for his actions, but she found no place on the ship where she could escape the sound of his screams. She was only grateful to Hanno, who sometimes seemed to know her better than she did. He'd told the pilot just what he said he would, with no mention of how the sailor had threatened her. The man's punishment wasn't for risking *her* life, but the whole ship. And, Sabra decided, it was better that way.

After six days of rough sailing they arrived at the harbor of the great city of Carthage. They'd had no further trouble from the sailors; the man who had threatened Sabra had been kept chained to one of the massive oars, since the crew needed every available hand. If he muttered against Sabra to the other sailors, no one showed it. Still, Sabra could barely wait to reach land and get off the ship. She never would have believed that being on the open sea could feel quite so claustrophobic.

Hanno watched her with relentless attention as they left the ship with the rest of the crew, but Sabra had finally reconciled herself to the voyage and didn't even threaten to leave his side. If she had to go to Rome, then perhaps she could do something for her city there, even if she didn't really believe any of the four rulers could manage their way out of a grain sack. Diocletian could, perhaps, but as far as she knew, he was in Antioch, on the other side of the Empire. But even if the great Roman war machine proved incapable of helping them to defeat a god, perhaps they could help her struggling city. Prevent riots, restore order, boost their trade. Anything would be better than nothing.

She and Hanno wandered the streets of the city closest to the harbor while their surly shipmaster made his trades and adjusted his cargo. Everywhere they went they got curious glances from the traders and sailors who filled the streets around the docks, but Sabra felt a sinister edge to their curiosity. It felt nothing like the subdued reverence the people of Cyrene showed her, but a darker sort of mistrust. She knew they must have looked strange—the tall, muscular slave and the thin, dark-robed girl, neither of whom seemed to belong in the city. They might have even looked like runaways, and Sabra watched one of the merchants murmuring to a Legion centurion with a sudden spike of fear.

"Hanno," she whispered. "We're not going to make it to Rome like this. I wish I had the rest of my priestess raiment. At least then these people wouldn't look at me like I'm a beggar."

"Your father sent some clothes with you," Hanno said. "But they don't belong to your office."

"What do you mean? What kind of clothes?"

Hanno shrugged. "I think they belonged to your mother."

Sabra's mouth dropped open. "Oh. No, I'm not going to wear that. I can't."

"Do you think if a Legionary stopped us, he would believe that you're actually a priestess? You don't look anything like those Roman Vestals."

"Do you think I don't know that?" she hissed. "What am I supposed to do? Look, if we stay out here much longer, I won't have a choice but to try to explain."

He sighed. "We should go back to the ship, I guess."

She pursed her lips, but she knew he was right. No one would ever believe her claims of office; they would have no reason to. She didn't even have any way of proving that she was the daughter of the Cyrenean governor. Hanno's neck ring had been engraved with the initial letters of her father's name, but that meant little enough this far away from Libya.

In the end she gave up and they headed back to the ship. They stayed up on the deck, watching the crew trade fish and ivory for *amphorae* of wheat and salt. Most of the sailors ignored them, all but one who glanced at them from time to time. He was one of the younger crewmen, with thick, knotted dark hair that grazed his broad shoulders, and a smile too wide and bright for the hard work he was doing. Sabra stiffened, fearing a repeat of her earlier run-in with a sailor, but at least this one didn't seem hostile. Not from this distance, anyway.

"Maybe I should pretend that I can't speak," she whispered.

Hanno stared at her, bewildered. "Eh…why?"

"I'm not allowed to speak to men," she said blandly. "Everyone in Cyrene knew that, but how can I explain that here?"

"I'll tell them," Hanno said, shrugging smoothly.

She bit her lip. "But it's no use anyway. I'm going to have to speak to someone eventually. After all, we're going to Rome." She smiled ruefully at him. "I don't know how many people there will speak Punic."

His face fell. Obviously he hadn't considered that.

Sabra sighed and leaned over the rail, watching the foamy waves slapping the hull. The sun shone down full on them through a heady midday haze, warming away the bone-chill of a week's winter travel at sea. But even the cold had been good for her. In the time she'd spent aboard the ship, her skin had finally lost some of its death-like pallor, warming to a faint burnished tan. She still looked pale in comparison to Hanno, but at least she didn't feel quite so much like a walking corpse. In fashionable clothes she might almost pass for a normal person.

But could she ever speak as freely as one? Her whole life she'd been taught to be silent, to speak only as the god instructed her except when talking to slaves. She'd probably abused that privilege by keeping a friend like Hanno—she wasn't sure the old priestess would have approved of the long conversations they'd had over the years. But the priestess had never been overly specific on that point, and Sabra had never questioned her. Sometimes it was better not to ask.

She brushed the long sleeves of her robe up over her elbows, soaking the sun into her skin. The sea wind gave a chill undertone to the sun's warmth as it scattered her long hair across her face. She brushed it back. Then, slowly and with faltering fingers, she tied the wind-tangled strands into a knot at the nape of her neck. Hanno watched her quietly.

"I'm not the voice of the god anymore, not here," Sabra said. "They left his worship long ago here in Carthage, and in Rome I don't know if they've even heard of him. If I'm going to get help for Cyrene, I can only be the voice of the governor."

He smiled slowly. "They'd be fools not to listen to you."

Sabra laughed.

"Should I bring you those new clothes?"

"Not yet. We've still got another five days at sea. I wouldn't want to ruin them. Bring them to me when we get to Portus."

He nodded and settled against a heap of rope, pulling the hood of his cloak down over his eyes. "If you don't need me for anything right now…"

"Enjoy it," she said, and crossed over to the bulwark that overlooked the city.

The storm cloud of a ship's pilot stood on the stone dock, shouting orders to the slaves and sailors handling his cargo. Most of the goods they'd brought from Apollonia had been pulled off, and only a few more *amphorae* of wheat waited to be loaded into the ship's hold. Sabra was so caught up in watching the procedures on the dock that she didn't hear anyone come up beside her until she heard a voice in her ear.

"Some of the men say you offer human sacrifices."

She whipped around, finding herself face to face with the dark-haired sailor. His brilliant smile was gone, but he spoke openly, casually, as if he'd asked her if she preferred the summer to winter. A cold rush of dread washed over her. Her instincts begged her to deny it—the words were horrific, barbaric…and true. Nausea followed the dread, and she jerked her gaze away.

And then, to her shock, she heard herself answering.

"Only presumptuous young men who bother me when I want to be left alone."

The sailor laughed, loudly. Sabra noticed Hanno shifting his hood back to look at them, but she held her hand subtly by her side. He stayed put, eyes closed but still listening. It didn't bother her if it gave him a purpose; he had to be restless after days cooped up on the ship with nothing to do.

"Are you a priestess then?" the sailor asked.

She tipped her head back to study him, lips pursed.

"All right, don't answer that," he said. "My name is Gavros."

"Sabra," she said, glancing at his offered hand and refusing to accept it.

He lowered his hand and took a step back. "A pleasure," he said. "I should get back to the cargo."

She turned without replying and went back to studying the docks, waiting until she could no longer hear the sound of his bare feet slapping the wooden deck before letting out her breath.

"You could be a little more polite," Hanno muttered.

She shifted around to stare down at him, hands on her hips. "That was the first man besides my father I have spoken to in my own name since…ever. I think I handled it remarkably well."

He smirked at her and closed his eyes again.

"If I'm going to go prancing around like some governor's daughter, you need to be more respectful," she said, nudging him with her foot. "What will people say?"

29

THE IONIAN SEA

OROSIUS MADE GOOD TIME BRINGING the merchant vessel south across the wide expanse of the Ionian Sea, but the waters were rough under a near constant churn of storms. Three days out from Corinth, Menas finally surfaced from the cabin, wrapping a spare sail over his head to keep the weather at bay. Jurian watched the giant stagger across the deck, wincing every time the boat pitched and almost sent him stumbling into the rail.

Menas stared blearily through the sheeting rain until he caught sight of Jurian. His face turned several shades whiter.

"Jurian! What are you doing?"

Jurian shrugged, keeping half an eye on the experienced movements of the sailor standing beside him. "Plying the oar," he called. He grinned. "At least I'm trying to be useful."

"I was being useful too," Menas said with a scowl, finally making it to the rail that divided the deck from the crinolines where Jurian balanced, barefoot, on the wet planks. "I was staying out of everyone's way."

"Where's Mari?"

Menas waved back toward the stairs of the deck. "She's in the cabin. Praying, I think."

Jurian squinted at the sky. "The wind's calming a bit," he said, then shouted, "Alypius!"

One of the sailors down in the hold glanced up and saw Jurian's wave, and came to take his place. Jurian climbed over the bulwark and headed down to the cabin to get warm by the cooking fire. Menas followed gratefully.

"Do you want me to get Mari?" he asked, stooping in the narrow corridor.

"No, she's fine where she is. Menas, I've been talking to the sailors. One of them has a brother in the Legion. Apparently my good friend Casca is on his way to Rome. He's...always been good at getting himself noticed."

Menas ducked through the low door and sat on the floor—the only space large enough to fit him. "I've been trying to tell you, boy. We should just forget about going to Rome."

Jurian groaned and dragged a hand through his hair. "Not this again," he muttered. "Why are you so set against Rome?"

Menas leaned back against the wall, thrumming his fingers on his knees. For a while he didn't say anything at all, but measured Jurian in enigmatic silence.

"Let's just say I don't have many friends in Rome," he said. "Or rather, I have all too many enemies. And I'm not exactly the best at...blending in."

"Casca isn't going to stop me," Jurian said, colder than he meant, "and neither are you. What else am I supposed to do with Mari? Our only family worth speaking of is in Rome. If I'm going to join the Legion, I can't take her with me."

"Why are you so set on the Legion?"

Jurian glanced away. As long as he could remember, he'd promised himself that he would follow his father's footsteps. At first it had been a matter of expectation—sons of Legionaries became Legionaries, and that was just the way the world worked. But somewhere along the way the Legion had come to represent everything noble and courageous that he knew. Then, with his father's death, it had become a matter of honor. A matter of proving to the world that the name Lucius Aurelius was worth something after all.

"I don't know," he said. "But I don't know what else to do."

I just want to defend my family, he thought, but the words wouldn't come out. *And she's all that's left.*

"Keep traveling," Menas said. "Go to Alexandria, or Antioch. You're a man of action—I've seen that from the first day I met you. I know you'd never settle down to live like Nikolaos. You seem to enjoy the sea. Sail to Britannia!"

Jurian knew Menas was exaggerating, but he bent his head and said, "I mean to go to Britannia. Have I ever told you about the dream I keep having?"

Menas arched a brow. "No…"

"I'm in Britannia. I don't know how I know it. Maybe it's the trees. The trees are the tallest I've ever seen, taller than I could even imagine. And there's a man. He looks old, but…not. Like he's lived a thousand years in the span of forty. He's not dressed like a Roman, but he speaks perfect Latin. He is speaking to me, but I can never remember what he said when I wake up."

Menas waited a few moments after Jurian fell silent, then asked, "That's it?"

Jurian shot him a peeved look. "It feels a lot more intense when I'm dreaming it," he said sourly.

"Eh…" Menas said, shaking his head. "So you dream about trees and that's enough to make you take a four-month voyage?" He shrugged. "Well, to each his own…"

"I could see myself, too," Jurian said, voice dropping to a near whisper. "In the pool of water."

"What pool?"

"Just a pool, I don't know. It's a dream. It all bleeds together. But I can see myself, and I'm wearing Legion armor."

Menas slapped a hand on his thigh. "Well, that settles it then. I suppose you have no choice."

"Menas!" Jurian cried. "Why are you being so difficult?"

"There's a darkness in Rome."

"Oddly prophetic for a man who discounts dreams."

"I don't discount them," Menas growled. "And I mean what I say. Nikolaos said as much. Rome is a bad place to be."

"But I made a promise to Mari, to help her find the bones of the rock."

Menas jerked back, eyes wide. "The bones of the rock? What gave you that idea?"

"Our mother. She kept saying it, and led us to believe we'd find out what it meant in Rome. We made a promise."

Menas chuckled and rubbed his beard. "That is a worthy pilgrimage, I'll grant you that."

"You know what it means?"

"You don't?" Menas asked.

Jurian shook his head, biting his cheek in frustration.

"You speak Greek. Was she saying *the rock* precisely?"

"No," Jurian said. "It was an odd form."

"*Petros*, correct?"

"How did you—"

"*Petros*. It's a name. *The bones of Petros*, or, in the Roman way, Petrus." Menas eyed him steadily. "You're looking for a tomb."

AFTER A FEW days of sailing up the Italian coast, Jurian was one of the first on deck to spot a gleaming octagonal port jutting out into the Tyrrhenian Sea. Just south of it lay the ruins of the old port of Ostia, long-abandoned after the mouth of the Tiber had silted up. Portus had taken its place, and Jurian could only stare in awe as they sailed closer. A massive lighthouse towered over the harbor, flanked by the arms of the port that stretched out like a breakwater, creating a deep mouth of calm waters where the merchant ships and navy triremes could dock.

Orosius' oarsmen steered expertly between the lighthouse and the northern mole, bringing the ship into the wide sweep of the Port of Claudius where dozens of vessels dotted the water. Mari leaned over the bulwark beside Jurian, wide-eyed with amazement, and even Menas emerged from the ship's cabin to see the view. Buildings crowded up to the mooring points—warehouses, temples, harbor offices, even an amphitheater and a complex of Roman baths. Brightly painted statues lined the walkways, and there were people everywhere.

Orosius didn't bring the ship in to dock, but directed it past a smaller lighthouse and into a newer interior harbor he called Trajan's Port. There the crew brought the ship to moor and harbor slaves rushed to raise a gangplank. Orosius let the dock official come aboard to take stock of the ship's cargo, and, while the man was busy, Orosius climbed up to the deck to his guests.

"If you make your way past the warehouses, you'll come out on the canal that leads to the Tiber. That's where the river barges wait for cargo. It shouldn't be hard to get passage on one heading up to Rome."

"Thanks," Jurian said. "We've got a contact to look for."

"Who?"

"A man called Dionysius?"

Orosius laughed, hard, slapping his palm on his thigh. "Dionysius the Celt? Hah! That man is a piece of work. You'll like him." He cast an amused glance over the three of them. "He's odd like you."

"We're not odd!" Mari cried.

Orosius winked at her, then said, "He's a good man. Tell him I've got some oil for him. I'll be in Portus a few days. If he doesn't mind, I've a wish to share wheat and wine with him, if you know what I mean."

Jurian frowned but nodded. Orosius clasped his hand briefly and hurried away. Once Jurian, Mari and Menas had gathered their belongings, they threaded a path through the chaos of slaves and sailors down to the paved walkway. Just inland from the harbor they stopped for a bite to eat at a market stall, then headed for the channel. After the brightness of the sea and the sun-soaked stones of the outer harbor, the channel seemed dim and cold, sheltered between tall buildings and high banks. As Orosius had predicted, several broad river barges floated gently beside the walkway, waiting as slaves loaded them down with cargo.

Mari snatched Jurian's arm. "I'd wager anything that's Dionysius," she whispered, and pointed discreetly to their left.

Jurian surveyed the knot of people and immediately spotted the man Mari had seen. He grinned. The man was uncommonly pale and tall—thin enough that he would have looked gangly if he hadn't carried himself with quite so much elegance. He didn't wear a toga or white tunic, or even the ordinary dark workman's tunic. His was a strange rusty hue, short as a Legionary's tunic and revealing a pair of *braccae* in the plaid pattern of the Celts. His sandals laced up almost to the hem of the pants, and he wore a tall, rounded hat in the Persian style. For all his strange confusion of fashion, he walked with confident swagger, and everyone around him made room for him.

"He's wearing *pants,*" Mari whispered behind her hand, stifling a laugh. "It's barely even cold here!"

"He's wearing a hat," Jurian said, "and I don't think he's a Persian *or* a slave."

Menas scowled. "*That's* the merchant Nikolaos told us about? He looks like a peacock."

"Only one way to find out," Jurian said, and headed toward the man. He waited until the merchant had finished speaking to one of the slaves, then cleared his throat and said, "Are you Dionysius?"

The man spun around, hands flashing up in surprise. "Of course I am!" he said, his voice richer and deeper than Jurian expected. He stared at Jurian's hair. "And…who are you?"

"My name is Jurian."

A brief disappointment flashed over Dionysius' face, then his brows lifted in an elegant arch, almost distasteful. "Oh. Germanic boy?"

"No. My father was Greek."

"Oh. That's odd then. Err, fine. That's fine."

"Jurian is what most people call me, but…my Roman name is Georgius."

If possible, the man's pale face turned even whiter. "Georgius?" he whispered.

Jurian's hand brushed the hilt of his *seax*. Had this man heard about him? Had Casca already gotten to Rome and started searching for him? But if Nikolaos trusted him…

Dionysius laughed suddenly—the sound a little too forced. "What can Dionysius do for you? In the market for wine? I've got the finest vintage from Lutetia." He eyed Jurian closely. "Lutetia? Parisii? No…? Still don't recognize it?"

Jurian shook his head, bemused.

"Veh," Dionysius sighed, his voice dropping as if he were talking to himself. "That's the sort of day it is. No one even knows where I'm from, let alone what vintage I've got. Remarkable people even know what *wine* is around here…"

"You're from Gaul?" Jurian asked.

Dionysius heaved another great sigh and waved a hand. "Eventually."

"We were directed to you by a man in Myra, named Nikolaos. He said you could get us up the river."

"Nikolaos! How did he even know I was going to be in Rome? It's not my usual time to be here, though the weather is quite nice compared to Gaul…" His voice trailed off and he shivered. "Don't answer that, though. I know well enough. He's told you about his messengers, I'm sure? No? Oh well, come on. You caught me just in time. We're setting off at once."

"Just a moment," Jurian said. "I need to get my sister and my friend."

Dionysius waved his hand again and turned away, calling, "Cyricius!" before hurrying down the walkway.

Jurian watched him go in baffled silence. Finally he shook his head and went back to Mari and Menas, only to find Mari nearly in tears.

"What's wrong? Did something happen?"

Mari bit her lip, and Menas sighed and said, "I'm not going to Rome with you, Jurian. It's too risky. I don't want to put you in danger, all right?"

"What will we do without you?" Mari asked. "You're part of our family now!"

He laid a massive hand on her dark hair, smiling down at her. "You gladden my heart, girl," he said. "But my mind's made up. I'll try to lay low here at the harbor. Perhaps if I spot that Casca I'll put a hitch in his journey."

"Are you going to go back to Anatolia?" Jurian asked. His

gaze drifted unconsciously toward the pole of Menas' *sarcina*.

You'll know when to give it to him, Nikolaos had told Menas. But Menas had a death grip on the wood. Apparently nothing was prompting the giant to give up the staff now.

"Saints, no. Not just yet. I need to get my strength back," Menas said, patting his stomach. "And besides, you'll be back soon. I can make myself useful in the harbor until then. Just come and find me when you're ready to go..."

"Menas," Jurian interrupted. His own throat felt tight, but he swallowed and forced through it. "The next time I leave, who knows where I'll be going? I could be going anywhere. I don't even know if I'll be leaving by sea. If you won't come with us, then I can't ask you to stay here where you're in danger of being recognized. You should go back to Anatolia."

Menas folded his arms. "You'll be back. And I'll be here."

Mari embraced him, not even trying to hide her tears. "But Menas, when will *I* see you again? What if I never do?"

"Don't say that," the giant rumbled. "You never know." He bent down and murmured, "Maybe you can convince Jurian not to join the Legion, and you both can come back and we can travel the world together. Maybe we can go to Britannia. Eh? How does that sound?" She nodded against his chest and he kissed her on top of the head. "Go on now. I think that peacock is back looking for you."

Jurian bit his lip, staring up toward the broad sweep of the Tiber. Some deep worry festered in the back of his mind, fed by the ominous whispers of so many people along their way.

"Mari," he said finally. "Why don't you stay here, too? I could go and scout out the situation in the city, and then come back and get you when I know where we need to go."

She shook her head violently. "No. I'm going with you."

Jurian glanced over his shoulder. Dionysius and another man, shorter and more subdued, were standing at the edge of the barge waiting for them. He sighed and nodded.

"Fine. Let's just go."

"Goodbye, Menas," Mari whispered. "God protect you."

Jurian clasped Menas' arm without a word, with only a long, hard look in the eye. Then he turned away, and took Mari by the shoulders and guided her toward the barge.

THE VOYAGE UP the Tiber took only a few hours. Dionysius regaled them with tales of his travels, while the merchant he worked with, Cyricius, directed the driver of the mule team to guide the barge up the river. Mari and Jurian sat on sacks of grain near the stern of the barge, watching the land sweep by in frost-covered waves.

"What are your plans once you reach Rome?" Dionysius asked after they'd ridden some time in silence.

"I'm not entirely sure," Jurian said. "We're looking for our father's brother. His name is Caius Aurelius Brocchus. Do you know him by any chance?"

Dionysius scrubbed his fingers against the tuft of his blond beard. "Brocchus? Not sure. Is he…that is, I assume if Nikolaos sent you, that you're…"

"Christians?" Mari whispered. Jurian bit his tongue as she added, "Yes."

Relief flashed over Dionysius' face. "I thought so. I took one look at you and thought, *Ah, fellow travelers*. Well, not one look. I suppose it was the third or fourth. But eventually I did look at you and think, *Ah, fellow travelers*."

Mari stifled a laugh.

"And the answer to the question I think you were going to ask is no. Brocchus and his family aren't…*fellow travelers,* as far as I know," Jurian said.

"Ah, then no, I probably don't know them. I don't spend much time in Rome. Just a few days here and there when I've got special deliveries to make and time to visit old friends."

"By the way," Jurian said. "The ship's pilot who brought us from Corinth…"

"Orosius?"

"Yes. He said he's got some oil for you. And that he wants to meet you for wheat and wine."

"I may be able to arrange that," Dionysius said, a faint smile on his lips. "And you? Will you be back in Portus at the end of the week?"

"I doubt it."

"Ah well." Dionysius shrugged smoothly. "I suppose you'll have others to offer thanksgiving with you, being in Rome. Just be careful. There are eyes and ears everywhere."

Jurian exchanged a glance with Mari, who seemed to know exactly what Dionysius was talking about.

"Well, since you don't know where your relations are, I've got an idea where you can stay. There's a good family that lives at the outskirts of the city. Justinus is a stone cutter. They don't live in the city flats, but have a small *domus* where I'm sure they'll be happy to let you stay while you get your bearings."

"Thank you," Jurian murmured.

After a moment he noticed Dionysius staring at his hair again. As flamboyant as the man was, Jurian wondered briefly if he were jealous of its startling redness.

"What?" he asked finally. "You keep looking at my hair."

Dionysius shifted his gaze to Jurian's face, staring at him blankly. "Hmm...?" He gave a quick shake of his head, as if to snap himself out of some thought. "Oh. No...it's just a...remarkable color, that. Like fire, one might say?"

"So I've been told," Jurian muttered.

"You'll want to see the *pappas* while you're here, I assume?"

Mari's mouth dropped open.

"I suppose so," Jurian said, curious. "Is it hard to see him?"

"Very," the merchant said. "So much intrigue and suspicion. He's in hiding these days, the new *Petrus* where the bones of the first *Petrus* were once hid."

"What did you say?" Jurian gasped.

Dionysius winked and started to turn away, but Jurian was on his feet in a flash, grabbing the man's shoulder.

"Explain what you meant, just now."

"Steady there," Dionysius said, gently extracting himself from Jurian's grip. "I'll show you. In due time, *frater*, in due time."

"I'd really like to know now."

Dionysius' gaze jerked toward the two other crew members on the barge and shook his head. "There's a time and a place. This is neither."

He gave Jurian a piercing look, then sauntered toward the prow to have a word with Cyricius. Jurian watched him pointing and gesticulating at the east bank. Cyricius nodded and shouted something to the mule team driver. In a few moments, the mules stopped and the barge butted up against the bank.

"Come on!" Dionysius called. "Cyricius will take the barge the rest of the way. I'll take you to see Justinus."

He hopped lightly from the barge to the bank, holding the boat steady with his foot as Jurian and Mari stepped across. They climbed the bank and came into a clean, quiet district, far enough away from the city center to be free of the crowds and noise. Dionysius led them straight to a small stone house, unremarkable except for the fish carved low on the building's front wall. They waited at the door, Jurian half-expecting to see a slave come and let them in, but instead they were greeted by an elegant woman who had to be the matron of the household.

"Dionysius!" she cried. "We weren't expecting you. Justinus is at the basilica. Some legal matter, I don't know."

Dionysius smiled and ushered Jurian and Mari forward. "That's no matter. I'm not here on my own business. I have a favor to ask."

"You don't need to ask," the woman said briskly, and smiled warmly at them.

Jurian noticed Mari fidgeting with the fabric of her tunic, a faint blush coloring her cheeks. For having been at sea for over a week, he thought they both looked remarkably well, but Mari was probably more sensitive to that sort of thing than him.

"*Matrona* Aemelia, these are my good friends, Jurian and…"

"Mari," she whispered.

"Jurian and Mari. Good friends, for the last five hours anyway. They've come looking for family, but need a place to stay for the present. Would it be too much to ask if they could stay with you until they find their relatives?"

"Of course not!" the woman cried, reaching out warm hands to Mari. "Poor things. Have you really had to spend five hours with Dionysius?"

Dionysius gave them an elegant bow in the eastern manner, and Mari laughed.

"He knows I mean no harm by him," Aemelia said in low tones to Jurian. "He's cherished by all of us, as much as his own flock in Lutetia."

"Flock?" Jurian asked, regarding Dionysius with surprise.

Dionysius only smiled and took a step back. "I'll leave you in her care, then. If you need any more from me, I'll be back and forth between Rome and Portus all this week. Just come find me at the *emporium*."

30

ROMA, ITALIA

THE REST OF SABRA'S JOURNEY to Rome passed without incident, the surly pilot proving his skill as he navigated around the worst of the winter squalls. When the ship swept into the sprawling harbor at Portus, Hanno took Sabra down into the ship's cabin where he had stowed a chest of their belongings.

She gasped as she pulled out the garments her father had sent with her. Brightly colored silks fluttered in her hands—a delicately striped yellow tunic and an embroidered wrap of emerald green shot with gold and russet. There were beaded sandals and an ornate headdress of brightly colored glass beads and copper disks, a heavy golden choker and more bracelets than she had ever seen in one place.

"You have got to be joking," she said, holding the choker out to Hanno. "He expected me to wear all this?"

"Your mother wore this when she was offered to your father as a bride. She was Roman, but she honored his heritage in wearing this." He shrugged. "Most people in Libya just dress in the Roman fashion, so it meant a great deal when she had this made."

Sabra ran her fingers over the intricate embroidery on the veil. "It is beautiful. But if I stood out before in this old priestess robe, I'm going to stand out even more in this."

Hanno grinned. "I believe that was the idea, wasn't it?"

She glared at him and took the whole pile of cloth into the narrow berth she had been provided for the voyage. Her old robe had gotten so weathered from salt spray and rain that it almost disintegrated as she took it off. With uncertain fingers she pulled on the delicate tunic and wrapped the long embroidered cloth around her waist, belting it and leaving it alone as she did her best to situate the intricate headdress over her hair without the help of any sort of mirror. When she was satisfied it wouldn't fall off, she added the choker and bracelets, then drew the long end of the embroidered wrap over her head like a veil.

Feeling self-conscious and a little foolish, she pushed back the curtain and stepped into the cabin where Hanno waited for her. She wasn't quite sure what reaction to expect from him. A laugh, maybe, or an approving smile. She didn't expect him to drop to his knees and touch his forehead to the floor.

"Hanno," she hissed. "What are you doing?"

He stood up, grinning, and turned without a word to leave the cabin. She followed, hesitant, and found him waiting for her at the bottom of the ship's ramp. It was just after sunrise but a sizable crowd milled about the docks—traders and merchants and money traders—and she felt a hundred pairs of strangers' eyes fix on her as she stopped at the top of the ramp.

"May I present you," Hanno said, his melodic voice carrying his broken Latin easily over the crowd, "the princess of Libya."

Sabra felt the blood drain from her face. Only her long schooling in silence kept her expression neutral, while inside she was screaming at Hanno.

Princess of Libya? Why? What are these people going to think of me?

The crowd murmured quietly, some drawing back respectfully, others pushing forward to get a better look at her. That wasn't so different from being in Cyrene in her priestess regalia, so she acted the same as she did there—she walked slowly down the ramp, chin up, eyes down, until she thought that keeping her gaze lowered might make her look weak or vulnerable. She glanced up then, fixing her attention on some point at the end of the dock, refusing to meet the eyes of any of the ragged sailors or merchants around her. The wind blew in hard off the sea, fluttering the layers of her silk robes. At least the gaudy costume involved enough fabric to keep the wind's bite from reaching her.

Hanno led her toward the covered canal that cut a channel to the sweeping Tiber, where barges waited to be loaded with merchandise bound for Rome. Slaves with handcarts transferred cargo from the merchant vessels after they'd been checked and measured by the dock officials. The activity died down as she approached, then picked up again as she passed, and she felt her cheeks burning with embarrassment.

"I could kill you for this," she muttered. "Libyan *princess?*"

"Sorry," he said, and didn't sound the least bit sincere. "My Latin is not very good."

"Non-existent," she retorted.

"Well, if these people think you're a princess, so much the better. It'll make my job easier."

"And mine that much harder."

"I have confidence in you," Hanno said with a smirk.

Sabra resisted the urge to punch his arm. They approached a pilot whose barge looked a bit better kept than the others they'd seen, and Hanno, acting the part of princess's bodyguard with enviable flair, gave the man a cold look and folded his arms on his chest.

"The princess requires passage to Rome," he said, pitching his melodic voice as low as he could.

"The *princess* does, does she—" the pilot started, then he turned and saw Sabra standing behind him and his face turned several shades whiter. "Oh. Of course, *domina*. Just give me a moment to make some preparations, and we can take you at once."

Sabra said nothing, and the man bowed deeply and darted away. She watched with some amusement as he called a handful of slaves to set up a small stool and a silk shade near the stern of the boat, well back from the mast and its heavy tow ropes. Cargo was shifted to the edges of the ship to make a path for her, and moments later the pilot himself returned to take her hand and lead her to the seat.

Sabra walked stiffly beside him, all too conscious of her hand in his, and allowed him to hold the stool steady for her as she sat down. He gave her another profound bow and retreated to the prow of the ship, where he called to the driver of the mule team to move out. The barge glided steadily up the canal to the Tiber, where for a while the sea current helped guide the boat toward Rome.

Sabra watched the land drift past, staring in awe at the frost-coated fields that spread endlessly on either side of the river. She had never seen an expanse of land so wide and flat, or so empty. Every now and then they passed under the daunting shadow of a Roman watchtower, the rising sun glinting off the Legion guards' helmets and spearheads. Occasional vineyards spread in barren rows, speckling the fields as far as she could see. Sometimes she saw slaves burning back the vines, sending up plumes of pungent smoke that made her eyes water and her lungs burn.

By early afternoon the empty fields began to give way to low stone buildings, then all at once the city of Rome sprang up around them. The mules pulled the barge to the right of a tiny island covered with low buildings and a small, brightly colored temple, and, around another sweeping curve of the river, drew up to dock at a narrow pier. Here were buildings taller than any she had ever seen in Cyrene towering over her, shadowing the wide, paved streets that wound up the hill into the city. And so many people. She had never seen so many people in all her life.

"Gods," she whispered. "What am I doing here? What can I possibly do here?"

"The princess will wish to disembark here," the pilot said. "I have to take the barge back down to the *emporium*, but the warehouses are not what the princess will wish to see. We're close now to the forums. You should be able to find someone to take you up to the Palatine."

Hanno escorted her off the barge and paid the pilot handsomely for his services. The man blubbered his appreciation, turning Sabra's indifference to disgust. Once Hanno had finished, he called a young slave boy lingering nearby and sent him to fetch a litter. Sabra grimaced. As priestess she had been accustomed to walking wherever she needed to go. Being carried around by slaves felt embarrassing, but she knew she couldn't just stride through the streets of Rome in all her finery.

"What am I supposed to do now, Hanno? Ask to see the *Imperator*?" She laughed at the foolishness of it. "They'll turn me away at the gates."

Hanno scratched his head, looking remarkably discomposed. "We can go to the palace. I've got a letter from your father introducing you."

"Oh," she said, her brows shooting up in surprise. "Why didn't you tell me that before?"

He shrugged. "Didn't see a reason to."

"You're impossible," she said, but smiled.

31

Roma

Aemelia ushered Mari and Jurian into the house, leading them through the tiny atrium and into a modest peristyle flanked by sleeping quarters. Aemelia chattered comfortably as she walked, telling them about her own children who had grown and married, leaving her house empty and her days quieter than she liked. She showed them each to a bedchamber, then instructed a servant to heat water for them to bathe.

"This is Rome," Jurian said, curious. "Don't you use the baths? Aren't there half a dozen of them in the city?"

"Oh, mercy," Aemelia said. "Stay away from those places. Hotbeds of vice and everything filthy in the world."

Jurian frowned. All the Legionaries he'd ever heard praised the *thermae* in Rome. He'd never stepped foot in the baths in Satala, but everyone said they were nothing compared to the vast complexes in Rome. None of the soldiers had ever talked about vice or filth, but then, Jurian was starting to understand what Menas meant when he told Jurian that they saw the world differently than the Romans.

In the end, he contented himself with the hot water Aemelia provided them, washing the brine and rain and sweat from his body and scrubbing his tunic clean in the process. Aemelia had been kind enough to lend him one of her husband's clean tunics to use while his own was drying. He tugged it on and then, hesitating, he wrapped himself in the toga that Nikolaos had given him. He'd watched his father put his on more times than he could recall, but draping it properly was much more complicated than it looked. When he left the washroom, Aemelia smiled and came to help him adjust the folds.

For one brief moment, the woman's dark eyes and gentle smile reminded Jurian so much of his own mother that his throat burned, and he ducked his head to hide his grief.

When Aemelia stepped away from him he cleared his throat hoarsely and said, "Will you tell Mari to wait for me here? I'm just going to go up to the forums to see what I can see."

She nodded. "What do you know of your uncle, Jurian?"

"Not much. His name. He's of the equestrian rank, from military service. I think he's an administrator."

"Then the basilicas would be a good place to start. That's where most of the leading men like to spend their time."

Jurian hesitated. "I'm not sure I know how to get there."

"Oh," she laughed. "Go north. Follow the crowds. Most everyone will be heading to or coming from the forums."

"Thanks," he said, and slipped out of the house before he could start second-guessing himself.

As he followed the road toward the city center, he quickly realized what Aemelia had meant. The narrow streets were crowded with people, most of them pressing their way north. Every now and then a few slaves carrying a litter would push through, sending everyone scrambling to get out of the way. Eventually he came to a broader street lined with tall, elegant buildings that leaned over the road, trapping shadows and noise. The towering aqueducts he'd seen from the Tiber traced a snaking line over and between the buildings below. Vendors manned tiny carts on every spare scrap of road, selling cheap pottery and greasy food.

Just when Jurian decided he was thoroughly lost and completely claustrophobic, the road opened to reveal the largest building he had ever seen. It was oval like an amphitheater, but it couldn't possibly be *just* an amphitheater. It was too huge.

It dwarfed everything below it, even the massive statue of Sol standing poised in its shadow.

"That's the Flavian Amphitheater," someone said, noticing his stupor and stopping beside him. "They call it the Colosseum on account of that great statue, the Colossus of the Sun."

So that *is the Colosseum,* he thought. He'd heard Legionaries talk about it, but he'd always assumed they were exaggerating when they described it.

He let the crowds usher him down a narrower street, past a number of temples and finally passing under a triumphal arch to deposit him in the Roman forum. Jurian stopped to stare again, oblivious to the people jostling him on all sides and the nasty glares they gave him as they passed. Temples of all shapes and sizes sprang up on every side, crowding over each other in haphazard arrangement while the massive Temple of Jupiter Capitolinus towered over them all high on its hill.

Everywhere he looked, people stood in knots, talking and debating, while someone spoke from the raised *rostrum* to a small group of listeners. There were no merchants, no stalls or shops, no trade of any sort, and for a while Jurian just watched and tried to figure out what everyone was doing. As far as he could tell, they were all just standing around and gossiping. Maybe that passed for a hard day's work in Rome.

He swallowed and adjusted the folds of his toga. Besides the togaed men engrossed in their deep arguments, there were Legionaries everywhere—more soldiers in that single space than in the whole *castra* of Satala.

"Watch out, boys," someone laughed from somewhere to his left. "That one might catch you on fire if he gets too close."

Jurian turned and spotted a group of young Legionaries standing nearby, stifling laughter as they stared at him. He gritted his teeth. The Legionaries of the *Apollinaris* were seasoned soldiers, men who'd fought countless battles and lost more friends than most people had in a lifetime. These Legionaries…they probably didn't even know which end of their sword to hold. They looked little more than children, though they all had to be at least a few years older than him.

"Talk about me like that again, and I just might," he said, walking up to them, hand casually on his *seax*.

One of them arched a brow at his friends. "Well, he's got fire inside and outside," he said. He surveyed Jurian briefly. "You don't look like you hail from Rome."

Jurian hesitated on telling him the truth. Finally he settled for saying, "No."

The Legionary grinned. "I'm Vitus. Marcus Barrius."

"Lucius Aurelius Georgius," Jurian said, accepting Vitus' offered hand.

Vitus shot a glance at one of the other Legionaries. "Lucius Aurelius?" he repeated. "Eh, Falco, any relation?"

The other Legionary swaggered forward, eyeing Jurian up and down. He was a little shorter than Jurian, with a round face that looked rather boyish behind his impish grin.

"Aurelius is hardly a unique *nomen*, Vitus," he said, languid. "We probably share it with a thousand frontier families. Still, Lucius Aurelius? Sounds familiar. I'm Falco, by the way, if you weren't quick enough to catch that. Caius Aurelius Falco."

Jurian took a step back. "Highly unlikely, I know, but is your father Brocchus?"

"The very."

Jurian laughed. He couldn't help it. Of all the people in that crowded forum, he would stumble on his cousin by utter chance. Falco regarded him skeptically.

"My father was Lucius Aurelius Gerontios."

Apparently Falco knew his uncle's name; he threw his head back and laughed, then grabbed Jurian in an enthusiastic embrace. "Well met, cousin!" he cried, and whispered conspiratorially to Vitus, "My cousin. Father's brother's son. Frontier people. *Barbarians*." Then, to Jurian, "What're you doing in Rome?"

Jurian shook his head. There was too much story to tell, and he wasn't sure how to start, or what he should say. And even though the only activity in the Forum seemed to be talking, it didn't feel like the right place to him.

"Looking for your family, actually," was all he said. "My sister Mari is with me."

Falco strained to peer past Jurian's shoulder. "Where?"

Jurian grimaced. "Not *here*. I left her with some acquaintances. Thought I'd see if I could find your father first."

"Eh, he's in the basilica," Falco said, waving toward the sprawling building across the forum. "Stuffy business matters. But you got to town just in time! Word has it, *both* the emperors are coming to Rome. Imagine! Not sure what about. Imperial business, always such a mess. But what a time to see the city."

"Is that why it's so crowded?"

Vitus laughed out loud, and Falco grinned as he said, "What, no! This isn't crowded. This is normal, less than normal! I'm surprised, actually."

"Well," one of the other Legionaries said, pointing, "maybe we'll see more foreign royalty like that."

Jurian glanced over his shoulder. A few slaves were carrying a covered litter, but the occupant had drawn back the curtain to get a view of the Forum as they passed. Jurian's breath caught in his throat. The occupant was only a girl, maybe a year younger than him. She had a quiet sort of mystery about her as she peered past the silk curtain, and her eyes were a startling gold, vibrant against the pallor of her skin. Those eyes suddenly rested on him, meeting his gaze for one endless moment. Jurian's pulse pounded in his ears, and it wasn't until the girl abruptly dropped the silk curtain back in place that he realized he was still holding his breath.

"Gods above and below," Vitus whispered, and gave a low whistle. "Did the moon-goddess Diana just pass by?"

"I don't know, but she seemed to be drawn to the sun," Falco said, sticking his hands roughly in Jurian's hair.

Jurian jerked his head away and stared after the litter. "Too bad it's such a big city," he muttered.

He paused, his eyes searching the crowds that had moved aside for the litter. Had he seen a flash of dark blue, the rich, deep color of the tunic Nikolaos had given to Mari? But that was ridiculous. He could see half a dozen women at least who wore similarly colored tunics.

"Well," Falco said. "I suppose I can take you to my father."

But no sooner had the words left his mouth than a horn blast rang out over the Forum. Everyone froze, then turned to gape as an imperial procession wound its way down the Via Sacra. The emperor Diocletian *Augustus* came riding down like a general for a triumph, his chariot flanked by hundreds of imperial guards on horseback. Jurian and the Legionaries stood and stared. After a moment Jurian realized he was holding his breath again, and he forced himself to let it out, slowly.

The emperor of the world was riding past, only a dozen or so feet from where he stood.

Jurian didn't realize that everyone else had dropped to their knees. By the time he noticed that he was the only one standing, it was too late; Diocletian had noticed too. He drew his chariot to a stop and gestured to an imperial guard walking alongside him. The young man nodded and strode over to Jurian.

"The Divine Emperor Diocletian *Augustus* wishes to speak with you," he said, his voice low, lightly accented.

Jurian glanced up to catch his eye—with his height and build, not to mention his blue eyes and pale skin, the man looked like he should have come from Britannia, not Antioch. Jurian tried to read in his eyes any warning or encouragement, but the man just stared back at him impassively. Not wanting to risk the emperor's impatience, Jurian nodded slowly and stepped toward the chariot. He knew he should bend his head as well as his knees, to avoid looking the emperor in the eye, but he didn't.

This man had once called his father *friend*, and Jurian wanted to know what manner of man he was.

To his surprise, the emperor looked nothing like his statues. They all showed a rugged, bearded face, strong and implacable, but the Diocletian standing before him was cold rather than strong, and dominating rather than implacable. He wore no beard and his hair was cropped short, not curled over his forehead like the sculptors showed. His face wasn't rugged but it had a strange kind of beauty to it, remote and dangerous. Jurian wasn't surprised that most of Rome considered him a god.

Diocletian's ice-blue eyes held his, measuring him steadily. At first Jurian thought he saw anger simmering behind his stare, but it shifted to curiosity, then, slowly, to something like respect.

"You dare to meet my gaze?" he asked quietly.

His voice was impressive even at a murmur, like calm waters veiling the rise of a maelstrom. Jurian's mind chased after something to say, but words slipped away, meaningless.

"Why should I not?" he heard himself ask.

Diocletian's mouth twisted in a faint smile. "Because I am the divine *Augustus*, god and master of the known world."

"But you came into the world from a woman just like every man," Jurian said.

And I know only one Man born of a woman I would call God, he thought, and wanted to say it, but couldn't force out the words.

The tall guard who had summoned Jurian let out his breath in a sharp hiss, but Jurian kept his gaze on Diocletian. The emperor leaned back, brows lifted in surprise, then turned to the guard and said, loudly,

"If I had a hundred men like this under my command, Constantinus, the Empire wouldn't be tearing apart at the seams."

He regarded Jurian another long moment, then, with a veiled smile, reached to lift his horses' reins. Jurian swallowed and took a half step forward, suddenly wanting to mention his father, to give his name, to do something to make the emperor recognize—and remember—him. But the guard, Constantinus, reached out a gloved hand and pushed Jurian back sharply.

"Stand back now," he said. He stayed there a moment as the chariot rumbled into motion, eyeing Jurian curiously. "Some would say you're lucky he didn't have you killed." He paused, then lowered his voice. "I'd say you would have been luckier if you hadn't won his interest." He clasped Jurian's hand, pressing something cold into his palm. "Take this, and perhaps next time you will remember the face of your *Augustus*."

He turned and strode after the chariot, his armor shining in the cold sun. Jurian stood rooted until the entire procession had wound its way up to the Temple of Jupiter Capitolinus. When the last horseman disappeared up the slope, he let out all his breath and staggered a step back, opening his palm to reveal a coin imprinted with Diocletian's image. He remembered the Legionaries then, and turned to find them all staring at him, eyes wide and mouths agape.

"Dear gods, man," Vitus said, and rubbed his hands over his face. "You have got some…courage…to face him like that."

One of the Legionaries snickered, but Vitus ignored him.

"I don't know any Legionaries who would be that bold, and you're…you're in a *toga*."

"Only until I'm able to join the Legion," Jurian said, hot.

Funny, he thought, that something he'd once thought represented everything it meant to be a man was now somehow inadequate. He was more grateful to Nikolaos than he could ever say, but somehow it didn't keep a little flare of jealousy from his heart as he eyed the other boys' armor and polished swords.

"Well, you heard the emperor," Falco said. "You're as good as in already. Just need to make it formal."

"You think so?" Jurian asked.

"Worth a try, anyway."

"All right, brothers," Vitus said. "Let's go to the villa. My father's in the country, so I'm sure he won't mind us using the place for our entertainment! We can celebrate with our new friend, eh? What do you say?"

The other Legionaries laughed and Falco slapped Jurian on the back. Before Jurian could say a word, the soldiers strode off, jostling him along with them until he gave up even wanting to stay behind. A curl of satisfaction wove through him. He was in Rome. He'd found his cousin. He'd found Legionaries who weren't determined to kill him or ruin his name. He'd even found the emperor, and somehow managed to impress him. For the moment he would forget about all the gloomy pronouncements of well-meaning but insulated people, whose pessimism had made this whole journey an exercise in agony so far.

The Legionaries settled down as they headed up what Vitus

called the Patrician Way, through a well-to-do district of villas and fine houses. It was early evening, and the wind turned colder as the sun sank behind the buildings of Rome. Jurian hesitated, glancing over his shoulder as he walked. He hadn't realized how late it had gotten, and he hated the thought of Mari or Aemelia worrying on his account.

Falco threw an arm around his shoulders. "What's wrong, cousin? You don't look happy to be invited to dinner."

"Oh, I am," Jurian said. "It's just…my sister. I think she was expecting me back by now."

Falco plucked at Jurian's toga. "You're the man, aren't you? It's none of her business what you do, or how late you stay out. She's safe, right? So, don't worry about her."

Jurian bridled his anger. Yes, he knew he was a man here… but to him that didn't give him leave to do as he pleased. He had a duty to Mari, not to anyone else.

"Come on," Falco said. "Just for a few hours. Surely she wouldn't resent that."

"Falco!" Vitus called. "Go round up the others, will you?"

Falco patted Jurian's shoulder. "Don't insult Vitus. Usually he only invites fully enlisted Legionaries to his events." He backed a step, spreading his arms. "You should be honored!"

He swung away and sauntered back down the street, leaving Jurian with Vitus and the other Legionaries.

A few hours, he told himself. *What harm can a few hours do?*

Vitus led them to one of the larger villas, with a wide front portico and a shaded walkway. Slaves greeted them with deference, but Jurian caught a faint sense of disdain from some of them as they eyed the raucous young men spilling into the peristyle. Vitus called for refreshments for his guests, and soon the wine was flowing as more and more Legionaries arrived. Jurian disliked the taste of the wine, even mixed with honey and herbs, but he accepted a dish anyway and sipped at it while the other men downed theirs in single gulps.

"No, no! Don't worry at all. It's a pleasure, really," Jurian heard Falco saying somewhere behind him. "Look, you're not the only one here who isn't under the eagle." Then he called to Jurian, "Cousin! I brought you some company."

Jurian turned around. His stomach plunged.

Casca.

Before he could stop himself, he lunged forward, fist swinging. It took Casca only a moment to recover. He let out an undignified shriek and ducked back, and only Vitus' arms around Jurian kept him from getting struck.

"Gods, man! What's the matter with you?" Vitus shouted.

"Get him out," Jurian hissed, pointing a finger at Casca. "That man is a mur—"

Casca shook himself free of Falco, who had caught him, and took two strides toward Jurian. His hand lashed out, driving a fist hard into Jurian's stomach. Jurian doubled over, coughing hollowly, but twisted his arms out of Vitus' grip and returned the blow with two solid punches that made Casca stagger a few paces back toward the long pool.

"Break it up!" Vitus shouted. "What's wrong with you? Gods, you're not even soldiers, but you've practically got a private little war going on here."

"You have no idea," Jurian hissed.

Casca recovered and favored Jurian with a nasty smile. "I saw you earlier, you know. In the Forum. Did you really think you could curry favor with the Emperor? *You?* As soon as I get my chance to talk to him, he'll know *exactly* what you are."

Jurian stiffened, but forced himself to stay calm. He smiled sympathetically at Casca, saying, "Oh, don't be jealous, Casca. I'm sure the Emperor overlooked hundreds of would-be sycophants today. Not just you."

Casca's face turned a deep red as Vitus stifled a snort of laughter. "I guess he just focused on the worst of them," he spat.

"I've no desire to curry favor with anyone," Jurian said, his voice turning cold. "What are you doing here, Casca? Did your father finally kick you out of Satala?"

Casca sniffed, straightening the folds of his toga and pressing his hair back into place. Jurian noticed that the fool had grown a sparse beard, and with the curls of hair on his forehead, it was only too obvious that he was trying to look like the sculptures of the emperor. Repulsive.

"I'm here to begin my career," Casca said. "Unlike some people, I don't run away from my problems and leave the people I love to take the fall for me."

Jurian lunged at him again but Vitus grabbed hold of him.

"By the gods," Casca sniffed, "Such a terrible temper. I don't remember you being so beastly. Didn't your mother ever teach you manners?"

"Should I remind you?" Jurian growled. "Maybe we could revisit how we first met all those years ago."

Casca's face paled. "Fine," he said, brushing his hands off on the front of his toga. "Just don't ruin the party, *Georgios*."

He turned and slipped away with that odd, fluid gait that Jurian had always found repulsive. Jurian didn't watch him go. He jerked his arms free of Vitus' grip again and pulled his toga back into place. A headache pounded in his temples, and he turned to walk along the enormous pool with its mosaic basin and candles floating among the lilies.

The place should have been beautiful. Even the *praetorium* in Satala was nothing compared to the grandeur of this villa. But Casca's appearance had left a sour taste in his mouth, and now nothing seemed pleasant. He knew that Casca wouldn't leave off the fight so easily. Now that he knew Jurian was in Rome, he would find a way to finish what he'd started back in Satala.

"Now Jurian," Falco said, coming up suddenly beside him. "Don't be glum. Sorry about bringing that simpering idiot around. If I'd known you were old enemies…"

"It's fine," Jurian said. "But I should probably be going. Sorry for the fight."

"You can't leave! Not now!" Falco cried. He stood on his toes to look down the length of the pool, to where a few of the Legionaries were talking louder than the others. "What's that? The evening entertainment? Eh, I'll wait. Come on, have some more wine with me!"

Jurian bit his tongue on mentioning that Falco seemed to have had too much already. He just shook his head and edged past him, making his way through the chattering throng.

"Did you see the girl?" he heard one Legionary ask another.

Jurian's thoughts drifted back to the exotic girl in the litter, and he smiled.

"No, which one?" the other asked.

"Some girl is here. Says she's trying to find her brother." The Legionary snorted with laughter. "I'm sure that's what she's looking for!"

A knot of dread twisted in Jurian's heart, and he grabbed one of the men's shoulders. "Who? Where?"

"Pretty little thing," the Legionary said, shrugging. "Making her rounds. Think Dion and Marsis are…helping her."

He pointed down toward the far end of the peristyle. The blood drained from Jurian's face. There were the two Legionaries, Dion and Marsis, no doubt.

And there, elegant and stunningly beautiful in a dark blue tunic, was Mari.

32

ROMA

"NO, NO," JURIAN HISSED TO himself. "Foolish girl!"

He turned to stride toward her, anger simmering up in his veins.

What is she doing here? What is she thinking, walking into a crowd of half-drunk Legionaries who think she's the evening's entertainment?

If one of them so much as laid a hand on her, he didn't know what he'd do, but he was fairly sure it wouldn't help his chances with getting into the Legion.

The soldiers thronged around him, making a maze of his path to her.

Don't do anything stupid…don't do anything stupid…

He wasn't even sure who that thought was directed toward, but his hand dropped to the hilt of the *seax* buried under the folds of his toga as he pushed his way through the strangling crowd. Then the burn of anger in his blood vanished, and cold, cold dread seeped over him as he watched Casca step up to Mari, his face twisted in an ugly grin. Casca's mouth was moving but Jurian couldn't hear his words, only see the surprised faces of the Legionaries around them.

"Mari," Jurian whispered.

It all happened too fast. Too fast, but too, too slow.

He saw Casca's hand reaching for Mari, saw her face turning

aside, toward him, and her thumb reached up to brush her forehead. And for the briefest moment, her eyes found Jurian's, and she smiled.

He never even saw the knife flash in Casca's other hand. He only saw the color seep from Mari's cheeks. Then she was falling, and no one reached out to catch her. Her body crumpled into the starlit pool, her arms drifting wide as her blood stained the water crimson.

Someone screamed her name.

A moment later Jurian realized it was his own voice. He couldn't even feel it tearing from his throat. He couldn't feel anything. The crowds gave way around him and he rushed to the pool, reaching and reaching, but he knew he would never catch her. Somehow he pulled her to the rim of the pool and dragged her out, her blood washing over the whiteness of his toga. He touched her cold cheek, brushing the water from her eyes, but she didn't open them.

Gently, slowly, he laid her down on the mosaic floor, smoothing her wet hair off her forehead. His lungs had forgotten how to breathe, and deep inside he felt his heart trying to beat—trying, and failing. He pushed himself off the ground and turned to face Casca.

"What have you done?"

In the thundering silence in his mind, it seemed he screamed those words, but they came out in a growl.

Casca, pale and petrified, only stared at him.

"He said he was doing Rome a favor," one of the Legionaries whispered. "Cleanse her of the Christian filth. The girl was a Christian. Did you…did you know her? She said she was already betrothed. We didn't mean harm by her. But that man seemed to know her."

Jurian's body shook with rage as he stared at Casca. "You killed her. In cold blood. You just appointed yourself judge and executioner, and *killed* her. Right here."

"Just…finishing some business that should've been taken care of months ago," Casca said. "And they'd have done it if…if

I hadn't first."

He pointed at the Legionaries, who backed away from him with their hands up. Jurian closed the distance between them until his face was inches from Casca's.

"What about me, then?" he hissed. "Will you do the same to me? Come on, then, you *coward,* and finish it!"

"No, no…I'd rather bring you down so the whole world can see your shame."

"Then I'll bring you down with me."

Casca's face paled, then flushed red with anger. It was the only tell Jurian had before Casca stabbed forward with his knife. Jurian grabbed his wrist and twisted as hard as he could. Casca screamed in pain as his strength gave way, and Jurian stumbled forward as the knife sank into Casca's belly. He pulled away, sweating and shaking. With a groan of disbelief, Casca toppled to the ground.

Jurian didn't wait to see if Casca would get up again. In the dim light he saw his hands running red with blood, his toga stained with it. He turned and knelt by Mari's side, oblivious to the silent, confused crowd around him. After a moment he felt a hand on his shoulder and found Falco bent over him, eyes wide with horror.

"Georgius, you…what did you do?"

"He killed her," Jurian whispered. His throat knotted and he stared, disbelieving, at the quiet lines of her face, the smile frozen on her lips. "Oh God," he choked. "My sister…"

He lifted her up, strangling a scream of rage as he clutched her to his chest.

Just move…just move, please…don't abandon me now…not after everything…

He pressed his face into the tangle of her wet hair but he held back the sobs. In the muddle of his thoughts, all he knew was that he had to leave. One of the bodies lying there had been his doing, with a hundred Legionaries as witness.

It was over.

All of it.

Mari was gone, and nothing else mattered.

"Come on," Falco murmured, dragging his arm. "Bring her. Come on."

Jurian lifted Mari gently, following Falco out through the slave's door at the back of the villa.

"You're lucky most of those men were all drunk," Falco said. "And those who weren't probably didn't see what happened."

"Why are you helping me?" Jurian asked, numb.

"Because you're my cousin. And because I know she was all the family you had left. And because it was my fault Casca was even there. And—"

"I get it," Jurian snapped. "What will you do with him?"

Falco shrugged. "He obviously stabbed himself. Maybe it'll be ruled a drunken accident. I'll fetch a physician. Gods know how it'll turn out."

Jurian let his breath hiss out. Falco led him across the dark street, past the villa opposite Vitus'. Beyond it lay a low slope of frost-covered grass, dotted with occasional small houses and cut by the winding colossus of an aqueduct.

"You should come back to my father's house," Falco said. "We live a little farther up the road, on this side. Do you want me to take you there?"

"No," Jurian said, adjusting his grip on Mari's body. "Please, I don't want to involve your family, too. I'll…I'll go back to the friends we were staying with."

"Where was that?"

"South of the Forum, near the river."

"That's your direction then," Falco said, pointing. "Come find me if you need anything. Anything. Burial cult, whatever. I'll do my best to help."

Jurian bowed his head in gratitude, then turned without another word and headed toward the river. He skirted well wide of the palace grounds, winding his way past a few outlying temples and doing his best to stay in the shadows. It wouldn't be difficult to find Justinus' house again, but part of him wasn't sure if he wanted to. If he didn't want to involve his own family in his disaster, he certainly didn't want to involve a stranger's. But he had nowhere else to go. There was nowhere he could go, carrying a body with his toga stained with blood. The first guard he saw would arrest him on sight.

He drew a thin, shallow breath and stumbled the remaining distance to the fish-carved house. For a few moments he stood irresolute in front of the door, clutching Mari protectively to his chest, every part of his mind and body completely numb. Then, before he made up his mind to knock, the door swung open and Aemelia stepped out to greet him. She took one look at them, and her hand flew up to cover her mouth. Without a word she reached and grabbed Jurian's arm, and pulled him inside.

"CASCA KNEW WE were Christians," Jurian said softly.

He sat with Aemelia and Justinus in their tiny peristyle, gathered close around a coal brazier against the night's chill. Aemelia had brought Jurian a warm woolen blanket, but for all that, he still felt numb. Mari lay on the stone floor at the foot of a small shrine—a simple sort of thing, with only a candle and a stone-cut cross. Jurian couldn't look at her. Looking at her made him fret about her lying on the cold stone, made him worry that she was uncomfortable, made him fear that she would fall ill again. Looking at her proved everything that was wrong with the world.

Everything that was wrong with him.

She'd needed him, and he had failed her. Just like he'd failed his mother. If only she had spotted him sooner. If only she hadn't followed him at all. If only he hadn't been stupid and vain and gone with the Legionaries, or left her behind in the first place. If only he could go back and rewrite all of the mistakes of his life.

Is God punishing me? Or is He just as capricious as the gods of the Romans?

Mari would have known how to answer that.

A sob tore his chest and he bent his head, ashamed, but he couldn't force back the shaking breaths. Aemelia wrapped an arm around his shoulders and somehow that only made everything worse. He clutched the blanket as if he could tear it between his bare hands, and everything inside him burned and burned until he wished he would catch fire and make an end of it all.

After a few moments he got his breathing under control and lifted his head. "He was there when my mother died. He killed her and our priest. Ordered them run through…then burned their bodies alive. He's been tracking us all the way from Anatolia."

"Did your sister…" Aemelia began, then cleared her throat gently and said, "Did she disappoint him? Reject him somehow?"

"He never cared for her," Jurian said. "He doesn't know the meaning of love. He only knew how to hate, and I was the one he hated more than anyone. I knew what he was. I knew things about him…things he wanted kept secret. And he knew that I knew them." He scrubbed a hand over his face. "I don't know what to do now. I thought…I thought my life would begin when I got to Rome. I didn't think this would be where it ended. Was I wrong?" He lifted his head. "And I don't regret what I did to Casca. Is that wrong?"

There was a long silence. Jurian could feel that Justinus and Aemelia were exchanging some sort of wordless communication, but he couldn't focus enough to try to understand what.

"The right thing isn't always what feels right, or what makes sense," Justinus said.

Jurian had the good grace not to glare at him. Justinus was a large man, kind and quiet, and he had said nothing so far to rebuke Jurian. But these words felt like a rebuke, like a judgment.

"Would you have stood by and done nothing?" Jurian asked. "What if it was your wife?"

Justinus studied Jurian quietly. "I don't know what I would have done, which is why I'm not trying to condemn you. Casca obviously went through his life planning and scheming ways to hurt you. That's the difference between you."

"You said Casca was trying to stab you," Aemelia said.

Jurian let out his breath like a snort. "Yes, I wish I could take self-defense as my excuse. But the truth is…I provoked him." He buried his face in his hands. "Oh, God. What am I going to do now?"

"Go and find Dionysius if you can," Aemelia told her husband. "I think Jurian will want to see the Father."

The mention of Dionysius reminded Jurian of their trip to Rome, and suddenly a shard of pain stabbed into his heart.

"Menas," he whispered. He bit down hard on his lip, squeezing his eyes shut. "How can I tell him? He'll never forgive me."

33

Roma

In the massive dining hall of the *Domus Flavia*, relegated to a corner near the windows where she could see the courtyard's fine oval fountain, Sabra was not in the mood to be polite to anyone. She was surrounded by arrogant imperial guards, patricians and senators with their gaudy wives and their overinflated senses of their own importance, and high-ranking Legion officers who had accompanied the Divine *Augustus* in his triumphal march, and she could have sworn that every single one of them had come to greet her over the last half hour. Her mouth hurt from smiling, and, even though none of them had given her the chance to utter so much as a syllable, she felt like she'd been yelling all night.

And she'd never seen chaos like that dining hall. It was, of course, elegant and refined chaos, but somehow that made it even worse. Her head ached intensely, and the only thing that wanted to occupy her thoughts was the slow mental countdown of the days until the next sacrifice—*her* sacrifice—was supposed to take place in Cyrene.

It should have encouraged her, seeing that she had arrived in Rome apparently on the very same day as the *Augustus* of the East—she knew most people would say it was the gods' work. But, she thought sourly, refusing yet another wine-serving slave, none of that mattered since the *Augustus* was too busy to even receive her introduction. How could she ever intercede for her city if she couldn't even beg for ten minutes of the emperor's time? And it was no use trying to ask the *Augustus* of the West. He was even busier and less interested than Diocletian.

She groaned and kneaded her fingers against her temples. It was intolerably bright in the *triclinium*, from its myriad of candles and oil lamps and blazing fires, to its polished marble walls and floors and massive Corinthian columns. All the white stone reflected the light, until Sabra found herself longing to be underground in her damp, silent Temple again.

Hanno stood just behind her with his arms crossed, and when she glanced up at him, she scowled at the smug smirk on his face.

"I get the feeling you're enjoying this," she muttered.

"That I am," he said. "And I am so grateful that my Latin is as bad as it is. I can tell just from the way these people talk that they all think they're the gods' gift to humanity."

She snorted. "Be careful. You might not speak Latin, but someone here might speak Punic."

She was interrupted by the approach of a tall young man, likely in his early twenties, with short golden hair and skin almost as pale as her own.

"*Domina*," he said, bowing to her. "Flavius Valerius Aurelius Constantinus."

When he stopped and eyed her expectantly, she swallowed hard, realizing he actually intended for her to say something in return.

"That's quite a lot of names for an imperial guard," she said.

The man smiled. "Diocletian *Augustus* keeps me as part of his retinue, but I belong in the north with my father, *Caesar* Constantius. I should be in Britannia right now. Instead I've been… stuck…in Antioch…almost as long as I can remember."

The last sentence he spoke haltingly, turning to the window to gaze out at the oval fountain. He kept one hand behind his back, shoulders straight, and even with his head bowed he had a pride about him, a presence that no one could ignore. Sabra stared at him. This was the son of Constantius? She'd heard rumors, of course, of how Diocletian had essentially taken the young son of his western *Caesar* hostage, raising him in his own court to keep him loyal—and to keep his father Constantius loyal. She'd just never imagined that the boy had actually grown up at some point, and turned out to be such a noble man.

"I don't even know where Britannia is, *domine,*" she said honestly, folding her hands in her lap and lowering her gaze.

Constantinus laughed as if she'd said something witty. "Did I hear you introduced as the princess of Libya?" he asked.

Hanno shifted his weight, and Sabra stifled a smile.

"A slight misunderstanding," she said. "I'm only the governor's daughter, not a king's."

Constantinus turned back to her, holding out his hand. She hesitated, then extended her own. He took it elegantly and kissed it. "I would have believed you were a princess," he said. He smiled at her shocked expression and straightened up, his gaze flashing to someone across the room. "Ah, it looks like I'm being summoned. It was a pleasure to meet you, *filia regis*."

"Oh," Sabra said, struck with a sudden thought, and held her hand out toward him. He turned back to her with no sign of impatience, and she said, "I'm sorry, *domine*. I don't mean to be presumptuous, but I'm here on behalf of my father. I'd hoped to receive an audience with the Divine *Imperator* Diocletian *Augustus,* but…I've been told he has no time for me. I…"

"You were wondering if I might take your plea to the *Augustus*?" he asked, a little smile playing at the corners of his lips. "For you, *domina,* I would be happy to do anything."

Sabra watched him leave, feeling a sudden warmth creep over her cheeks. Behind her Hanno crossed his arms and cleared his throat.

"Don't get any ideas," he muttered. "Those people are all the same."

"Oh," she said, mocking. "And you would know that, Hanno?"

"Everyone knows it."

"Well, we'll see who's right when he gets me an audience

with the emperor."

Hanno gave an undignified snort but didn't answer.

SABRA WOKE WELL after sunrise the next morning, taking a moment to remember where she was. Even in the palace in Cyrene, she had never slept on a bed quite as comfortable as the one she had in her guest chamber in the *Domus Flavia,* and after days at sea, she didn't want to leave it. She was buried under an intricately woven blanket of a far softer wool than any she'd ever felt, and the mattress beneath her was thick and luxurious, nothing like the palm-stuffed mattress of her own bed. But a slave was already bustling around her chamber, laying out her clothes, so with a sigh she got up and allowed the woman to help her dress.

The slave had just finished wrestling Sabra's headdress over her hair when someone knocked outside her chamber. Sabra's heart launched into her throat as she sent the slave to answer the door. Moments later the woman returned with a scroll in her hands.

"*Domina,* a message for you," she said, handing her the scroll with a low bow.

Sabra nodded and opened the letter, barely scanning the contents before bursting out of her chamber in search of Hanno. She found him just outside her door in the peristyle, already standing like he expected to see her.

"I saw the messenger," he said. "Is it from him?"

Sabra flapped the paper at him, shaking her head with pursed lips to keep from crying. "No, not *him.* From some...Piso. His secretary, I suppose. He..." Sabra's voice died and she pressed the backs of her fingers against her mouth. She wanted to just give Hanno the letter to read himself, but he read Latin even worse than he spoke it. "He apologizes, but the emperor will not be able to see me. He says that Cyrene...Cyrene is not worth the Empire's notice. He says he is sorry for our troubles, but..." She unfolded the letter and began to read, "*The city of Cyrene has already become a burden to the Empire, both financially and politically, being unable to offer trade of any value and offering no political advantage in an already stable region. Word has already reached us of manifold disturbances in the area, culminating now in armed uprisings in the city itself and its surrounds. The city is a liability, and while we grieve the sufferings of your people, we are unable to offer assistance of any sort at this time. We pray to the gods to alleviate the city's difficulties. They may help you, but we will not. No further inquiries regarding this region will be heeded by the Divine Imperator Diocletian Augustus."*

She managed to read through the entire thing without her voice breaking, but when she finished she covered her face with her hand and wept quietly. Hanno muttered under his breath and clasped her arm briefly, but she pulled away.

"What did I think was going to happen?" she cried. "Did I think I could make any difference? That I could traipse into Rome and pop in to visit the emperor, and he would send his armies to save us? And now there are rebellions in the city? My father could be in danger and…and I can't even be there to stand by him! It's all my fault. The god is angry, and no one is there to placate him…"

"Mistress!" Hanno said, sharp. "Your father had a suspicion that a plea to the emperor would go unheeded. He just wanted you away from the city."

She froze, staring at him. "Why? Why Rome? I don't understand!"

Hanno hesitated, scuffing the sole of his sandal against the colored stones. "You couldn't be happy here?"

"Happy?" she echoed. "*Here?* What are you talking about, Hanno? I just want to go home."

"But this city is so beautiful, isn't it? All the temples and the villas, and the theaters…"

She crushed the letter in her hand, shaking it in her fist at Hanno as she glared up at him. "It's dirty. It's ugly. It's crowded. It smells, and it's cold. I don't like it here. I don't want to stay here. I just want to go home and put things right."

"Your father sent word ahead to your mother's sister," he murmured, bowing his head. "She is apparently a senator's wife. That doesn't mean so much anymore, I suppose, but she is highly respected. Your father was hoping that she would...take you in. Bring you into society. Take care of you, so you could leave Cyrene and its troubles behind and not worry anymore."

"He wouldn't dare," she hissed. She strode a few steps away from him, then spun back and gestured at her ridiculous dress. "Is this what he wanted of me? He expected me to prance around like a painted doll in Rome, while my city suffers? While *he* suffers? Does he even know me at all?"

"Mistress, listen!" Hanno cried, desperate. "If there are rebellions, it must be that the people found out about the lottery. If you go back, you'll die. They'll chain you up on that mountain—"

"Good!" she said. "I hope they do!"

Before he could argue, she turned and strode back into her chamber, slamming its door shut behind her. She sat down on the narrow sleeping couch, digging her hands into her hair under the heavy coins of her headdress.

I have to get out of here. They can't keep me here like a hostage, like Constantinus in Antioch. I have a duty to my city.

And somewhere, deep inside, she thought she heard another voice...not the snide internal voice of her own imagination, but something...darker. Deeper.

You should sacrifice the slave, it whispered. *He defies the will of the god. He is unworthy of your friendship. He must die...*

She sprang off the bed, shaking all over. Her hands reached up and tore off the headdress, letting the coins clash to the ground.

*No, no, no...*she told herself, taking her mental self by the shoulders and giving her a solid shake. *Forget that. That's not right. That's not true...*

But against her will, a dark image flickered deep in her mind of Hanno bowed before the god's altar, whispering apologies as his blood gushed out over the white stones.

"NO!" she screamed out loud, throwing herself on her knees by the bedside and scraping at her forehead to dig the image out. She heard someone pounding on her door but ignored it. "I will not. I will not even think it! Oh, gods, help me."

You will think it. *And you will do it, because you know it is the god's will. Has affection ever stopped you before? You know they are all meaningless, worthless. Only the service of the god matters.*

Sabra dragged the heavy wool blanket over her head, weeping and praying for the voice to go away.

It's the voice of the god, her inner voice whispered. *You can't actually want to ignore him?*

"I don't know that!" she cried. Then, comforting herself with the sound of her voice in the heavy silence, she went on, "I'm leaving. And I won't tell him. I'll sneak past him and slip away before he knows I've gone. It's the only way. I have to do it, to protect him from me. I just need…a little time."

34

ROMA

DIONYSIUS ARRIVED AT JUSTINUS' HOUSE early the next morning, barely after dawn. Jurian was already awake—or still awake. He wasn't sure if he'd slept at all. But he knelt still next to Mari's body, praying every prayer he knew even when he didn't know what he was praying for. He was fairly sure Mari didn't need his prayers anymore, but maybe she did. Or maybe it would make her glad, even if she didn't need them, to see her brother praying.

He barely looked up when Dionysius came into the peristyle. His eyes were heavy, gritty and tired from his long vigil, and he was afraid that if he so much as blinked, he would fall asleep. Dionysius knelt down beside him, clasping his shoulder firmly.

"I am so sorry, Jurian," he murmured.

He reached over and signed Mari's forehead, the same *signum* that had gotten her killed. Jurian wanted to feel angry about that, but somehow he thought his anger would dishonor Mari's death more than anything else he could do. In his mind, all he could see, over and over again, was how she had looked at him and smiled.

He rubbed his forehead to drive back the pain and nodded. Words were pointless.

"Come on," Dionysius said. "I have somewhere to take you, a place I think Mariam would have wanted to see. When we have finished, we'll take her to the catacombs on the Via Appia. We can bury her there, where we have buried so many of our faithful."

Jurian gritted his teeth but gave permission with a wave of his hand. Dionysius pulled him to his feet and escorted him out the door, leading him down to the banks of the Tiber where Cyricius had left them only the day before. Had it only been a day? The whole world had changed in a day.

Cyricius was waiting for them with a smaller boat than the barge, more like a fishing vessel plied by oars. He and Dionysius held it steady as Jurian climbed in, then the two men each took up the oars and headed up the river. They passed the sprawling Circus Maximus and the Palatine Hill, and slipped silently under a number of stone bridges. A curve in the river brought them near a tiny island crowned with a number of small buildings and temples. Jurian eyed it curiously but the boat never stopped. The men rowed steadily, continuing north as the river serpentined through the hills. Jurian watched the city center of Rome drift away, the gentle rocking of the boat nearly sending him into sleep. Just when he started to nod off, the boat scraped up against the western bank of the Tiber, and Dionysius was shaking his arm.

"We get out here, Jurian."

"Where are we?" Jurian asked, stepping awkwardly out of the boat. Directly in front of them towered a massive stone building in an impressive circular design, all marble and brick with a garden growing from the roof around a gold sculpture of a four-horse chariot. "Is that where we're going?"

"Saints, no," Cyricius said, climbing out after him. "That's the mausoleum of an emperor. Or emperors. Several are buried there, I'm told. Houses for the dead grander than the houses of the living," he added with a shake of his head. "No, our destination is not so grand as all that, by what the eyes can see."

Jurian didn't even have the heart to roll his eyes at Cyricius' enigmatic statement. He just bit the inside of his lip and followed the two men along the narrow paved road between two sloping hills. On their left lay the ruins of a massive stadium, not quite as grand as the *Circus Maximus* under the Palatine Hill, but daunting all the same. Parts of it had been carved out to make room for graves, continuing the necropolis that covered the slopes of the hill to their right.

"Why have you brought me here?" Jurian muttered. "Do you think I need a better acquaintance with death?"

Dionysius smiled sympathetically at him. "No. But perhaps it will give you a new perspective on life."

Perspective, Jurian thought bitterly. Eventually Cyricius stopped and pointed at the base of the wall of one of the pagan mausoleums.

"What do you see there, Jurian?"

Jurian frowned at the wall. "Some graffiti, it looks like. Greek? It spells fish but it looks...strange."

"*Ichthus,*" Dionysius said. "Tell me you know what the fish represents."

Jurian shrugged. "I've seen it all over the world, but I thought it was an oddity."

Cyricius chuckled. "Yes, it's an oddity. It stands for something, each Greek letter. *Iesous Christos THeou Uios Soter.*"

"Son of God, Savior," Jurian murmured, translating the last few words. "I never knew."

And then, suddenly, he understood. The stone Nikolaos had given to Mari. His words to her—*I pray it give you strength and courage for what is to come.* Jurian reeled back against the wall, clutching his head.

"Nikolaos," he breathed, choking on tears. "Nikolaos, you knew. You knew!"

"Well, now you do too," Dionysius said, baffled. "Sometimes you'll see the letters, sometimes the symbol. It's all the same. It's a signpost to anyone who knows to pay attention."

He gestured for them to leave the road, and they walked up the hill along the footpaths among the tombs. They passed several more of the fish symbols as they went, and finally they descended a narrow staircase into what felt like a hidden vault, where they found themselves facing a plain red wall painted in red plaster. Two marble columns supported a small frieze, and a burning oil lamp rested under the narrow roof beside a slightly diagonal slab of rock.

"What am I looking at?" Jurian asked.

"On the barge you asked me what I meant, about the bones of the first Petrus once being taken into hiding. Not too long ago, another emperor, Valerian, began a persecution of our kind. Mostly he targeted presbyters like Cyricius and me. But to preserve what we hold precious, this monument was excavated and its contents were moved to the catacombs. They were moved back a few decades ago, and the faithful still come here to pray, as you can tell by all the graffiti on the walls."

You're looking for a tomb, Menas had told him.

"The bones of the rock," Jurian whispered, a sudden flash of cold washing over him. "This is…this is the tomb of Petrus?"

"Petrus was crucified in that stadium," Cyricius said, pointing at the ruins where, in its very center, a tall, pale obelisk scraped the sky. "His followers took his body and buried him here, as close as they could get to the place of his death. It's a poor man's tomb. A fisherman's tomb." He glanced over his shoulder at the Mausoleum of Hadrian still visible behind them. "A simple brick wall marks this man's grave, but what he built will outlast what the greatest emperors of Rome achieved in all their glory."

Jurian knelt down, brushing his hand over the plain, cracked slab of stone as his mother's last delirious words ran through his mind. So this was what she had meant. This was what she had invoked, time and again, repeating it like a prayer or a warning—*the bones of the rock.* And this…this was what Mari had come to Rome to see.

Look, Mari, he murmured in his thoughts. *Did you expect it would be this? When we set out for Rome I had no idea what we would find. I'm sure I didn't expect this. I'm sure I didn't expect any of it.*

He drew a careful breath and sat back on his heels.

"I was supposed to light a pair of candles here," he murmured. "I wish you'd told me this was where we were coming. I would have brought them."

Dionysius said nothing, but dropped Jurian's pack beside him.

Jurian stared at it, then at him. He hadn't even noticed Dionysius picking it up at Justinus' house, let alone carrying it all the way to this tomb. He thanked him quietly and rummaged through his few belongings, finally pulling out the thick beeswax candles that Blasios had given him.

"What should I do with them?" he asked, softly.

"Light them," Cyricius said. "Say a prayer. You can lean them against the wall and leave them to burn away."

Jurian nodded and lit one of the candles from the oil lamp. "God," he whispered under his breath, feeling awkward even after Cyricius and Dionysius stepped back. "Please help me. I don't know what I'm supposed to do. Blasios told me to ask You for guidance. I don't know what dark paths he thinks I'm going to walk, but…please, be a light to me." He leaned it against the wall and lit the other taper. "For my friend Menas, please strengthen him. You showed him the burden of the Cross before. Whatever burdens he will have to bear, help him carry them as he once carried You."

He propped the candle beside the first, and his thoughts drifted back to Blasios. Blasios, who had found them in the wilderness, who had brought them in and had cured Mari when she should have died. His throat closed and he covered his face with his hand. What was it all for? She had died anyway.

But could he say it had been for nothing? He knew she would not have thought so, but he wasn't sure he understood the world the way she had seen it. She had died like their mother. Like Petrus. So many had died, so many would die.

He shut his eyes and tried to calm the frantic race of his pulse, but the awful premonition tore through his body, leaving him shaken and numb.

The light blotted out and he watched the wings of a massive eagle shrouding the sun, only it wasn't an eagle at all, but a dragon. Its wings spread and stretched until its shadow blanketed everything, and in the sharp blue of its eyes Jurian saw Death. The blood of thousands of innocents ran through its claws.

He gasped and scrambled to his feet, heart pounding, sweat

streaming down his back despite the chill. Dionysius and Cyricius looked at him in alarm.

"I've visited the old Petrus," he said, shaking off the vision and squaring his shoulders. "Now take me to the new."

35

Roma

They returned first to Justinus' house, and with the stone-cutter's help they laid Mari on a straw pallet. Just before they draped a dark linen cloth over her, Jurian lifted the small pouch at her waist and spilled its contents into his open hand. Three gold coins, all that remained of the wealth that Nikolaos had given her.

She must have given it all away on her way to find me, he thought, and a smile tugged at the corner of his mouth. It would have been just like her.

In the midst of the coins lay the object he'd hoped to find.

The smooth, dark stone, with the silver-threaded *ichthus* etched on its face. He clutched it in his hand, then slipped it somberly it into the pouch at his own belt.

"It gave you strength," he murmured, lifting the dark cloth and hiding her peaceful face. "Maybe…now that I don't have you…it will give me courage too."

Jurian glanced up to see Aemelia looking on, her hand over her mouth and tears in her eyes.

"I told you about my children who'd gone and married," she murmured. "I didn't tell you of the ones I lost. I wove that mourning *pallium* when my first son was taken from me."

Jurian stood and took her hand, kissing it in silence. He didn't know how else to express his thanks when his voice had betrayed him. She sighed and laid her hand on his head, and the four men lifted their burden and carried it into the street in silence. Justinus hitched a team of mules to the wagon he used to transport stone in the city, and they laid Mari in its bed. They traced a slow, somber route down the Via Appia, far outside the city of Rome, where catacombs had been dug to house the dead.

They descended a narrow set of stairs into the catacombs, guided only by the light of a few flickering candles. A cold, clammy breeze drifted over them, and the sound of their steps echoed between the rough-hewn stone of the close walls. Burial niches lined the corridor. Jurian held his breath; the whole place smelled of death and incense. As they made their careful way through the maze-like tunnels, Jurian caught the faint murmur of voices from somewhere deep underground. He drew up, alarmed, but Dionysius only smiled.

"We're close now," he said.

Jurian frowned. Everything looked the same, in front of them and behind. But Dionysius had barely spoken when the corridor opened up into a small antechamber. Shadows shifted in the corridors beyond, and Jurian's hand went instinctively to his knife.

"No need," Cyricius said. "We're among friends here."

They laid Mari's bier on the rough stone floor, and Cyricius disappeared down one of the branching corridors. Dionysius gave Jurian an encouraging smile. Jurian wondered why—was something supposed to happen? After a moment the murmur of voices grew louder, then Cyricius returned with a young, bearded man and two older women, veiled under somber *pallas*.

"These women will see to Mari's burial," Cyricius said.

One of the women clasped Jurian's forearm briefly, murmuring, "Please, make your farewells. We will do her the honors due those who have gone before us."

Jurian stared at her in alarm. It sounded so final. With grief burning through him, he dropped to his knees beside Mari's body and laid a hand on her cold forehead. All in a rush he remembered everything…her cheerful laughter, her strength, her infuriating stubbornness. Her insufferable teasing.

"I was supposed to chase a hundred Legionaries away from you," he whispered through the sick knot in his throat. "I always knew none of them were worthy of you. No one was. But that didn't mean I wanted this for you. Why, Mari? Why did you have to leave me now? I can't go on without you. You were all the strength I had. You were the light on my dark road…the joy of my heart. Wherever you are now, watch over me, as I couldn't watch over you. Please light my steps…please don't forsake me. And wait for me at the gate to welcome me home."

His voice broke and he buried his face in his hands, breathing shallowly to fight back the tears. Dionysius clasped his shoulder, but no one else moved or spoke until Jurian gritted his teeth and straightened his shoulders, and nodded at them.

"All right," he said. He took one shuddering breath and kissed Mari's forehead. "Goodbye, *cara mea*. Pray for me."

He stood and followed Dionysius and Cyricius into another tunnel. They walked a while in silence. Even Jurian's mind was quiet, as if the weight of the tombs had stifled his thoughts. They passed a number of brightly painted tombs—family mausoleums for the pagan dead—and some narrow niches with names and inscriptions carved in stone. One caught Jurian's eye, drawing him forward almost without his realizing it.

There wasn't much to catch his gaze, but he stared at it, magnetized. He sensed Dionysius beside him and pointed.

"That," he said. "Whose tomb is that?"

Dionysius smiled sadly. "That is the tomb of Sebastianus. I knew him when I was younger. He died a little over ten years ago, at the emperor's hand." He shook his head. "He was a good soldier, and a good man. God knows we need more men like him."

Jurian laid his hand against the stone above the burial niche. "He was a soldier?"

"Well favored by the emperor too, I'm told. He made him captain of the Praetorian Guard here in Rome. But Sebastianus knew where true honor lies, and for that, he died."

Jurian swallowed hard and turned away. They continued on, soon arriving at another small chamber. Jurian stopped in surprise. A number of people had gathered inside, some sitting on the stone floor, others standing along the walls. In the center, on a low brass stool, sat a man. He wore a simple tunic and toga, with a dark *stola* over his shoulders, but nothing about his dress or appearance singled him out as anything remarkable. And yet when Jurian saw him, he was struck with far more fear than even the sight of Emperor Diocletian had stirred in him.

Dionysius stepped forward. If Jurian didn't know better, he would have thought the man looked almost giddy.

The man on the stool beckoned him and Cyricius forward, saying, "Greetings to my beloved sons."

They kissed his hand and Dionysius said, "*Pappas,* I found him." He turned back to Jurian and said, "From the first to the last, this is Petrus. *Pappas* Marcellinus, bishop of Rome. *Pappas,* this is Lucius Aurelius Georgius. His father was Greek, so I suppose we might say…*Georgios.*"

The man rose from his stool, staring curiously at Jurian. Under the weight of his gaze, Jurian felt small, insignificant, and he bowed his head. Without even realizing it, he dropped to his knees. Marcellinus rested a hand on Jurian's head, and when he removed it, Jurian glanced up to find him smiling.

"Fire-headed *Georgios,*" the *pappas* murmured. "So, it's finally come."

Jurian's brows twitched in a faint frown. "I'm sorry. I don't understand."

Marcellinus hesitated, then gave a gentle gesture to the people crowded in the room. They left at once, with only curious glances at Jurian as they went. Once they were alone, Marcellinus returned to his bronze stool and bowed his head.

"It's a prophecy, nearly two hundred years in the fulfilling," he said.

"Prophecy? I thought prophecies were superstition. Pagan."

Marcellinus gave him an enigmatic smile. "Not all prophecies are. This one comes from a man, the uncle of *pappas* Linus, successor of Petrus. Linus was the son of Caratacus, chieftain of a formidable tribe in Britannia who battled against the Roman invaders of his land. But Caratacus was defeated and brought to Rome, where he ought to have been killed, but instead he made such an eloquent appeal to the Senate that they pardoned him. He embraced the Christian faith, and, as I said, his son Linus became the second bishop of Rome after the first Petrus."

He fell silent, and Jurian, hoping it wasn't impudent to speak out of turn, said, "You mentioned Linus' uncle."

"Yes. At least, the legends say he was Linus' uncle, but we know very little about him. A strange, enigmatic man. They called him Myrddin in their native tongue, but we call him *Merlinus*. According to legend, he had fantastical powers, one of which seems to have been the gift of foresight. When Caratacus was still a boy, long before he was conquered and taken hostage to Rome, Merlinus crafted a sword for him. He called it a sword of kings, forged of steel and water and air. No one knows how he crafted it. As far as we know, he was not a smith, had no training in the art of forging steel. But even after two hundred and fifty years, that blade is still as sharp and spotless as the day it was forged. Caratacus gave it to his son Linus, and he in turn passed it on to his successor. So you might say the sword has been hidden in the rock for over a century."

Jurian smiled, and Marcellinus gestured to Dionysius.

"Do you see that niche along the back wall? It is a tomb not for a body, but for steel. Bring me what you find there."

Dionysius faded into the deep shadows at the back of the chamber, returning moments later with a long bundle wrapped in crimson wool. Jurian watched him curiously—Dionysius was a strong man, but he seemed to be struggling with his burden.

"Lay it there on the floor," Marcellinus said. "I don't want to hold it." As Dionysius set the object on the ground, Marcellinus beckoned to Jurian. "Unwrap it and tell me what you see."

Jurian cast a quick glance at Cyricius, but the man only gave him a faint, encouraging smile. Trying not to think about how strange all of this was, Jurian knelt down and unwrapped the crimson wool. Candlelight rippled over the flawless blade of a massive sword, at least twice as long as a Roman *spatha*. It had a long hilt, large enough to accommodate two hands, with a crosspiece that extended farther to either side of the blade than any he'd ever seen. It was plain, too, un-ornamented, but Jurian thought the sword was the most beautiful, and the most terrifying, piece of craftsmanship he'd ever seen. Wrapped around the blade above the hilt was a piece of vellum. Jurian touched it lightly, afraid it would disintegrate under his fingers.

"What is this?" he asked.

"Read it."

He unwrapped it and smoothed it open. The text was written in Latin with a few words of Greek, the script fine and even.

"I shall pass from hand to hand, from *Petrus* to *Petrus*
Until, from *Petrus* I shall return to *petra*
In Britannia but not alone
Keep vigil for the one who must take me up
The fire-headed worker of earth—"

Jurian paused and shook his head. "No, not *worker of earth*. That's my Greek name. *Georgios*." He stared at the scroll as if it might bite him, then twitched his head again and continued,

"The fire-headed *Georgios*, the *eques*
Whose banner is the Cross.
The red dragon awaits.
The dragon will fall.
The eagle will fall.
A phoenix from the fire will rise.
Unchain her and free the world.
In Britannia will rise the eagle whose sign is the Cross.
In Britannia will rise the chief dragon whose sign is the Sword.
Take me to Britannia so from stone to be freed
For Georgios by Linus to Linus from Linus.

Merlinus Ambrosius
in the second year of
Emperor Claudius Caesar of Rome."

Jurian dropped the scroll, snatching his fingers back as if it had burned him. "What..." he started, but his tongue faltered and he barely managed to say, "What...was that?"

Marcellinus smiled. "I was hoping you would tell us."

"Why do you even think this has anything to do with me?" Jurian cried, standing and backing away from the sword. "Just because I have red hair and my name is *Georgios?* Maybe it was really meant for some Celtic farmer in Britannia."

Dionysius chuckled, but Marcellinus didn't seem offended by Jurian's outburst. "No, I believe he was seeing a specific time and place in history. What do you make of that last line?"

Jurian thought for a moment, then a flicker of understanding opened his eyes wide. "Oh! I think I see. By Linus...because the sword was crafted by Mer-*linus.* To Linus, because it came to *Pappas Linus* from Caratacus. From Linus, because it's now to be given from...Marcel-*linus*. From you."

"To *Georgios,*" Marcellinus concluded, his gaze penetrating. "So unless you can bring me another Christian *Georgios* with red hair, I believe he was referring to you."

36

Roma

Jurian stared at the sword lying in its red wrap, like a silver snake lying in bloody grass. In that deep underground space, the silence was complete, so thick that Jurian couldn't even hear Dionysius breathing where he stood close behind him.

"And the rest of it?" he asked finally. "What does the rest mean?"

Marcellinus only folded his hands and kept his gaze fixed expectantly on Jurian. When Jurian realized the *pappas* would say no more, Jurian bit his lip and bent to pick the scroll up again.

"All right," he said. "From the beginning, it's obviously talking about the sword as a sort of inheritance, passed down from *Petrus* to *Petrus*. But what is this rock in Britannia it refers to? Is it a literal rock?"

"Possibly," Marcellinus said. "We don't really know."

"Well, then it talks about me, presumably," he said, half under his breath, brushing the words aside as soon as he'd said them, "and then there's all this talk of dragons..." His jaw snapped shut and he scanned the scroll again. "The dragon! In Cyrene...there's been talk of a dragon terrorizing the city."

"Yes," the *pappas* said, his voice heavy. "It is more powerful than you realize. There's a great darkness over Cyrene. The persecution has begun there already, and it will only spread. Why do you suppose I am in hiding here, rather than dwelling up in Rome, tending my flock?"

"They've threatened your life?" Jurian gasped. "But—"

"It makes perfect sense to them. After all, I am *Petrus*. Why should they give me a better fate than that which the first Petrus received?"

Jurian rolled the vellum into a tight scroll, his grip so firm he almost crushed the leather. "I want to stop it."

"The dragon, or the persecution?"

"All of it. The dragon first. Nikolaos…a friend of mine…he said I would go to Cyrene."

Marcellinus sat very still for so long that Jurian was almost afraid he'd fallen asleep. Then he noticed his lips moving, and realized he was praying.

"Then you will need to take it up," he said finally, nodding at the blade, "as the sword itself requests."

"I will kill this dragon," Jurian said. "Even without a blade."

"I'd warn you against pride, but I know that is not your weakness. A wise philosopher once said that the great-souled man knows his own worth and does not doubt it, not out of pride, but honesty."

"Apparently he wasn't talking about me," Jurian muttered.

"That is precisely my point. You trust too much in yourself, Georgius. The world does not rise or fall at your behest, but if you have a responsibility, a duty, you cannot falter. Do all that you can, and pray as if you can't."

"I'm not worthy of responsibility. Every duty I've been given so far, I've failed at."

Marcellinus regarded him quietly. "Come here."

Jurian approached him and knelt down, bowing his head.

"Give me your hands."

Jurian held them up, like a supplicant.

"There is blood on your hands."

Jurian snatched his hands back and snapped his gaze to Marcellinus' face. But the *pappas* only searched his eyes calmly, with no hint of anger.

"I attacked the man who killed my sister," Jurian murmured, the words halting at first, then pouring out in a rush. "He might have died. I think…I think he probably did. And I was willing to kill him. I goaded him into attacking me, then turned his attack on him."

"Why did you want to kill him?"

Jurian stared at him. He'd mentioned that Casca had killed his sister, but Marcellinus seemed to know that, although that might have been enough to provoke the attack, it wasn't the only thing that had. Anger simmered in his veins.

"He dishonored my father and slandered my family. He made ruining my life his sole purpose, and he instigated the attack that killed my mother and our priest. He hunted us across Anatolia and slandered my name among the Legions. And then he killed my sister to get to me. And the worst part of it all is that I don't even really know why."

"Are you sorry that you attacked him?"

"Wha—no!" Jurian cried, but he choked back bile and bowed his head again. "Yes," he said, gritting the word through his teeth to keep from screaming it. "Yes I am…oh, God."

He wasn't even sure if it was just the fear of losing everything he'd counted on, but he stared with revulsion and horror at the memory of Casca's face, eyes wide with surprise, mouth agape, hands vainly trying to catch his own blood. Had he been the cause of that? He'd done it without hesitation…and so much anger. How could this Marcellinus even stand to look at him, let alone show him any kindness?

"Can you forgive me?" he whispered.

"My forgiveness would mean nothing," Marcellinus said. "But God forgives, and does not remember." He rested his hand on Jurian's head, then traced the *signum* on his forehead. "I absolve you of your sin, *in nomine Patris, et Filii, et Spiritus Sancti. Amen.*" He clasped Jurian's shoulder. "Take up the sword now, and go in peace."

Jurian couldn't speak, so he bent and lifted the sword. It felt surprisingly light in his hand for so ungainly a weapon. Its weight was perfectly balanced, like an extension of his arm.

"Is there a scabbard for it?" he asked.

Marcellinus glanced at Dionysius, who, with an embarrassed apology, went back to the niche where he'd found the sword. He brought back a strange scabbard attached to a belt that looked like it might have fit Menas. Jurian took it tentatively and twisted it around, frowning.

"I believe you'll want to wear that sword across your back," Marcellinus said, miming placing the belt over his shoulder. "It's too long to carry comfortably on your hip."

That made much more sense, so Jurian wrapped the belt experimentally across his chest, buckling it on the wide leather belt he already wore. When it was fitted to him, he reached the sword over his shoulder and found it slid quite easily into the scabbard, which was little more than a buckle for the hilt and a sheath for the last foot or so of blade. Once in place, the scabbard held the blade securely against his back.

"That sword will be useful to you on foot or from the back of a horse," Marcellinus said. "You've received a great calling. You will be an *eques Christi.*"

"Do you mean," Jurian started, almost afraid to ask, "that I shouldn't join the Legion?"

Marcellinus tipped his head to the side, studying Jurian thoughtfully. "You saw the tomb of Sebastianus, didn't you?" Jurian nodded and the *pappas* said, "Go and do in like manner."

Jurian bent to kiss Marcellinus' hand again. "Thank you, *Pappas,*" he murmured. "For everything."

"Make it all worth something."

Jurian reached to pick up his bag, and feeling its weight he remembered Nikolaos' commission. He dug around in it until his fingers brushed the leather sack of coins. Pulling it out, he pressed the bag into Marcellinus' hands.

"This is from Nikolaos, the presbyter in Myra. He asked me to give it to you to support the faithful in Rome."

"Thank you," Marcellinus said, staring at the bag in surprise. "It will be put to good use. Thank Nikolaos for me, if you see him again. And here, this should go with the sword." He handed him the vellum. "It's up to you to decipher the rest of that. It's out of my hands now." He sighed heavily, as if a great weight had been lifted from his shoulders. "Godspeed, Georgius."

OUTSIDE THE CATACOMBS, Jurian took a deep breath of the cold, biting air, clearing his lungs of the musty stench of smoke and death down below. The sword already felt like a comfortable, familiar weight on his shoulder, but as he stood with the other men, he realized they were watching him strangely.

"What?" he asked.

"Never would have imagined I'd stumble on a prophecy's fulfillment in Portus, that's all," Dionysius said.

"I just can't get over how large that sword is," Cyricius said, an almost pained expression on his face that Jurian thought might be horror or poorly veiled amusement.

"Why, do I look strange?"

Cyricius exchanged a glance with Dionysius and laughed, not in mockery but something like amazement. "You already had people looking twice at you with that crown of fire you wear. Now they won't be able to stop staring. They'll likely think you're some sort of Celtic conqueror from myth…in a Roman tunic."

Jurian smiled for what felt like the first time in years. "Dionysius? Would you be able to take me back to Portus? I need to find my giant and go slay a dragon."

37

ROMA

SABRA PACED BACK AND FORTH in her chamber, watching the line of light under her door for any sign of someone approaching. Surely the servant would come back eventually, especially if Hanno could communicate with her enough to send her in. Her stomach growled, resenting the loss of breakfast, but she refused to leave.

Soon.

When she was sure it had almost reached midday, the light under the door flickered out and a moment later there came a heavy knock on the door.

"Domina?" came a woman's voice that Sabra recognized as the slave's.

"Enter," she called.

The woman slipped into the chamber, stopping in surprise when she saw Sabra sitting on the edge of her couch, hands folded in her lap, the ornate headdress pooled on the floor at her feet. She opened her mouth—Sabra thought she looked ready to rebuke her for still being in her chamber so late in the day—but at the last minute she snapped her jaw shut and bent wordlessly to pick up the headdress.

Sabra sat with her chin up and her gaze fixed on the wall across the room, and said, "I need your clothes."

The slave lurched upright so fast Sabra was afraid she'd fall over. "Wha—" she started. "*Domina!* I don't understand!"

Sabra stepped down off the bed and crossed demurely to the chest of belongings Hanno had brought from the ship. Inside she found a small bag of imperial coins that her father must have entrusted to Hanno, to pay for their journey.

"I will gladly pay you for them," she said, dumping a few coins into her hand. "Yours, or any plain tunic and *palla* that might look like yours."

The woman licked her lips, staring from Sabra's face to the coins as if she weren't sure if Sabra was lying or crazy. "I can get you a tunic, *domina*. For this much, I could get you a very fine tunic."

"No no no," Sabra said, pointing a finger at her. "You don't understand. I don't want a fine tunic. I want a tunic like yours."

The woman's eyes widened, horrified. "But *why?*"

Sabra grasped the woman's arm, staring her very earnestly in the eye until the woman dropped her gaze. "I'm the princess of Libya," she said, lowering her voice. "But right now, I'm in *Rome*. And I can't see any of it because everywhere I go there are litters and slaves and people staring and crowds and all this heavy jewelry...have you felt how heavy that headdress is? I get a headache just thinking about it!" She squeezed the woman's arm. "So, if you *promise* not to tell anyone, I'm desperate to slip out...just for a while...and see the sights without...being a sight to see myself. Do you know what I mean?"

The woman patted her hand, eyes twinkling as she caught on. "I see. A little disguise and you have your freedom. All right, *domina*. Let me see what I can do for you." She crept toward the door, smiling conspiratorially over her shoulder at Sabra. "Don't you move an inch. I'll be back in no time."

The woman was true to her word. Sabra had only just finished dividing out enough money to get her home to Cyrene—as near as she could guess, anyway—when she heard the familiar firm knock on the door. The slave bustled in a moment later, carrying a plain tunic and *palla* with a woven belt and sandals, the sort of fashion any slave or commoner might wear. Sabra's face lit up and she gave the woman a huge smile.

As soon as she had exchanged the overly fine regalia she'd been wearing for the comfortable tunic, she gripped the woman's hand and said, "Which way can I go to get out without being noticed?"

The woman directed her to the slave's entrance at the back of the *Domus*, which led to a narrow street ordinarily only used by the slaves and merchants who did business at the palace complex.

"Thank you," Sabra whispered. "That's all. You can go now."

"Good luck, *domina*," the slave whispered back. "Enjoy the city!"

Sabra waited until the woman had ducked out of the chamber, then gently folded up all the pieces of her finery—her mother's finery. She laid them in the chest and then, using a wax tablet and stylus she found at the bottom of the chest, she wrote a brief note to Hanno in Punic. She pressed out the letters five times before settling on something to say. Part of her wanted to go without a word, without a trace, but she couldn't bear the thought of how upset, how betrayed, that would make him feel.

"I'm going home. Don't try to stop me," she said as she gouged the letters into the soft wax. "There. Short and simple."

She laid the wax tablet on top of her clothes and closed the lid. Hopefully it would take him some time to find it, and by then… by then she should be on her way back to Cyrene.

SHE FOUND HER way back to the Tiber with little difficulty. Securing passage on one of the barges was more of a challenge—the first three barge pilots she hailed took one look at her simple tunic and the money in her hand and shoved away from the river bank without so much as an apology. Sabra gritted her teeth. If she'd dressed any nicer, she might have been taken seriously…but she knew she would have aroused more suspicion too, because well-bred ladies didn't beg rides on river barges all on their own.

Finally she managed to come up with a convincing enough story to persuade a barge pilot to give her a ride. He chattered at her the whole way down the Tiber, gossiping about this senator and that patrician's wife until Sabra's head was spinning. They couldn't get to Portus fast enough, but as soon as they arrived and the pilot helped her off the barge, her heart sank. She'd had problems getting a ride on a barge. Now…

Now she saw nothing but hundreds of merchant vessels bobbing on the water, and she hadn't the faintest idea where any of them were going. It was useless. What had she been thinking? She'd be wandering the docks for hours trying to find someone to listen to her, and by then, Hanno would have figured out where she'd gone, and he'd come looking for her.

Not that he'd be likely to find her, though, she thought with some smug satisfaction. Portus was enormous, crowded with more people than she could possibly count. Almost everyone was dressed like her, in tunics dyed dark for work. With her *palla* draped over her head, he might walk past her a hundred times and never notice her.

She struck out for the docks with a determined stride. She was safe in Portus. Even if Hanno came, he'd never find her. Even if it took her weeks, she would find a ship. She would finally go home.

38

Portus, Italia

It was late afternoon when Dionysius' barge drifted up to moor in the channel at Portus. Jurian took his leave of Dionysius and Cyricius, who insisted on sending a skin of their fine Gallican wine with him—for the road, or for a bribe, they said.

"Give my thanks to Justinus and Aemelia," he said, clasping Dionysius' arm. "I'm sorry I didn't get to thank them myself."

"They'll understand. Godspeed, Jurian. I wish that your stay in Rome had been a happier one."

Jurian bent his head and nodded. "So do I," he said. And that was all there was to say.

Cyricius clasped his shoulder. "If you ever need wine, or a friend, come find us. We're good for both."

Jurian smiled. "Thanks." He shuffled a step back. He'd never liked farewells, and was finding less and less to like about them as time went on. "I guess I'd better go find Menas."

He turned without waiting for a reply, only holding up a hand as he went in farewell, and he didn't look back. As he made his way back to the main ring of the inner harbor, he wondered how he would ever find Menas. It couldn't be that hard to track down a giant, though, even among the thick crowds. But it turned out he didn't have to look at all, because he'd barely stepped out under the cold winter sun at the water's edge when an enormous voice boomed behind him,

"Jurian!"

He turned and braced himself as Menas barreled toward him, crushing him in suffocating embrace. Jurian coughed and punched Menas' arm until he let go.

"Saints, Menas, I was only gone…"

God, was it only yesterday that I went to Rome? Could so much have changed so fast?

"Well, I'm still happy to see you," Menas rumbled. "Eh, Jurian, what's that on your back? Looks like a sword made for someone my size."

Jurian smiled. "I'll tell you, but first—"

"Did you get Mari settled in with your relatives?"

He flinched, and he felt the blood drain from his cheeks, turning traitor on him. Menas must have noticed, because he took a step back, slowly.

"Jurian? Is Mari all right?"

It's your fault! Jurian wanted to scream. *If you hadn't been so stubborn about staying here and making us go alone, you could have protected her!*

"Jurian?"

He closed his eyes. "Menas…Casca found us, in the city. I was…I wasn't where I should have been, and Mari was alone. He saw me first, and we argued…then he went after her."

"Is she—"

"She made the *signum*, Menas. Right in front of him and two Legionaries. Told them she was betrothed. And Casca…" His voice shook, but he forced the words out, "He killed her for it."

Menas stared at him, his expression like stone, dark with rage. Jurian had never seen him so angry. He took half a step back, but suddenly Menas dropped to his knees there on the dock and covered his face with his hands. Jurian's heart wrenched and he crouched beside him, resting his hand silently on Menas' upper arm. He couldn't blame Menas. The giant had done no wrong… there was no one to blame but himself. And he wouldn't even have blamed Menas for hating him for it.

"I'm so sorry," Menas said, looking up. He took Jurian's head in his hand, his face etched with grief. "I wish I had been there. I should have been there."

Jurian took Menas' hand and clasped it briefly. "Don't blame yourself, Menas. She wouldn't want you to."

Menas gave him a penetrating look. "Follow your own advice. I can see that guilt in your eyes. Let it go. She is in God's hands." He stood, giving Jurian a hand to pull him to his feet. "What is your plan now? Are you going to join the Legion?"

"Not yet," Jurian said, wiping a hand over his mouth to banish the last of his sorrow. "I have business in Cyrene."

Menas made a low rumbling noise in his chest. "Cyrene? After everything everyone's been telling you about that place?"

"That's exactly why I need to go," Jurian said. He explained as briefly as he could about the sword's scroll, with its description of the dragon. "So, I think I'm meant to go there, to try to defeat that creature."

"What if it meant Britannia?" Menas asked. "After all, it says the chief dragon will rise in Britannia, and there's rumor of war brewing up there."

"There's always war brewing in Britannia. And I think they're two different dragons. One will fall, and one will rise." He shook his head in irritation. "It's hard to explain. But I need to help those people. Mari was right. They're suffering so much, and no one will raise a hand to help them, and they're certainly not going to do it themselves if they think it's a god they're facing. But I *can* do something. I have to try."

Menas grumbled. "How about a bite to eat? There's a wonderful *taberna* across the port. I've made the acquaintance of some Celtic sailors who plan to winter here in Italia. And they're fellow travelers." He started walking as he spoke, guiding Jurian along with him. "You don't think it's a coincidence, do you? Celtic merchants from Britannia, here! They already told me they would sail us there, if we wanted to go."

Jurian said nothing.

"Are you certain you want to go to a godforsaken place like

Cyrene?"

"Absolutely," Jurian said. "Cyrene first. Then Britannia."

His gaze drifted over the knots of people milling around the quayside. He could hear some kind of commotion nearby, but couldn't quite locate it. Finally he spotted a knot of Roman Legionaries, with a small crowd gathered around them. Jurian smacked Menas on the arm and pointed.

"What's going on there, do you suppose?"

Menas drew back, turning a bit pale. "I'd rather not find out. Come on. Only a little further."

Jurian frowned at him, but Menas planted his legs like a mule and Jurian knew he'd never be able to get him to move.

"I'm going to go have a look. I'll meet you at the *taberna* if you don't want to come with me."

"What, you have a sword on your back and now you think you're some kind of avenging angel?" Menas grumbled, scratching idly at the leather band on his arm.

"Preserver of the peace," Jurian said with a faint smile.

"I'll stay right here."

Jurian shook his head and made his way toward the arguing crowd. His stomach wrenched, sending a shower of cold through him. What if it was another Christian soldier being beaten? Could he stand by and do nothing? But he wasn't sure he knew how to get involved without becoming guilty himself.

He pushed through the inner ring of citizens and found the Legionaries surrounding, not one of their own, but a girl about his own age, who might have been strikingly pretty if not for the mud and dust streaking her cheeks. Something about her seemed rather familiar to Jurian—the pallor of her skin, maybe, or the gold of her eyes—but he couldn't place it. The girl was dressed like any commoner, but she wore no slave bracelet or choker. Still, that seemed to be the brunt of the Legionaries' accusations against her.

"Where is your master?" one of them asked.

"We know a runaway when we see one. What commoner has that much coin to try to get passage on a ship?"

"And what business has a girl got traveling by sea, alone?"

The girl's eyes flashed. "It's my business, not yours," she snapped, her voice lower than Jurian expected. "How dare you accuse me of being a slave?"

"She doesn't even speak very good Latin. Do you hear that accent? She must have been brought in from some conquered tribe somewhere. Where are you from, girl?"

The girl looked ready to keep fighting, but Jurian knew she was facing a losing battle. Once the Legionaries decided they'd found a runaway slave, they wouldn't stop harassing her until they'd taken her away in chains. He sighed and grabbed two of the Legionaries by their shoulders, driving them aside.

"You found her!" he cried.

The two Legionaries turned to look at him, their gazes snapping immediately to the sword's hilt at his shoulder.

"What's a boy like you doing with a weapon like that?" one of them asked.

"First you call her a slave and now you call me a boy?" Jurian said, hot. "Are you blind?"

One of the other soldiers chuckled and whispered something to his neighbor.

"Do you know this girl?" another asked.

Jurian caught the girl's wide-eyed gaze and held it briefly. "Of course I do," he snapped. "She's my…" His voice caught on the word *sister*, but he recovered quickly. "Cousin."

"Your cousin?"

"Are you deaf too? That's what I said. Come on…Lucretia," he said to the girl. "Your father's been looking for you everywhere."

She glared at him so fiercely he almost stepped back, but instead he just reached an impatient hand toward her. With a mutter under her breath, she gave the Legionaries a bitter look and took Jurian's hand.

"All right?" Jurian asked the men. "This is not your concern."

One of the men jerked his head at the others, and with one final, long look at the pair of them, they turned away. Jurian watched them out of the corner of his eye, but when he realized none of them had moved too far away, he gave the girl's hand a tug and started toward the market stalls across the harbor. He steered clear of Menas to try to keep the Legionaries from seeing him—for whatever reason, the giant seemed terrified of being discovered by the army, and Jurian wasn't about to put him in the way of that happening.

"Let go," the girl hissed suddenly, yanking her hand back.

Jurian swung toward her, so fast that she almost ran into him. "Look around," he said. "Those Legionaries are still watching. I've got no idea what trouble you were in with them, but if you want to stay out of it, at least let me get you over to that crowd so you can disappear."

"I don't need your help," she said.

Jurian dropped her hand abruptly and took a step back. "All right."

He heard her let out a thin breath as he turned away, and just as he expected, a few steps later she come up beside him.

"Fine," she said. "I'll walk with you to the market. But that's all."

Jurian stifled a smile and glanced down at her. The girl strode quietly beside him, chin up and eyes down—a strange combination. Most of the noble women he'd ever seen kept their eyes up, and most slaves kept their heads bowed. The girl had confidence and some kind of dignity, but he couldn't make sense of it.

"You're not a slave," he said presently.

Her gaze flashed to his, her strangely luminous golden eyes bright with indignation. "Of course I'm not."

"What are you doing in Portus?"

"I didn't agree to come with you so you could ask me questions," she muttered, staring at the ground again.

He shook his head. "Will you tell me your name?"

She bristled but said promptly enough, "Eva." She sighed and added, "All right. I'm a freedwoman, but I came to Rome with my mistress. We got separated in the city so I came back to Portus."

"Do you think she'll find you here?" Jurian asked. "Perhaps you should go back to Rome."

Eva laughed bitterly. "What chance do you think I'd have of finding her there?"

Jurian shrugged. "Just trying to help."

"Jurian!" an enormous voice called, and Jurian winced as he glanced over his shoulder to see Menas striding toward them.

"All right," he told Eva, gesturing at the market stalls around them. "You should be clear now. Good luck."

She didn't move. For a moment she just stood staring, one hand covering her mouth. Finally she managed to whisper, "That man is a giant."

"Well, don't gawk at him," Jurian said. "That's my friend, Menas."

Eva made a little affirmative noise in her throat.

"Jurian," Menas said, lumbering up beside them. He took one glance at Eva and narrowed his eyes, but then he remembered himself and inclined his head to her. "Jurian, I found us a ship bound for Apollonia. Or, not exactly. Ship's pilot said they would go to Carthage and Leptis Magna, and then to Alexandria, but I, eh, convinced him to make a stop at Apollonia while he's in the area."

Jurian flicked a glance at Eva. The girl had gotten very still, paler than usual, and suddenly she pressed a hand to her face and said,

"Please, *domine*, take me with you!"

Jurian folded his arms. "I thought your mistress was in Rome."

She bit her lip, her eyes shining with tears. "That wasn't entirely true. She *was* in Rome, and I got separated from her, but I think she's already gone back to Cyrene. We were meant to sail this morning. I…I didn't make it back in time to find her."

Jurian exchanged a glance with Menas. "You're from Cyrene?"

Eva nodded. "Please. *Please*. Don't leave me here on my own. I'll gladly pay you to escort me back."

Jurian turned aside, gritting his teeth. The last thing he wanted on this journey was baggage, and yet, deep inside, he knew that wasn't what bothered him the most.

He wouldn't do it. No matter what Marcellinus said…he

didn't want to be responsible for anyone else. Not now. Not yet.

"No," he said, and touched Menas on the arm. "I'm sorry."

Eva trailed after them. "I won't be in the way. I promise. You won't even know I'm there."

"Don't beg from me," Jurian said, more harshly than he meant. "It won't change my mind."

Her eyes blazed and her hands knotted in fists, but whatever she meant to say she choked back at the last moment. "All right," she said, cold. "Just tell me which ship is making the voyage and I'll negotiate my own passage with the pilot."

Jurian closed his eyes and tipped his head back, letting his breath out in a faint hiss. "Fine," he said. "Stay with us if you must. I don't care."

"Gods, you're rude," she said.

"He's had a long day," Menas said, giving her a warning look. "He needs to eat. You look like you could use some food too." He pointed down the promenade to a dimly lit tavern. "Eh? It's not much, but the fish stew they serve is tolerable."

Eva wrinkled her nose but apparently knew better than to object. Jurian gave Menas a long look and shook his head, but kept his thoughts to himself as they headed toward the *taberna.*

39

Portus

It was funny, Sabra thought, how things could go impossibly wrong and improbably right all at the same time. She stared at the backs of the two men as she followed them down the walkway, the giant who could have crushed her with his bare hand, and the fire-haired young man with the massive sword strung across his back like some conquering king from legend.

The younger one she'd seen before, she realized. She had spotted him in the Forum in Rome. Hair like fire, eyes like the sea—a rare combination. He'd intrigued her then; now she was more intrigued by the coincidence of meeting him again, here, in this situation. They were going to Cyrene. And though she'd hated to lie and beg—and her face still burned at his rebuke about that—she would soon be on her way home with them.

At least once they got on the ship, she could steer clear of them. The young man confounded her. He might have been a year older than her, but that made him, apart from Hanno, the only man around her age that she had ever met. And he was nothing like Hanno. Being around Hanno was comfortable, but this boy felt dangerous, like fire.

You should not be associating with people like that, the deep, sinister voice in her mind whispered. *He has no love for the gods. Heathen infidel, unbeliever.*

She frowned and shook her head, grateful that both the men were in front of her so they couldn't see it. Luckily the voice stayed quiet after that, and too soon she found herself swept along with them into the dark, cramped interior of the *taberna*.

A few sailors and dock workers crowded around one of the tripod tables, but farther in the back was another chamber curtained off from the main room. Sabra held her breath and prayed that the tavern served food only. The giant snagged back the curtain and Sabra peered past her fire-headed companion, only to see a handful of sailors gathered around a larger table.

These men looked nothing like the ones in the main room. They dressed strangely, in *braccae* and multicolored tunics. One, a large man with scarred hands, had some kind of animal fur draped over his shoulders, and two of them had braids twined in their thick beards. They were fair-skinned enough to make even her complexion look warm.

"Ah, Menas. Was wondering if we would see you tonight," said the one with the fur, speaking a Latin even more strangely accented than hers must have been. He peered curiously at the boy and Sabra. "You've brought us guests?"

"I have. Jurian, this is Bleddyn, the pilot of the ship I told you about. And this young lady..."

"Eva," Sabra said, a blush touching her cheeks to find herself the sudden center of attention.

"We just met Eva too," Menas said by way of explanation.

"A pleasure," Bleddyn said. "My crew. Colwyn and Offyd there, the brothers with the braids in their beards. The young one hiding back there is my son, Glyn, and my older son beside him, Dafydd. The surly one with the dark hair is Ivor."

As soon as he'd finished, Sabra promptly forgot all the foreign names he'd recited, apart from Glyn, which was easy enough to remember...and pronounce. A few slaves interrupted them then, bringing in bowls of something hot—the tolerable fish stew, Sabra realized with a sinking feeling. She despised fish but it seemed to be the only thing to eat anywhere near the ocean. She'd had enough of it on her voyage from Cyrene to last her a lifetime.

The slaves also brought a few bowls of something that smelled like lamb and horn drinking cups filled with *posca,* neither of which was any use to her. But they also brought in dishes of dried fruits and nuts, and she quietly asked one of the slaves for a cup of water. The man regarded her strangely but nodded as he disappeared.

She reached for a handful of nuts and realized Jurian was offering one of the bowls of stew to her. She shook her head.

"Do you want the lamb instead?"

"I don't eat meat," she said.

Menas stared at her aghast, but she just lowered her gaze and calmly ate a few almonds. Jurian watched her curiously a moment, then shrugged and took the bowl for himself.

"That sword," Bleddyn said, after they'd eaten a few minutes in silence. "It doesn't look particularly Roman."

"It's not. It belonged originally to someone from your island. Someone named Caratacus."

Bleddyn's eyes widened. "That's the sword that Myrddin made?"

"You know it?"

Bleddyn laughed. "Every Celt knows the story. Myrddin made it for Caratacus when he was still a boy, when his father had recently retaken the city of Camalodunum. We all knew Caratacus had taken the blade with him to Rome, but it was lost to legend after that. How did you come upon it, lad?"

Sabra had forgotten about eating. She'd never heard stories of Celtic Britannia, and Bleddyn's words hummed with a strange sort of power, drawing her in. Beside her, Jurian bowed his head, then his sea-green eyes flicked a quick glance in her direction. She might have thought he looked embarrassed, but she couldn't imagine this boy being ashamed of anything.

"Menas," he said quietly, before answering the Celt. "You said they were…?"

"Yes. They like the fish." Sabra gave the giant a quizzical glance, and almost jumped when he turned his impassive stare on her. "And you, Eva? Are you a fellow traveler?"

She snorted. "I'm going to Cyrene with you, aren't I?"

Menas and Jurian exchanged a look.

"Well," he said. "Caratacus' son, Linus, stayed in Rome. As a…fisherman."

Bleddyn nodded gravely. "So I'd heard."

"Caratacus handed the sword on to Linus, and Linus to his… heirs."

"You're the heir of Caratacus?" Sabra cried before she could stop herself.

Jurian gave her a strange look and shook his head. "No. Linus' last heir gave the sword to me, yesterday. Said that Merlinus had prophesied that it should come to me."

Menas whistled. "Jurian, foretold by prophecy? I never would have believed it."

"Nor I," Jurian said softly.

"What's it like to be named by a prophet?" Bleddyn asked, laughing.

"Terrible," Sabra whispered.

They all stared at her. Hot blood rushed to her cheeks and she didn't dare to meet anyone's gaze.

"I mean, I imagine it would be. Almost like you had no choice in your life, as if everything were already settled."

"That's the thing about prophecies, I suppose," Jurian said. "They're usually vague on the matter of success."

She made a noise like a snort and kept her mouth shut, grateful that Bleddyn seemed more curious about the sword than her.

"Can I see it?" he asked.

Jurian surveyed the tiny room skeptically, but he shrugged and got to his feet, drawing the sword carefully. He started to hand the sword to Bleddyn but the man jerked his hands back.

"Oh no. I know the legends. Put it there."

He pointed at the table, and the Celts cleared the bowls of stew to one side to make room for the sword. Sabra watched the whole enterprise with something between humor and annoyance.

Men and their swords, she thought. *Leave it to them to find weapons more interesting than food.*

Jurian laid the sword on the table and everyone—even Sabra, to her chagrin—leaned closer to look. Glyn's brother pointed at a Latin inscription on the blade, just above the hilt.

"What is that? I can't read Latin."

Jurian glanced at it. "*Take me up.*" He flipped the blade over, the metal hitting the wood of the table with a deep gong. "There's another inscription here. *Cast me away.*"

"*Tolle me...emitte me,*" Sabra echoed under her breath, trying to match her Latin to the boy's fluid accent.

"And here?" Glyn asked, touching the metal of the cross-piece that had a few Latin letters carved across it.

"It's just initials. Romans like to initial everything on inscriptions," Menas said, frowning. He tapped each abbreviation as he read it, "Ex. Ca. Lib. Ur.."

Jurian looked pensive a moment, then, worrying his lip he said, "I remember the first three—they were in the prophecy too. *Ex calce liberandus.*"

Sabra frowned. "What does it mean—*from stone to be freed?*"

"I don't know," Jurian said.

"And what of the *Ur.*?"

Jurian shook his head. "That wasn't in the prophecy."

"*Urso,*" Ivor said, eyes dark. "*By the bear.*"

"The bear? What bear?" Jurian asked.

Glyn glanced at his older brother, and Sabra heard him whisper in a language she didn't recognize, "*Artos?*"

Daffyd waved a hand to silence him.

"On our island we like to name our swords," one of the braided-beard brothers said. "Sounds like that might be this sword's name. A name, and a prophecy."

"What, *from stone to be freed?*" Sabra asked, incredulous.

He waved a hand. "The inscription, just as it's written. *Excalibur*. Who knows. Maybe it will make sense in time."

Jurian leaned back while the others marveled over the sword, watching them with a peculiar expression that was almost amusement.

Glyn tried to pick up the sword and grunted when he failed

to raise it more than a finger's breadth from the table. The light of the oil lamp trickled down the blade's surface, and Glyn dropped the blade with another resounding clank.

"Look! There's more! What *is* that? That's not even Latin!"

"I've never seen any writing like it," Jurian said, tucking his hands behind his head as he leaned back on the wall.

Sabra pursed her lips and tried to get a better look. Sure enough, the length of the blade was etched with curious, runic figures. Menas grumbled and sat back, but all the Celts turned to look at the stern-faced man on Jurian's other side. Ivor, she remembered. The surly one. The man folded his arms and nodded toward the blade.

"It's called Ogham," he said, his voice so deep Sabra thought she felt it more than heard it. "It's an ancient script."

"I can see that," Bleddyn said with feigned impatience.

Ivor only met his gaze darkly, no hint of amusement on his face. "The language it writes here is a Celtic dialect."

"And…?"

There was a long silence, then Ivor said slowly, voice low, *"A 'm dal draig lladawt ef."*

Bleddyn's face turned a ghastly shade of white. Sabra shot a furtive glance at Jurian, but he was studying Ivor curiously and had missed it entirely. Even Menas was too busy staring at the sword to notice.

"Well," Bleddyn said, his voice thin. "You can put that sword up now, Jurian. My stew's gone cold."

Jurian lifted the blade off the table without comment, but then he glanced at Sabra and her face must have betrayed her alarm, because he lowered his brows and said, "You look like you've seen a ghost."

She felt Bleddyn's gaze fix on her, but she just smiled faintly and said, "No, I was just curious about the words."

"What *did* they mean?" Jurian asked, swinging the sword back into its scabbard.

Ivor shrugged smoothly. "Hard to say. Runic inscriptions rarely say anything straightforward, I find."

Jurian let the matter drop, but Sabra was burning with curiosity. She couldn't understand how he could go back to eating cold fish stew so blithely, when the air hummed with so much tension, so much power? Couldn't anyone else feel it?

Menas slurped the rest of his soup and ended with a loud belch. She grimaced, but Bleddyn, who'd apparently forgotten all about the runic script, laughed out loud and slapped him on the shoulder. Menas had the grace to look embarrassed, but that just made the other Celts laugh harder. Jurian's mouth twisted in a faint smile, but Sabra felt he stood apart too, an onlooker who didn't quite fit in. Maybe they had something in common after all.

"All right," Menas said, silencing the Celts by thumping his hand on the table. "Jurian, Eva, the ship's pilot told us to sleep on board tonight. They've got to be ready to sail whenever they get a favorable wind." He got up but almost knocked his head against the doorframe, so he stooped over as he clapped Bleddyn on the shoulder. "Thanks for letting me help your men."

"The help's always welcome," Bleddyn said. "Are you sure you don't want to stay and work through the winter, and sail up to Britannia with us in the spring?"

"It's his choice, not mine," Menas said. "I go where he goes."

Sabra's brows jumped at that, but Bleddyn just grinned at Jurian. "No chance of convincing you? That sword's meant to go home, you know."

"I'll bring it back, don't worry," Jurian said. "But it has something to do first." He leaned over the table to clasp the ship pilot's arm. "I'll look for you when I come back, if the offer still stands then."

"We're at your disposal. Good luck, Jurian. Eva."

Eva dipped her head, waiting impatiently for Menas and Jurian to stop talking and leave the thick air of the *taberna*. She'd felt stifled since she walked through the door, and sitting at table with a crowd of barbarians hadn't done much for her mood. But part of her mind kept turning over those strange Celtic words, and she pondered any number of ways to trick the translation out of one of the men. Preferably not Ivor—that man terrified her. As Menas and Jurian stepped out of the small chamber, she saw her chance. The boy Glyn slipped out behind them, sent to get more wine by his father, but Sabra grabbed his arm before he could pass her by.

Menas and Jurian were already at the tavern door, and she only prayed they wouldn't forget about her.

"Glyn," she whispered.

The boy stared at her, wide-eyed and open-mouthed. Now that she thought of it, he'd been staring at her wide-eyed and open-mouthed through the whole of their meal. She bit her lip and pressed on quickly.

"What did the inscription say? I need to know."

Glyn scrubbed his hands over his ruddy cheeks. "I don't know. I mean, I know, but I don't know if I should say it. My father didn't want it translated."

"Why not?"

"Because it sounds like a curse!"

She took a step back. "What do you mean?"

Glyn jerked his gaze from hers, his eyes roving over the dim room. "All right, listen. But don't tell the swordsman, all right?" He bounced on his toes and said, "The literal translation is this. *Who me holds the dragon will kill he*. Or *him*."

Sabra waited a moment, but Glyn said nothing else. "Wait, that's it? Why is that a curse?"

"Because," Glyn said, tugging his dark blond hair. "Because! Weren't you listening?"

"Look," she snapped. "I don't speak…whatever language it was written in, but it doesn't sound like a curse to me. And what was that *he* or *him* supposed to mean?"

"*Ef! Ef!*" He glowered at her. "It doesn't translate. In Latin you have to say *him* or *he*, but it doesn't work that way in this inscription." Glyn puffed out his cheeks. "Ivor and my father both interpreted it as *him*. I'm sorry. It says he's going to die."

"That's a stupid thing for a sword to say," Sabra snapped.

Glyn shook his head. "I don't think it's that simple," he said. "Think about it. It was written ambiguously on purpose. That one phrase could mean so many different things, and it can mean them all equally, all at the same time."

"You're not making sense," Sabra said.

As she said it she glanced over her shoulder for any sign of Menas or Jurian. She'd wanted a quick answer, not a linguistic debate. But the two men had left the tavern, and even the other rough sailors had gone their way. In the common room, no one remained but a greasy-looking man in Eastern-styled black robes, who sat sneering at a plate of figs as if he could reduce it to ash by the power of his hate. Sabra shook her head and glanced away before the man caught her staring at him.

"I mean, what if the sword means all of it?" Glyn said. "*Draig* is also a word we give to chieftains, kings, powerful warriors and lords of men." He waved his hands dramatically. "So, it could mean 'the one who holds the sword will kill the dragon.' And 'the dragon—chief—who holds the sword will kill...someone.' *And* 'the dragon will kill the one who holds the sword.' It could mean different people, or all the same person, or both. Listen, that sword was made by *Myrddin!*"

Sabra shook her head to show her ignorance.

"Myrddin was the greatest seer in all the world. Some people say he's already lived the future. Don't you think he'd know how to write an inscription?"

"But..." Sabra's voice dropped to a whisper as the greasy man stood to leave. "What's the dragon?"

"There are prophecies...myths about two dragons in Britannia. A red dragon and a white dragon. Perhaps those are the ones the inscription means."

Sabra shuddered. "Why did you say I shouldn't tell Jurian all this? Seems like something he ought to know."

"He'll hear the curse. He may not hear the rest of it. He's got a responsibility, but if he thinks death is waiting for him in Britannia, he may never bring the sword back, and he *has* to bring it back. But what person in his right mind would willingly go to meet his death?"

Sabra bit her tongue and said nothing.

"Anyway, there's also a belief that if someone is told a prophecy about themselves, it will have to come true. That they may even make it come true by trying to avoid it."

"Enough," she snapped. "You only just met him. Do you already doubt him so much?"

"You only just met him too. Are you that quick to trust him?"

She pursed her lips and took a step back. "Thanks for the information, Glyn."

Without waiting for a reply, she turned and stalked out of the tavern. To her relief, Jurian and Menas were standing against one of the portico's marble columns, deep in conversation. Jurian glanced up when she came out, his face impassive.

"Thought you might have changed your mind," he said. "No such luck."

She narrowed her eyes but swallowed her retort, trying not to notice how the evening sun slanting behind him turned his hair to a crown of fire.

"Are you ready?" Menas asked.

Sabra hesitated. It might have been her imagination, but…she could have sworn she heard someone calling her name. Someone with an unmistakable voice, warm and melodic…

Hanno.

"Gods, no," she hissed under her breath.

40

Portus

Jurian watched the color drain from Eva's cheeks as she twisted around suddenly to scan the milling crowds.

"Is everything all right?" he asked, voice low.

He tried to follow her gaze, and after a moment he spotted a tall Libyan slave pushing through the crowds. Every once in a while the man stopped, staring around in desperation and shouting someone's name. With the wind blowing the wrong direction, Jurian only heard the last "a" of the name. Eva reached out frantically and grabbed his arm.

"Please. Let's go to the ship."

"What's going on?" he asked, pulling his arm free. "Is that man looking for you?"

She hissed in annoyance. "If I wanted to be found, do you think I'd be asking to leave?"

"*Are* you a slave, Eva? Tell me the truth."

"I'm *not*. But that doesn't mean I want anything to do with that man."

Jurian contemplated the value of continuing their argument, and finally shook it off with a dismissive wave.

"I honestly don't care who or what you are, but don't ever lie to me."

She pursed her lips and strode off toward the ships. Menas

caught her after a moment and steered her in the right direction, and Jurian took one more look at the Libyan slave before following them. They arrived at the ship and were greeted by the pilot, a thin, grey shard of a man who called himself Kleon.

"I didn't know there would be three of you," he said, eyeing Eva suspiciously. "I've taken another passenger already, and haven't got berths for so many guests to have their own."

Jurian was about to tell Eva she would need to wait for the next ship to Cyrene, but Menas held up a hand and said, "I'll sleep on deck, if it's all the same to you. Those ship beds are a bit small for me anyway."

Kleon shook his head and waved them on board. Jurian took Menas' *sarcina* and his own pack to one of the berths under the deck and came up just as the sailors started pushing the ship away from mooring.

"Did we get that wind already?" he asked Menas, leaning on the bulwark beside him.

Kleon overheard him and said brusquely, "No. But we're putting out into the Claudian harbor to wait for it."

Jurian exchanged a glance with Menas. "Not too obliging, is he?" he muttered under his breath.

"You know, that girl over there could say the same about you," Menas said. "You could try to be more considerate."

"Something about her is off," Jurian said. "I don't know what it is. But I don't buy her story about her mistress leaving without her, especially when that slave showed up."

"That, Jurian, is none of our concern. But a little charity goes a long way. Whatever the reason, she's on her own. No friends. No one to give her a hand. Maybe she deserves it, I don't know. But that really doesn't matter, does it?"

Jurian pushed himself away from the bulwark and strode away, not even bothering to reply to that. He walked the entire length of the ship and stood a few minutes in silence beside the watchman at the prow, then paced back again, grateful for the firm floor laid over the hold that spared him from navigating a treacherous path between barrels and crates and *amphorae*. When the ship dropped anchor in the outer harbor, most of the sailors wrapped themselves in blankets in the ship's hold. Menas had already set the example for that; Jurian found him stretched out alongside the bulwark in his traveling cloak, the hood pulled so far down over his face that the fabric ruffled as he breathed.

Jurian sighed and crossed to the other side of the ship, leaning out over the rail to peer into the infinite darkness of the sea below.

"Can't sleep?" a quiet voice beside him asked.

He ground his teeth and glanced down, realizing he'd almost stepped on Eva. She was huddled against the bulwark in her dark *palla,* blending so well with the shadows that he hadn't seen her at all.

"No," he said, though he'd rather have said nothing at all. "Are you anxious to be home?"

She smiled faintly. "Anxious. That's a good word for it. What about you? Are you on your way home?"

"I have none," he said.

"No family?"

He prodded his tongue against his teeth, fighting the sudden ache of loneliness in his heart. "No. Not…not anymore."

She didn't say anything for some time, and when he finally glanced at her he found her still staring at him. After a moment she scrambled to her feet and braced her hands on the rail.

"I'm sorry," she said.

Jurian shrugged; what could he say to that? Fortunately he didn't have to say anything; the girl didn't have any trouble keeping her mouth shut.

"Why are you going to Cyrene?" she asked. "No one goes to Cyrene these days."

"There's something I have to see for myself."

She gave him a haughty look. "Coming to gawk at us? Mock our misery?"

"Hardly," he said. "But if it makes you feel better, you're free to think that."

He saw her bristle and gave himself a mental slap. If Menas had heard him, he'd be in for another lecture.

"Sorry." He bent his head and dug his fingers through his hair. "My sister died yesterday, in Rome," he murmured suddenly, without even knowing why. What business did this strange girl have knowing his private troubles?

Her hand flew up to her mouth and she took a step away from him. For half a moment he thought she looked ready to throw her arms around him, but thankfully she didn't move.

"What happened?" Eva asked. "Was she sick?"

Jurian laughed quietly. "No, no…that's the thing. She was perfectly…perfectly well." He noticed her curiosity and waved a hand. "It doesn't matter. I'm sorry I troubled you with it."

"No," she whispered. "That's all right. I don't mind."

Jurian gave her a strange look and pushed away from the rail. "I'm going to bed. Good night, Eva."

He left her standing there and headed into the ship's cabin, wishing with all of his aching heart that he would find Mari in the berth, ready to tease him about the golden-eyed girl from Cyrene. He would have been so mad at her too, and that would have only provoked her to tease him more. With a thin sigh he pushed back the curtain to his berth, and stopped in surprise.

Right in front of him, sitting cross-legged on the floor, was a thin, awkward looking man. Looking at him, all Jurian could think of was a spider—all gangly legs and narrow body. He had his forearms resting on his knees and his head bowed, a greasy mop of long black hair dangling in front of his face. The whole berth stank, too, like leather and unwashed flesh.

"I didn't know I had a berth-mate," Jurian said, folding his arms.

The man almost jumped out of his skin. He scrambled to his feet, brushing his hair from his face with long fingers and sniffing as he scanned Jurian head to toe.

"You weren't supposed to, but I got ousted from my private room because these heathens have put a girl on this ship. Of course *she* had to have a berth to herself. Harlot. They should make her sleep in the hold with all the other heathens."

Jurian's hand clenched reflexively on the hilt of his *seax*. "That girl, Eva? She's with me. And she's *not* a harlot. So be careful what you say."

The man made a smug face and took a step back. "Do what you like. I've no care for anything."

Apparently, Jurian thought, but managed to keep the thought to himself. Instead he edged around the man.

"Did you already claim one of these bunks?" he asked.

Because I really don't want to touch anything you've already touched.

"The bottom one," the man said. "I don't care."

Jurian glared at the man's back and unhooked his sword belt, tossing Excalibur up into the bunk before hoisting himself up after it. It was a narrow fit, but Jurian was used to it by now. The man kept the oil lamp burning below so Jurian pressed his eyes closed, running his fingers over the part of the sword's blade not covered with leather. The sword had a strange feel. It felt like something solid, something ghostly, something fluid, and all the while a faint buzzing sensation inched up his fingers from the cold steel.

His mind would not settle enough to let him sleep. Even after all that had happened, and with as little sleep as he'd gotten the night before, he couldn't stop the bewildered racing of his thoughts. Prophecies, dragons, mystical swords made by mystical men? And *he* was supposed to do something about all of it? It seemed ridiculous to even accept that he was the person named by the prophecy—and more than ridiculous, it seemed incredibly arrogant.

Still, he now had a sword, and even if he wasn't a Legionary yet, he still had a commission to fulfill. And he would fulfill it.

What would Mari say if she saw me now?

41

THE MEDITERRANEAN SEA

THE GENTLE ROCKING OF THE boat finally lulled Jurian into a strange half-sleep. He could hear the greasy man on the floor muttering to himself—snatches of words in a lilting tone that sounded like a prayer. But it wasn't any prayer Jurian had ever heard, and when at last he lost track of the man's voice, he slid into uneasy dreams.

The ground was hard and dry under Jurian's feet, and for a moment, he felt he was back in the catacombs of Rome. The sickly smell of death and some kind of incense wafted over him, and his feet crunched in something that wasn't stone. He glanced down, saw bits of broken skulls and crushed garlands of flowers.

He staggered forward, up a hill toward a pillar that gleamed silver-white, though the sky was dark with clouds that threatened to smother the earth. There was something wrong with the sky now…it was red, red like blood. Red like fire.

Something was coming, scorching the ground under his feet, bleaching the skulls in shimmering heat. He had to get to the pillar, but his feet wouldn't move properly. A weight pressed him down, forcing him to the earth. He dragged himself through the skulls on hands and knees. The weight of the sword on his back pressed him into the earth. But he struggled on, propelled by some intense urgency.

He crested the hill, and found that the pillar was no longer empty. A woman in a white gown stood chained to it, a crown of flowers in her hair. And the clouds roiled away, revealing a dark shape in the sky—wings, a head with horns. As the creature exhaled, the woman turned to face him.

It was Eva.

Jurian jerked himself awake, slamming his head painfully on the low ceiling of the cabin. For a moment he sat there, propped on his elbows, his heart hammering and a cold sweat soaking through his tunic. Gradually, the guttering lamplight and the gentle rocking of the ship soothed his tattered nerves.

What does it all mean? he wondered as he settled back, his hand resting on the hilt of Excalibur. *The dreams, the prophecies, all the mysteries...*

So many mysteries. Since he and Mari had left Satala, it felt as if his entire world had shrouded itself in mist. Everything he thought he knew—everything he thought he'd ever wanted—had twisted somehow into something new and strange. Here he was, a fire-headed half-Greek Roman with a Germanic name from the borderlands of Anatolia, heading across the sea to the Libyan coast with a Celtic sword clutched in his hand.

He had to smile at that. Maybe he was a bridge after all.

"You make too much noise," the greasy man said suddenly.

Jurian rolled onto his side and peered down at the floor. "Are you still down there?" he asked. "And I'm not the only one in here making noise. I can't sleep with all your muttering."

"Because you are weak." The man snorted. "I do not need sleep."

"Everyone needs sleep."

"Why should I sleep, when I can contemplate the things that matter the most?" The man took a deep breath, tipping his head back and closing his eyes. "The body keeps us from truth. It is a wretched evil, a cursed weight."

"You don't look like you weigh much to me," Jurian said.

The man's eyes snapped open and he glowered up at him. "Sleep if you must," he said, "but leave me in peace to contemplate the higher things and follow the path to illumination."

"That sounds like nonsense," Jurian said. "Have you been drinking?"

"I don't touch wine. These things are for the unclean and the uninitiated. All luxuries of the body are abhorrent to me."

Jurian started to chuckle, then realized that the man was glowering at him, dark eyes fierce under pointed brows. "What's your name?" Jurian asked instead.

"I am called Innai. I have lately been in Persia, where I was initiated into the elect that follow Mani."

"Never heard of him," Jurian said. "Is he some god of the Persians?"

Innai clicked his tongue. "Stupid boy," he said. "Mani is *the* Prophet...the Incarnate One. The Manifestation of Truth."

"You really believe that?" Jurian asked. "Some man from Persia is supposed to be the—what did you call him?—Manifestation of Truth? How can he be the manifestation of truth when apparently all he speaks are lies?"

"Your ignorance does not do you credit."

"Nor yours."

Innai pressed his fingertips together and measured Jurian. "You are not like the heathen pagans aboard this ship," he said. "There is something of the light about you. But you have not yet realized the truth."

"What truth would that be?"

"There is a great darkness coming. The Dark Power is struggling for ascendancy. The balance of the universe is tipping."

"What are you talking about? What Dark Power?"

Innai shook his head. "There are two powers in the universe—Dark and Light. Body and Soul. Don't you see? And the Dark Power is rising."

Jurian thought about his dream, about what had happened to Menas...about Casca and Mari. Something dark *was* coiling its way into the heart of the world. But the man's vision of things rang with a false note, something that struck Jurian as hollow.

"You believe that they are evenly matched...this Dark Power

and the Light?" Jurian asked slowly, wishing Mari were there to give him the words he needed. He closed his eyes, whispering a prayer in his heart for guidance. "And you say that the body is evil…and only the soul of a man is good?"

"Yes, yes. Perhaps you aren't as stupid as you seem," Innai said, nodding his head.

"So tell me, then. Which power gives life?"

Innai hesitated. Jurian watched him with interest, surprised as much at the question as at Innai's sudden uncertainty.

"Well?" Jurian asked after Innai was silent for several minutes.

Innai shook his head, muttering something about infidels and the uninitiated. After another glare in Jurian's direction, he unfolded himself from the floor and took the lamp outside. Jurian settled back into his bunk, considering the strange man and his stranger beliefs.

But he's right about one thing, he thought. *A dark power is rising…and it will reveal itself in Cyrene.*

THE NEXT MORNING dawned cloudy and chill. The churning waves were capped with white, as if donning furs against the bite in the wind. Jurian stumbled up the narrow steps to the deck, bleary and aching after a poor night's sleep. He found Menas and Eva already awake and standing at the bulwark, pointing out slivers of lightning in a distant bank of clouds. Innai, he realized with some annoyance, was awake too—if he'd ever fallen asleep. He sat cross-legged in the shadow of the deck on a coil of rope, even the violent wind failing to stir the oily length of his hair.

"Good morning," Menas said cheerfully.

Jurian shivered and tightened his father's cloak around his shoulders. Eva had brought a blanket from the cabin and had it pulled up over her head and puddled at her feet. She peeked at him from under the makeshift hood, eyes bright.

"Jurian. Honestly. You look terrible," she remarked.

"Thanks." He leaned on the rail and ducked his head from a blast of wind. Times like these, he might almost believe what

Innai said about the body being evil.

"Didn't you sleep?" Menas asked.

Jurian pointed at the man sitting below them. "I had to share a berth with that one."

"I saw him in the tavern," Eva said, making a face. "Nasty, unpleasant-looking man."

"Just as nasty and unpleasant on the inside, too." Jurian crossed over to the other side of the deck, just to make sure the man wouldn't overhear him, and the others followed. "Claimed to be the follower of some man he called Mani. Apparently this *prophet* teaches that there are two gods, Light and Dark, and that everything in the world is bad, only spiritual things are good."

"I've seen enough evil in this world that it almost makes sense," Eva said, very quietly.

"You too?" Jurian asked, just as soft.

She regarded him in surprise, but he lowered his gaze to the sea.

"Steer clear of snakes in the grass like him," Menas warned. "They mix just enough truth with lies to make their teaching seem reasonable…and then the trap is sprung."

"And once sprung, escape is almost impossible," Eva murmured.

Jurian glanced at her, curious. "You've been saying things like that since we left Portus," he said. "What was your business in Rome…and what is Cyrene to you?"

"Cyrene is home," Eva said. There was a startled look in her eyes that Jurian didn't quite understand.

"Then perhaps you could tell us something of what is happening there," Menas said. "In our travels we've heard rumors of strange things…of dragons, and sacrifices, and a cult to a dark god." He peered at Eva. "Do you know anything of this?"

"These rumors…" Eva stopped, then began again. "Do they fault the cult of the god for the trouble in Cyrene?"

Jurian shook his head. "No. Incredibly, they blame the Christians."

Eva flinched, and Jurian exchanged a glance with Menas.

"Does that surprise you?" he asked. "All the ills of the Empire, it seems, are to be blamed on the Christians. And many pay for it with their lives."

His breath caught and he stared out across the wind-swept sea. The girl beside him was suddenly quiet, and not just because she was silent. She was just…still. Like a flower that had closed itself against the chill of night.

"You do know something of all this, don't you?" Jurian asked her. "Please tell us. We are heading to Cyrene to help, if we can."

At this, Eva raised her eyes to his, her sudden guardedness thawing just a bit. "You…care about Cyrene?" she said. "Why?"

"We don't always get to choose the roads we travel," Jurian said, his mouth twisting in a grin. "Sometimes, it seems, they're chosen for us."

Eva was silent for so long that Jurian thought she would never speak. But finally she said, "There is some dark power in the hills above our city. We have been offering ritual sacrifice for ten years, attempting to appease it. But the earth is filled with tremblings, and the Kyre—our spring—is withering." She took a breath, then continued, "My mistress discovered, just before we left for Rome, that her own name had been drawn in the lottery as the next sacrificial offering. But her father, the governor, called another name in her stead. I fear that my mistress has run back to Cyrene against her father's wish…and I think she means to take the girl's place before the god is blasphemed."

"And is that why you are running back to Cyrene, then?" Menas asked, eyes keen. "To…do what, exactly?"

"I…don't want my mistress to die alone," Eva said. "I am her assistant. She needs me."

"You speak of this dark power as though it was divine," Jurian said. "Is it? Or is it just some brute beast that crawled its way out of the sea?"

Eva shook her head. "No one is certain."

"Have you seen it yourself?" Menas asked. "Do you know what it is?"

Jurian watched the girl's face grow pale under their scrutiny.

She knows more than she's telling, he thought. *I just hope she tells us what she knows before it's too late.*

He remembered his dream then—the sight of her pale face against the smooth stone of the pillar, a wreath of flowers in her hair. Without thinking, he reached up to brush his fingers over the hilt of his sword.

"They told me what it meant," Eva blurted. "The Celtic sailors. They told me what the inscription said."

Jurian regarded her with interest. "Oh? And?"

"It means, 'the one who holds the sword will kill the dragon.'"

Menas clapped Jurian on the shoulder. "That's a positive message for you," he said.

"That's not all," Eva said. "It could also mean, 'the dragon will slay the one who wields the sword.'"

Jurian grimaced at Menas. "Not so positive, that last one. I'd like to *not* die by dragon fire, if I can avoid it."

"It's an ambiguity," Eva said. "The voices of the gods so often are shrouded in mystery."

Tell me about it, Jurian thought. Aloud, he said, "Then we make our own destiny…and let history decide the right reading."

42

Carthago, Africa

Three days later, the ship put into port at Carthage. As the sailors traded out their cargo, Sabra, Jurian, and Menas headed down to the docks.

"We should stay close to the ship," Menas said under his breath. "I do believe that ship's pilot might make a break for it while we're on land if it meant he could avoid putting in at Apollonia."

Sabra glanced over her shoulder and found the captain watching them steadily from the side of the ship, and shuddered.

"This place doesn't seem very friendly anyway," Jurian muttered.

Their strange party drew many interested stares from the sailors and dock workers bustling around them—and not all of them were friendly. But when they saw the hilt of Jurian's sword above his shoulder, and the quiet confidence in the way he carried it, they moved away without a word.

The three of them wandered across the busy street that edged the harbor, guided toward a row of food stands by Menas' appetite. Sabra followed, lost in memories of walking these streets with Hanno, when Jurian suddenly laid a hand on her back and propelled her down a dark alleyway that stank of rotting fish. She hissed in protest, but he jerked his head, laying a finger on his lips. Menas followed, too wary to grumble.

Once they were in the shadows, he left her near the wall with Menas and edged to the corner of the building.

"What's wrong with you?" Sabra asked.

Jurian waved a hand at her to be quiet, and she crossed her arms and glowered up at Menas.

"Is he always like this?"

Menas didn't answer, but kept his eyes trained on Jurian's back. After a moment, Jurian left his vantage point and returned to them.

"There's a knot of Legion troops over there," he said quietly. "Standing not two ships down from where our vessel is docked." He exchanged a glance with Menas, worry in every line of his face. "Do you think...could they have found us so quickly?"

"Are you in some kind of trouble with the Legion?" Sabra asked, her heart jumping in alarm. The last thing she needed was to bring more trouble home with her...especially trouble with Rome.

Jurian ignored her. "What should we do?"

"We should get back to the ship," Menas said evenly. With a woeful smile, he lifted his shoulders and said, "There's no disguising me, Jurian. We can't hide out in the city forever, or we'll be left here in Carthage."

"I can't stay here," Sabra interrupted. "We have to get back to Cyrene...even if I have to go alone."

"You're not going alone," Jurian said. He tapped his finger against his lip and paced the alleyway for a moment, then returned to the corner of the building. "They're not paying much attention to the street. We might be able to make it if we go now—"

A sudden shout rang out from the far end of the docks. Sabra and Menas rushed to join him, all three of them peering around the corner of the building. The Legion soldiers were running toward a scuffle, but Sabra was too far away to see what was happening.

After a moment she realized Jurian was tugging her arm.

"Come *on!*" he hissed. "We have to go, now!"

"But—"

She swallowed the retort and followed him. Menas had already made his way to the ship, and once on the street, Jurian held Sabra to a casual stride. She could hear him breathing thinly and knew he'd rather run than walk, but he was smart enough not to make a scene. The boy was clever; she had to give him that.

Once they made it back onto the ship, all three of them climbed up onto the deck for a better view of the docks. Menas leaned low over the bulwark to hide his height, but Jurian stood tall and shielded his eyes against the light, muttering under his breath.

"I wish we could have gotten closer," Sabra muttered. "I can't see anything, Jurian."

He flinched and stared at her, face grey as the grave, and Sabra's heart jerked strangely.

"What?" she asked. "What's wrong?"

He bit his lip and shook his head. "Nothing. It's just…my sister… Never mind."

His voice trailed off and Sabra hesitated, wanting to comfort him somehow, feeling ill-suited for the task. Instead she focused on the scuffle at the end of the dock, where the Legion troops had pushed back the crowd to clear a space to settle the dispute. A small man stood in the middle. He looked youthful, but his head was bald save for a thick, dark beard. He had a bright smile on his face, and Sabra couldn't figure out why. A drunken sailor staggered in wobbling circles around him, shouting abuse, but the man just kept smiling and smiling.

Finally, the Legion commander threw up his hands and seized the sailor by the neck of his tunic, flinging him out of the circle of bystanders and gesturing for him to get back to whatever hole he'd crawled out of. The small man immediately sat down on the ground, cross-legged, and held out his hand to the crowd.

"Coin for the poor traveler?" he said, his voice reaching Sabra's ears with surprising clarity. "Coin for the poor?"

One of the soldiers flipped him a coin. "Read me my fortune, fool," he cried with a loud laugh.

And then, for no reason whatsoever, the bald man lifted his

gaze, bright and piercing, and stared straight at her across the crowded dock.

"Chains may bind, but words may loose."

Sabra caught her breath. The man seemed to be speaking straight to her, not to the soldier who stood waiting for his words.

"That's it?" cried the soldier. "Nothing else?"

The man smiled up at him. "I say what I must, and no more than I must."

The soldier rejoined his troop, and slowly the bystanders trickled away from the scene. Just before the eddy and swirl of the crowd hid him from view, the bald man smiled at them and raised a hand in salute.

Sabra heard Jurian's sharp gasp and glanced at him. His face was a ghastly white, like he'd seen a spirit, and he turned away to lean back against the bulwark.

"Menas," he said. "Did you see…? That's not…that's not possible."

Menas chuckled. "It is. With him, it is. It wouldn't be the first time he's gotten me out of a mess." He rubbed his beard, exchanging an amused glance with Jurian. "Eh, maybe that's how he gets all his money."

"What do you mean?" Sabra asked. "Do you know that man?"

Jurian only got to his feet and moved away to the other end of the boat. Sabra watched him go, then turned back to Menas.

"Can you please tell me what is going on? Who was he?"

"An old friend," was all Menas would say. "A powerful friend."

That little bald man? she wondered, bemused, and turned to scan the crowds again, hoping for another sight of him. There had been such a kindness in his smile, and she couldn't banish the sense that he had been speaking to her. She didn't know what the words meant, but they comforted her somehow.

Maybe that's what he means by powerful?

Do you still know nothing of power?

She winced and focused on each face on the street to drive the sinister voice away. And then—her breath caught in her throat, and her blood turned to ice. There…on that merchant ship just putting into port…

No. It's impossible. We left him in Portus. There's no way he could have followed us…

"Cast off lines!" the captain shouted suddenly, breaking through her panic. "Oarsmen!"

Sabra ducked down behind the bulwark, smiling when Menas gave her an anxious look.

"I never like this part," she whispered.

He smiled and dropped heavily down to the deck beside her. "Me either." He jerked his head toward the stern behind the cabin. "I think we lost our greasy traveling companion."

"Gods be praised," she muttered.

AFTER ANOTHER SCANTY evening meal of fish and dried fruit, Sabra decided she never wanted to eat fish again. Or raisins. Particularly not in combination. She stood up from the mound of rope she'd been sitting on and leaned over the ship's rail, feeling the wind pick up and whip across her like a stinging lash. It was evening already, but it seemed too dark too soon.

"Storm's coming," one of the sailors shouted at them. "Come on, clear off the deck!"

Menas and Jurian were on their feet in an instant to follow him, and Sabra stared in terror at the sea as she trailed Menas down the steps. She thought of the sea storm on her way to Rome, but that was nothing compared to this. The waves churned, pummeling the hull of the ship and showering them with an icy spray. A tattered rack of clouds was building on the horizon.

With Innai gone, Jurian invited Menas and Sabra to sit together in his berth. Sabra climbed up into the upper bed, where she could see out the small window and watch the approaching storm. Jurian and Menas settled on the floor in the darkness. The sailor had forbidden them a light, explaining that if the storm got too wild, a broken lamp or an unguarded candle could set the whole ship alight.

After a few moments of silence, a roll of thunder set the cabin walls trembling. Lightning knifed through the sky, and the ship pitched. Below her, she heard Menas groan and Jurian chuckle softly.

"You're just never going to get used to this, are you?" Jurian's voice said in the shadows.

"They call me River Walker and not Boat Rider for a reason," Menas growled.

The ship pitched again, more steeply this time, and Sabra heard the sailors on the deck above begin to shout. She closed her eyes, murmuring a prayer under her breath.

"Menas," Jurian began, his voice unnervingly calm as the ship twisted beneath them. "I've been meaning to ask you something."

Sabra stumbled over her words, then forgot about the prayer altogether as Jurian began to speak.

"I asked Innai which power gives life—the Dark or the Light... Body or Soul. He said that the Light was the Good, and the Dark Evil. He said that the body was evil. And when I asked him the question, he couldn't answer me...but I don't even know why I asked it. I wish..." His voice trailed off. "I just wish Mari were here to explain it."

When Menas spoke, Sabra could hear the smile in his voice. "But you haven't asked a question yet, Jurian."

"I suppose...if God is good...and you say that the Christ is the *via et veritas et vita*..." Jurian's voice faltered.

"Go on," Menas prompted him gently.

"Then how is it that He demands death?"

Sabra pressed a hand to her mouth to keep herself from gasping. Was it true, then, what the Romans said? That the Christians took victims of their own for dark sacrifices? If it were true, then perhaps the God of the Christians and her own dark god weren't that different after all.

"Why do you say that?" Menas was asking.

"Because...Mother and Eugenius...and my sweet Mari...they all died. They had to die. God...God *required* them to die, Menas. And if He is supposed to be Life...then I don't understand. Why would He not want them to live? And why would they want to die?"

Menas was quiet for a long time, and Sabra waited, breathless, for him to speak. "There's something you need to understand, Jurian. About love."

Love? Sabra thought.

"Love?" Jurian asked at the same moment, as if he'd read her mind.

"Let me ask it this way. If Casca had given you the time or the choice, would you have offered to die in your sister's stead? If you knew it would save her, would you?"

"You know I would. You know I wish I had."

"Why?"

Sabra edged closer, wishing she could see Jurian's face in the swallowing darkness. Lightning flashed outside the cabin and thunder followed almost instantly. The ship heaved and rolled beneath them.

"Because I love her, Menas," Jurian said. "And I would want her to live."

"And what is the greatest gift that you could give your sister?" Menas asked.

"My own life."

Sabra felt the tears running down her cheeks. She thought of Ayzebel, her hands burning with coals, her back torn with lashes, her face pale and amber eyes still and empty as she hung dead in her bonds in the square. She thought of Elissa, smiling from the pillar of sacrifice.

"When your mother and Eugenius accepted death…when Mari witnessed with the *signum* and accepted her death…it wasn't because they hated life, or because God required death." Menas paused for a moment. "It was because they *loved,* Jurian. They loved God beyond everything else. And when your love is strong, you don't fear…and you don't waver."

Sabra drew a shaking breath as quietly as she could manage. Everything about the sacrifices they offered the dark god in Cyrene was an execution. The god was a god of blood and death, and he demanded those things. He was a maw…a gaping, devouring hell-mouth.

But that's not what I teach the children, she realized suddenly. *I have taught them about sacrifice…to be willing victims…to offer their lives for the sake of the city, for their own families…for everything they love…*

"That's why we make the *signum,*" Menas continued. "That's why it is the sign of our faith. It is the Sign of Love, Jurian. The Love that sets men free, the Love that conquers death, the Love that banishes evil."

As the lightning flashed through the tiny window, Sabra saw Menas' large hand gripping Jurian's shaking shoulder. As the darkness swallowed them again, she heard Jurian's broken breath and realized that he was weeping too.

"I never knew," he managed, voice taut with tears, "that love could hurt so much."

"Stay the course," Menas told him gently. "Death is not the end."

The ship suddenly pitched so violently that Sabra was nearly flung off the bed. She heard Menas grunt as he crashed over, and Jurian's muffled cry.

"All hands!" a sailor's frantic voice screamed from the deck. "All hands!"

A moment later, another sailor appeared at the doorway of the cabin. "You two!" he shouted, his voice hoarse from salt spray and barking orders. "Get up here or we're done for! We've lost three men to the sea tonight, and we can't hold her head steady without help!"

Sabra recovered herself just in time for Jurian to thrust something into her hands.

"Keep this safe for me," he said.

Sabra wrapped her hands tightly around the scabbard of Excalibur as Jurian and Menas clambered out of the cabin and onto the deck above.

43

APOLLONIA, LIBYA

WHEN THE BATTERED SHIP FINALLY limped her way into the harbor at Apollonia, the surviving crew members made her fast and staggered ashore. They had meant to put in at Leptis Magna, but the storm had driven them too far off course. They were well past the port when the storm had finally cleared, and the captain had made the decision to press on for Apollonia.

The harbor was practically deserted, all but a Roman trireme drifting out at anchor. Unlike the bustling trade markets of Carthage and Portus, full of people and wares, Apollonia was a ragged outpost. Jurian stared out at the crystal blue waters, gently lapping against the sea wall that protected the little harbor. From this vantage, the place was lovely—all deep greens and blues and white sand. But when he turned and looked at Apollonia itself, he shuddered. The port city looked like it had been broken by some giant hand and left to crumble into the sea.

Beside him, Eva drew a deep breath, and he glanced down at her. There was something sad and almost wistful in her gaze, but the grim shadow that had always lurked deep in her eyes had faded.

"I didn't know," she murmured. "I'd heard rumors…but I didn't know the city had fallen to such ruin."

"You haven't been here before?" he asked, frowning. "But

how did you get to Rome? You must have sailed from here."

She blushed and turned away. "It was night when I came through. I was…attending to my mistress. I didn't see."

"Ah," Jurian said, eyeing her skeptically.

She darted a glance at him and, seeing his expression, gave him a dazzling grin that caught him utterly off-guard. He scrubbed a hand through his thick hair, and caught her stifling a laugh.

"What's so funny?"

"Nothing," she said. "Just mind you don't burn yourself."

He gave her a mock glare and her laughter bubbled over, a low musical sound, like a spring of deep water. Jurian realized with a start that it was the first time he had heard her laugh. She was so different from Mari, and yet…somehow similar. Somehow familiar.

Menas joined Jurian and Eva at that moment, hefting his small sack of coins and scowling.

"Captain charged me double what he should have," he mumbled. "I think he faults us for the storm…and he certainly faults us for making him put in at this port."

Their business settled, they hefted their packs and headed into the city. Eva stumbled more than once on the broken ground. What used to be paved streets had crumbled into near oblivion, their stones cracked and scattered. Buildings crouched in half-toppled mounds, and what remained of their stone walls bulged suspiciously, as though just the movement would dissolve them into heaps. There wasn't a soul to be seen.

"This doesn't feel right," Menas grumbled. "Something's not right in this place."

Eva shifted her small pack, frowning. "This land is plagued with earth tremors. It's part of the god's curse on our land, they say. And trade hasn't been what it used to be in recent years. We have nothing to offer Rome…and so Rome passes us by."

"You seem to know a lot for a slave," Menas said.

"My mistress…she speaks to me sometimes."

"That's not forbidden?" Jurian asked, frowning at her.

Eva shrugged. "She's lonely, I think. She needs someone to

trust. Someone she can speak to and unburden her heart."

They continued in silence, past more ramshackle buildings than Jurian could count and past great fissures in the earth that reeked with a foul steam. In the central *agora* stood a massive stone fountain. Its central pillar was carved with the forms of dolphins and griffins—a tribute to the god for whom the port city was named. It was the only thing in the city that seemed untouched by the destruction around them.

But when Eva saw it, she stumbled forward with a cry.

"No!" she gasped. "No, no!"

She dropped her pack beside the fountain and plunged her hand into the basin.

Jurian and Menas ran to catch up with her. "What is it?" Jurian asked. "What's wrong?"

Eva stared up at him, her face stricken with terror and grief. The basin was dry and filled with dust.

"Please…" she whispered, but not to him. Her eyes seemed to stare straight through him. "Don't let me be too late…"

"Too late for what?" Jurian asked.

"We have to hurry," she said. "There's no time."

They moved through the empty agora and came to the massive, crumbled temple of Jupiter. Its columns had tumbled into what had been the nave, and a pile of rubble taller than Menas marked all that was left of the roof.

On the stone steps before what had been the door sat the only other living person they had seen since they left the harbor. He was a ragged man, bones jutting out everywhere, his feet withered and bare. His eyes, cloudy and bleared, stared vacantly across the square.

Mari would want me to do something for him, Jurian thought. He fumbled in the pouch at his waist and drew out the three last coins from Mari's bag. As he stepped forward to place them in one of the man's upturned hands, the man cried out.

"Which of you carries the sword?" he croaked.

Jurian recoiled. "What sword?"

"The sword from over sea and under stone."

Jurian and Menas exchanged glances.

"That would be…me, I guess," Jurian said.

The man's hand snaked out and caught Jurian by the wrist, his grip stronger than Jurian would have imagined.

"The dragon god waits for you," he said, lifting his other hand and pointing south. "Through fire and blood the sword must pass, then make its journey over a sea like glass…bring it to rest in house of stone, until the orphan boy takes crown and throne. Rome from Rome will pass away, and Rome from Rome will rise."

The man dropped Jurian's wrist, his eyes once more fixed across the square. Jurian dropped the coins into the man's other hand and backed away.

"What does that mean?" Eva whispered.

Jurian shook his head and pointed south. "It means we have business with a dragon," he said.

As they left the shattered port behind them and headed south into the wilds between Apollonia and Cyrene, Menas began to grumble. Jurian's anxiety grew, and he kept glancing back over his shoulder and around at the barren and parched landscape. The grasses were like straw, crunching under their feet and pricking their legs. Small stands of short, shaggy trees pocked the flat expanse of the sea plain, and the shadows beneath them seemed somehow darker than shade should be.

In the last light of the evening, Jurian called a halt under the cover of one of these pockets of shelter.

"Not right, not right," Menas mumbled. "Evil, that's what it is." He made the *signum* across his forehead. "Can you feel it, Jurian? It's thick as wool in this place."

"Why are we stopping, Jurian?" Eva demanded as he shrugged off his pack.

Menas leaned his *sarcina* against a tree trunk and set about gathering dried wood for a small fire. Eva stubbornly refused to set down her own things, Jurian noticed, as he fished in his pack for his flint.

"Jurian," she said again. "We have to go! We're so close…we

can make it tonight. Please, we have to try!"

"I won't risk that tonight," he said. "We don't know what lies ahead. I'd rather not face it in the dark if I can help it. This land is too uneven to cross without a light anyway."

"You don't understand!" Eva cried. "There's nothing but darkness…it won't matter. But if you don't get me home in time…" Her voice trailed off. "Please?"

"I'm sorry, Eva," Jurian said firmly. "We stop for tonight. We'll get you there in the morning."

Eva dropped her pack and sank down, drawing her knees up to her chin and wrapping her arms around them.

Jurian and Menas made a small fire, and they gnawed a few strips of dried meat and a handful of nuts. Eva refused to eat, but sat huddled with her head on her knees at the edge of the firelight. Jurian watched her thoughtfully, crunching an almond.

"I have this feeling," he said softly to Menas, "like we're being followed."

"It's this cursed place," he said. "There's something here. All around us. I haven't felt the like since…" His voice trailed off and he held his hands out to the fire.

Jurian nodded slowly. Menas didn't have to elaborate. He remembered the giant's story all too well, and his skin prickled. They sat a long while in silence, until the fire burned low. Finally, Menas stirred and jerked a head towards Jurian's pack.

"Get some sleep," he said. "I'll watch tonight."

Jurian gratefully rolled himself in his cloak. With one last glance at Eva, who seemed to be asleep, Jurian closed his eyes.

He woke to the sound of shouts and wild bellows.

At first he thought their camp was being attacked by a feral beast. He thrashed out of his cloak and drew his *seax*, tumbling into a crouch and facing what was left of the fire.

His heart jumped into his throat.

Menas was on his knees. Four Legion soldiers held his arms pinioned behind him, and a fifth stood over him, smiling triumphantly. Jurian watched in horror as the man brought his knee up into Menas' face. Menas leaned over and spit blood into the dirt.

With their attention on Menas, somehow, miraculously, the soldiers seemed not to have seen Jurian. He edged quietly into the deep shadow under the tree just behind him, catching the pole of Menas' *sarcina* just before he sent it crashing over into the undergrowth.

He scanned the little camp desperately, but couldn't spot Eva anywhere. She had disappeared, probably when the fight started. A thin sigh of relief escaped him—at least she hadn't been caught. Still, he wasn't sure if he wanted to blame her for cowardice or praise her for quick thinking. She knew these hills; maybe she was going for help.

He wormed his way around the tree, testing the grip on his *seax*, calculating the angle of his attack.

"Menas, you are under arrest for treason," the captain said. "It is the will of the divine Diocletian that you stand trial for your crime." He twisted his fingers into Menas' hair, jerking his face up. "Otherwise," he said, "I'd kill you right here, right now. Desertion is punishable by death." He dropped Menas' head again and stepped back, folding his arms across his chest. "Bind his arms and legs. Make sure the beast is secure."

Jurian shifted his position to get better purchase for his attack, but at that same moment Menas lifted his head. His eyes locked with Jurian's, and he mouthed a single word.

"Run."

44

Libya

Jurian froze, his hand still hovering over the hilt of his *seax*, but the cursedly rational part of his mind knew it would be suicide to rush into the fight.

"Where are the others?" one of the Legionaries asked. He was a few minutes lighting his torch, then he swung around to pace the perimeter of the camp. "Didn't you say he traveled with a boy and a girl?"

Jurian swallowed hard. A few more steps and the Legionary would find him, and then it would be over. He could see Menas' face taut with fear and anger, still mouthing that one word at him in a desperate effort to make him move.

"I'll come back for you," Jurian whispered.

He turned to run, but as he did, he noticed something in the flashing torchlight, conspicuous only because it was different. The leather band on Menas' arm was gone. And on the slightly paler skin it had hidden, Jurian saw the mark of the Legion in black and crimson.

He reeled back like he'd been struck, and for a moment he just crouched there in the shadows, staring. At the last minute he remembered the prowling soldier, and he backed slowly away from the tree.

"He's here!" someone shouted behind him.

He felt hands on his arms and threw himself into a roll, ducking under the man's grasp with his hand clutching the comfortable grip of his *seax*. The soldier stumbled, unbalanced, and Jurian slashed back at the tendons behind his knees. Not waiting to see what the other soldiers would do, he turned and threw himself into the shadows.

Shaking with rage, he barely managed to keep himself from crashing through the undergrowth like a maimed bear. He forced himself to breathe slowly the way his old friend Leptis had taught him, to put everything out of his mind except his immediate situation. Running became the whole world. Everything reduced to abstract simplicity. Step, step, breathe, duck, weaving between trees and over uneven earth. Finally, when he could no longer hear the sounds of fighting, he threw himself on the ground at the base of a tree and dragged shattered breaths into his exhausted lungs.

As soon as the desperation of escape faded, the rage came roaring back. He'd run away. He'd run and left his closest friend to the mercy of the Legion, and he'd barely even tried to stay and fight. It didn't matter that Menas had wanted him to run. It didn't matter that he would have died if he'd stayed. He had abandoned Menas. Just like he'd abandoned everyone else who had ever needed him.

He ground his teeth, exerting every ounce of his will to keep some semblance of control. Slowly, slowly, his breathing steadied and his hands grew still. The sharp burning anger faded to a numb, sick ache in his chest.

When he was sure of himself, he got to his feet and peered blindly through the darkness. He had a vague sense of the way he'd come, so he started backtracking along what he assumed had been his path. Whatever happened, he would never live with himself if he forsook his friend so easily. He would go back, and he would fight to the last beat of his heart to free him.

SABRA CROUCHED BEHIND the narrow trunk of the tree, breathing hard. Behind her, she could still hear the sounds of the scuffle, faint above the pounding of her pulse. She risked a glance back but couldn't see anything in the night darkness.

This is your chance. If you stay, you'll have to tell him who you are. You'll have to see his hatred.

She bit her lip and banged her head against the tree. Menas… that kind, impossibly kind man…he could be dying, and she was sitting behind a tree thinking about herself. And Jurian? If he was as rash as he was stubborn, he might try to fight off the Legionaries to save his friend. He would never survive.

Did you really think coming back to Cyrene would involve anything other than death? You knew from the beginning how it would end. Does it matter if they die? In a few hours, you will join them.

"Shut up," she whispered, and pushed herself to her feet. "My fate has nothing to do with theirs."

She cast her head back to see the stars, searching for something familiar. When she found the moon she turned her steps southeast, and headed straight across the broken countryside toward Cyrene. It was the way she would have brought Jurian. Now she wondered if he would ever find his way, if he would even last long enough to get lost. She tried to silence the corner of her mind that whispered she should be glad—he was a burden. He would have interfered. He would never have understood what she had to do.

For all that, she knew it was a lie. Jurian did know what it meant to sacrifice.

That didn't mean he would have allowed her to do what she had to do. And worst of all, his words kept ringing in her ears, weakening her resolve, making her doubt everything she believed she could accomplish. No wonder the old priestess had forbidden her from talking to men, she thought, though deep inside she knew her doubts had crept in long before.

She pushed the thought aside and focused on her feet. The rocky ground here was treacherous, overgrown with rangy scrub and dotted with knotted trees like ink stains against the stars. She circled well to the southeast, desperate to avoid the hill of the god before her time came. By the coming night, the god…the beast…

whatever he was, he would have his feast. He would have her blood, and it would be over.

Am I still innocent? she wondered. *After all I have done, with all the blood on my hands…what if he no longer wants me?*

Your name was chosen. Your blood is still required.

She drove the voice back. After running for what felt like an eternity, her lungs burned so violently in the cold air that she had to stop and catch her breath. Legs shaking with exhaustion, she pressed on at an unsteady walk. Her foot slipped on a loose bit of stone and she skidded to the ground, scraping her hands on the dirt. For a minute she sat where she'd landed, drawing her knees up and pressing her forehead against them. Her whole body shook but she barely felt it. She barely felt anything. Everything about her felt numb, and she knew it had nothing to do with the cold.

I am not afraid to die. I'm not. I won't be afraid to die.

I am afraid.

She screamed through her teeth and got up. The earliest tinge of morning twilight lit the eastern sky, just enough that she could start to see the colors of everything around her. As the light steadily strengthened she picked up her pace, scrabbling down low hills and up mounds of crumbling rock until a thin glaze of sweat covered her neck.

There was too much to do; she had to hurry. It had to be tonight. She didn't know how the city planned to sacrifice Jezbel without her there to conduct the rituals, but she was back now, and if her mental calculations of the days were accurate, the sacrifice should happen tonight. She only prayed she hadn't made some mistake, that she hadn't missed a day in her reckoning. If Jezbel had already died, for nothing, she would never forgive herself.

The first contour of the sun had just broken the horizon when she caught sight of the city of Cyrene spreading in the valley below her. She let out a stifled sob and started running, pulling her tattered *palla* over her head as she went in case she met any farmers or merchants on her way into the city. But this early, the city and its surrounds were still quiet, and no one was on the Roman road when she reached it.

She slowed to a walk, kneading her hands together as she mentally rehearsed everything that would happen. First she would need to sneak into the palace, and hope to avoid her father. Then she would need to prepare herself. She hadn't even had time for any of the usual prayers or rites. She hadn't prepared the ritual feast, hadn't burned the incense or chanted the long chant in the *adyton* of the temple. But she was giving the god her blood—she only prayed that would be enough for him, even without all the proper rites.

As she got closer to the city, a sick dread crept into her veins. She could see the signs of recent turmoil even from outside the gate. It didn't seem like she had been gone that long, but it felt like an era had passed. If not for the familiar sight of guards on the outer watchtower, she might have thought the city had been abandoned long ago.

"Halt there!" one of the guards shouted from the tower.

She stopped, clutching her *palla* close at her throat and bowing her head. The guard clattered down the stairs and came out to question her. Sabra was only glad that the sun was rising behind her, throwing her face into shadow.

"You've been abroad at night?" the guard asked, sounding alarmed or amazed, she couldn't tell.

She frowned. It wasn't the question she'd been expecting. "Yes," she whispered, keeping her eyes down. Even in the dim light, the guard might recognize her by the color of her eyes.

"And you came safely? You weren't troubled or in danger?"

"You mean the god in the hills?" she asked. "He was quiet tonight."

"Ah," the guard said, shifting uncomfortably. "Perhaps he is satisfied."

Sabra's blood froze. "Was the girl…was the girl sacrificed? I'm sorry, I don't know what day it is."

She felt the guard's incredulous look but didn't raise her gaze to meet it. "No, no. That happens tonight. I only meant the god might be content to wait for that, rather than chase down more difficult prey."

Sabra swallowed back bile. "Is everything all right in the city? It looks so different from the last time I was here."

"No. We're coming apart at the seams. Even the nights aren't always quiet any more. People are threatening to kill the governor if he tries to go through with the sacrifice. They heard what happened with his own daughter, and they're furious. Say he's been hiding the truth from them all this time."

"Well," Sabra said, voice thick. "Maybe they will be delivered in a way they least expect."

She raised her gaze enough to see the confusion on his face. For a moment he just stood there, frowning at her, until Sabra grew impatient.

"May I enter the city?"

"Of course. Just try to keep from getting killed. The burial cults are overtaxed as it is."

She nodded silently and slipped past him, walking the long-familiar road into the city and up toward the governor's palace. If she wanted to sneak in, she would have to go around the back through the garden where the slaves' entrance was. It was early enough yet; she might just be able to make it to her chamber without running into anyone.

Before she got too close to the palace, she slipped off the road and traced her way along the steep slope of the hill to the back of the complex. The slaves' gate was unlatched and she let herself into the garden, the smell of bay and thyme following her as her robe brushed the fragrant plants. She slipped past the *culina* without trouble, and soon reached her own chamber.

Holding her breath, she entered as quietly as she could—but not quietly enough. Her new slave, Acenith, burst out of her tiny sleeping chamber and stopped short, staring at Sabra as if she'd seen a ghost.

45

LIBYA

JURIAN STOPPED AT THE EDGE of their camp, frozen with shock and grief. After losing his path more times than he cared to recall, after blundering for hours through the dark collecting cuts and bruises, he'd finally made it, but he was too late. There was no sign of the Legion, no sign of Menas. Just the earth scored with signs of the struggle, a patch of dark blood where he had cut the centurion's legs. Even the fire was cold ash by now, scattered over the ground as if someone had fallen into the fire ring. There was no sign of Eva.

Finally Jurian moved, stepping slowly, quietly. The hairs on the back of his neck prickled as if he were being watched, but the forest was silent around him and growing steadily brighter. He made his way to the fallen log where Menas had been sitting and dropped to his knees, running his hands over the disturbed soil.

"This is all my fault," he whispered. "Where'd they take you?"

He pressed the heel of his palm against his forehead, shoulders shaking. He'd failed him. Just like his mother and Eugenius, just like Mari. Just like Eva. He'd let down everyone who had ever depended on him, everyone who had ever trusted him to help them. Whose life had he ever touched that he didn't destroy? And now he was foolish enough to think that a two-hundred-year-old piece of paper and a sword could turn him into some sort of hero? Whoever this Myrddyn was, he'd picked the wrong person to carry the sword.

Maybe that was the meaning of the prophecy. Maybe Myrddyn knew all along that he would try and fail, and die a failure and a disappointment.

So be it, he thought bitterly. *I have nothing left to lose.*

He moved to sit on the log, and as he did, he spotted Menas' *sarcina* tucked behind the trunk. With a heavy sigh, he reached for the pole, but the *sarcina* caught on the undergrowth and tugged free, sending Jurian reeling back as the pole released. The early light flashed on something metal at its tip, and for one long moment Jurian just sat and stared at it. The tip of the pole was a burnished steel, leaf-shaped point almost half again as long as his hand. He brought the metal blade close and ran his fingers over it.

The pole was not a pole at all. It was a *spiculum,* a Legionary's spear.

Suddenly, a number of things clicked into place. Menas' obvious disappointment over Jurian's plans to join the Legion. His discomfort around the soldiers. His refusal to go into Rome.

Menas had been a Legionary. *Had been*. But he had concealed his Legion mark and hidden his *spiculum* in a bundle of belongings, and forsaken the army. Jurian had thought the centurion was accusing Menas of being a Christian when he called him a traitor, but that wasn't it at all. Menas was a deserter.

The thought should have filled him with revulsion, but Jurian only felt a great gnawing sorrow in his heart. He could only imagine what Menas had been asked to do in the Legion. How much of Menas' shadowy past had been lived under the Legion's eagle? How many atrocities had he committed in the Legion's name? He shuddered to imagine.

Exhaustion washed over him in a sudden, unstoppable rush. He slid off the log to lean his back against it, cradling the spear across his chest, and his thoughts drifted incoherently away.

SABRA STARED AT Acenith, praying every prayer she knew that the woman wouldn't start screaming. But to her credit, she didn't.

She took a few running steps forward and clasped Sabra's arms, peering tearfully into her face.

"Is it you, mistress?" she whispered. "I prayed and prayed to the gods to deliver you and bring you back to us. I *knew* you hadn't just abandoned us for Rome. What happened?"

Sabra drew a thin breath. "My father was trying to protect me. I...made a decision, and he thought I was being rash, so he had me taken away to keep me from following through with it. But," she said, and smiled, "I'm too stubborn for that to work."

"What...what did you mean to do?"

"I mean to give myself to the god in sacrifice," Sabra said, very quietly. "I believe only my blood will save this city, once and for all."

Acenith's hand flew to her mouth, stifling a cry of dismay. "No, mistress! You can't mean that!"

"I do. And no one will stop me. But please, don't let anyone know that I'm here. I need to get myself ready. I'll show myself to the city before the time of the sacrifice. Maybe that will get them to stop this pointless bickering." She paused, her gaze drifting to the narrow room that the victims used. "Where is Jezbel?"

Acenith bowed her head. "She was allowed to stay with her parents, after you disappeared."

"Which means she is long gone from the city," Sabra said with a sigh. "What would my father have done, if he'd gone to find her and she wasn't there?"

"I don't know, mistress. But fear will tear this city apart. They hate the sacrifices but they rely on them to feel safe. In one breath they condemn the cult and all who participate in it, but in the next breath they would cry out for vengeance if the rites fail."

"They're only human," Sabra murmured. "Acenith, I believe my father still has some of my mother's things. After all, he sent some of her regalia with me to Rome. Can you find the white tunic she wore on her wedding day?"

"And the orange veil as well?" Acenith asked, her face very pale.

"No. I will need a white veil. Silk, preferably. I will wear my priestess sandals."

"Very well, mistress," the slave whispered. "And may I bring you some food?"

"No," she said. "Not until tonight. Then I will need you to bring me wheat meal mixed with honey and oil, and fresh grapes and olives. That will be my ritual feast. I should eat it in the Temple, but I'm not purified for the *adyton*."

She sighed and turned to her small bed, sitting on its edge and easing her feet out of their sandals before Acenith could move to help her.

"Why are you still here, Acenith?" she asked. "Didn't my father dismiss you when he sent me away?"

"He tried," Acenith said. "I just didn't listen. I knew you'd be back."

She ducked her head and disappeared from the chamber. As soon as she was gone, Sabra lay back on the bed, folding her hands over her stomach and closing her eyes to wait.

46

Libya

Jurian woke some hours later, disoriented and numb in mind and body. The sun was high overhead, and for a moment Jurian panicked. How long had he slept? Was it morning still, or already afternoon? Then the anxiety faded and he slumped back against the log. He didn't even know what he meant to do, now. Go after Menas? Try to find Eva? Go and challenge a dragon destined to kill him?

He pressed his hands against his eyes and groaned. Obviously he couldn't sit there against that log forever. His hands drifted over the length of the spear again, and suddenly he stopped and held it out in a pool of sunlight. Nikolaos had done something to the *spiculum* in Myra. Menas was supposed to give it to him "at the right time," but Menas hadn't had a chance.

"Now is as good a time as any, I suppose," Jurian muttered.

He twisted the pole back and forth, but the wood was unbroken and smooth, weathered by constant handling and exposure to the elements. With a grimace he turned to the tarnished spearhead. Obviously Nikolaos hadn't put the spearhead on—it was much too old and worn to be a gift for anyone. But as he examined it, he twisted it a little and the metal shifted in response. He frowned and twisted harder, and all at once the spearhead snapped off. Jurian cursed under his breath, afraid he'd broken the thing, but as he lifted the spearhead, something slipped out of its cavity. He caught it deftly and frowned.

It was a piece of delicate parchment, far finer than anything he had ever seen, and on the back it was sealed to something with a bit of white wax. He turned it over and peered at the object. It looked like a splinter of cedar wood, barely the length of his smallest knuckle and no thicker than his bowstring. One end was stained dark by something that looked suspiciously like blood. He frowned and flipped the paper over to read the tiny Latin text inscribed on it.

Jurian—hail! You stand at a crossroads. Your night of agony has passed, but the long journey is only beginning. Have faith. Victory is not won by great deeds or strength, but by quiet, immovable fortitude that never falters. This splinter of wood was carried to Cyrene embedded in the palm of a man named Simon, a Cyrenean who was forced to bear the Cross with ICHTHUS. Now it is for you to carry up the hill of sacrifice. I am praying for you, my son, at this very moment. Godspeed, and peace to you.

Jurian's grip faltered on the parchment. He flipped it back over and stared at the splinter, his heart hammering painfully in his chest. Slowly, tentatively, he moved his finger to brush the fragment of wood. A shock tore through him, throwing him back blinded and winded. His blood raced with pain or power, and for a few long moments he just leaned against the log with his eyes closed, trying to calm the frantic pace of his heart.

When he could move again, he tucked the parchment back inside the spearhead, careful to avoid touching the wood again. He secured the spearhead to its shaft, hoping the blade wouldn't fall off. But a *spiculum* wasn't meant for multiple uses. He would carry it with him, and if he had the chance to use it, he would have only one chance to use it.

Jurian sat quietly for a long time once he'd fitted the spear back together. In his mind he remembered the story of the Christ, crucified by the Romans. It was the one story his mother had told him when he was quite small that he had never forgotten. The whips. The thorns. The spit. Women crying in the streets. The dusty road. The heavy cross. Simon the Cyrenean. Nails. The spear. Blood. Water. Love.

Love.

For love He had endured the impossible without complaint. And if Jurian was to be His *eques*, and if he was supposed to carry His Cross as his banner…could he expect to face anything other than this—to suffer, to face a bloody death, to die victorious?

He bent his head, whispering to the forest, "I don't know what to do."

You trust too much in yourself.

With Marcellinus' words echoing in his thoughts, Jurian got to his feet and picked up the spear, tugging Menas' *sarcina* free of the brambles. He concealed the spear tip under the bundle again, and, letting his breath out, set off into the forest.

He had walked for what felt like hours when he realized that he had assumed it was already afternoon. But as the sun finally began to creep lower in the sky, he discovered his mistake—it had still been late morning when he started out. He was headed northwest. With a muttered curse he swung around and tried to trace his way back the way he had come.

After losing sight of the sun altogether in the thickest part of the forest, Jurian finally caught a scent of char on the wind, the last faint evidence of the previous night's campfire. His senses sharpened and he focused on the smell, ignoring the sun and everything else that tried to confuse him. He brushed his fingers over a broken twig, spotted a streak of mud where his shoe had slipped. All at once the trees gave way, and he found himself once more on the edge of the camp.

In the middle, kneeling over the cold ashes and weeping, was a man.

Jurian stared at him. The stranger couldn't have been more than a year or two older than him, but his head was shaved and a slave's collar around his thick neck glinted dully in the fractured light. But what puzzled Jurian more than anything was the feeling of familiarity. He recognized the man. Where had he seen him before?

The memory flashed over him at once—the bustling docks of Portus, Eva's insistence on going with them…a man shouting from the crowds.

He stalked from the undergrowth, crossing the camp in two strides and grabbing the man's shoulder to twist him around. The man gave a cry of surprise and fell back onto the ground, staring up at Jurian wide-eyed. Then his eyes darted over the clearing, panicked.

"Where is she?" he whispered in broken Latin.

"You've been following us, haven't you?" Jurian asked, ignoring his question. "I saw you in Portus. And I think Eva saw you in Carthage too. What is your business with us?"

The slave straightened up, keeping a wary eye on Jurian. "Forgive me," he said. "I don't speak Latin."

Jurian let his breath hiss out, then gestured emphatically between himself and the slave. "I saw you in Rome. Rome?"

"Yes."

"You followed us here?"

"I go to Cyrene. You lost her. Where is she? Is she in Cyrene?"

He could only mean Eva, so Jurian shrugged and said, "I suppose that's where she's gone. She disappeared last night. I haven't seen her since."

The man seemed to have a hard time following that. He frowned and rubbed his jaw, eyeing Jurian with a look somewhere between suspicion and hope.

"I must save my mistress," he whispered. "You go to Cyrene? Come with me."

Jurian hesitated. He wondered if the slave and Eva served the same mistress; curiosity prickled in his mind, wondering what danger she was in. If she had something to do with the dragon in the hills…perhaps he could help the slave along the way. He nodded and held out his hand to the man, pulling him to his feet.

"All right, I'll come with you. My name is Jurian, by the way."

The man grinned. "I am Hanno."

He turned and struck off into the woods, walking so quickly that Jurian had to jog to catch up with him. After a few miles,

Jurian was grateful for the slave's company—Hanno seemed to have an uncanny sense of direction and a keen awareness of the landscape. He led Jurian around the most treacherous stretches of land, through the sparsest parts of the forest, and finally, as the sun was starting to set, they stepped out of the trees to look down at the city of Cyrene.

ACENITH BROUGHT SABRA'S ritual feast in the late afternoon, and for a while she stood and watched as Sabra slowly ate the food.

"That's a feast, is it? Looks like fasting rations to me," she remarked.

Sabra glanced up at her. She'd never spoken to anyone during the meal, and Acenith seemed to understand that, because she bobbed her head and retreated to the far end of the room. As soon as she had finished eating, Sabra stood and beckoned her.

"I need you to do two more things," she said. "I need you to find a child who is willing to come with me. Boy or girl, but I would prefer a girl. She must be very brave and willing to face the unseeable. All right? And I need to send slaves out into the city to act as messengers. Tell all the people to come here to the palace instead of to the Temple of the god. I will address them from here."

Acenith nodded and withdrew, looking so pale Sabra feared she would faint on the way. As soon as the woman had gone, Sabra pulled off the slave's tunic and *palla* she'd been wearing, and washed herself as best she could with the jug of water Acenith had left for her. Then she slipped into her mother's white wedding tunic.

It fell a little long; her mother must have been a few inches taller, but Sabra belted it as best she could with the plain corded belt and the white-woven girdle with its ornate knot. The tunic was beautifully made of white linen, embroidered and beaded all along the neckline and hem with pearls and cut glass that caught the light. She buckled her beaded priestess sandals on, her heart twisting strangely at the sound of the tinkling bells. Acenith had already styled her hair in the fashion of Roman brides, but Sabra didn't drape the silk veil over her head just yet.

She studied herself in the bronze mirror, frowning. She'd always assumed that she would never wear a bride's tunic. It certainly had never occurred to her that she would wear it on the night she went to die.

Her stomach curled. For so long now, the idea of dying had been so far away, so abstract. She dealt with death regularly, but never her own. Was this how all those children had felt, while she was dressing them up for their sacrifice? She couldn't even comprehend the depth of the dread and revulsion she felt, every fiber of her being recoiling from the thought of death. In a few hours, it would all be over.

In a few hours, Sabra would no longer exist.

And she wouldn't even have the satisfaction of knowing if her sacrifice had been effective. Perhaps she would die, and the god would turn and destroy the whole city anyway, and everything would have been for nothing.

Don't think like that. Not now. You have to believe.

Believe what you like. The god does not bow to your whims and desires.

She shuddered and turned away from the mirror. Acenith returned a moment later, leading a young girl by the hand. The girl must have been at least thirteen, tall for her age with luminous dark eyes and a look on her face that the greatest Stoic philosophers would have admired.

"Mistress, this is Flavia," Acenith said. "She is willing to serve you tonight."

"Are you brave enough?" Sabra asked, putting an edge to her voice. This girl wasn't one of her victims, and she wasn't a child like Elissa. She didn't need placating; she needed certitude.

Flavia, to her credit, met her gaze with equal intensity. "I'm willing to do what you need."

"To walk up the hill of bones with me? To turn away and leave me to die?"

The girl swallowed. "Yes."

"Very well. Acenith, is everyone here?"

"Many are. Some are still coming in."

"I'll go now. It's getting late. Flavia, there on the bed are my veil and the wreath of flowers. Carry them for me."

The girl went silently to pick them up, her fingers resting briefly on the white asphodel flowers. Sabra drew a deep breath and smiled at Acenith.

"Where is my father?"

"He's in his *tablinum*, mistress. He stays there under guard most days."

"Under guard?"

"For his own protection. People have sworn to kill him if he shows himself."

Sabra swallowed. "Very well."

She left the chamber and walked slowly across the peristyle. Her throat burned. Everywhere she looked she saw memories of her life; walking with Hanno, playing ball with Elissa, disappointing the Legion Tribune. So many hours she had spent in that courtyard, staring at the stars and listening to the fountain. And she would never see it again. She let her hand brush the tall pillars as she passed them one by one, her fingers touching the pedestals of the statues in between each of them.

As she came into the atrium, she heard the noise of the uneasy crowd gathering on the steps outside. They obviously didn't know why they had been summoned away from the Temple. They probably assumed it was some new impiety concocted by her father. She would put it all aright. Her father wouldn't need to live in fear any more. Her city wouldn't need to live in fear any more.

"What in the name of all the gods is going on out there?" someone cried behind her, and Sabra froze.

"No," she whispered. "Stay inside. Don't come and see me now…"

But it was too late. The curtain door of the *tablinum* swung open, and Sabra's father strode out, only to stop, paralyzed, as his gaze fell on her.

"Sabra…what…"

"Don't blame Hanno," she said. "He tried to stop me. I tried to get Rome to help us, but no one will come. No one will save us, but I can. And nothing you could say will stop me now."

"Sabra...please."

The grief in that one word stung Sabra to the core of her heart, and her eyes burned with tears. Her father stepped closer to her until he could reach out and take her hands.

"I wanted to save you from this," he murmured.

"I know," she said. "I know you love me. Now let me save *them*, because I love them."

She could tell he was doing everything in his power not to break down in front of her. He kept his expression rigidly neutral, but it was a fragile thing. She knew that what she was about to do would crack that veneer, but she couldn't go into the darkness if she didn't.

She leaned in and kissed his cheek, and whispered, "Father, I love you more than anything. It's you I want to save most of all."

She turned away without looking at him, and tried not to hear the sound of his tears as she strode out of the palace. As soon as she appeared in the lamplight at the top of the steps, the crowd erupted. She couldn't tell if the cries were of dismay or anger or joy. On one level, it didn't even matter.

"People of Cyrene!" she called, her voice silencing the crowd at once. "I know that these have been dark days. They have been days of confusion, and bitter strife, of fear and suspicion. I know you have been bowed under the weight of so many innocent deaths, and bowed still further under the weight of so much fear of divine punishment." She paused, then, lowering her voice, she said, "I am going to end it all tonight. You see me here in a bride's raiment, in a victim's mantle. I cannot bear to see you all suffer. If I can save you by my blood, I will willingly, gladly, shed every single drop of it."

She took a breath and scanned the crowd that now stared in dumbfounded silence at her. Some of the women were weeping, and even some of the men.

"All of you who have suffered the loss of a child," she said, "all of you who have suffered with them, suffer now with my father, and do not blame him for what he did. He did what he thought the god wanted. You know he would lay down his life for Cyrene. I've asked to have that privilege for myself. You came out tonight to honor a victim's path into the hill. Please, if you are willing, be a light for mine."

One of the men standing closest to the palace came up the steps, staring at Sabra long and hard. At the last moment he bowed, and handed his unlit torch to one of the slaves gathered on the porch. The slave lit it and handed it back to him, and one by one the torches and candles flickered to life until the whole city gleamed.

Sabra glanced over her shoulder at Flavia and nodded, and the girl reached up to lay the veil over her head and fix it in place with the wreath of flowers. Sabra tightened her hands in knots to keep them from trembling, but she was afraid to breathe too deeply. As soon as she was ready, she reached to her belt and removed the chain she had fastened there for the time being.

"Flavia, I need you to carry this for me," she said, and handed it to the girl.

Flavia took it, her hands shaking just a little.

Smart girl, Sabra thought. *Only a fool wouldn't be afraid at a time like this.*

Somewhere in the distance the musicians began to play, the shrill wail of the flutes echoing the terror in her mind, the frantic drums matching the beat of her heart.

47

Cyrene

On the slope of the hill, Jurian crouched down to get a better look at the city of Cyrene. It was nearly dusk, but one of the roads in the city, stretching from one hill to the other, was all lit up with a forest of tiny lights.

"What are the lights?" he asked, pointing.

Hanno's face turned a sick shade of green. "Oh gods," he cried. "Oh gods, I will be too late. We must hurry! Please help me save her!"

He grabbed Jurian's arm and bolted down the hill, so fast that Jurian almost lost his footing on the loose stones.

"Where are we going?" he cried, trying to use Menas' spear for balance. "I thought we were going to the city?"

"No," Hanno cried. He stopped suddenly and turned to face Jurian, his face a perfect mixture of grief and horror. "My mistress…Sabra, the priestess…she is going to give herself to the god and she will die, and I'm too late!"

He muttered something in Punic and continued on, pointing toward the hill as he went. Jurian slowed, staring up the ragged hillside. The low hill shouldn't have been very impressive, but Jurian couldn't help staring at it with dread. Deep, primal fear curdled his blood. There was something wrong with that hill, something very, very wrong. Every instinct he had was screaming at him to run, to get away, to save himself.

"Hanno," he said, sharply enough that the slave stopped his mad rush toward the hill. He forced his voice to be steady. "Is that where the dragon is?"

"Dragon?"

"The destroyer? Your god?"

Hanno's face blanched. "Yes. Up there."

He turned and pressed on, while Jurian stared after him, too numb to think.

He slid the spear's shaft through his hands and brushed his fingers over the blade, whispering, "Not by my strength."

Somewhere up the hillside he heard a deep rumbling, as if the earth itself were growling, and the rocks trembled beneath his feet.

THE TREK ACROSS the city and up the hill took longer than Sabra had ever felt. Each step felt like a step through mud, and her body shook with exhaustion and fear. More than anything, she trembled with rage at herself.

Coward! How many innocents did you lead up this hill to die, and you never once felt these pangs of fear? They were victims, you said, so you wouldn't have to feel. Did you ever try to imagine the dread they faced? No, only when it is your own death you're facing. At least you are supposed to die, unlike those children. Theirs was a pointless sacrifice, and you never even blinked.

"Oh, God," she whispered suddenly, and she didn't even know what deity she meant to invoke.

Flavia glanced at her, looking as if she wanted to say something, but Sabra shook her head and they pressed on in silence.

What would Jurian say if he saw me here? Would he hate me? But he knows...that God he follows, that is a God of sacrifice. But...they didn't follow their God for fear. They followed for love. Like Ayzebel. How else could anyone die joyfully? I wish I understood. I wish I had a little of her strength.

I wish the god I serve were the kind of god who could be loved.

Don't be foolish, the deep, sinister voice in her mind whispered.

You are powerless before me. You are nothing. Life and death are meaningless, and love is a lie. All you can offer me is service. And the only service I desire is your death.

Sabra stifled a strangled sob and focused on forcing each step.

Please accept my sacrifice. Take my blood and spare my people.

The voice didn't answer. Only silence.

They reached the end of their path, and Flavia stumbled when she saw the line of bleached skulls with their faded garlands.

"Mistress," she whispered. "I can't do this. I can't."

"You have to," Sabra said, hoarse with fear. "Please. I can't trust myself not to run if you don't chain me up."

Flavia nodded, tears streaming down her cheeks as she followed Sabra to the mouth of the cave. Sabra wasn't sure if she was imagining it, but she thought the depths of the cavern didn't seem as black as usual, as if some sort of light burned deep within. The foul gases crept over the broken earth, and Flavia coughed until she gagged.

Sabra stood before the cavern and chanted the sacrificial prayer, focusing on the rhythm of the words to steady her pulse. When she finished she crossed to the pillar, stumbling as her legs grew weak.

"Come here, Flavia. Come and chain me up."

"No, mistress," Flavia said through broken sobs. "Please don't make me. Don't make me leave you to die. I can't!"

"You can. This is your chance. What you do here can save the city," she said, cursing herself as she recognized the same encouraging words she had always offered the victims in the past. "Please."

The girl nodded, and, her body shaking with heaving sobs, she looped the chain behind the pillar and bound Sabra tight. Sabra's breath came faster and faster, wanting to lose control, but she closed her eyes. She wanted to pray but her whole being curled away from the thought of the old god, with a revulsion verging on hatred.

Please...Jurian's God, if You deign to listen to my prayer...please let my sacrifice work. Please don't let my people perish when I'm gone.

Flavia returned from behind the pillar, staring at Sabra as if willing her to ask to be released.

"Go," Sabra said, "Don't be afraid. Just go. And pray for me."

Flavia turned to go, but her feet stopped, and her hands dropped loose at her sides, her gaze riveted on the shadowy fissure of the cavern. The blood leeched from her cheeks. A voice deep in Sabra's mind ordered her to look and see what the girl had seen, but she couldn't tear her gaze from Flavia's death-white face. She couldn't look away; she couldn't look at the cave. Couldn't.

Suddenly Flavia screamed, paralyzed where she stood. Sabra winced and she heard her own voice join the girl's, shouting her name or senseless noise, she couldn't say—it all sounded like death. Flavia never heard her. Her voice gave out all at once and she staggered a step, hands rigid at her sides, then her body dropped to the earth like a broken statue.

"Flavia!" Sabra cried. "Flavia, get up, go!"

But she knew it was no use. The girl's eyes stared straight at her, empty, seeing nothing. Sabra gulped air, her lungs jerking with strangled sobs that left her reeling with dizziness.

"Flavia!" she screamed again. "No! No…that's not fair… that's not fair! I'm here! Why did you take her too?"

She turned to stare at the mouth of the cavern, willing the god to come and finish it. She couldn't see what had scared Flavia to her death, but she felt the deep, visceral fear in every inch of her body.

And then, somewhere down the hill, someone shouted.

48

Cyrene

Jurian and Hanno had made it halfway up the ragged hillside path when they heard the girl scream. Hanno dropped like a bolt, shaking all over and white with fear, but for all that, his eyes burned with a rage that Jurian had never seen…but somehow understood.

"Can't you feel it?" Hanno gasped. "Oh gods. Oh gods. Everything wants to die."

Jurian shuddered. He felt it through every inch of his body, dragging him down to the earth, the dead earth, the swallowing earth… Fear pulsed like shadow at the corners of his vision and his mind reeled with vertigo. He bit down hard on his lip to shake the feeling, but the taste of his own blood only made the terror surge through him like a torrent.

"Come on," Jurian gritted, one hand tight on Menas' lance, the other reaching slowly, awkwardly, to grip Hanno's arm. "Come on, get up. Let's go. Your mistress needs you."

But Hanno's body pressed like a deadweight against the rocks, and he couldn't or wouldn't raise his head to meet Jurian's frantic gaze.

Jurian tried one last time to pull the slave to his feet. His own legs buckled as a fresh wave of fear crashed over him. He couldn't even tell if Hanno was breathing any more. Blood seeped from beneath the arm he had pinned beneath him, dark like shadows.

Just give up, give up, turn away...none of this is your concern... Why should you suffer for their sins?

Jurian realized he had sunk to his knees and he lurched violently to his feet. He laid a hand on Hanno's shoulder.

"Don't be afraid," he murmured. "I'll save her."

Oh, you will, will you?

Jurian flinched. That voice in his thoughts...he'd never heard anything like it. It crushed him with terror, snapping the frail bit of freedom he'd just won, sending him staggering back to his knees. His hand inched up the length of the spear until it found the blade and he pushed the fear back, inch by inch, until he felt the terror recede from his limbs.

As soon as he could move again, he unslung his bow and quiver, his pack and Menas' *sarcina,* leaving them on the path beside Hanno. Then he turned, and, drawing in a deep breath, forced his legs to run the rest of the way up the hill, shouting the name of the slave's mistress.

"Sabra!"

His steps faltered as he reached the top of the rise. The road was edged for some distance by a morbid display—children's skulls crowned with flowers, more than he could count, like a gruesome memorial or macabre talisman against the evil that had killed them. He stared at the skulls, his stomach churning with the memory of his dream, then he shook his head and kept going. The dead were not his concern. He only hoped Hanno's mistress didn't number among them yet.

He stepped out onto the ledge and stopped short. In the middle of the ledge a girl lay dead, her face fixed in a look of terror as a low fog of some foul-smelling vapor curled around her like water. She couldn't have been there long, and Jurian felt a sudden sick certainty that he was staring at Hanno's mistress. But then a flash of brightness caught his eye and he glanced up, caught between relief and despair. There, dim in the growing dusk, he saw a young woman chained to a pillar on the far side of the ledge, dressed all in white, like a bride...just like that horrific dream.

The cold wind clawed at her veil, blowing it across her face.

He thought he heard her sob a word, "*No...*"

And then the veil drifted back into its place and Jurian's heart jerked strangely in his chest. He would know those luminous golden eyes anywhere.

"Oh God," he whispered. "Eva?"

She bit her lip, face strained with grief and fear. He ran over to her, reaching out to lay a hand on her shoulder, but she pulled away from him.

"Don't touch me, Jurian. Please don't."

He froze, hand outstretched. "I thought I would find Sabra up here."

Her eyes widened. "How did you know that name?"

"A slave, Hanno. We came to save his mistress Sabra."

"Oh, Hanno," she whispered, closing her eyes. Then she opened them and gave a little sigh. "I am Sabra."

"Priestess? Of...Vesta?"

She bowed her head. "No," she said, and jerked her chin toward the mouth of the cave. "I serve the old god who lives in that hill."

Jurian felt the blood drain from his face. "The *dragon?* You serve...Eva! You serve that monster?"

Her shoulders crumpled, shaking with violent sobs.

"And now you're sacrificing yourself to it?"

He braced a hand on the pillar and tried to see behind it, but though he could see the chains, he couldn't see any way of unfastening them.

"I do what I must to save my people."

He paused, mentally rebuking himself as he suddenly realized why she had always looked familiar to him. He *had* seen her before, in the Roman Forum, dressed in exotic regalia. The thought made him marvel. She had been borne into the city like a queen, with a beauty and grace that could have launched her to the peak of Roman society. But instead she had run away... taken on the aspect of a slave, and returned to her city to die. To die willingly, because she believed she could save her people by pouring out her blood for them.

Jurian came back around the pillar to face her. "Listen," he said, as gently as he could. "That thing in there, whatever it is... it's not what you should be serving. It can't save your people, or destroy them. If they are destroyed, it'll be their own doing."

He would have kept talking but the ground beneath them quaked suddenly, and Jurian snatched the pillar again to stay upright.

"You shouldn't be here," Sabra whispered. "You'll get yourself killed."

"Well, that's what the prophecy promised, wasn't it?" he said with a forced smile.

Her mouth dropped open. "I thought...I thought you were going to Britannia to face a dragon. This...this is what you came to Cyrene for?"

He nodded. From the look on her face he could tell she would have gladly slapped him if her hands had been free.

"You came to kill a god?"

"Not a god," he said. "I came to kill a dragon."

Before he could give himself a chance to doubt himself, he turned and strode toward the mouth of the cavern.

"Jurian, no!" Sabra screamed. He stopped at the threshold and glanced back. "I've seen the god. He is more terrible, more terrifying than even you can imagine. He'll kill you! Please. Don't make me the cause of your death too. Listen...I think..." Her voice died and her face became as pale as bone. "He's evil, Jurian! He delights in death and laughs to see us suffer. I don't want to serve him...I only want to make him leave my people alone forever. But that can only happen if I die."

Jurian hesitated. Memories of Menas' story of his past flashed through his mind, and suddenly he understood exactly what he had to do.

"If I meant to face him with my own strength, I'd say you were right. But I won't." He held her gaze steadily, wishing he could give her peace, wishing she could give him some of her impossible strength. "Listen, Sabra. I don't fault you for what you were taught all your life to believe. I even admire what you want to do. But don't you understand? Someone else has already shed His blood so you don't have to." He held up the spear in a salute. "By His *signum* I will triumph."

He swallowed his fear and stepped into the cavern.

49

CYRENE

AT FIRST HE COULD SEE nothing. The darkness was total and unyielding, pressing around him with almost tangible force. All of his senses seemed to abandon him, except smell—and that was the one sense he would gladly have given up. The air reeked with a stench like death and ash and something far fouler besides. His heart hammered relentlessly, while his mind raced through imaginings of dragons.

How could he prepare to fight something that was only supposed to exist in myth? It was ludicrous to even try to form a strategy. He was little more than a boy, unarmored, carrying only a broken spear and a sword that foretold his own death. If the dragon had the power of fire as some myths said, he wouldn't stand a chance. If it was the size of a ship with teeth the length of swords, he would die before he could land a blow.

His mind flashed back to Sabra, weeping and terrified outside, more vulnerable than he had ever seen her. He would die in this cave, and she would have to face the dragon's wrath anyway. If he failed, she would die.

He drew a thin breath and kept feeling his way forward. The passage was narrower than he'd expected, just wider than the breadth of his outstretched arms, and it curved tortuously over rough and broken ground. After he had walked a few minutes, he realized suddenly that he could see the head of his spear shining with a dull, reddish gleam. He shifted it, wondering if it was somehow giving him light, but then he noticed he could see his hands too, and the rocks beneath his feet.

The rocks that, at that moment, started to tremble and groan. A chunk of stone dislodged from the ceiling above him, landing a few feet in front of him. Jurian winced. As if clawing through a treacherous tunnel in search of a dragon wasn't enough, now he had to fear the tunnel collapsing over him too. Gritting his teeth, he pressed on. The light grew gradually stronger, suffusing the whole corridor with a warm glow. He couldn't tell what was causing it; as far as he could see, it cast no shadows as the tunnel snaked forward. It just…lingered.

All at once the light was gone, and the quiet shuffle of his steps turned to a sudden startling echo. Somewhere far in the distance he could see a flicker of light. If it was a fire, Jurian couldn't imagine how big that chamber was. He pushed forward doggedly, shuffling blindly over the stones toward the light that never seemed to come closer.

He reeled to a stop. The light wasn't a distant fire. It was a candle, and it was directly in front of him, barely illuminating the figure of a man. Jurian stared. The man stood robed in imperial purple, his head covered with a fold of his toga like an emperor at a sacrifice. And his face…

The candlelight glinted off his face, with its strange, almost feminine beauty, and those piercing blue eyes.

"Diocletian?" Jurian whispered. The emptiness swallowed his voice and he took another step forward, curious.

The man smiled, and Jurian felt his fear fade behind a quiet flood of relief and comfort.

But something was wrong. Something about the complexion was off…it was a little too perfect, a little too smooth, its lines mercurial in the unsteady light. There was a brightness about him, but at the same time, the closer Jurian looked, the more he could see something like shadow moving beneath his skin.

As the immediate recognition faded to horror, the relief he'd felt eroded. He froze where he stood.

"So, at last," the man said, his voice low and sinuous. "The mighty Lucius Aurelius Georgius has deigned to visit me?"

He lingered over each syllable of the name, drawing them out as if he were tasting them.

"How did you know my name?"

The candlelight flashed over his teeth as he smiled. "It's written in your blood, boy." He bent his head to regard the candle. " And now tell me. What gift have you brought me?"

"I've brought you no gift," Jurian gritted.

"That blade there on your back? Give it to me."

"It's mine."

The man lifted his head, lips closed to cage a laugh. "Oh, is it? And what have you done in your life to deserve that blade?"

Jurian bristled.

"Let me name your accomplishments. I see you have a few. When your father died, you failed to step into his role. You cast yourself into isolation and...*training*...pretending that it would mean something, while your family suffered without your father's presence. Or the presence of anyone who could be considered a man. You failed to comfort your mother in her sickness, and despised her teachings, never looking back to see the tears of disappointment in her eyes when you ran away from her gatherings. You ignored your sister's failing health. You stood by and watched as your mother and the priest were murdered, and didn't even try to avenge their deaths. You dragged your sister across the country and over sea, only to stand by and fail to defend her when she needed you most. You let down your closest friend and abandoned another, and now your failure with me will kill the girl and all the city she loves. And was it all worth it? You set out with so much to prove. Jurian the man. Jurian the hero. Jurian the *failure*."

He spat the last word, his blue eyes blazing across the shadows. Jurian couldn't move. Even his thoughts were stagnant, numb. It was all true. Every word the man had said. And he'd been running from that truth more than anything, all this time.

"Oh, come now," the man said, his voice irresistibly gentle. "It isn't all bad, is it? You've learned your place. You know that everything you touch will turn to dust, so it's better to stop now before you hurt anyone else."

The last words sharpened to a bitter sword-point, stabbing Jurian deep in the core of his heart.

"You thought you could conquer dragons with a broken spear and a sword that prophesied your death. Do you see the error of your ways?"

Jurian flinched. His hand found the buckle of his sword belt, feeling its smooth contours. It would be so easy…if he just walked away now. He hadn't asked for the sword. Thought it was a foolish fancy right from the start. Surely another could fulfill this task just as well, or better. Certainly better. After all, he doubted anyone could do worse.

"Jurian," the figure said, turning the name over like a tender rebuke. "All your life you've been chasing a purpose, but did you ever think what it would cost you? Of course not. You were never worthy of their love anyway. And do you think your God has any place in His court for failures like you? You're a disgrace to your faith. At least your sister died with *some* dignity."

Jurian's hand clamped into a fist, blood boiling up in his veins. "Don't talk about my sister."

"Too painful? Too hard to remember how much you let her down? How did that feel, when she looked right at you and realized you weren't going to move to help her?" The man pondered that a moment, then lifted his brows in mockery and shook his head. "I can't imagine her disappointment. You broke her heart. Oh, and let's not forget what happened next. You challenged her killer…but you only attacked him when he promised to bring you down. But that's just typical for you. You only move when it's to your advantage, you only strike to raise yourself up, and only run when you can save your own life."

"Are you finished?" Jurian gritted, the words so low, he almost couldn't hear them himself.

"Are you? You bore me. You're a waste of my time. I don't

even know if I should bother killing you. Maybe I should let you live, so that when I devour the girl and destroy her city, you'll be there to watch."

Jurian let out his breath. "Why did you want my sword?"

"Does it matter?" he asked, bemused. "That sword is powerful. I'm intrigued by it."

"It could be no use to you, so you must only want it to keep it away from me."

"Oh, please," the man said, passing his long fingers over the candle's flame, indifferent to its heat. "Don't pretend to use logic against me. I'm far cleverer than you."

"I'm not using logic against you," Jurian said. "I'm using it against myself."

The man paused and glanced up at him, barely stifled mockery in his eyes. "Oh? Is it working?"

Jurian ignored the jibe. "Perfectly," he said. "You want my sword for its power, but you've said nothing about my spear."

"That bit of refuse? A relic of a man's betrayal?" The man snorted. "I've no use for such tawdry things."

"Then you're not as clever as you think you are. But, your kind never could see real power, could you? Is that how you know so much about failure? Personal experience?"

"Don't trifle with me, boy. You know nothing of my kind."

"I know enough. I know exactly how to defeat you."

"You?" The man tipped his head back and laughed, a low, rumbling chuckle that reverberated far more through the cavern than it should have. "You still think you can defeat me?"

Jurian smiled, the shaft of the spear warm beneath his hand. "No," he said. "Not me. But I don't come in my own name." He drew the sword from its sheath on his back, holding it upright by the blade below the hilt. "This is my banner."

The man stared at him long and hard, then, without a word or a warning, he turned his head and blew out the candle.

50

Cyrene

Darkness crashed over the cavern with the roar of a wind and shaking rocks. Jurian took a step back, extinguishing the first faint surge of triumph before it could take root in his mind. He hadn't won. The man hadn't left him; he could still feel his presence tangibly somewhere in front of him. The wind buffeted him like a hurricane, and somewhere in the blind emptiness of the cavern he could hear that low rumbling sound like laughter and the voice of a nightmare.

"I walked back and forth in the midst of the fiery stones. I was the seal of perfection, full of wisdom and perfect in beauty. I was in the garden of delight. Every precious jewel became my covering. The sardius, the topaz, and diamond, the beryl, onyx, and jasper, the sapphire, turquoise, and emerald. I was bedecked in gold. I sounded the timbrel and played the pipes. I dwelt on the summit of Holy Mountain. I bore the light. I was the anointed cherub who covered the Presence. I am the Phosphoros. I am the Luciferus. I am the Shatan."

In the midst of the noise, the red light blossomed from the darkness like blood, pooling over the stones until even Excalibur was awash with it. And as the light grew, the rushing wind died, and Jurian's heart stuttered to a painful halt. There, not fifteen feet in front of him, leered the face of a dragon, its head a mass of cruel horns, the crimson light spilling off its scales like water. Its piercing blue eyes stared at him, the pupils slitted like a lizard's, and its mouth hung open to reveal teeth and shadows writhing like a thousand tiny snakes. Growling laughter erupted from the inferno of its deep chest.

Jurian didn't give himself time to think. He didn't have any time. If he waited for the dragon to make the first move, it was all over. He gritted his teeth and broke into a run, shifting the spear to a throwing grip, his heart galloping wildly in his chest. As soon as he moved the dragon's jaws snapped shut and it loomed up, flashing its wings out like smoke and shadow. Its sinuous body moved faster than Jurian could follow, long neck and tail all curling snakelike around him. The earth shook and the dragon's head reared toward him, and before Jurian could even flinch, its broad forehead slammed full into his chest.

For one, endless moment, Jurian felt himself weightless, the air rushing around him. Then his back slammed into the wall and gravity tore him down, and down, until he crashed on the jagged rocks of the cavern floor with the breath shattering from his lungs. His ears rang with the heavy clang of metal on stone as Excalibur flew from his grip and landed somewhere in the darkness beyond. Somehow he'd managed to keep hold of the spear, but he had landed with the spear—and his hand—pinned under his body. As soon as sensation crashed back over him his stomach reeled with the pain. He couldn't unclench his fingers; he knew without looking that they were bloody and crushed.

Sucking in a shallow breath, he staggered to his feet, but no sooner was he upright than the dragon's head rushed toward him. He braced himself for another blow but the dragon's mouth curled open, showing its fangs. At the last moment, Jurian dove aside. He felt wind rush past as the dragon's mouth missed its mark, but then it swung its head back toward him and Jurian watched its horns driving toward him like a boar's tusks. Still gulping air into his empty lungs, he waited, and waited, and just before impact he ducked into a roll and scrambled away into the shadows, his hands scouring the rocks for his sword.

Don't think you can hide in the shadows, little one, the deep, resonant voice muttered, more in Jurian's head than as any audible sound. *I am the darkness. Come and behold me.*

Jurian felt a presence behind him, but even as he tried to slip away, one of the dragon's taloned forefeet grabbed him and threw him on his back, slamming down on his chest. He felt the claws curling against his skin, tapping against his ribs the way a scholar might tap an ancient text.

Foolhardy, the voice hissed. *You do know there's a difference between courage and foolhardiness?*

"It's a fine line," Jurian growled.

The foot shoved down suddenly, harder and harder, squeezing the air from his lungs. His already mangled back pressed into the jagged stones, sending a shower of stars across his vision. He tried to reach for his *seax* but the blade was pinned under his hip, and he couldn't move enough to free it. His lungs struggled, wanting to gasp. But with the dragon's foot like an anvil on his chest, he couldn't draw the faintest breath, and his head hammered as he slowly ran out of air. He kicked his legs, trying to find purchase on the rocks, and his fingers scrabbled desperately over the broken ground, reaching and stretching until finally he felt the very tip of his sword's hilt. His fingertips clawed over the knob until they could take hold of it, but then he left his hand where it was, out of the dragon's line of sight.

I've had you trapped from the moment you crossed my threshold.

Jurian winced as he tried, carefully, to shift the grip of his mangled fingers on the spear shaft. Pain flashed through him, but he knew it should have hurt more. Everything was fading, even the pain. The dragon leered over him, lowering down to stare him in the face until it was so close its breath scorched against his skin, and Jurian could see the inferno within its throat. The claws dug in harder, moments from tearing the flesh over his heart. Jurian closed his eyes and let his gaze drop to the dragon's chest. Through his wavering vision he could just make out the fleshy patch of skin under its elbow, revealed by its outstretched leg.

Give up now. Give up, and I'll let you live. I'll let you witness the great destruction, the darkness that heralds the end of all things.

"You..." he choked, and the dragon released just enough pressure to let him speak. "You should have paid attention."

He tightened his fingers around the spear shaft, screaming through his teeth in pain, and, with the last fragments of his strength he drove the spear forward. It slammed into the dragon's chest with more power than Jurian could have imagined, the force of the impact driving his shoulders back to the earth. The dragon reeled away, its claws dragging over Jurian's chest as a wash of darkness poured from its wound. Jurian rolled and grabbed the sword, and thrust the blade straight up under the dragon's jaw as it writhed above him. The dragon bellowed in wrath or pain, and Jurian felt it fading all around him, withering as it collapsed from the inside.

Jurian staggered to his feet and backed away. His tunic was drenched in blood, but as he felt over the skin of his chest, he realized it was the dragon's blood he felt. Apart from three raised welts over his heart, his skin was intact. But the dragon writhed as if he'd poisoned it, and a moment later he understood why. The spear shaft had shattered into a hundred pieces, but its head must have pierced all the way to the dragon's heart and lodged there. The dragon's head snapped back, blood streaming down its throat. Jurian could hear its screams in his mind as it thrashed to stay alive, and under its weight the ground began to quake, knocking him to his knees.

Jurian stared at it, watching its edges blur in its own light, and a sudden sick dread washed over him. If he let the dragon fade... if he walked out with nothing to show...the people would never believe he had killed the dragon, their god. They would never believe he wasn't just a liar, and Sabra along with him. Nothing would have changed.

"You!" he shouted, his voice rattling in his battered chest. "By the wood that pierced you, I adjure you to stay as you are."

But this body dies, the voice whispered.

"You chose it," Jurian said. He leaned over his knees, struggling to draw a solid breath. "Now, follow me."

51

CYRENE

SABRA BRACED HERSELF AS THE earth quaked beneath her feet. She hadn't heard anything since Jurian had disappeared into that cave, and it felt like he had been gone a lifetime or more. Surely if he had found the god, he would have been killed at once for defiling the god's dwelling, but time had dragged on, so long, so silent. Then came the earth's rumbling, and Sabra clutched the pillar behind her for strength.

"Why do you cling to that pillar, daughter?"

Sabra bit her tongue on a scream as she snapped her gaze up, searching the darkness. For a moment she saw nothing, then, slowly, she made out the figure of a small, slim man standing on the ledge across from her. Dusk had long since fallen, but she could see him clearly enough, with his thick black beard and bald head. Her mouth dropped open. She had seen that man before. He was the one who had seemed to appear out of nowhere in Carthage to clear the docks for them. What was he doing here?

He approached slowly, casting one long look at the cavern mouth as he passed. Then he nodded as if satisfied, and with a faint smile, he stopped in front of Sabra.

"You can let go now," he said. "Come away from there. All will be well."

"But..." Sabra started, and sputtered, unable to think of anything to say. Finally she managed, "But I can't come away. I'm chained."

He gave her a knowing look. "I said *let go,*" he said, and with an enigmatic smile, he turned and disappeared into the shadows.

Sabra stared after him, bewildered. After a moment she relinquished her death grip on the stone behind her and cautiously tried to bring her hands forward, waiting for the inevitable pain when her wrists hit against their fetters. But the pain never came. She brought her hands in front of her and stared at her empty wrists.

"What…" she started, but it was no use. The man was gone.

The ground tremored again, nearly throwing her to her knees. She leaned a hand on the pillar and stared in dread at the mouth of the cavern.

I can't run. Even if that's the god coming to devour me, I can't. Jurian wouldn't run, no matter what.

A moment passed in devastating silence, then the darkness fractured and the dragon slithered from the hole in the mountain. Sabra clapped her hand over her mouth, barely choking down a scream. The dragon turned its head toward her. It was more massive than she remembered, but instead of the piercing stare she recalled, its ice blue eyes rolled back to show the whites. And suddenly Sabra saw the blood dripping from under its jaw, and then Jurian stepped out of the cavern behind the dragon.

She gasped when she saw him. He had lost his spear and now had nothing but the long-bladed sword, which he held curiously upright by the blade. His hair hung in damp curls over his forehead, and his tunic had been shredded and drenched in blood. His left hand was a mangled mess, but he was alive, and he was walking on his own.

Some strange mixture of guilt and shame and admiration washed over her, and before she could stop herself, she ran to him, and threw her arms around his neck, ignoring the dragon altogether. She half expected him to shove her away and give her some stern rebuke, but he didn't. He let her embrace him, and all at once he gave a shuddering, exhausted sigh and leaned into her hold, letting the sword slip through his hand to rest point-down against the rocks.

"You defeated him?" she whispered. "How? How is it possible?"

You will bow to me, a sinuous dark voice hissed in her thoughts. *You are my slave. Give me worship.*

She withdrew her arms from Jurian's neck and turned to face the dragon that glared at her, its body twisted and bloody. After so many years as the voice and hands of the god, Sabra could only stare at the dragon in horror and revulsion…and contempt.

"I will not," she said.

The dragon bared its fangs but winced suddenly, writhing against its pain. Jurian walked slowly around to face it, undeterred as it snaked its head back and forth not inches from his own.

"Jurian," Sabra whispered. "What did you do to it? How did you defeat it?"

Jurian stared at his sword, an enigmatic smile playing around his lips. "I didn't. The dragon bested me."

Sabra stared at him, her relief churning into dread. Was this some kind of sick mockery?

Jurian seemed to read her mind, because he glanced up at the dragon and said, "I carried the *signum* against the dragon. My Master defeated it, not me."

"Was it your God's *signum*? A talisman? What was it?"

Jurian grinned. "A splinter of wood."

Sabra gaped at him. "You brought down the dragon…the old god…with a splinter of wood?"

"The wood of salvation," Jurian murmured.

"I've heard that before!" Sabra gasped suddenly. "The prophecy of the Oracle…she said, *your city's salvation awaits the wood*. Where is it now? Can I see it?"

"Sadly, no. A man of your city carried it here in his palm. I carried it here in the head of a spear, and now that dragon carries it in what's left of its heart. The spirit possessing that form was going to fade away back in that cavern, but I have bound it to the dragon's form. It is nothing but an empty shell, now. A husk. It has no more power, and it will die as soon as I give it leave."

Sabra hesitated, waiting for the voice in her mind to contradict him, but none came. She frowned and waited a little longer, but still, nothing.

"What power could silence the god?" she whispered.

"That being was no god," Jurian said. "I'm sorry. I won't say you served nothing, because that would be a lie. You did, and I know you thought you were doing well. But that being was not worthy of your worship." He regarded her in sudden curiosity. "But that's not the most interesting question."

She tore her gaze from the dragon to give him a quizzical look.

"How did you get free?" Jurian asked.

"Your friend was here. I suppose he came with you?"

"Menas?"

Sabra shook her head. "No, the other man. He was very short…black beard, dark eyes? Dressed in a dark robe?"

"*Nikolaos?*" Jurian cried. "But that's…that's not possible."

"Well, he was here," she said. "He told me to let go, and I did." She smiled suddenly and murmured, "It's just like he said: *Chains may bind, but words may free.*"

"When did you ever speak to him?" Jurian asked.

Sabra's smile widened. "He spoke to me. In Carthage."

Jurian stared at her for another moment, then shrugged. "It's Nikolaos," he muttered. "I don't know why I should be so surprised."

"Jurian," Sabra said, "my people need to see this. I may be free now, but they aren't. Not yet. Not until they see this. I want them to see him brought low, and I want them to mock him. It's all the honor he deserves."

Jurian contemplated the dragon's broken body for a moment. Then, suddenly, he swung the sword over his head in deadly silence and drove the blade straight through the dragon's neck. The sword cut true, severing bone and sinew in a wash of blood and fire, and the dragon's head crashed to the earth. The rest of its body shuddered in a last contortion as it fell. Smoke and shadow poured like blood from the wound. And for just a moment—though she may have imagined it—she thought she saw something writhing snakelike from the shadows under the dragon's head. Then it was gone.

Sabra stumbled a step back, wrenching her gaze from the dragon's corpse to Jurian standing quietly beside it, sword loose in his hand, head bent and face somber.

"And now," he said, lifting his eyes to hers, "I think he is fit to be seen by your people."

A sudden scattering of rocks on the hillside path startled her from her numbness, and she glanced up to see Hanno limping his way toward her. He clutched one arm against his chest—it was mottled with blood.

"Mistress," he called, and she ran and threw her arms around his neck. "Mistress, you're not allowed—"

"Oh, Hanno, I've never been so glad to see you! But where were you? What happened? What's wrong with your arm?"

His face paled and he twisted his arm to regard the strange pattern of wounds. "I…I don't know. That terrible fear…it weighed me down, so heavy, and I was lying on my arm on the rocks. Can fear do that to someone? I thought I was going to die. No." He shook his head. "I…I *wanted* to die."

She watched as his gaze fell on Flavia's body, and he covered his face with his hands.

"Don't be afraid," Sabra said. "There's no more reason to fear."

From the moment she'd caught sight of him coming toward her, she'd noticed that he was avoiding the gruesome sight of the dragon. But now, at her words, he shuddered and risked a glance at the severed head. His gaze drifted past it to the broken body, then over to Jurian, who stood calmly cleaning the long blade of Excalibur.

"It's over?" he whispered.

"It's over," she said. "The old god is dead, and my priesthood is ended."

She watched Jurian sheathe the sword and stoop to lift Flavia gently in his arms. Her throat burned with grief and regret as she reached out and laid her hand on the girl's cold forehead.

Why did you have to be so brave?

"Come on," she said. "Let's go put an end to this."

They made their way down the rocky path in silence. The drums and flutes echoed off the face of the cliff, a jarring cacophony that set her teeth on edge more now than ever. The sound mixed with cries and lamentations, the great noise of a city awaiting its destruction. They rounded the corner onto the main road of the city and the ritual music jarred to a stop. Then, little by little, the shouts and weeping died into silence as the entire city stared at Sabra and the fire-haired boy with the girl in his arms.

52

Cyrene

JURIAN WAITED QUIETLY AS THE people tried to make sense of what they saw. He could see their fear and confusion, the faint stirrings of hope that were too fragile to blossom.

"You defied Molech!" someone shouted suddenly. "You'll bring his destruction on this city!"

Other cries shattered the silence, and the people stirred restlessly, staring at the group on the road with hostile suspicion. A woman pushed her way clear of the crowd, sobbing inconsolably. Jurian's heart ached when she stretched out her hands to the girl in his arms. He carefully gave her the child's body, sinking down to a crouch with her to clasp her around the shoulders as she wept.

"Father!" Sabra cried suddenly.

Jurian glanced up to see a man in a fine toga burst into the open street, running to meet her and folding her into a warm embrace.

"I was certain I'd lost you forever," he murmured. "What happened?"

Sabra gestured to Jurian, and the man studied him curiously under lowered brows. Jurian gave him a few moments to gather his thoughts, but when he realized the man wasn't going to speak, he turned to face the crowd.

"People of Cyrene!" he shouted, pointing at the dreaded hill. "Go and behold your god!"

They stared at him, stunned speechless. A few glanced up the hillside, but for one endless moment, no one dared to move. Then Sabra's father straightened up and faced the path. Another man pushed free from the crowd and stepped up beside him with a hard challenging look.

"I'll go with you so I can be sure you report the truth to the people," he snapped.

The two men took torches and disappeared up the hill. The crowd waited in breathless, murmuring quiet, broken only by the sobs of the woman still weeping over her daughter. Hanno and Sabra both crouched beside her, trying in vain to comfort her.

He delights in death and laughs to see us suffer. Jurian shuddered, recalling Sabra's words. What sort of being could be so capricious, so cruel? And how could anyone pay him the reverence owed to God? Thinking of that, Jurian turned back to the crowd, throat tight.

"Your Molech was no god," he called. "You served a monster. You served a dark power, a being more powerful than you even imagined by calling him a god. But he was never worthy of your worship. He was never worthy of the innocent blood you shed in his name."

A few moments later the two men reappeared, walking slowly and pale-faced back into the city. A murmur rippled through the crowd.

"It's true," Sabra's father said, so quietly the people hushed of one accord to hear him.

"What did you see?" someone shouted.

"A lie," the other man said.

"Dignianus—" Sabra's father started, but the man held up his hand to cut him off.

"Don't misunderstand me," he said. "That god, that dragon… he was no more than a lie. False religion. No wonder Apollo was angry with us."

Jurian saw Sabra bite her lip but she said nothing, and he only shook his head.

"How did you destroy him, stranger?" Sabra's father asked. "He has plagued our city for over a decade, and you brought him down all by yourself? With just a sword?"

"Not with the sword," Jurian said quietly.

"Then how—"

Jurian glanced at Sabra, giving her a little nod.

She tipped her head to regard him, and Jurian wondered briefly how she would explain it.

She said, "Not all the Legions of Rome could do what this man did on his own. Or..." She darted a quick look at him, smiling. "He would say he didn't do it on his own, but he did it by the power of the *signum* he carried. The *signum* of a conqueror."

"What conqueror? Was it the *signum* of the Emperor?"

"Diocletian has no power that wasn't given him," Jurian said. "I serve the One who gives power, not the one who borrows it."

For a moment there was silence. Then, somewhere in the crowd, someone began to laugh...a laugh of pure relief. Then someone whooped and raised his hands over his head in a slow clap. The stunned stupor of the crowd dissolved into a sudden chaos of cheering, shouting, laughing. Even Hanno was standing with his head cast back to the sky and arms lifted, calling out something over and over again in Punic.

"What is he saying?" Jurian asked Sabra, who was watching the slave with faint amusement.

"He says, *blessed the man*." When Jurian just frowned she laughed and laid a hand on his forearm. "It's a prayer of praise," she said. "He's honoring you for your deed."

"He'd do better not to praise me," Jurian said quietly.

He folded his arms, watching the crowd dissolve before him. Nobody went back to their homes, though. They divided off into groups, some trickling up the hill in small clusters to see the dragon's corpse for themselves, others lighting bonfires in the streets and bringing out food as if for a feast. The ritual musicians began to play again, but this time they left the harsh noise of their ritual songs and played a beautiful, haunting song that somehow caressed pain into joy.

Sabra's father turned to her, taking her face in her hands. Jurian glanced away when he saw the tears streaming down his cheeks, but he couldn't help overhearing his words.

"Can you ever forgive me, *filia?*" he asked. "I've done so much wrong by you. I've caused you so much pain..."

Sabra wrapped her arms around his neck and held him tight. "I forgive you," she whispered. "And don't blame yourself for sending me away. If I hadn't gone to Rome, I wouldn't have met Jurian, and we may never have been saved at all."

He smiled and took her hands in his, kissing them fondly. Then he turned to Jurian, extending his arm to him. "I don't know how to thank you, *domine*."

"I'm no lord," Jurian said, but he clasped the man's arm warmly. "I'm not worthy of that title."

"You delivered us from out of the mouth of our own destruction," he said. "It may be we put ourselves there in the first place, but I'm sure none of us knew how to get back out again."

"Just see that you don't make the same mistake again," Jurian said, his voice sterner than he expected.

He turned, walking away from the mayhem and all the noise. On the other side of the road, toward the city gates, everything was dark and quiet, and he found himself on the road leading out of the city. Near the gate he stopped and glanced back at the joyful chaos, then as he turned east again, he found himself face to face with Nikolaos.

"You!" he gasped. "But how...how can you be here?"

"You did well, Jurian," Nikolaos said. "I'm only sad that you left the splinter of the Cross in that heart of darkness."

Jurian didn't bother to ask how Nikolaos knew that much, but he winced in regret. "I suppose I could dig it out again."

"That heart is not its tomb," Nikolaos said, regarding him keenly. "And life will rise from the ashes."

"Nikolaos," Jurian said, throat tight. "Menas..."

"Is far from you," Nikolaos said. He clasped Jurian's arm. "If you want to find him, you must be ready."

"For what?"

"What you will face at the end."

Jurian sighed and pressed his fingers against his forehead. "Why—" he started, but when he opened his eyes, the road was empty.

A moment later he heard a shuffle behind him and turned to find Sabra standing there, uncertain. She had taken off the garland and veil, and the wind had tugged some of her dark hair free of its ornate styling. Despite the cold night air she wasn't shivering, but stood with one hand clasping the other's upper arm, her head bowed to avoid his gaze. Jurian waited for her to speak, marveling at how anyone could look so impossibly strong and yet so vulnerable at the same time.

"And what about me, Jurian?" she asked finally.

He frowned. "What about you?"

"Can you forgive me for what I've done? Or do you despise me too much? I know you barely thought well of me before you discovered what I really was." She lifted her eyes to his, holding him breathless for one long moment. "And now that you know…I could understand if you hated me."

He took a step closer to her. "How can you think I would hate you?" he asked. "Do you think I don't see what you've been through? What you've suffered? What you did, you did because you love your people." He smiled down at her. "Somehow—impossibly—you served the darkness without losing yourself in it. That is strength that I don't think I'll ever know."

"I don't understand it," she said softly, shaking her head. "How can weakness be strength, and strength weakness?"

"Because," Jurian said softly, taking her shoulders in his hands, "it's when we're weakest that love can be strongest. And it's love that conquers, Sabra. Just love."

She laughed softly, tipping her head back to study him. "Just love," she repeated. "You're an impossible man, do you know that? You and Menas. Just like Ayzebel was impossible. Your faith makes no sense, but it makes more sense than all the world."

53

Cyrene

THE CELEBRATIONS IN CYRENE LASTED an entire week, and inside the governor's palace, it felt like they would never end. There were days Sabra believed she would never quite accustom herself to her new liberty. She was no longer The Priestess…but now she had to learn how to be Sabra. She shied away from strangers, but found herself seeking Jurian's company as often as she could. He was quiet, like a sea after a storm, and his quiet suited her.

Maybe it's because he's only ever known me as Sabra, she realized one day as they sat together in the peristyle. *And maybe it's because he knows what it is to be broken and remade.*

Jurian was tending to his weapons, and she watched him check the arrows in his quiver and oil the string of his bow, his left hand still awkward from his injuries. A heaviness settled on her heart as she watched his face, saw the grim line of determination between his brows, the intensity in his eyes.

He didn't mean to stay. And she didn't quite know what she would do when he was gone.

One day she caught herself reckoning the day of the month, wondering if this was the day the winnowing was supposed to take place, but the thought opened a gaping wound of grief and shame in her heart and she drove it away. That life was gone. All its forms and rituals and gnawing dark loneliness—these weren't a part of her any more. At first the loss of her priesthood seemed enough to drive her mad, but she couldn't ignore the feeling of relief and peace its absence left her with.

As the week wound to a close, Sabra found herself warming to the people who swarmed the palace for the evening feast. She watched them crowd around Jurian, watched his patient smile, and marveled. Whatever had happened in that cavern, he had come out changed. Even the way he moved, the way he spoke or didn't speak, the way he seemed to measure a person's soul with a simple look...everything he did seemed born of some strange inner fire, and the whole city was captivated.

On the fifth evening of feasting, Sabra found him in the peristyle with a cup of honeyed wine forgotten in his hand, staring at the fountain with the strangest expression on his face. She almost hesitated to approach him, but before she could slip away, he glanced up and fixed her with a quiet look.

"They're finally leaving you alone?" she asked lightly, taking a few steps closer to him.

He smiled wryly. "They'll be back. Unless you stay and talk to me."

She could feel the blush creep up her neck. "Do you want me to stay?"

He gave a quiet laugh and regarded the wine in his cup. "I'm not used to all this. I used to think that this was what I wanted." He glanced at her again. "All those years after my father's death, all I wanted was to restore our family to the dignity we deserved. I wanted us to be welcomed by our city...wanted so desperately not to be an outcast. And I used to imagine being high up in Diocletian's court, following him everywhere, being looked up to as a friend of the emperor." He sighed. "I just don't know if I want that anymore."

"There's a storm coming in the Empire," she said. "And that man will be at the heart of it."

"I know," Jurian said quietly. "I know better than you can imagine. And it's already begun."

"So what will you do, then?" Sabra asked. "If that's not what you want any more, is there something else?"

She clapped her mouth shut abruptly, her heart pounding. Had she really just said that to him? And what did she hope he would say?

He glanced up abruptly, studying her with steady attention for a few long moments. "I'm not sure," he said slowly. He stared across the peristyle, then he sighed and turned back to her. "And what about you, Sabra? What will you do with yourself now?"

She should have expected the question, but it still surprised her, and she wasn't sure how to answer. Everything she'd ever known, or thought she'd known, had been turned on its head, and she still wasn't sure which way was the surface.

"I don't know either," she said finally. "But I think…I think I'll try to help my father put Cyrene back on its feet. It's time for us to move forward now, but the way is full of hazards."

He turned toward her suddenly, eyes bright and intense. "You'll have to be careful, Sabra. There are people in this city who won't be favorable to change. Don't let them drag you down with their pride. And please, whatever you do…please take care of my people here."

And with that, she knew he wouldn't stay.

"You mean to go, then?" she asked softly. When he held her gaze but didn't answer, she dropped her head and nodded. "I always knew you meant to."

"Sabra—"

"I'll do my best to protect them, Jurian. And there's a man here, Theodorus." She smiled up at him, trying to hide the strange brokenness she felt inside. "Maybe he will teach me more about this conquering victim you worship."

He turned back to the fountain, rubbing a hand over his jaw. Sabra wondered if he even noticed the shadow of a beard he'd grown. It made him look older than when she'd first met him… but then she realized it had nothing to do with the beard, and everything to do with the shadow in his eyes.

"You keep looking at the fountain," she said, gently. "Is something wrong with it?"

The muscle at the corner of his jaw tightened. "I told you I lost my sister in Rome," he said after a long silence. "When she was killed, she fell into a pool like this one. I can't look at it without seeing her blood among the lilies."

Sabra's breath caught in her throat and she laid a hand on his arm. "I'm sure she's proud of you, Jurian."

"I hope so," he said. His eyes were fixed on her hand, and she slowly withdrew it, suddenly unsure of herself. For a moment, Jurian didn't speak, but suddenly, he smiled at her, brushing his finger against her cheek. "You have so much to give, Sabra," he said softly. "So much to give."

And without another word, he turned and left the peristyle. Sabra realized she was holding her breath, and as she lost sight of him in the shadows, she reached up and touched her cheek.

"So do you," she whispered after him.

AS THE WEEK of feasting drew to a close, Sabra's father called her and Jurian into his *tablinum* before the evening's guests had arrived. Jurian looked restless, Sabra noticed, but he stood patiently behind her father's desk, waiting as the governor finished reading a parchment.

"I hope you are enjoying your stay with us, Jurian," he said finally.

"I have, *domine*," Jurian said. "But I'm anxious to be on my way. I hope you'll excuse me saying so—I mean no disrespect to your hospitality or your household."

"I understand," the governor said quickly, to spare him the embarrassment of trying to explain. "Though I heartily wish we could keep you here with us."

"A friend has need of me," Jurian said, quiet.

"I wish I could offer you something in thanks for what you've done for this city." His gaze flickered for a moment at Sabra, then returned to the pile of scrolls on his desk. "And there is only one thing in my possession that is precious enough to express my thanks." He straightened and gestured toward her. "My daughter Sabra."

The blood drain from Sabra's face. "What?" she stammered.

She didn't dare look at Jurian. He hadn't so much as moved, and she couldn't sense at all what he must be thinking.

"Sabra, if you're willing," her father, "I will offer you to Jurian as a bride as a token of my gratitude."

Sabra swallowed hard. *My willingness has nothing to do with it, she wanted to say. He means to go…and I can't make him stay.* She had already accepted that fact, but it didn't make it easier to bear the emptiness that threatened her every time she thought about it.

She had no idea how Jurian felt about her. He was warm and kind, thoughtful…but to take her as a wife, was that enough?

"*Domine,*" Jurian said, and cleared his throat. "I cannot thank you enough for your generous offer, though I could never think of your daughter as a token to be given away." He paused, then added, "If you'll permit me, I'd like to discuss this with your daughter in private."

Her father's eyes widened, but he only nodded and dismissed them with a wave of his hand. Jurian turned and held back the curtain for Sabra, then followed her out of the *tablinum*. Sabra hesitated in the atrium, but Jurian just turned and headed into the peristyle. He sat down on one of the low bronze benches under the shade of the portico, then, surprisingly, patted the seat beside him. Sabra sank down gingerly beside him, careful to keep a disinterested distance between them.

"Sabra," he said softly. "I can't stay. You know I can't."

"I know." Her voice sounded small, and she wondered if he could hear it tremble.

"I am so honored that your father would think me worthy of you," he went on, his eyes flickering at her for a moment, then returning to rest on his hands. "I don't want to disappoint him after the kindness he has shown me."

Another pause. With every silence, Sabra's heart jumped into her throat, but she couldn't find any words to say.

"And…I don't want to disappoint you."

A hundred things she might say suddenly tumbled into her mind, but all she could manage was, "I know."

He looked up at her then, and Sabra felt the tears burning behind her eyes. His face softened as he studied her. "It will disappoint you, won't it?" he said.

Sabra couldn't speak. She clasped her hands in her lap and just tried to breathe without letting the tears fall.

"I'm so sorry."

There was such a weight of sorrow in his voice that she had to look at him again. When she caught his eyes, he fumbled a smile. "You mean more to me than you will ever know…but I can't stay. I made a promise to a friend…and beyond that, I don't know where my road will take me. Prophecies are funny things, you know?"

She managed a little laugh that caught in a sob. "I know. Believe me, I know."

He reached up and tucked a stray lock of hair behind her ear. "I wish I could stay, Sabra. But I can't. And I don't know if my road will ever lead me back to you again. How could I ask you to wait for me?"

She seized his hand in both her own. "I would wait for you, if you asked me to," she said. "I've been waiting all my life."

"And that's why I can't ask you to wait any longer. But…" His voice trailed off and he laid his free hand over hers. "Remember me, will you? In your prayers. As you will always be in mine."

He leaned forward and kissed her gently on the forehead, and then he was gone.

54

CYRENE

AFTER THE LAST DAY OF feasting had finally ended, when the city had gotten over most of its shock and some of its excitement and had returned to petty squabbles and lawsuits and trade agreements, Jurian gathered his few belongings in his pack and tied it together with Menas' for when he would find him. The governor had offered him a new toga but Jurian had refused. He had his tunic and his military cloak, and that would serve him well enough until the day he could take on a Legionary's armor.

He sighed, thinking of Menas and the Legion *spiculum* he had carried. Menas had left the army because he had to, for the good of his own soul, but others joined to fight for the souls of others. Like Marcellus and Sebastianus. He didn't fault Menas for his choice, but his choice was not the same. He would fight. Whatever battle, on whatever front, against devils or barbarians or his own *Imperator*. He would fight.

A low knock sounded at the door of his chamber, and he found Hanno waiting there.

"My master would see you," he said.

Jurian nodded. He'd broken the news to the governor as gently as he could that he would not be accepting Sabra as a bride. The man had taken it with good grace, but Jurian could tell he was disappointed, and a little offended when Jurian suggested that he should leave Sabra's decision about marriage to her. The girl had been cut from her father's rule years ago; it didn't seem right to suddenly start making those decisions for her again. Sabra was an incredible young woman, fearless and strong in a way he wasn't sure he would ever be, and he knew she would find her purpose, just like he had.

So he followed Hanno to the atrium with some anxiety. He didn't want the governor to waste his breath trying to convince him again, but he couldn't imagine what else there was to discuss. He drew up in surprise when Hanno didn't take him to the *tablinum*, but headed instead for the front door.

"Where are we going?"

Hanno thought a moment, then shrugged and beckoned him without a word. Jurian set his teeth and followed him out into the city, winding toward the less inhabited part of the city to the northeast where the old Greek Temple of Zeus towered over an expansive hippodrome.

Is he going to ask me to burn incense to the gods? Jurian wondered, frowning.

He had made it clear to the governor that he was a Christian; when he'd refused Sabra, the governor had asked if there was anything else Jurian wanted, and Jurian had asked him only to show mercy to the Christians in his city. He'd agreed. Like Sabra, he even seemed interested in learning more about the religion at the heart of his city's salvation...so why was Hanno taking him to a pagan temple now?

At the last minute Hanno veered away from the temple, instead heading toward the stables near the hippodrome. They stepped through the massive doorway into a building of light and stone, thick with the smell of hay and sweat and leather. Dust motes drifted hazily through the low winter sunlight, and everywhere he could hear horses stomping and snorting. The governor stood at the far end of the aisle, leaning on one of the pillars of a wide stall. Hanno led Jurian to him and bowed.

"Ah, Jurian," Lucius Titianus said. He leaned into the stall, slapping the shoulder of a white horse.

Jurian moved around to face him, casting a quick, appreciative glance over the horse. This was no small, stocky horse like the Legion cavalry in Anatolia rode. He'd heard of this breed, desert-bred, light and fast and enduring as the desert itself. The horse was tall, fine-boned, with faint smudges around his eyes that made him look strangely wise. Other than that, he was entirely white, his coat brushed to a high gleam. With a snort the horse regarded him briefly, then turned to claim the last bits of hay from his wooden trough, tapping one hoof on the dusty ground with something like impatience. Jurian's mouth quirked in a smile.

"He's a fine animal, isn't he?" the governor asked.

"Beautiful," Jurian said. *Mari would have loved him.*

"He's the finest horse in Libya. I'd wager Africa, but that might be a bit presumptuous. Four years old. He's stubborn and high strung, rather like someone I know."

"Me?" Jurian asked with faint surprise.

The governor laughed. "No, I meant Sabra."

Jurian grinned and held out his hand. The horse came around and snuffled at his palm, snorting when he found nothing of interest there.

"Is he named?"

"No," the governor said. "I only name horses I've ridden, or that I've entered in the races. Haven't had a chance with this one yet." He turned and measured Jurian. "I know it's a poor replacement for my daughter, but I was hoping you would accept him as a gift."

Jurian's mouth dropped open and he started to shake his head, but the governor held up a hand.

"This friend you were telling me about? You said the Legionaries captured him?" The man sighed. "I'm wagering they'll take him over land. There are plenty of amphitheaters spread along the path from here to Antioch, and I would guess they're going to try to take him to Antioch. It's closer than Rome, anyway, and that's where the *Imperator* Diocletian normally lives. If your giant is as impressive as you've described him to be, they'll be shoving him in the arena to fight the beasts every chance they get on the way to bringing him before the emperor."

Jurian sighed. He hadn't told the governor that Menas had deserted the army. But that would be just one more reason his captors would want to take him to Antioch.

"Anyway," the governor continued, "if you want the best odds of catching him, you should follow over land. You won't get anywhere on foot." He gestured to the horse. "Take him. He's the fastest and strongest in my stables."

Jurian swallowed hard. "I don't know how I would thank you for such a gift."

Lucius Titianus laughed. "The horse is a thank you. You owe me nothing. Now take him before I change my mind."

"Thank you, *domine*. He's trained to ride under saddle?"

"He is. And you? Can you ride?"

Jurian's mouth quirked in a wry smile. "More or less. I'm sure I'll get used to it in a hurry." He studied the horse a while longer, the smile spreading slowly to a grin. "Marcellinus said I would be an *eques*. Now I'll look the part."

JURIAN RETURNED TO the palace to gather his belongings, staying long enough to share a noon meal with the governor and Sabra before taking his leave. The governor clasped his arm warmly and welcomed him to return and stay at any time, then turned away without another word or backwards glance. Jurian picked up his belongings, slinging his bow and quiver over his shoulder alongside the sword, then shrugging his pack over the other shoulder. Hanno chuckled behind him, and he caught Sabra grinning at something the slave said in Punic.

"What did he say?"

Sabra laughed. "He said you look like a pack horse."

Jurian arched a brow at Hanno in mock severity, then grinned and clasped Hanno's arm. The slave looked startled, darting a nervous glance at Sabra.

"Most people don't say goodbye to slaves," Sabra said quietly, seeing Jurian's uncertainty. "You show him a great honor."

"I would never have found you in time if it hadn't been for

him. Tell him that. He deserves the honor."

"I understood that," Hanno said with a broad grin. "Thank you, *kyrie*."

Jurian smiled and turned to Sabra, his heart heavy. "I hope I didn't offend you, domina, with how everything turned out."

She shook her head and embraced him briefly. "You saved me and my city, and overthrew a cult that wasted its worship on an unworthy being. That is all I could ever have wanted from anyone."

"Be strong, Sabra," he said, clasping her hand in both his own. "The darkness isn't gone entirely, and your people will need grace and mercy in the days to come."

"Well, that's one way to spoil the cheer," she said, but she smiled as she said it. "No, I know you're right. Take care of yourself, Jurian. I hope you will find Menas soon, and find out what that prophecy about the sword meant. Write to me about your travels, if you would, and if I can ever do anything to help you… money, supplies, a place to stay…just ask. I'm at your disposal." She suddenly seemed to remember something, and put her hand to her heart. "Oh, Jurian, I almost forgot. I do have something for you to take with you."

She gave him an insufferably smug smile, then lifted something from beneath her tunic. He cocked his head, catching the flash of sunlight on a small cedar wood and bronze case dangling from a thick chain.

"What is it?"

"Did you wonder what happened to the dragon's corpse? They hauled it away outside the gates and set it on a huge pyre, not to give it any honorable passing, of course. Just to get rid of the body. Well, they burned its body all that night and it was still burning the next day. When the fire finally died and the pyre was cold, one of the men found this in the ash. It should have burned, but it didn't, so I imagine it might just be the wood that killed the dragon. I took the liberty of having a case made for it."

He stared at her, lips parted in shock, until she had to grab his hand to give him the pyx. The metal felt warm to his touch, and he opened the case gently. It was lined in gold, but there, tucked safely in a piece of fine linen, was something far more precious—the splinter of the Cross. Jurian bit his lip, throat burning.

"I never thought I would see it again," he said. "But...perhaps it should stay with you in Cyrene. After all, it first belonged to a man of your city."

"And I'm sure he would like nothing better than to pass it on to the man who saved it."

He bowed his head in thanks, unable to call up his voice. The chain slipped easily over his head, and he tucked the little case under his tunic. It pressed against his skin with a weight that was both familiar and strange.

"Thank you," he murmured, and that was all he could say.

He gave her a rare smile and then, with just a lift of his hand in farewell, he turned and left the palace.

The stable slaves had brought the white horse to the base of the palace steps, all tacked up in what looked like Roman cavalry equipment—a deep saddle with tasseled edge and a silver harness decorated with intricately embossed buckles, an ornate bridle with the thin reins dangling free, ready for him to take up. The men helped Jurian fasten his bags behind the saddle, but he kept the weapons on his back. Once everything was secure, a slave offered him his knee so he could swing onto the horse's back.

Jurian swallowed. He'd felt more confident about this before, but now that the moment was on him, he could only think about just how many years it had been since he'd ridden. And a crowd had gathered too, of course. Jurian could only picture himself getting on the horse from one side only to fall off the other, and the image made him laugh as much as blush.

The horse arched his neck and glanced back at him, shaking his head as if to say, *This is the man they expect me to carry?* Jurian grinned and pulled himself into the saddle. The four high saddle horns helped him feel a little more stable, and the horse danced under his weight as he gathered up the reins.

Jurian glanced over his shoulder and found Sabra and her father at the top of the steps. He grinned and gave a sharp wave like a salute, and, with only the lightest pressure from his calves, moved the horse through the townspeople. They cheered as he passed, making him feel strangely self-conscious, but the horse seemed to enjoy the attention enough for the both of them. The crowd thinned as they reached the city gate, then there was nothing but the open road ahead.

Jurian left the road after nearly an hour, turning the horse up a long, low hill. At the crown they could barely see the smudges of the highest buildings of Cyrene behind them, and ahead of them, a vast, flat stretch all the way to the sea. Jurian kept his seat on the horse's back, suddenly anxious about getting down and not being able to get back up, or having the horse bolt as soon as his feet hit the ground.

"We've got to be partners now, you and I," he muttered to the horse. "No throwing me off or bolting or running away, all right, horse?"

The horse flicked its tail at his legs and shook his head.

"Aster," Jurian said. "Since I suppose it's odd to call you *horse*."

He sighed and leaned on the double pommels, staring out at the endless sea where it met the endless land. Somehow the horse, unimpressed though he seemed by the whole affair, lessened the weight of isolation that threatened to sink him. He was alone, but he wouldn't stop moving forward. Menas was out there somewhere, possibly awaiting execution, probably doubting that he would ever be found.

"Not while I'm still breathing," Jurian murmured. "I promise you that. You found me in the wilderness and saved me. Now let me do the same for you."

The late afternoon sun slanted down on them with a memory of warmth, casting Jurian's body in a long, thin shadow that pointed like a finger toward the east. He nudged Aster forward, riding along the ridge of the hill, while the whole world spread beneath their feet.

EPILOGUE

Roma

The sun was setting over Rome, slanting pools of warm amber light through the narrow windows as Diocletian paced back and forth in the grand *tablinum* he'd been given to use. The room should have impressed him—even his own *tablinum* in Antioch was nothing compared to it, with its bright frescoes and towering pillars, and a writing table that was entirely too large to be reasonable. Coal braziers scattered around the room drove away the winter chill, but nothing could shake the darkness in Diocletian's mind, and he wasn't in the mood to be impressed by anything.

This business in Rome was taking too long; he needed to be in Antioch. Having him and Maximian *Augustus* in the same city threatened to fracture the stability of the Empire, as if they had to stand on its opposite reaches to hold it in balance.

And he could feel the Empire shifting beneath him, like rock splitting under the force of an earthquake. The tremors were small yet, but he didn't need auguries or the divinations of the *haruspex* to understand what was happening. He'd barely managed to salvage what he did of the old Empire, and now, all his years of hard work rested on the edge of a precipice.

He was still pacing and muttering under his breath when a guard appeared in his doorway. As soon as Diocletian gave him leave to speak, the man bowed and stepped inside, ushering a rather unfortunate looking young man in behind him. The man walked with a little limp that Diocletian wasn't sure was genuine, and he kept one hand flopping limply across his stomach.

"What is this?" Diocletian snapped. "I've no time to give audiences right now."

The guard bowed again and said, "This man claims to have information that you will want to hear. Divine *Imperator* Diocletian *Augustus*, may I present Marcus Valerius Flaccus Casca."

EXTRAS

Bonus Content for the First 3000 Copies of
Sword and Serpent:

THE DREAM OF NIKOLAOS

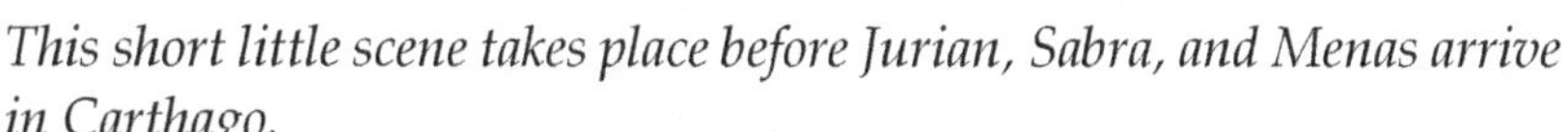

This short little scene takes place before Jurian, Sabra, and Menas arrive in Carthago.

A GREY DUSK HAD FALLEN over Myra and the wind blew in from the sea, heavy with the energy of an impending storm. Nikolaos sat cross-legged on the ground outside his home, staring toward the water. Worry prickled in the back of his mind like the nearness of lightning, but it was shapeless, formless—a need to act without knowing what to do.

With one hand clasping the simple wooden cross he wore at his neck, he closed his eyes, trying to find understanding, trying to find peace. The brine-sharp wind buffeted him, then died. The wild chattering of his thoughts calmed, and he breathed deeply.

A slow coldness threaded through his veins, something of surprise, something of joy.

He could smell roses—a delicate sweetness that filled him with the peace of memory and hope. But roses, here? Here, in the path of the sea-wind, where nothing but scrub grew anywhere near?

Holding his breath, he opened his eyes, and flinched when

a soft light flooded across his vision. He'd expected…he hadn't expected this.

He hadn't expected *her*.

"Mariam?" he asked.

The girl stood quietly right in front of him, her hands folded across her stomach. She was dressed in a simple white tunic, a garland of roses on her head, but in the grey-shade of dusk, those roses stood out in a vivid blood red. She was smiling.

"How are you here, daughter?" Nikolaos asked. "I'm usually the one standing in your place."

Her smile brightened. "I don't have your gift, *pater*, though I have need of it."

"I don't understand," he said, uneasiness settling in the pit of his stomach. "If you haven't come in my manner…then how are you here?"

"You were right," she said, instead of answering. "You foretold my wedding day, and I have embraced it. I met my Bridegroom, and He crowned me with this crimson crown of love."

She moved her hands then, and Nikolaos drew back, pressing a hand against his mouth. There, where her hands had rested, was a single stain of deepest red. A sick ache clawed at his heart, and for a moment he forgot to breathe.

"Mariam…" he began, but his voice broke and he bowed his head.

"No need to weep, *pater*," she murmured, laying her hand gently on his head. "All is well with me. I do not need your tears now."

He hid his face behind his hand, unable to swallow back his grief. He whispered, his voice shaking, "You are all beautiful, daughter, and clothed in glory, for you have loved justice and hated iniquity." He took a slow breath to steady himself, and glanced up at her. "But your brother and the Christophoros? Are they…"

"Alive, and well. But they need you."

"Not you?"

"I would rather be here where I am now than there with them.

I can help him here more than I ever could from there. But you… you can help him from there."

He frowned faintly. "I will pray for them, of course, unless—"

Mariam raised her hand, stirring the scent of roses again. "Tomorrow, when you can smell the roses again, I will come and take you to them."

She took a step back, and he stretched a hand toward her. "Mariam, I beg of you…"

"Yes," she said, her whole face lighting up with a smile. "Yes, pater, you must beg. Beg for their lives."

He stared at her, bewildered, but she only leaned forward and clasped his hands in both her own.

"When the time is right, tell Jurian I love him. Tell him not to be troubled—he did all he could. He saved my life so many times and I never even knew it. But now it is my turn to repay the favor."

"When the time is right?" Nikolaos echoed.

"You'll know. The words will be given to you." She took another step back. "Tomorrow," she said.

NIKOLAOS LURCHED FORWARD, the darkness of midnight crashing over him in a rush. The wind raged around him, scattering the loose folds of his dark robes, cold on the dampness of his cheeks. He lifted his fingers and touched his face.

"A dream," he murmured, but his heart caught at the word.

But a true dream, he thought. *She has received the crimson crown. Oh, daughter, how is it possible to grieve and rejoice with the same breath?*

He got to his feet, shivering and stretching the stiffness from his limbs, and headed into the courtyard. The fire in the brazier had died to embers; he must have slept longer than he thought. He stoked it up and sat close to its warmth on one of the bronze benches, staring sadly at the other where Jurian and Mariam had sat laughing and talking, their faces bright with the glow of hope and candles.

Jurian, I pray that I may be some help to you. God protect you. I cannot walk with you into the darkness, but perhaps I will see the way cleared for you to get there.

A cold scattering of raindrops blew across him, startling him from his thoughts, and he stumbled into his small bedchamber. There he fell into a restless sleep, not waking again until the pale greyness of a stormy morning brought a frail light to his room. He pushed himself to the edge of his narrow bed and leaned over his knees, rubbing his hands over his face. His eyes felt heavy, gritty from grief, but for a moment he struggled to remember why.

Then the memory of his dream rushed over him, and his breath caught in his throat.

Mariam, he thought.

And as her name formed in his mind, the smell of roses drifted in on the breeze.

Lexicon

Agora — a Greek marketplace for buying and selling goods, as well as a public meeting place.

Amphora — a clay urn or jar used to carry oil, grain, wine, etc. Also a unit of measurement.

Atrium — the front room in a Roman house. It had an opening in the ceiling where the rainwater would drain in; see *impluvium*.

Augur — a priest who practiced divination by observing the flight of birds.

Augustus — in the four-fold division of the Empire called the Tetrarchy, the two higher-ranking emperors were called *Augustus* (Diocletian in the East, and Maximian in the West).

Bracchae — short pants that reached about the knee; worn by Germanic tribes in the north and adopted by Legions stationed there.

Caesar — in the Tetrarchy, the two subordinate emperors were called *Caesar* (Galerius in the East, and Constantius in the West).

Caesareum — a temple devoted to the imperial cult, usually housing statues of the *genii* of the Emperors.

Cara — dear one; a term of endearment.

Castra — a Roman Legion camp or permanent fort.

Catacombs — underground burial sites. By the laws of Rome, these had to be situated outside the city limits. During the persecutions, these became places Christians would hide and practice their faith.

Christophoros — Greek for *Christ-bearer;* Menas' title and Christian name.

Culina — a Roman kitchen. Related to the word "culinary."

Decurion — a cavalry officer who commanded a unit of ten horsemen.

Diolkos — a railway-like construction between the ports of Cenchreae and Lechaeum, which enabled ships to be transported by land over the four mile isthmus of Corinth instead of having to sail around the Peloponnese peninsula. It stopped being used for transporting ships in the 1st century AD, but the track continued to be used to transport merchandise between ports.

Domine — lord; used as a title of respect for those in positions of authority, like "sir"; *domina* — lady; *domine meus* — my lord!

Domus Dei — house of God; a Christian church.

Emporium — a massive complex of warehouses for storing and distributing goods.

Eques — horseman; more specifically, a Legion cavalryman, the precursor to the medieval knight.

Filia — daughter; *filia regis* - daughter of the king, i.e., princess.

Flaccus — flabby, fat; the name of a very old Roman family.

Fornax — an oven used for cooking. Related to the word "furnace."

Forum — an area of a Roman city set aside for public discourse. People would gather in the forum to transact business, discuss new ideas or politics, or hear public addresses.

Frater — brother

Genius — similar to later concepts of "soul" — all creatures had them. In the case of the emperors, the *genius* was considered divine. Statues of the *genius* of the emperor often depicted him in idealized form, not as the man really appeared.

Haruspex — a priest who practiced *haruspicy*, or the study of animal entrails for divination.

Hippodrome — an oval stadium used for horse races.

Hyssop — an herbal remedy for coughs and respiratory sicknesses; also, it was a plant branch used by Moses to sprinkle blood, and used by Christians to sprinkle holy water.

Ichthus — the Greek word for "fish." A symbol of early Christianity because the Greek letters form an acrostic of "*Iesous CHristos THeos Uios Soter*" meaning "Jesus Christ, Son of God, Savior."

Imperator — emperor.

Impluvium — a depression in the atrium floor to collect rainwater.

Kalends — the first day of the month.

Kyrie — lord; the Greek equivalent of *domine*.

Legate — the *legatus legionis* or Legion Legate was the highest ranking officer in a Legion. He often acted as a civil ruler, especially along the frontier.

Mare Nostrum —our sea; the Roman term for the Mediterranean Sea.

Matrona — matron; the female head of a household.

Mensor — a dock official responsible for measuring the cargo imported on merchant vessels.

Narang — Persian word for "orange." Oranges were rare in the Empire, not becoming popular in Europe until the Middle Ages.

Necropolis — "city of the dead"; a massive burial site usually situated in a hillside where the dead were housed in mausoleums or tombs, often highly decorated.

Nomen — a name. Roman men had three names, which changed in meaning and importance throughout the Republic and Empire. In Jurian's time, the *praenomen* and *nomen* (for instance, Lucius Aurelius) designated a family, while the *cognomen* was what we would consider a first name (Georgius). Some men would choose to use their father's *cognomen* in addition to their own to add to their prestige, especially if it had been in the family for a long time (hence

Marcus Valerius Flaccus Casca). With the expanding Empire, it became increasingly common for the *cognomen* to be of non-Roman origin.

PALLA — a long rectangular piece of fabric worn as a veil or wrap by Roman women.

PAPPAS — a Greek word meaning "father"; this was the common title for all bishops in early Christianity, but gradually became associated in particular with the bishop of Rome.

PERISTYLE — an inner courtyard that served as the main social area of a Roman house. It was often decorated with statues, columns, a fountain or a pool, and fruit trees.

PIETAS — a concept of piety that, for the Romans, went beyond religious faith, and concerned devotion to Rome herself.

POSCA — a bitter mixture of vinegar and wine popular among Legionaries and sailors. This was probably the drink given to Christ on the Cross.

PRAETORIUM — the building where the Legion Legate would live with his family, and where Legion business was conducted.

PROCRUSTES — in Greek myth, Procrustes would force-fit guests to their bed, either by stretching those who were too short or cutting the legs of those too long.

PRYTANEUM – a building where government business was conducted.

QUINTANA — a market within a Roman camp or fort where Legionaries could buy food. Related to the word "canteen."

ROSTRUM — a raised platform used for public speaking.

SAPSARIUS — a Legion field medic.

SARCINA — a bundle Legionaries used to carry their provisions. It was attached to a pole called a *furca* and carried over one shoulder. It usually carried a cloak bag, a pot, a mess tin, a basket, a satchel, entrenching tools, and provisions for three days.

SEAX — an ancient Germanic weapon, longer than a dagger but shorter than a sword.

SIGNUM — a sign. This had many meanings, from the eagle emblem of the emperor that his envoy might carry to the *signum crucis* or "sign of the Cross" that early Christians used to recognize each other.

SILPHIUM — a variety of fennel used in herbal medicine. It was Cyrene's major export, harvested almost to extinction in the first century AD, but was still at least in existence in the 5th century.

SPATHA — a Roman sword which became popular in the first century AD. It was longer than the *gladius* which it replaced, and could be used by infantry or cavalry.

SPICULUM — a heavy Roman spear that became popular after 250 AD.

It had a shorter tip than the earlier *pilum*. The length is uncertain, but likely between six to eight feet.

TABERNA — a tavern or public eating house popular with travelers.

TABLINUM — a small office in a Roman house usually situated between the atrium and the peristyle.

TAU — the Greek word for the letter "t." For Christians, the letter symbolizes the cross. See also Ezekiel 9:4, "Go through the city of Jerusalem and put a TAU on the foreheads of those who grieve and lament over all the detestable things that are done in it."

THERMAE — public bath houses, which were centers of Roman social life throughout the Empire

TOGA — the outer garment of Roman male citizens. For ordinary adults it was all white, but the emperor could wear a purple toga called a *toga purpura*, and priests and children both wore a purple-edged toga called a *toga praetexta*. A boy marked his entrance into manhood by laying aside the *praetexta* and assuming the white toga.

TRIBUNE — A high-ranking Legion official, usually second-in-command to the Legion Legate. These were usually young men in their late twenties, who often aspired to a senatorial career.

TRICLINIUM — the dining room in a Roman house, often arranged so the men would eat reclining, and the women sitting in chairs.

TRIREME — a warship of the Roman navy.

VEXILLUM — a standard or banner which displayed a particular Legion's device. The *vexillum* of the *Legio XV Apollinaris* was likely a griffin.

VITIUM — vice or defect; in Roman sacrifices, any error in the priest's action or blemish in the victim could ruin the sacrifice.

ABOUT THE AUTHOR

Taylor Marshall, PhD, is a former Episcopalian priest and the President of the New Saint Thomas Institute, an initiative offering theology classes to over 1,300 students in 24 nations. He is the author of *The Crucified Rabbi, The Catholic Perspective on Paul, The Eternal City, Thomas Aquinas in 50 Pages,* and *Saint Augustine in 50 Pages*. He blogs, publishes videos and podcasts at taylormarshall.com where he has 147,203 daily followers. He and his wife Joy have seven children (four boys and three girls) and make their home in Dallas. To learn more, please visit taylormarshall.com.

ACKNOWLEDGMENTS

Eight years ago this book was conceived as short stories at the bedside of my then four-year-old son Gabriel. They began as adventures centered on knights, weaponry, and horses. Gradually, I introduced the characters of Saint George and eventually, Saint Christopher, Saint Nicholas, Saint Blaise, and others. This book is dedicated in a special way to Gabriel. He was my first and best literary critic, even before he knew how to read.

Father Bill Stetson encouraged me to write down these short stories and the bedtime tales would never have become a book without his suggestion.

My method for developing this book was to test characters and stories with my children at bedtime. Then, after I tucked them in, I would drink a snifter of Grand Marnier and type out the tales on the MacBook. Still to this day, the smell of Grand Marnier elicits my love for Saint George.

The year during which the original manuscript was written was a difficult and depressing one. It was my first year as a Catholic. In some ways, my own battles echo in the struggles and insecurities of Jurian/Georgius.

When the book was complete, I began to shop it around. New York Times bestselling author Sandra Brown asked her agent to look at the original manuscript. New York Times bestselling author Raymond Arroyo of EWTN also had his agent look at the manuscript. Their response and the response of other agents was that the original book was great but that it still lacked a "strong female presence."

I am especially grateful to J. Leigh Bralick and S.K. Valenzuela. They proposed a plan to introduce the needed female character. They successfully allowed Sabra to come to life in a way that rivals Jurian's character. Their general influence throughout the novel adds dramatic suspense and greater historical accuracy. The novel is richer thanks to their hard work.

I am grateful to all the captains, men, and young men of the Troops of Saint George. You remind me that the virtue of Saint George has not been forgotten.

My wife Joy encouraged me all along to write and complete this project. Without her, this book would not exist.

As more and more babies came along, the initial audience grew. The story of Saint George will always be chiefly a story for our children. It is dedicated to Gabriel, Mary Claire, Rose, Jude, Becket, Blaise, and Elizabeth (and those to come, d.v.) with the hope that they will slay dragons and find their peace.

Taylor Marshall
Feast of Saint Martin of Tours
November 11, 2014

A special thank you to my Saint George Launch Team who read advanced copies and helped us with promoting Sword and Serpent. I am so very grateful to each of you!

Godspeed,

Taylor

Davis Aasen, Maggie Abernathy, Zaballero Aidan, Pierangelo Alejo, Gonzalo Alvarado, April Anide, Sheila Appling, Dwight Arnott, George Arokia, Doug Austretm, Maureen Aviles, Kevin Bailey, Gemma Balcomb, Bob Barnhouse, Nathan Barontini, Jonathan Barrett, David Bartlewski, Orland Daniel Batongbakal, Veronica Beauclair, Melanie Behnke, Deacon Stephen Bennett, Mary Berglee, Ernesto Berumen, Carmello D'Jay Bigol, Timothy Black, Paul Boer, Mike Bonin, Eric Boutin, Lisa Bowe, Max Bradicich, Ted Brauker, Anne Bremer, Christopher Brown, Pam Brubaker, Jakov Busic, John Paul Busag, Michael Bunardi, Paul Burdett, Patrick G Burke, Juan Camargo, Matthew Cantrell, Mark Cappetta, Bernadette Capuyan, Jessica Carney, Tony Charo, Jimmy Chilimigras, Claire Chretien, Bob Clancy, Dean Clarke, Fr Laurent Cleenewerck, Alanson Cleveland, Andrew Cody, Annie Coffey, Brock Cordeiro, Daniel Cornell, Nancy Cousintine, Dante Cuales Jr., Sean Cunningham, Becky Darling, Romeo de Guzman, Richard de Lorimier, Roderick DeAguero, Fr Paulo Maria Del Carmen, Bill Kevin Del Rosario, Allaine Dela Cruz, Traci Dempsey, Cinthia Deniz, MacBeth Derham, Jim DeSart, Mike DeWitt, Froilan Diaz, Tomas Diaz, Maria Doane, Raymond Donnelly, Jonathan Dooley, Pilar Dougall, Therese Dougherty, Bill Dowdell, Darren Duffield, Marie DuMabeiller, Brian Dvorak, Tru Dymm, Christi Edwards, John Egerer, Kathy Elias, Cathleen Fakult, Gregory Fast, Mayur Fernandes, Adrian Fernandez, John Fiffick, Jason Fitch, James Florio, Robert Frank, Albert Garcia, Arnie Garcia, Jane Garcia Bernal, Robin Garrett, Ray Garza, Deborah Gaudino, George Gehring, Valerie Giggie, Michael Gill, John Githinji, James Glover, Thomas Goh, Jane Gonzales, Richard Gonzales, Don Gonzalez, Mishka Gora, Jon-Mark Grussenmeyer, Steve Guillory, George Gussy, Tamara Haas, Ryan Hall, Kevin Hall, Sheelagh Hanly, Sarah Harder, Janice Harper, Chris Harvey, Laura Hastie, David Hatch, Michael Healy, Christin Hebert, Matthew Heffron, KM, Mark Helgeson, Teresa Hemphill, Phil Henneman, Darlene Hinman, Marius Hiu, Stanley Holmes, Chris Hora, Richard Hudzik, Andrea Huza, William Hynd, Helton Iaraney, Pamela Idenya, Colette Ivers, Rolden Jacob, Kathy Jenkins, Bantang Johnrob, Terry Jones, Birgit Jones, Julie Jordan, Kelvin Jukpor, Rachel Jurado, Andrew Kaldas, Maurice Kelly, Eric Kelty, Thomas Kennedy, Greg King, Ceryl King, Luke Kippenbrock, Kristopher Kirkland, Ed Kise, Leo Klump, Mark Knickrehm, Patricia Koenig, Brian Kraft, Melissa Kristine, Jaison Kunnel Alex, Zau Doi Lahtaw, Allen Landes, Margie Larson, Lillian Marie Laruan, Peter Lassiter, Maccario Lawrence, Michael Leau, James LeBert, Joyce Lenardson, Foster Scott Lerner, Tom Lewis, Leonardo Ljuljduraj, Catherine Loft, Donna Lohr, Christopher Lushis, Rodel Luyao, Juralyn Macabodbod, Mario Magasa, Julie Maguire, Jim Maguire, Sophia Malakooti, Alex Maldonado, Cathy Malo, Charles Mangerian, Michael Manuszak, Richard Marchessault, Fr Cajetan Maria, Amber Marshall, Joy Marshall, Christina Martin, Linda Martin, Annabelle Maso, Daniel Massuto, Julie McCabe, Jay McCurdy, Erin McGahuey, Thomas McIntyre, John McKenna, Andrew Medina, Victor Melendez, Jhunry Mendez, Mark Michalski, Angela Miller, Victoria Mitchell, Richard Mitzel, Michael Mondragon, Umberto Monteverde, Brian Mood, Lorraine Moody, Laura Morched, Michele Morgan, Brad Morse, Andrew Musano, Alan Nadeau, Jeremaia Naigulevu, Chris Nash, Zophia Newborne, Dalia Nino,

Abraham Nunez, Tami O'Brien, Patrick O'Brien, Tom O'Brien, Mark O'Brien, David O'Connor, Laura O'Neill, Brian O'Reilly, Banjamin Oben, Maggie Ohnesorge, Erich Ohrt, Suzanne Ohrt, Peter Okafor, Andrew Olson, Julie Onderko, Aileen Osias, John Ott, Tristan Ralf Pacheco, Nick Padley, Mirielle Palacios, Tammy Palubicki, Kevin Paquette, Joseph Paragone, Diane Pascaretti, Fra Colin Pasqualetto, CPMO, Cheryl Passel, Sarah Passman, Dr. Joe Pastorek, Grace Peladeau, Emilio Perea, Johnny Perez, Diana Perez, Mario Perez, Yves Pernet, Brent Pierce, Barbara Pierre, Patrick Pineda, John Pramberg, Amanda Pritchard, Luke Procter, Hayden Raines, Carlo Franco Rapay, James Rauch, Dawna Reandeau, Marie Reidy, Joan Reiley, Patti Revelle, Melissa Reynoso, Maura Rieland, Pam Riley, Maria Socorro Rivera, Lisa Roberts, Osvaldo Robles, Ephren Robles, Andrea Roche, Deborah Rodriguez, Ramiro Rodriguez, James Rogers, Alfredo Roldan, Nathan Rolf, Dorianne Romero Plihon, Eric Rose, Ernest Ross, Jacques Rothmann, William Rowe, Richard Ruesch, Christie Rushenberg, Wayne Rusinek, Karen Rutigliano, Patrick Ryan, Nowellyn Ryan, Phyllis Ryan, Audry Salvador, Roy San Buenaventura, Cesar Sanchez, Lindy Post Santiago, Victoria Santucci, Ryan Sayles, Angela Schade, Mike Schramm, Jason Schreder, Daniel Schuler, Abby Schult, Todd Seiler, Robert Shea, Elizabeth Sheehy, Teresa Shrader, DanKelley Sicard, Megan Silas, Jeffrey Singer, Ante Skoko, Alyssa Smeltzer, Michael Smith, James Smith, Fr Hugh Somerville-Knapman OSB, Debbie Spech, Jeff Spiegelhoff, Chris Spiller, David St. John, Romualdo Jr. Sta.Ana, William Stallings, Jeremy Steck, Diane Steenburg, Pauleen Subido, Sheri Talbot, Erin Teter, Wendy Thomas, Marc Tinsley, Lawrence Todd, Viktor Torres Airava, David Trana, Nicholas Trandem, Winnie Tresaugue, Ann Trimble, Charles Trujillo, Janine Tryban, James Tull, Donal Turrentine, Vanessa Ugwuoke, Alison Ujueta, John Usalis, Joseph Valadez, Teo van der Weele, Antonia Van Male, Ant Vassallo, James Vaughn, OFS, Luis Vazquez, Eduardo Villarreal, Dr William von Peters, Jeff Walczak, Christine Walnohas, Catherine Walton, Louis Warfel, John Wasko, Gregory Watson, Miriam Webb, Thomas Weigel, Dominic West, Fr. Jeffrey Whorton, Chris Widhelm, Lance Williams, Michael Wilson, Lauren Witzaney, Debbie Womack, Melissa Woulfe, Stephen Yelletz, Leslie Yetter, Jennifer Yuen, Marilyn Zayac, Sara Zewrvos, and Robert Zimmerman.

Made in United States
Orlando, FL
02 February 2023

29399223R00246